# Barging In

EMILY BANTING

**Barging In**
**Copyright © 2025 Emily Banting**
**Published by Sapphfic Publishing**
**ISBN: 978-1-915157-21-8**
**First edition: September 2025**

CREDITS:
Editor: Hatch Editorial
Proofread by: Suzi Vilkman


1 2 4 5 6 7 8 9 10

# ABOUT THE AUTHOR

Emily Banting is an award-winning and bestselling author of contemporary sapphic romance featuring LGBTQ+ characters and plenty of British humour. History obsessed, she throws her sapphic leading ladies into historic buildings and environments at every opportunity and strongly believes in representing women over forty in literature.

www.emilybanting.co.uk

# FIND ME HERE

I love to hear from my readers. If you would like to get in touch you can find me here…

www.emilybanting.co.uk

Or follow me here…

f facebook.com / emilybantingauthor

instagram.com / emilybanting

X x.com / emily_banting

BB bookbub.com / authors / emily-banting

g goodreads.com / emily_banting

a amazon.com / author / emilybanting

bsky.app / profile / emilybanting.co.uk

tiktok.com / emilybantingauthor

threads.com / @emilybanting

# ACKNOWLEDGMENTS

I love cake!

It's long been a weakness of mine. When I was little, the best part of my birthday was always the cake, and it still is! My mum used to make a caterpillar cake every year. I don't remember a lot of things about the past, but I do remember that growing up there was always homemade ginger cake or flapjack to snack on. A lot of my memories are cake-based.

When my son was little, he loved making cakes — or more often sneaking a bit of the chocolate icing from the bowl! As I write these acknowledgements, he's just turned fifteen, and I'm multitasking by making his birthday cake. I can confirm he still does. Over the years, I've made all sorts of shapes for him: a Minecraft cake, a dinosaur, a BMX track, which was one of my greatest achievements! This time, I whipped up a simple chocolate loaf cake as he's less fussed these days. My regular bakes are banana bread, blueberry muffins, and, of course, the luscious lemon drizzle.

It was during a dog walk and a stop at a café that Christine's Chemical Cakes was born. I didn't think it possible to be offended by a piece of cake, but alas, it was. The chocolate cake tasted of nothing but chemicals and didn't even have the texture of a cake. Now, I stick to homemade.

It was inevitable, therefore, that one day I would write a book about cakes. Of course I had to combine it with my passion for historic buildings and my fascination with the transport of the Industrial Revolution. Don't ask!

The book isn't just about cake, unfortunately, but also about stale relationships. I'm always struck by how many women are stuck in abusive or coercive relationships, or are simply unhappy, unloved, and unappreciated, craving more for themselves but unable to make a change. Even when the world is screaming at them to act, and deep down they know they need to, sometimes for their own survival, they stand frozen. This can be for financial reasons, fear of reprisals, judgement, or losing children.

Many stay in marriages to the detriment of their own physical and mental wellbeing, often holding the world together for other people. If you are one of them, I hope this book helps you see that there is light at the end of the tunnel and that the grass can be greener on the other side. Be brave.

As always, thanks go to Conny, my trusty sidekick who keeps pushing me when things get tough. Also to Lou, for her thoughts early on, my editor, Jess, and proofreader, Suzi.

My final thanks go to my new work colleague, Otto, who gently snores beside me as I write, and reminds me to take breaks. I miss Maddie and her enthusiastic outlook on life, but our furry friends can only travel with us so far, and then it's another dog's turn. Otto is very different — he'll happily get up at midday, devour something dead, have a slow sniffy walk, and head back to bed. As I get older, I find I appreciate his pace.

I hope you all enjoy the slow pace of the English waterways and the emotional journeys of Victoria and Clem. I certainly enjoyed writing it, almost as much as eating the cake that fuelled it, and I'm glad to have you along for the ride.

*To my teen,*
*For always being patient when I'm writing.*

# CHAPTER 1

Clem Wentworth drank in the sun-dappled, silty waters of the canal ahead. The first warm, sunny day of the year had brought families out to stroll the towpath after their Sunday lunches. Children wobbled on scooters, dogs strained against their leads, and everyone smiled and waved at her as she passed them at a snail's pace.

Wild garlic carpeted the woods on either side; its invigorating aroma was so strong it drifted over the canal. Clem inhaled, eyes half closed, letting the punchy scent fill her lungs. An avenue of willow trees lined the banks ahead of her. Their drooping branches and long leaves rose and fell with the breeze sweeping along the cut. The whispering and rustling accompanied the rhythmic drumming of Florence's 1.5-litre diesel engine.

A happy engine was always a welcome sound. Its low drone reminded Clem of the air-conditioning unit that had hummed through the open-plan office where she had spent her career. Like all background noise, it soon faded, sinking into the fabric of the day until she barely noticed it.

She still couldn't believe she'd walked away from it all. Corporate life was behind her now, and if everything went to plan, she wouldn't be going back. Ahead stretched a new kind of future: just her, Florence — her bright orange narrowboat — top-notch coffee, homemade cakes, and the steady rhythm of the waterways.

Tucking a loose strand of long, brown hair behind her ear, Clem tried to steady the excited voice that had brought her this far, knowing it would be no small task. If anything, the road ahead was going to be tougher. It was the end of being crammed onto packed commuter trains, wasting eight hours a day behind a computer and then handing over half her salary for the rent on a poky studio flat. But now, her survival — and Florence's — was dependent on her selling enough coffee and cake to keep them both afloat.

The cost of buying and refurbishing Florence had been steeper than she'd planned, leaving Clem with only a modest amount of her inheritance to live off and launch the business, far less than she would have liked. Catering kitchens and top-of-the-line espresso machines, even second-hand, didn't come cheap, and Florence had been in a miserable state when she found her.

Getting her head down and working hard was the only way forward now. She had to make it work; there was no safety net left. Hard work didn't scare her; it was the idea of spending the rest of her life trapped in the gears of some corporate machine that she couldn't stomach. What had begun as a temporary job straight from university had quietly solidified into something permanent that she had built her life around. It wasn't until the prospect of a promotion was dangled in front of her that she finally saw the truth: She was sliding straight into the world of corporate management. The thought made her shudder.

Admittedly, when Clem left university, she hadn't known exactly what she wanted from life. By her fortieth birthday last autumn, staring out at a supermarket car park from her office, surrounded by bumbling suits and the relentless click of high heels, she knew one thing for sure — she hadn't found it.

The only real joy that day came from watching her colleagues devour her beloved blueberry muffins and fight over slices of her luscious lemon drizzle. Her baking had become a highlight of office life, earning endless praise and comments that the world was missing out.

A call from her mum later that evening to say her dear great-aunt Maud had passed away felt like the final straw on what had been a crappy birthday. Yet in the following days, she learned that Maud — or Gram, as Clem affectionately called her — had left her a small inheritance. It wasn't a life-changing amount but enough to create an opportunity for herself. Following the funeral, she and her parents went through Gram's old photographs together, and that's when the idea formed. It was a way to blend her love of baking with the change she craved.

Two weeks had passed since she'd left her job and collected Florence from the outfitters. All fifty-seven feet of the narrowboat had been crane-lifted into the canal, ready to start their new adventure together. Rather than having her delivered, Clem had chosen to wend her way through the English countryside, where she and Florence could learn each other's quirks and those of the meandering waterways.

As their new mooring came into view, Clem slowed the engine and steered Florence towards it. The water lapped gently against the grassy bank as she manoeuvred the tiller and lowered the throttle lever towards neutral. She reversed in gentle bursts, and Florence slowed to a stop, her hull settling alongside the wooden jetty as the engine fell into silence.

She looked up at the house that had once been the heart of the family, where her mum had grown up after losing both parents at the age of ten. Grief-stricken by the loss of her younger sister, Gram had taken her niece in without hesitation. With no children themselves, Maud and her husband, Frank, had raised Clem's mum as their own. Although Maud was technically not her grandmother, Clem had always seen her that way, and Gram had always felt like the perfect name to bridge both roles. The memory of her drew a bittersweet smile to Clem's lips.

Disembarking with the centre line in hand, she tied it off with a cleat hitch to the bollard. It felt good to finally fasten Florence down. Anchoring a boat might be a simple task, but at the moment, small certainties mattered a great deal to Clem. She wasn't mooring Florence just anywhere; she was bringing her home, back to where she belonged.

Florence had been an eighteenth birthday present from Gram and Gruncle to her mum: a way to give her independence, a home of her own, with the comfort of knowing she could always return and tie up at the end of the garden whenever she wanted. Clem couldn't wait to see her mum's face when she saw Florence again.

Having a private mooring for the foreseeable future was certainly one less stress. Adhering to the continuous cruiser rules and moving along the waterway every two weeks would have proved challenging, especially with the steady stream of supplies she would need for her café. She couldn't imagine hauling pints of milk, dozens of eggs, and heavy bags of sugar and flour from distant supermarkets along the towpath.

Unlatching the gate, she wandered up the garden path.

Most of the three-storey late Victorian house would soon be hidden behind a maze of scaffolding. The builders were due to start work the next morning, beginning the process of making it habitable for her parents to move into by the end of summer.

She pulled her phone from her pocket and called her mum, who answered almost immediately.

"Clementine! Tom, it's Clementine on the phone!" her mum shouted, completely forgetting to cover the mouthpiece and making Clem wince.

"Mum," Clem huffed. "It's *Clem*. How many times do I have to tell you?"

"I don't understand why you insist on shortening such a beautiful name," she huffed.

"You named me after an orange, Mum. An orange! What happened? Did you give birth and then stare at a fruit bowl for inspiration?"

She tutted dismissively. "Just be grateful I didn't call you Tangerine. Now, how's the new boat? Is it behaving? Did you manage the locks all right?"

"Yes, everything's fine. And yes, I can handle a lock." Clem groaned, tired of her mum's habit of assuming she was helpless.

"I know you can, darling. It's just... they're harder on your own, that's all."

Clem had lost count of how many locks she'd piloted on her way south. They were manageable enough, especially now that some were electric, but they still interrupted the smooth rhythm of cruising.

"So the boat is running fine, is it?" her mum pressed, apparently not finished with her rapid-fire questioning.

"Yes, all fine," Clem confirmed again, her tone resolute.

"What boat did you say it was?" her mum added, trying to sound casual but failing miserably.

"You know full well I'm not telling you. You'll have to wait and see, like I told you last week. And the week before that."

An exasperated breath came back down the phone. "I don't understand why you're being so secretive about it."

"I just want it to be a surprise. Are you still coming on Saturday?" Clem asked, quickly changing the subject.

"Yes, but we'll need to head straight back Sunday afternoon. Our first guests arrive on Friday, and it'll take a couple of days to cruise back to the marina and get everything ready. I can't believe it's our last season."

"The end of an era," Clem exhaled.

Her mum hummed soulfully in agreement.

"I'm sure you should be more elated at the prospect of retiring, Mum."

"You know me. I need to keep busy."

"Finishing the house will keep you busy," Clem countered.

"There will be nothing left to do."

"I'm sure you'll find something to sink your teeth into," Clem said, trying to reassure her. "You can always come and help me in the busy season."

Her mum hummed again. "If it wasn't for your dad being so old—"

"Oi, Barbara!" came her dad's mock offended voice in the background, making Clem chuckle.

"—then we wouldn't have even contemplated selling *The Kingfisher*," her mum finished.

Although Clem's mum was only sixty-four, the ten-year age gap between her parents put her dad well past retirement age, something he had spent the last few years telling anyone who would listen. He often complained about his aching joints and how he was ready to hang up his skipper's hat, tired of running around after guests on their luxurious wide-beam hotel boat, *The Kingfisher's Rest*.

Inheriting the house from Great-Aunt Maud had presented Clem's father with the perfect opportunity to call time on his and his wife's successful business as it entered its twentieth year. With a full diary of bookings lined up to the end of August, though, they couldn't move straight in. It was just as well; at present, the house wasn't fit for purpose. Towards the end, Aunt Maud had become a bit of a hoarder, and with the house being so large, it had taken Clem's parents the whole winter to empty it out. Now that it was clear, it was the builders' time to shine.

Realising the line had gone quiet, Clem tried to make out inaudible whisperings between her parents as she gave a friendly wave to a passing narrowboat. Suddenly her mum spoke, making Clem jump.

"Your dad's reminded me: Watch out for that woman next door. She had the gall to have a go at us for obstructing the lane when we were clearing the last bits of furniture out a few weeks ago. It's not our problem that she has such a fancy car; she should learn to drive it properly."

A grunt of agreement sounded from her dad in the background.

"Then she asked us what we were doing. I told her to keep her sticky beak out of other people's business, didn't I, love?"

"Too right you did!" he shouted back.

"There's nothing quite like falling out with the neighbours before you've even moved in," Clem muttered quietly.

Her mum blithely ignored her comment and moved on. "When do you start work?"

"Tomorrow," Clem confirmed.

"Well, I wish you every success with it, darling, but you know how I feel."

Clem internalised a groan, wishing her mum had stopped halfway through her sentence. She braced herself as she continued.

"You had so much potential, such a bright future ahead with that promotion you were offered. 'Head of Social Media and Marketing' has such a nice ring to it. You worked hard over the years to get to that point, only to throw it away."

"I hated it, Mum."

That wasn't completely true. She loved elements of the job, just not the industry she was working in. She wanted to use her creativity for good, not to actively harm people by persuading them to buy overpriced fast food without an ounce of nutrition in it. Cakes weren't exactly nutritious either, but at least they could be made from real, wholesome ingredients, and were intended as an occasional treat. Her motto was simple: If it wasn't in a kitchen cupboard, it wasn't real food. Not that she ever said that out loud at the office.

"Most people hate their jobs," her mum said with a sharp tut. "Sometimes you need to knuckle down and get on with it to put a roof over your head."

Clem inhaled sharply, anger rising inside her, but she let it out slowly before saying, "And yet I *have* a roof over my head. I even own the roof."

"But you could have set yourself up with a nice deposit on a house with your inheritance."

"And be a slave to a mortgage the rest of my days? Sounds wonderful," she replied, sarcasm lacing her tone.

"I just want the best for you, and I hope this works out," her mum urged. A little pull in Clem's chest tugged at her until she added, "It's not like you've left yourself with any other option."

Clem rolled her eyes.

"We'll see you Saturday, love. I'll cook a lasagna and leave you the leftovers."

"Thanks, Mum."

Weekends were bound to be the busiest for her, so not having to cook dinner would be a bonus.

"Call me tomorrow to let me know how it all went, and send photographs of what the builders have done."

"I will," Clem assured her, wondering how much monitoring of the builders' progress her mum was expecting. "I'd best go. I've got a lot to do before then. Cakes won't bake themselves."

"Bye, love. Good luck tomorrow."

"Thanks."

With a deep breath, she hung up and pushed herself into motion. Slipping her phone into her back pocket, she headed around the side of the house to the front door. The call hadn't exactly given her the boost she was after, and now a sense of dread threaded its way through her veins.

Her mum was right. She didn't have any other option than to make her café work, but hearing it said so starkly made the burden feel heavier. Would anyone come by tomorrow? If they did, would they like her coffee and cakes?

Birds chattered in the large hedge separating Gram's property from the neighbouring one. The sound would usually have had a calming effect on Clem, but the knot in her stomach only tightened as she realised how much she needed to do. She had hoped to scope out the mooring she would be trading from, but with her grocery delivery behind schedule, her baking schedule was, too.

She slid the key into the lock and opened the front door, a ripple of trepidation washing over her as she entered the red-tiled hallway. A once-dominating staircase ran up one side of the home. It looked less impressive now, with its missing spindles and wallpaper lying across it. It must have come away from the walls since her parents' last visit.

Clem hadn't set foot inside the house since her parents had cleared the last of the furniture. On her last visit to Gram in the autumn, the place had felt cluttered and musty. Now stripped bare, it felt like an empty shell, the air somehow colder without her frail-framed, resolute great-aunt to greet her.

As she wandered through the dank, empty rooms, she realised she'd never appreciated the historical features before. Now it was hard to miss the wood panelling, parquet flooring, elaborate cornicing, and moulded ceilings, all of which had seen better days.

Her parents' plans for the house were courageous, especially given the timescale in play. Their architect had won them over with a proposal for a sympathetic restoration, including a large, Victorian-style conservatory extension at the rear, complete with a roof lantern. They just had to hope the builders would remain on schedule — and budget — and finish by the end of the summer. Considering the house needed complete rewiring and a new central heating system installed, they were cutting it fine. With the new owners of *The Kingfisher's Rest* taking ownership at the end of August, her parents could end up homeless if things didn't go to plan.

The sound of gravel crunching pulled her to the window. A grocery van was reversing onto the driveway. Finally, she could crack on with her baking and put the narrowboat's kitchen to proper use.

After dragging six grocery bags down the garden to

Florence — two of which split on the way, breaking three eggs — she decided she would need to invest in a trolley to get her produce to the jetty in future.

Once she'd cleared her rubbish bags from Florence to the dustbin on the drive and topped up the water tank from the garden hose, she carried two boxes of books and a suitcase of clothes to the garage to store. Now, it was time to strap on her apron and get to work.

# CHAPTER 2

*C*lem welcomed the builders onto the site the next morning, and Billy, the project manager, quickly reassured her that he had everything under control. She fired off a message with photographs to her mum, then steered Florence down the canal, flanked by hawthorn and blackthorn heavy with white blossom.

With no locks along the one-mile stretch to slow her down, she predicted the journey would take about twenty minutes — though she definitely wasn't counting it as a commute. At a speed of three miles per hour, it had the hallmarks of one, but with the light breeze on her face, coffee in one hand and tiller in the other, the resemblance ended there. The slow pace gave her enough time to gather her thoughts and prepare for the day, all while the morning sun warmed her.

The canals had been part of her life for as long as she could remember, so much so that they were woven into her sense of belonging. Their steady flow brought her a deep sense of calm, and nothing felt better than gliding along quiet waters. She had come into the world on the water and called it home until she was five. Then her parents had sold Florence and moved onto dry land, determined to give her access to a good school and a garden to run around in. Even then their annual holiday was spent frolicking on the canals, exploring a different network each year on a rented narrowboat.

She'd always sensed her parents regretted their move off the canal, even if her dad continued to repair boats on it. It was quietly confirmed when they sold up to buy *The Kingfisher's Rest* as soon as she left to study marketing at university. Now, even that chapter was at an end. They had come full circle once again.

Over the years, Gram's house had become a kind of sanctuary for the family. Clem spent most of her school holidays there and later her breaks from university since her parents had no home on land by then. During those long, hot summers, she would be in the garden, sunbathing while studying or devouring a good feminist book. One ear was always tuned for the sound of *The Kingfisher's Rest* drifting down the cut.

Her parents would take a two-week break from their busiest season to coincide with Clem's summer holiday. By the time they arrived at Gram's mooring, they had about a week together before they would sail back to the marina to welcome their next guests. In the years after Clem left university, they would meet out of season, her parents mooring up for weeks at a time with Gram and Gruncle.

Clem wasn't sure how her parents would adjust to retired life. Her dad would likely put his feet up with a newspaper, but her mum was unlikely to settle into a quieter pace. She was the type of woman who needed something to keep her busy. Clem worried that she herself might inadvertently become that *something* whilst living at the bottom of their garden.

Open fields stretched out on both sides of the cut. Lambs of all sizes frolicked in the grass, playfully butting their heads against their mother's bellies to nurse. As Clem neared a small town, the fields gave way to an imposing stone building with a sign on the side reading *Otterford Wharf*. She had arrived.

A line of narrowboats hugged the towpath opposite the building, so Clem reduced her speed to minimise the wash and not unsettle the other craft. A stone bridge stood ahead, connecting the wharf with the town on the right.

As she approached, an empty mooring right next to the bridge came into sight. It would make the ideal place to attract passing foot traffic visiting the wharf. She gripped the tiller and eased back on the throttle, hoping this would be hers. Then, she saw it — a bold, painted number seven on the bollard, the same number from her commercial mooring agreement. Her lips tightened into a grin — what a result!

With Florence moored, Clem took a moment to survey her surroundings. The building was beautiful, idyllic even. Perfectly proportioned and well maintained for its age. According to her mum, the wharf — once an old corset factory — had been converted into apartments in the last few years. It also housed some sort of heritage centre on the ground floor.

History had been one of Clem's favourite subjects at school, but a growing interest in marketing had steered her university studies. It hadn't dampened her love of history, though. She decided she'd wander over for a look sometime and see what the old building had to offer.

It was still early, and with only the occasional dog walker passing by, Clem figured she'd have enough time to film herself baking before opening. She also needed footage of Florence once everything was set up; with a quick edit, she'd have a video ready to post on her socials.

Whilst she hoped passing trade would bring in customers, building a loyal fanbase on social media was essential for growing her business. Beautiful photographs of her cakes would not only attract people but would hopefully help to spread the word that she was in Otterford.

She believed wholeheartedly in using fresh produce and aimed to bake as much as possible before opening. She'd thought about starting before leaving her parents' place but realised it made more sense to moor up as early as possible. Even if she wasn't open, passive marketing was always useful.

Thankfully, traybakes like brownies, rocky road, and chocolate flapjack had been easy enough to rustle up the night before, easing her first morning's workload. Blueberry muffins, a coffee and walnut cake, and a lemon drizzle were all she needed now. Judging the right balance of stock would be tricky. Baking too much increased her expenses while baking too little risked reducing income. Even if she ended up eating the leftovers herself, there was only so much cake one person could manage — and polishing off unsold stock wasn't exactly a sustainable business plan.

Heading to the stern, she grabbed her A-board and placed it on the grass beside the towpath. Taking out a chalk pen and her price list from her pocket, she attempted to scrawl *Clem's Coffee & Cakes* at the top, only to find it didn't fit well. She even managed to write the ampersand backwards. With a frustrated tut, she went back to Florence for a wet cloth to start over. She returned to her sign to find a youngish, lanky chap in beige chinos and a denim shirt, with long, brown hair and a short beard, inspecting it. He reminded her of a young Ozzy Osbourne.

"Would you like me to do that for you?" he asked, nodding at a chalkboard on the neighbouring boat.

It was elegantly scribed and legible — everything hers was not. She assumed it must be his. The sign read, *Vinyl for sale! 70s rock, 80s/90s grunge, and other stuff.*

"That would be amazing. Thanks."

She wiped the board clean, then handed him the chalk pen and price list. Leaving him to it, she retrieved two foldout benches from under the kitchen units and placed them on the grass between Florence and the towpath for customers to use. By the time she put the waste bin out for empty plates and coffee cups, he'd finished the sign. *Clem's Coffee & Cakes* beautifully filled one side of the board, complete with a cute sketch of a coffee cup and a slice of cake. He'd listed her prices neatly on the reverse.

"That's great! Thanks again. Could you find room on both sides for 'Open 10 till 3'?"

"Sure thing," he said, adding her hours with a flourish.

"You're talented," she remarked.

He stood back to admire his work. "I have an artistic streak."

"It shows. I'm Clem, by the way."

"I guessed you might be," he said, handing her the chalk pen. "I'm Max. I've not seen you around here before." He smirked as he added, "You got yourself the best spot, too."

Clem's cheeks flushed. She wasn't sure how she'd nabbed the best spot, but she hoped it wouldn't upset anyone. Making herself unpopular with the other traders on day one had not been part of her business plan.

"This area looks like a great trading spot," she replied.

"It is. It's fairly quiet during the week, but weekends

can get very busy. Just watch out for the woman who runs the wharf."

"Why?" Clem asked, intrigued. It was the second time she'd been warned about someone in the last twenty-four hours.

"She might not appreciate your offering. They have a café inside, you know."

"If she can't face a bit of competition, that's her problem," Clem said nonchalantly as she shrugged.

Max laughed in reply. "I like your attitude. I wish you luck with it."

"I won't need luck; you haven't tasted my bakes." To soften the boast, she added, "But you must, in payment for your skills. Coffee and a flapjack?"

"That would be amazing. Thanks."

She disappeared inside, eager to impress with her new Fracino espresso machine and premium bean blend. Although she'd completed a weekend barista course, the machine they taught on wasn't the same as hers, and she hadn't had much practice since picking up Florence. The machine also consumed a lot of energy when switched on, so she had been using the hob or the kettle for her own hot drinks when the stove in her bedroom wasn't on for heating.

"That is delicious," Max said, finishing the last bite of chocolate flapjack a few minutes later. "I can already tell you're going to be a popular addition to our little community. Business has been slow for us over the winter."

"I thought vinyl was all the rage again."

"It is, but physical media only appeals to a certain crowd. Hopefully, you'll attract people my way. With that colour, your boat certainly garners attention."

Clem smiled. "She does."

"A lot of people come from town via the footpath over there." Max pointed to a gap in the hedge further down the towpath. "Most head straight over the bridge and into the wharf without even noticing us traders. If you slow them down and have them queuing, that works for me."

"What other traders are here?"

"We've got a bookseller, vintage clothes, a woodworker, and one lady makes pottery."

"That's quite a mix."

Max nodded. "Some live aboard their boats; others come from the local area."

"Do you live aboard?"

"Yes," Max confirmed.

"Me too."

"I'm surprised you can fit everything in," he observed, trying to peer in Florence's windows. "You must need a lot of equipment."

"It's not too much of a squeeze. There's only me. Do you want to have a look inside?" Clem offered, already leading the way to the stern, knowing Max wouldn't be able to resist.

"I'd be lying if I said I wasn't intrigued," he said, following her onto the stern. "She's old."

"Yep. 1974," Clem said, patting the orange paintwork as she descended the steps.

Max took in the kitchen, his eyes darting around as he entered the boat. Stainless steel worktops stretched along both walls, stopping short on the port side to allow access to the serving hatch. Various mixing machines lined the surfaces.

"Wow, this is something," he said. "The kitchen must take up half the boat."

"It sure does. It's all second-hand, but it does the job. Come through; I'll show you the rest of her."

As they reached the middle of Florence, Max stuck his head out of the service hatch. "I should get one of these. It'd save me standing outside in the cold."

"You stay outside unless it's raining. It's good for business. You can engage with potential customers better."

Max grinned. "If you say so."

"I do." Clem gave a firm nod.

He turned to examine the partition wall, where her espresso machine stood, a statement piece in the compact space.

"Impressive kit. How do you run all this?"

"The hob and espresso machine run on LPG. The rest runs off batteries I charge overnight and keep topped up with solar panels," Clem said, pointing to the roof.

He nodded. "Will you be open through the winter?"

"Probably not. I moor up locally on a private jetty at the bottom of my parents' garden, so I was just going to batten down there."

The thought of her mum fussing over her every day was enough to have her cruising off into the sunset, though.

"A fridge and freezer?" Max asked, pointing to them under the stainless steel worktop on the starboard side.

"Yep. I hope it's enough. I've got a feeling Florence will turn into an oven in the summer."

"Guaranteed," Max said. He surveyed the space once more before pronouncing, "It looks like you have everything, including the kitchen sink and a spare."

"The small one in the corner is for handwashing only. There are a lot of food hygiene regulations to follow," Clem explained as she led him through a door into the other half of the boat. "Here are my living quarters." She opened a door to the right, revealing a newly decorated bathroom with a tiny shower cubicle, sink, pump-out toilet, and a washing machine all crammed into the space.

"Nice," he commented.

"And down here is a booth-style seating area that can double as another bed."

She was unlikely to have guests, but it had seemed sensible to make the table and bench seating multipurpose when the plans for her refit were drawn up. The C-shaped space was compact but cosy, complete with scatter cushions. An adjustable table served as a dining area and a coffee table when she wanted to work or relax there.

"And at the end is my bedroom," she said, gesturing for him to lead the way.

With a small double bed against the port side; slim-fitting wooden cabinetry on the bow wall; matching, soft furnishing; and vinyl flooring with a fluffy rug, the room felt homely if somewhat snug. A small TV was inset into one of the cabinets to the right side of the bow door.

"She's gorgeous! Sleek and modern yet still a classic. I love this tongue-and-groove," Max said, running his hand along the grey panelling that covered the lower half of Florence. "And the flooring's very stylish. This must've set you back."

Clem looked down. "I inherited some money from my great-aunt."

"Oh. I'm sorry for your loss," Max said softly.

Clem kicked at the floor with the toe of her Converse. "Thanks." Her eyes stung as the weight of the loss settled back in.

"But what a way to spend it, eh?"

"Yep, she's worth every penny," Clem said, her voice warm with affection for her great-aunt.

"What are you using for heating and hot water?"

"A Webasto diesel heater."

Max nodded. "Same as me."

"But I have the original stove," Clem said, pointing to an old, cast-iron Morsø squirrel stove tucked neatly in the corner behind him. "It should keep the living quarters warm enough through the winter, and I can always stick a kettle on top for a cuppa."

She unlatched the bow doors and stepped up onto the small deck. A small wooden table and two chairs were set up, though they barely fit into the space.

Clem breathed in the fresh air. "This is my favourite part of the boat. I love sitting out here with my coffee in the morning, watching the world drift by."

"My boat's nowhere near as glamorous, but you're always welcome to have a nosy," Max said, stepping onto the gunwale and hopping down onto the grass. "Thanks for the tour."

"You're welcome. I'm about to put a batch of blueberry muffins on. I'll bring one over for you when they're ready."

"Yum! I'm going to enjoy having you as a neighbour. Although I might have to increase my exercise." He patted his stomach and flashed her a smile.

Clem watched Max wander back to his boat, feeling quietly pleased to have made a friend already. She realised the time, though, so she strapped on her apron and got to work. It was going to be trial and error to see what sold well and what didn't.

As it turned out, everything was popular. She was completely out of cakes by early afternoon and kept herself busy serving hot drinks to a steady stream of customers until closing. Nobody even batted an eyelid at her wonky lemon drizzle — an unexpected quirk of baking in a floating kitchen. She needed to increase volumes for the next day and keep a close eye on supplies to ensure she had enough paper cups, plates, and forks for her customers.

As she folded her A-board and lifted it onto the stern, Max's voice called out across the towpath.

"Congratulations! First day done."

He handed her a glass, which he filled from a bottle containing a cloudy, orangey-yellow liquid.

"Don't worry, it's not what it looks like." He chuckled, filling his glass. "Try it."

Clem sniffed it cautiously. An intense aroma of apples filled her nostrils. She took a tentative sip and immediately coughed as the drink burned the back of her throat. "That's got some kick to it," she said, blinking through the cough as she dropped onto one of her benches.

"You'll get used to it." Max grinned, sitting beside her.

Clem took another smaller sip. "It's nice, though. What is it?"

"Scrumpy."

She nodded, knowing scrumpy was a name for a strong, home-brewed cider, one she'd never tried.

"Dare I ask the alcohol volume?"

"Ten percent," he replied with a smirk.

Clem's eyebrows shot up. He offered her a top-up, but she declined. High in alcohol and possibly high in sugar, she knew it would have a fast effect, especially on an empty stomach. She'd been kept so busy she'd only managed to eat a blueberry muffin.

"So," Max said, taking a sip from his glass and pulling a wry face, "how did your first day go?"

"I sold out far too early."

"Don't complain."

Clem laughed. "Oh, I'm not."

"But don't expect tomorrow to be as busy," Max cautioned. "It might be; it might not. It fluctuates a lot."

"How was your day?" she asked.

"Vinyl doesn't sell as fast as your cakes." Max quipped, drawing a smile from Clem. "It was okay," he added more seriously. "Could have been better."

"What sort of marketing do you do?" Clem asked, unable to help herself.

Max scrunched his lips together.

"Tell me you do *something*," she urged.

He grimaced. "I have my sign. Does that count?"

"No, not really. It's purely informative. Marketing's about influencing action. You have to understand what drives your customers and create a message that connects with them, ideally for the long term."

"I don't know much about it. I just rock up here and rely on passing trade. I take it you know about this stuff then?"

Clem chuckled softly. "You could say that. I assume you've heard of Facebook, Instagram, TikTok?"

"Of course!"

"Do you use them?"

Max shrugged. "I doomscroll."

Clem raised an eyebrow. "Cat videos, perchance?"

"You got me."

Clem laughed again. "I can see I need to bring you up to speed."

"That would be great," he said — and actually sounded relieved. "A marketing whizz and an amazing baker. What luck! That muffin you brought over earlier was sublime."

"Thanks," Clem said, wondering if her face was

warming from the compliment or the cider. "How long have you been making scrumpy?"

"About a year," Max said. "I'd love to make it properly and sell it, but I'm struggling to find somewhere to brew it in bulk. If I could sell my vinyl from there, too, then all the better. It's a pain in the arse lifting these boxes in and out of the boat twice a day."

"Oh, I bet," Clem said, remembering the weight of Gruncle's vinyl collection that Gram had once asked her to move. "I'd best get going," she added, glancing at the time and taking her last sip of cider. "I need to find somewhere to turn around."

There hadn't been a chance to look at her canal app for the nearest amenities, but her dad had assured her everything she needed was within easy reach.

"There's a winding hole about half a mile up where you can turn," Max said, standing. "And a pump-out station, too, plus water. You can use the bins for your trade waste. The marina where I stay is just beyond it."

She handed his glass back. "Great. See you tomorrow then, and thanks for the cider."

"You're welcome," Max said, ambling off.

Clem jumped back on board to finish cleaning, knowing it would need doing after dinner and again after her evening bake. By the time she'd completed her final wipe-down, getting ready for the morning's bake, it would be late, and so would begin her new routine. Her former nine-to-five, well-paid job was beginning to feel like a breeze.

# CHAPTER 3

Victoria Hargreaves crossed the driveway to her racing-green Jaguar E-Type but stopped just short of it. Taking a deep breath, she shoved her car keys into her handbag and set off down the lane on foot instead. She needed fresh air, and the walk to work might help her organise her thoughts.

Crossing the bridge over the canal, she briefly glanced back at the rear of her three-storey late Victorian house, smiling as she always did when taking in the building and its surroundings. A raft of ducks quacked on the water below, vanishing under the bridge and reappearing on the other side as she joined the towpath. They followed alongside her until a sharp-eyed swan sent them scrambling to the opposite bank.

The air was silent, broken only by the occasional quack and chatter of the birds in the hedgerows. It was a stark contrast to the endless whir of traffic, sirens, and horns she'd just endured in London. The city was a pigeon-ridden maze of overpriced coffee, nauseating pollution, and deluded tourists mistaking the sewage-filled Thames for something scenic. She'd be happy never to return. Having tied up loose ends and finished off her long-term projects, she hoped she wouldn't need to.

Although the team at the wharf weren't expecting her until the start of the following week, Monday was four days away, and she was eager to get started. Sitting idly by had never been her style, and even with the serenity of the house tempting her to linger, the pull to grab the bull by the horns and get the business on the right footing was too strong to ignore.

She couldn't help but wonder whether the business would be in such a precarious position if she hadn't split her time between two jobs in the first place. Would it be in better shape today had she committed fully from the start? The thought tightened her chest. What more could she do now that she was full-time? She was an architect, not a businesswoman. Was she fooling herself by pretending otherwise?

She tossed her head back; there was no time for such worries. Her husband, Drew, was threatening to pull the plug on the wharf if she couldn't turn things around by the end of the summer in just a few months. If he did that, she would lose everything. The wharf. Her future. Even the house she'd painstakingly restored. All of it would be sold off. Worst of all, she'd have to return to their ghastly London penthouse. To him.

Admittedly, it had been a slow winter, but everything stalled during the colder months. That wasn't a fair measure of success. The business hadn't quite finished its first year; it was far too soon to judge its popularity or long-term potential.

As she rounded the final bend, Otterford Wharf came into view, sending a warm shiver down her spine. She'd only been away a week, but she had missed it. To some, it was a cluster of old stones, but to her, it was so much more. When a place called to your heart, it didn't matter how long you were apart; it was the fact you had been that tugged at your insides and squeezed, only easing the moment you were reunited.

Her thoughts drifted back to the day the wharf had come into her life — when a bit of research into her ancestry revealed that her three-times-great-grandfather once owned a corset factory. Curious to see if the building still existed, she and Drew had driven out one weekend. To her amazement, not only was the factory still standing, but it was also for sale, though in dire need of saving.

Drew was immediately excited by the profit that might come from converting it into luxury apartments, but Victoria felt something deeper. She saw a tourist attraction that celebrated heritage while allowing her to pay homage to her corsetry roots. When she shared her vision — and the fact that she wanted to run it as such in the future — Drew was less than pleased. She was the best architect in his company, especially with historical projects, and he was reluctant to completely lose her.

Passing the row of narrowboat traders, she noticed a long queue near the bridge, something she'd never seen here before. Her heart fluttered in her chest as she prayed they were a crowd heading to the wharf. The sensation quickly waned as she noticed the queue was for a garish orange narrowboat moored next to the bridge.

Whatever the trader was offering, people were willing to wait for it. As she neared the bridge, she noticed a sign facing onto the path. Clem's Coffee & Cakes was advertising itself to all her customers on their way into the wharf.

Victoria could feel her lips pull in tight. *The damn cheek.*

Taking a deep breath, she convinced herself the queue

was a one-off. The narrowboat's owners were likely passing by and had moored here for the day. She crossed the bridge, letting the familiar sense of calm wash over her as it always did when she entered the wharf. Even on bad days, just being onsite grounded her. It gave her a sense of belonging, a connection to something tangible yet intangible — her past.

The nineteenth-century factory stood with a quiet industrial grandeur. Its weathered stone façade, softened by time, rose five storeys from the canal and stretched back in an L shape. Victoria would never tire of its towering beauty. Knowing she had played a pivotal role in bringing it back to life filled her with a sense of pride. Every decision she had made, every challenge she'd overcome, had helped restore it to its former splendour.

The large windows had deteriorated beyond salvaging, so she had replaced them with new Crittall-style steel frames. Multi-paned, double-glazed, and powder-coated in black, they contrasted well with the bright, freshly cleaned stonework. Their gridded design preserved the industrial charm while adding a modern sense of luxury to the apartments within.

Cobbles tested the strength of her ankles as she left the bridge and entered the site through a stone archway on the right side. She passed an undeveloped outbuilding to her right. It was a space on the property's grounds that she hadn't yet decided what to do with, not that she had the funds to do anything whatsoever. Drew had been clear he wasn't giving her anything more for such projects until she was making money from her endeavour. She used to dream the outbuilding would be converted into small units and house boutique shops; now it seemed destined to sit empty.

The outbuilding extended perpendicular to the canal,

meeting a stone boundary wall at the far end of the site. The wall then ran parallel to the water, stretching towards the main factory on the far left to form an enclosed courtyard. An opening in the centre of the stone wall allowed vehicle access from the road for staff.

She crossed the courtyard, passing a dominating stone fountain in the centre. Water spurted from the top, cascading down into a circular basin below. Passing half a dozen wooden picnic benches, she slipped inside the building, entering the reception area, which also served as a small museum shop. With a nod to Rachel at the reception desk, Victoria glanced through the museum's glass doors to her right. Much to her delight, people were milling about inside.

Turning left, she entered an open-plan café. She was particularly proud of the L-shaped space, which sat on the corner of the building, facing the water. Industrial lighting hung from the high ceilings, and exposed stone walls contrasted with the wooden floor and steel support beams. Brown leather sofas, wooden tables, and metal chairs created a warm, modern aesthetic.

Only a few customers were scattered around the spacious room; their low murmur of conversation mingled with the scent of coffee. It was a place she'd once envisioned filled with lively chatter and the sound of clinking cups. Now it felt empty and unloved. What could she do to fill the space?

As she crossed the floor, sunlight poured onto it through large windows at the far end of the room. They offered sweeping views over the canal from the adjacent tables — another of her ideas. She smiled at Emma, an employee who was currently clearing tables. She was young and relatively inexperienced but pleasant and hardworking; Victoria had high hopes for her.

Following the room around to the left, she traced the line of windows and exited through the door in the far wall into the wharf's staff-only area. It contained a staffroom and several offices, the largest being hers. She had chosen that part of the building specifically for the view of the canal and the bridge. It allowed her to monitor movement along the towpath and into the wharf from her office window — something she did a little too often.

No sooner had she sat down in her office and swapped her trainers for black, leather-heeled boots than the small frame of her catering manager appeared in the doorway. Petite and sharp-featured, Christine stood with her arms folded, her expression hovering between mild exasperation and patient resignation. Her dark eyes, always assessing, swept across the office with a cool scrutiny, reminding Victoria why she'd never warmed to the woman.

Despite her permanently put-upon demeanour, there was no denying Christine's efficiency. The woman ran the catering operation with military precision, ensuring everything was done exactly as it should be whether people liked it or not.

"Ah, Christine. Just the person I wanted to see," Victoria said, slipping off her jacket and hooking it over the back of her chair. "Any idea what's going on with that blasted orange boat?"

"That's why I came to see you. It's been moored there all week, poaching our customers." Christine's tone was hard and accusatory. "I was hoping *you* would deal with it."

"Have you got the café's sales figures for the week so far?" Victoria asked calmly, caution prevailing. She wasn't about to unleash hell on someone without the data to back it up.

Christine stepped forward and passed a sheet of paper to Victoria. "The quarterly report is there, too."

"Thank you. Leave it with me," Victoria said, her gaze drifting to the numbers.

The creases on Christine's face suggested she hadn't been expecting such a swift dismissal, but Victoria needed to analyse the situation in peace. She was mildly impressed that the woman could even manage to crease her skin with her hair so tightly pulled back in a bun.

Grateful that Christine made no argument beyond a loud huff and a firm shutting of the door, Victoria settled down to examining the spreadsheet. The weekly numbers spoke for themselves: The café's takings for the previous days had dropped off sharply compared to last week. The warmer weather over the last few days really should have boosted sales.

The total figures for the first quarter weren't much to look at either. She knew January and February hadn't been great, but she'd pinned her hopes on March bringing in more. Sadly, the café had barely broken even; she couldn't blame that on their new neighbour.

She threw the sheets of paper down, completely missing her desk and sending them flying across the room. With an exasperated sigh, she got up to look out the large window behind her desk, only to find herself in direct line of sight of the damned orange boat. With an even deeper sigh, she racked her brain for what to do. As much as she resented it, she wasn't one to crush free enterprise. Victoria wasn't even sure she had the power to move the woman along.

For now, she would do nothing. The museum and shop figures were due soon; only then would she have a clearer picture of the overall impact of the newcomer on the wharf. A week's worth of unanswered emails was waiting for her.

A loud cough at her door pulled her from her screen. A glance at the clock told her two hours had passed since she'd last looked up. Jasper, her museum curator and partner in crime, entered and placed a mug of steaming coffee on her coaster. His bright orange waistcoat paired with a white shirt and orange tie did not escape her notice. Why was everything orange suddenly?

"I thought you might need this," he said, perching on the side of the desk.

"Yes, I do! Thanks."

"So, how was London?"

"I did his laundry and cleaned the place top to bottom. It was filthy." She shuddered at the reminder.

"You're not his mother, Vic," Jasper said, rubbing at the stubble on his oval face. "You don't have to do that."

Victoria exhaled. "Isn't that what every man wants, though? Someone to replace their mother? And then they're surprised when the desire fades — because who can feel like a lover when they're treated like a parent?"

"I have no problem playing daddy," Jasper said, cocking his bald head with a coy smile.

The comment teased a crease from the side of Victoria's mouth. Out of all the elements that made the wharf so wonderful, she'd missed him most of all.

"So, he didn't put up one last fight about you being here full-time?" Jasper continued.

"He said I was more valuable to the company as an architect — like I was an asset, not his wife. Yes, financially it's better for us, but I'm nearly fifty, and this place has lit a passion inside me that I've not felt before."

She swivelled in her chair to look at the canal, only to spot the orange boat again. Her eyes narrowed. The trading pitches along the canal were intended to complement the wharf, draw people to it — not compete with it.

Jasper appeared beside her and lifted his black-rimmed glasses on top of his head. "It'll be great having you around more."

"As a buffer from Christine's moaning, you mean?"

He let out a light laugh. "She's been to see you already, then?"

"I'd barely sat down before she manifested in front of me. You could have called me to warn me about that, you know." Victoria pointed out the window.

"I thought you'd be having a hard enough time without me adding to it. You couldn't do much from London anyway." Jasper took some folded sheets of paper from the pocket of his navy suit trousers. "I assume you'll want these."

Victoria whipped them out of his hand. The figures brought some relief, just not as much as she would have liked. While the museum and shop numbers were fractionally down for the week, the drop was nowhere near the percentage the café had seen. She could chalk it up to seasonal fluctuations, which she expected. What the data revealed was that customers were still coming into the wharf, albeit full of Clem's coffee and cakes.

"Well?" Jasper asked cautiously.

"Any ideas how you sink a narrowboat?"

"That bad?"

Victoria nodded. "Drew's threatening to shut us down and convert the ground floor into apartments if we don't turn a profit soon. He knows it takes at least three years for a business to become profitable; he *told* me that, for pity's sake. The café is our biggest earner."

"Then why is he pushing?"

"I don't know," she exhaled.

"Is business bad for him, too? Maybe he's looking to recoup his investment?"

"I don't know," she repeated, her tone sharp. "He doesn't tell me anything." She took a breath. "Sorry. I didn't mean to snap. I just feel… out of my depth. Out of control. It's not something I'm used to. But one thing I do know is business and profits come first with him."

Jasper rubbed her arm. "We'll come up with something. We're a team. We started this together; we're not letting it end anytime soon."

His reassurance was comforting, but doubt lingered. From the moment her research had led her to Jasper, an esteemed fashion historian specialising in corsetry, and he'd agreed to join forces with her on bringing the heritage centre together, they'd faced every hurdle side by side, becoming firm friends in the process. Jasper was unshakeably optimistic, a steady force who never let her lose sight of the vision. This time, though, the worry was harder to ignore. To come so far and fall at the last hurdle would be gut-wrenching.

"Why don't we go and check out the enemy camp?" he suggested. "See what we're up against?"

Victoria's jaw dropped. "You mean try the goods?"

"Yes." He smirked. "I'll pay if it's too much for you to part with cash to a competitor. Come on."

# CHAPTER 4

*V*ictoria reluctantly got to her feet and trailed after Jasper, catching up with him on the bridge.

"You queue," she instructed him. "I'm going to sit and watch."

"What can I get you?" Jasper asked.

"Lemon drizzle if there is any, otherwise surprise me."

Victoria settled on a wooden bench a little way down the towpath, not yet ready to come face to face with whoever was causing the headache now pulsing behind her temples. She wanted to observe. Knowing one's enemy didn't simply mean sampling their wares; it was about understanding the person behind the product.

People heading towards the wharf paused at an A-board, eyed the boat, and joined the queue. The length of it didn't seem to deter them; if anything, it drew them towards the boat like a magnet. *Typical*.

Victoria's eye caught the hatch of the narrowboat, where a woman who looked to be in her late thirties frantically served coffee. A high ponytail constrained her long, brown hair, and a rather intriguing smile was flashed at every customer. Her eyes looked kind and genuine, and her face was so expressive that Victoria struggled to look away. Was this annoyingly attractive woman… Clem?

A couple of plastic benches sat in front of the narrowboat, crammed with people shovelling cake from paper plates into their mouths. They nodded to each other with satisfied smiles. A group of people stood up and wandered over the bridge into the wharf, where, under different circumstances, they might have headed into the café. Her stomach churned over the lost revenue.

Jasper finally joined her after ten minutes, presenting her with a small cup and a paper plate. "An espresso and a lemon drizzle."

"Thanks." The cake looked irresistible, making Victoria's mouth water.

"Shit," Jasper muttered, mid-bite. "That's the best damn coffee and walnut cake I've ever tasted. How's yours?"

Victoria remained silent for a moment, overwhelmed by the perfect balance of sharp, zesty lemon cutting through rich, buttery sweetness. The sponge was light and moist, soaking up the tanginess that seemed to seep into every crumb. The crisp sugar glaze gave a satisfying crunch before melting into lemony bliss. It was divine.

Jasper reached over, unable to wait for Victoria's assessment, and scooped a forkful into his mouth. "Oh, wow," he mumbled around the bite. "Who knew cake could taste this good?"

"Indeed," Victoria agreed.

"What the hell are we selling? Our cakes are like rubbery plastic compared to this."

Victoria winced. "Yes, thank you for that observation. Sadly, you're not wrong."

She watched as Jasper scanned a QR code on the side of the cup with his iPhone and then tapped the screen a few times. She could just make out the image of an orange boat on what looked like an Instagram page.

"You're not going to follow her, are you?"

"Of course not," he said, quickly shoving his phone into his trouser pocket. "Oh, she gave me this."

Jasper pulled a business card out and passed it to Victoria. One side displayed a logo with a website, an email address, and assorted social media logos. The reverse featured a QR code with the words, *Please leave a review.*

"She's friendly, too — very chatty," Jasper added through his last mouthful of cake. "We should leave her a review."

"We certainly will not," Victoria sniffed, shoving the card into her pocket as Jasper chuckled and took their rubbish to the narrowboat's bin.

Back at the wharf, Jasper returned to the museum, but rather than heading straight back to her office, Victoria stopped in the café. With her catering manager nowhere in sight, Victoria nodded at Emma behind the counter and headed into the kitchen.

"Ah, Christine, there you are," she said, spotting the woman standing at a stainless steel island, prepping for lunch. "As suspected, takings are down, so Jasper and I have been over to try the cake from the boat. They are far superior to what we offer. I assume you don't make ours fresh?"

"Of course not," Christine scoffed, slicing a cucumber with unnecessary force. "I don't have time to make cakes. I just buy whatever's available from our supplier. We're short-staffed enough without me spending my days baking."

"Can I see the cakes?" Victoria asked firmly.

Christine dropped her knife onto the worktop with a clatter that made Victoria pull in a breath. She let it out slowly and followed Christine to one of the large fridges at the back of the kitchen.

"There." Christine pointed at four large cakes in disposable plastic containers.

Extracting a chocolate one, Victoria examined the label and its long list of unpronounceable ingredients. "I don't even know what half these ingredients are. Do you?"

Christine gave her a flat look. "There's preservatives, so they keep longer; emulsifiers and stabilisers to improve the texture and consistency; and syrups to stop them drying out."

"And all this is necessary?"

"If you want to be able to store them, yes. They last for one to two weeks."

"I don't want to store them, Christine. I want to *sell* them!" Victoria snapped. She'd bet Clem's cakes didn't have a single additive — and didn't need them either. They probably flew out of her hatch within hours.

"Well, best get bums on seats then, hadn't you? Marketing is not my department," Christine bit back as she returned to her post and proceeded to chop cucumber regularly and firmly.

The problem, Victoria was quickly surmising, was that marketing wasn't anyone's department. If anything, the job fell to her, but she had no idea how to draw people in. She had assumed, naively, that people would flock in once they were open, but after an initial buzz, numbers dried up faster than Christine's chemical-laden cakes. There was also the question of finding the budget to hire a full-time marketing person; a part-time one would be a stretch, though she wasn't sure she could afford not to.

Lifting the lid on the chocolate cake, Victoria recoiled at the overly sweet, synthetic smell. Half the cake remained, and she could see the sponge was dense and unappealing. A shiny frosting coated the top, but on closer inspection it looked greasy. It was the sort of cake that promised indulgence but delivered disappointment on the first bite. Not that she was about to taste it. The only thing she was craving was another slice of Clem's lemon drizzle.

Her thoughts drifted to getting her hands on one, but she quickly shook the idea away. She needed that boat gone, not to be adding to its profits.

Victoria left Christine to her prep work, satisfied that she had made it clear she wasn't happy with what they were serving customers. She returned to her office with yet another dilemma playing on her mind. Changing how they ran things in the café would take work, especially if Christine wasn't on board. If they couldn't bake onsite, new suppliers would need to be found.

By mid-afternoon, her head was fuzzy and overwhelmed. Victoria kicked off her boots and slipped into her trainers, ready to head home. There was still work to do, but she could do it from a laptop with a glass of wine in hand. The bright sunshine and warm breeze beckoned her outside, and the stroll home might even prove productive.

It didn't, thanks to a group of noisy school children following behind her. As she crossed her driveway, she noticed the neighbouring house was now clad in scaffolding, which further soured her mood. The builders had better be quiet with whatever they were doing, or she'd give them a stern talking-to. With her work hours split between weekdays and weekends, she'd likely be around when they were, and builders were notorious for noisy radios, inane whistling, and shouting.

She kicked off her trainers and hung up her coat and bag in the boot room, then immediately headed to the kitchen with only one thing on her mind — a bottle of chilled New Zealand sauvignon blanc. She uncorked the bottle and filled a glass. The cool liquid trickled down her throat and soothed her instantly.

As she slid open the bi-fold glass doors of her large kitchen extension, fresh air and birdsong drifted inside, and the weight of the day began to melt away. Tucking herself into her armchair, she gazed out towards the canal, the greenery framing it like a scenic photograph.

She'd missed her house. Even though she'd only lived there for four years, it felt more like home than their London property ever had. The penthouse, perched at dizzying heights, was not for the fainthearted, and anything above a third storey certainly made her heart race.

Avoiding the floor-to-ceiling windows was near impossible, and when she tried to lower the blinds, Drew would complain she was ruining the view and raise them again. He never missed a chance to remind her how hard he'd worked to afford such a panorama. He would dismiss her concerns with a casual, "You'll get used to it." It was the same line he'd thrown out when announcing that they were to leave their four-bedroom Georgian house in Primrose Hill for a penthouse in Canary Wharf. He said he wanted to jog to the office in the mornings rather than be collected by the company car for the hour-long commute.

She had adored their Primrose Hill house, not least

because it had been her first project for Drew's construction company. Although she was already well established at the firm of architects, this had been a test, an opportunity to prove herself to her boss and his most important client, Drew. The firm had worked on several developments with him, and he was impressed by her style, particularly when it came to historical restoration.

He gave her free rein with the house, but she never imagined they would end up dating, let alone that it would become their first marital home. When the secondary bedrooms remained empty year after year, their hopes quietly faded until the answer came: Drew was infertile. The house they hoped to fill with children became a constant reminder of what was beyond their grasp. Every quiet room echoed with absence. Drew decided there was no point keeping a family home without a family to fill it. It had broken Victoria's heart to leave.

Going on to maintain what was essentially a bachelor pad — when Drew wasn't one — felt just as pointless to her. His commute may have shortened, but hers had increased from a fifteen-minute walk to Camden Town to a forty- minute commute with a Tube change. That was when he suggested she work for him directly rather than him employing her through her firm. It would be cheaper for the business and end her commute. He even suggested they could jog to the office together. So, she handed in her notice but declined the jogging, not quite ready to join the midlife crisis her husband appeared to be having.

Refilling her glass from the fridge, she picked up her phone from the kitchen worktop and settled back in her chair. It was time to make a call that might offer a solution to her Clem's Coffee & Cakes problem.

"Hi, Angela. It's Victoria," she said as soon as the call connected to the company lawyer. "Quick question."

"Hi, Vic. Fire away."

"When you drew up the legal agreements with Richard Armitage, was there anything about a no-competition clause for the traders along the towpath opposite?"

"Give me ten minutes to dig out the file, and I'll call you back."

"Thanks."

As she waited, sipping her wine, she took in her view over the beautifully landscaped garden. A stretch of lawn with neatly clipped hedges and borders sloped down to a weathered wooden jetty overlooking the canal. She'd fallen in love with the view first. Since leaving their Primrose Hill home, she'd longed to live beside a canal again. She missed her view over the Regent's Canal and her daily walk along it to work.

The house, although liveable, had been in a bad state when they bought it. She knew the wharf development plans were going to take at least a year to pull together before any real work could begin, so living nearby had been a no-brainer. Drew was happy that she'd be adding value to another property alongside developing the wharf; Victoria was just delighted to escape London and its bright lights, noises, and fumes.

The distant chug of a narrowboat caught her ear, drawing her gaze as it came into view. The familiar flash of garish orange made her jaw tighten. As it passed, she hoped never to see it again.

Pulling the card Jasper gave her from her pocket, she scanned the QR code with her phone. A total of seventy-seven Google reviews popped up, all of them five stars and all left in under a week! It must be a new business, she decided, and with a quarter of them failing in the first year, perhaps the problem would resolve itself in time. No business could be sustainable selling a few cakes and coffees. Not that she could wait a year for Clem's Coffee & Cakes to go bust. She'd be out of business herself by then.

The wharf had only managed forty-two reviews in the last year. With an average rating of 3.9, none of the reviews were as gushing as the ones she was reading now.

*"Absolutely fantastic coffee and the best lemon drizzle I've ever tasted! You can tell everything is homemade with love. A real gem of a spot!" – Lisa T.*

*"Lovely little café boat with delicious bakes and great coffee. The brownies are next level! Friendly service and a beautiful setting by the canal." – Melissa N.*

*"Clem's cakes are divine, as is Clem! Perfect balance of flavour and texture. Highly recommend the blueberry muffins – still warm when I got it!" – Emma P.*

*"Great coffee, gorgeous cakes, and a charming atmosphere!" – Daniel W.*

Victoria's stomach felt sour, and she wished she hadn't begun reading. The phone ringing brought a welcome interruption.

"So, no — there isn't, basically," Angela said as soon as Victoria answered. "It's mostly about bridge access and usage."

Victoria huffed. That wasn't what she'd wanted to hear.

"Did we miss something?" Angela asked.

"No, don't worry," Victoria reassured her. "It's nothing I can't sort out."

A boat selling coffee and cake wasn't something they could have foreseen. Back then, they'd been too preoccupied with hammering out access rights to the bridge during negotiations for the site. The seller owned it and the land opposite, along with the stretch of waterway and the towpath, so most of their legal energy had gone into that. Without pedestrian access across the bridge, the business would have missed out on a lot of custom from the town.

"I heard from Julia that Drew has put the wharf on her monitoring list," Angela said, her voice almost a whisper.

"Yes, but I'll turn things around," Victoria replied, hoping her tone at least sounded more confident than she felt. "Successful businesses aren't made overnight."

"True," Angela agreed.

"Anyway, thanks for your help."

"You're welcome."

They said their goodbyes and hung up.

Victoria felt a sharp pain in her hand before realising she was clenching her fist, her nails digging deep into her palm. Did everyone know? It made sense that Julia knew because she was Drew's number cruncher. Victoria had never wanted to be on her list, especially with Drew giving her until the end of the summer to make some changes. If she was on Julia's radar, did that mean he had already made up his mind?

The thought that everyone at the office knew the wharf wasn't thriving grated inside her. It didn't reflect well on her or her abilities. She pushed the thought aside, though, to focus on the task at hand. First thing in the morning, she needed to meet with Christine. If there was nothing they could do legally, she'd find another way to boost sales.

The familiar sound of a chugging engine pulled her attention back to the canal. The ghastly orange narrowboat was back, having turned itself around, and was now blocking her view by mooring next door. Was *this* her new neighbour?

"Hell no," Victoria growled.

This was war. Clem's Coffee & Cakes had to go, and she already had an idea forming in her head. She needed to speak to Christine now.

# CHAPTER 5

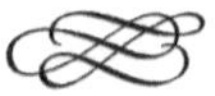

Clem peered out of Florence's serving hatch. Where was everybody? Every morning that week, she'd opened it to a patient yet eager queue. So far today, though, she'd only had three people and one hopeful Labrador. Thanks to the height of Florence against the towpath, it was easy enough for him to pop his head through the serving hatch to drool at the cakes on the worktop.

Deciding to take a closer look, she stepped outside. The weather was fine, and the towpath was busy enough, but everyone was heading into the wharf. Max was waving a customer off, so she caught his eye, and he wandered over.

"Is it me, or is it quiet today?"

Max scratched his beard. "Same as any other Friday. Busiest day of the week, bar Saturdays and Sundays."

"Every day this week I've had a queue, but today… barely a sniff. Do you think the novelty has worn off already?" she asked, trying not to sound too concerned but failing miserably.

"I think it's more to do with that sign." Max nodded to an A-board beside Clem's.

She approached it, only to find it was blocking hers. It read, *Free hot drink with every cake purchased.* An arrow underneath pointed to the wharf.

"What the hell?" she blurted out. "How long has that been there?"

Max shrugged. "It's not enough to make me go. Their cake is terrible, and the coffee isn't much better. They have nothing on you, but some people can't resist a bargain."

So many thoughts rushed through Clem's head that she struggled to organise them, but one stood out. Fight fire with fire.

"Could you redo my board, please?" she asked.

"Of course."

Fetching her cloth and chalk pen from inside, she returned to Max and wiped the board.

"Could you put 'Free hot drink with every cake purchased'? Don't forget the arrow."

Max smirked. "My pleasure."

Once he finished, Clem moved it in front of the wharf's sign. "That'll show them."

A few moments later, a loud voice echoed in the distance.

"How dare you move that sign?"

Clem turned to see a woman marching towards her along the towpath, her mousy-blonde, shoulder-length waves swaying with her stride. Dressed with subtle precision — in navy chinos; a crisp, white shirt; and a beige jumper casually draped around her shoulders — the woman was the picture of sophistication. Her outfit was nothing flashy yet perfectly curated. It took Clem a second glance at her fierce eyes to realise it was her shouting.

"I haven't touched your sign," Clem shouted back.

She recognised the woman; she'd been sitting on a bench a little further down the towpath from Florence the previous day. Although Clem had been busy serving customers, her eyes weren't too distracted to notice a beautiful woman. Not that it was her looks that had caught Clem's attention; it was her forlorn expression. There was something quietly arresting about her: sharp cheekbones softened by worry, eyes that looked tired, and lips that fidgeted as if caught mid-thought. She looked as though she carried the weight of the world on her shoulders.

Now it was clear she had been checking Clem out — well, not her, but what she was selling. A man had joined her. He'd ordered coffee and walnut cake and a slice of lemon drizzle. She remembered him distinctly; he'd visited every day since she'd opened for a latte and a slice of coffee and walnut. It was now her guess that they both worked at the wharf.

The angry woman, whom Clem would call Lemon Drizzle until she got a name, was picking up Clem's sign. Was she the boss?

"Hey! Get your hands off it!" Clem shouted, striding over to grab it back.

Lemon Drizzle twisted away, but Clem caught the edge of the sign and yanked it. A handbag slipped from her opponent's shoulder and dropped to the ground as she retaliated, gripping the other side of the A-board with both hands.

"Give it back!" Clem snapped, tugging harder.

"It's blocking mine!" the woman barked.

"Yours was blocking mine first!" Clem bit back. "Don't dish it out if you can't take it!"

Max moved to intervene. "Ladies—" he began, but the

furious tug of war only escalated, forcing him to jump back.

"I'm amazed you need a sign," the other woman sniffed. "Your horrid boat is so garish it would make a mole squint."

*Seriously?* Now she was coming after Florence.

"It's bad enough I have to see it at the bottom of my garden," the woman added.

The penny dropped, and Clem stopped pulling. "You're her."

The woman scowled. "What do you mean?"

"Nothing," Clem said, far too quickly.

"No, come on. Out with it, if you have something to say. Who exactly am I?"

"My parents' neighbour. They... erm... might have mentioned you."

Lemon Drizzle's skin pinked, likely remembering the altercation with them. With her opponent's guard down and an audience gathering, it was time to finish this. Clem yanked at her sign. It came freely — too freely for the force she'd exerted. Her heel skidded on the wet morning grass, and she slipped backwards.

"No, no, no—" she gasped, already falling.

She let go of the sign, which thudded to the ground and fell to the side. Her arms flailed, windmilling as she tried to stay upright. In a panic, she grabbed Lemon Drizzle's arm for balance. She shrieked as Clem's weight dragged them both backwards. There was a moment of horrified eye contact, then—

SPLASH!

The cold water hit Clem like a slap to her soul. The shock of it struck first, a blunt, icy force that sucked the air from her lungs and pricked her skin. Her boots were heavy with water, and her clothes clung to her like seaweed, weighing her down as she kicked to find the bottom to stand up. Once she found it, she stood, bursting through the water, coughing and blinking furiously as her sodden lashes blurred her vision. The murky water stank with a mix of oil, rust, algae, and something unidentifiable that made her gag. Her ears rang from the impact, and her whole body trembled from the cold.

Something splashed about nearby, reminding her she hadn't gone in alone. Great. Falling into the canal was bad enough, but accidentally dragging someone with her? The embarrassment was worse than the cold.

Noticing that a wide-eyed Max was rushing to the bank, Clem waded towards him. The woman's head appeared beside her, gasping, soaked, and furious. Expletives began tumbling from her shivering lips.

"Stand up," Clem shouted at the woman.

Lemon Drizzle emerged properly, water up to her chest, and reached up for Max's hand. He dragged her out and then lifted Clem onto the bank beside the startled, dripping woman.

Clem thought they must look like a pair of shipwreck survivors, chests heaving, hair plastered to their heads, clothes clinging in the most unflattering way. On second glance, though, Clem realised the way the woman's white shirt clung to her breasts wasn't entirely unflattering. The material was practically see-through, and her eyes took in everything it revealed.

"If you are quite finished," the woman said, fixing her with a steely glare from a pair of blue eyes.

If Clem hadn't been so cold, she would have felt a rush of heat from embarrassment at being caught ogling her hardened nipples. She watched the make-up–streaked woman pick up the fallen sign with trembling fingers and place it next to her own. Without a word, she grabbed her handbag and strode off towards the bridge, leaving a trail of water behind her.

Clem felt a sharp pang of guilt. She hadn't even asked if the woman was okay. She also noticed her jumper was no longer around her shoulders; it was likely waterlogged and sinking to the bottom of the canal.

Beginning to shiver uncontrollably, she turned to Max. "Would you mind keeping an eye out for customers whilst I clean up? I'll be as quick as I can."

"You take as long as you need to get that smell off you," he said, wrinkling his nose and desperately trying to withhold a grin. "You'll drive away the customers otherwise."

Stepping onto Florence's bow, she stripped off as many wet clothes as she could, fully aware people were still lingering after the — well, to call it what it was — the fight. She caught sight of the woman disappearing into the wharf and suddenly wondered if she should have offered her the use of her shower.

*Sod her! She started it.*

Throwing everything into the washing machine, Clem entered the shower and let the warm spray soothe her cold skin. She washed her hair twice with shampoo and scrubbed herself with soap, hoping it would be enough to erase the smell.

When she finally made her way to the kitchen, she discovered Max using the espresso machine.

He approached her and sniffed the air. "Better. I'd have another one later, though, just to be sure. You've had a few customers, mostly asking what happened, but they all bought something. I assumed the offer on the sign still stood, so I gave them hot drinks on the house." He reached into his pocket and extracted a pile of coins. "Here. They all paid in cash except one, but I have the same card reader as you, so it wasn't a problem."

Clem opened her mouth to speak only to close it again as she took the coins.

"You're wondering how I served two espressos, one cappuccino, and one latte?" he asked.

She nodded again, tying her damp hair back into a ponytail.

"I've done my time as a barista and as a barman."

"Thanks for helping me out," Clem said with a grateful smile. "I really appreciate it. You should get back; you might have missed customers of your own."

Max shrugged. "I ran over between making coffee and stuck a sign out asking people to pay here, so I'm good."

"Great. Let's see how good your coffee tastes, then. I'll have an espresso. Not even a hot shower has warmed me up after that dunking." She shivered. "I still feel cold inside."

"One espresso, coming up," Max said, springing into action.

Clem picked up her phone from the worktop, relieved it hadn't been in her pocket when she'd fallen into the canal.

"I can't get over the barefaced cheek of that woman to move my sign and then to fight me for it."

"That was Victoria Hargreaves," Max explained as the coffee grinder crunched through the beans. "She runs the wharf. I told you to watch out for her."

"So did my parents," Clem sighed. "She's their neighbour."

"Yikes."

"She was sniffing around here yesterday. Came to try my coffee and cake with some chap in a rather fetching orange waistcoat."

"Oh, really?" Max said, the corners of his mouth curling tightly. He nodded towards the windows overlooking the wharf. "She's probably there right now, watching you from her office and plotting your downfall."

Clem gave a light chuckle, then wondered how much truth there might be to his words. "Have you met her before?" she asked, wandering to the window and trying to guess where Victoria's office might be.

"No. One of the other traders warned me about her when I arrived. She's a stickler for keeping signage off the towpath — bit of a health and safety nut, perhaps."

"I get she doesn't want competition, but we all need to make a living," Clem said, her tone sharp with frustration.

Max hummed his agreement as he twisted the portafilter into place. "Living on the water is not as cheap as people think. By the time you've paid for insurance, licences, mooring fees, safety certificates, not to mention fuel costs for both you and the boat, it's a tough gig. A private landowner controlling the towpath pushes up the costs, too. Everyone wants a piece of our pie."

Clem let out a weary sigh of agreement as rich coffee ran from the spouts in two silky ribbons, filling the cup. Thankfully, her dad had sorted most of the paperwork for her; he was well versed in the rules of the waterways. She'd completed her food hygiene certificate and registered with the local council's environmental health department, but he'd handled everything else. She knew how much it had all cost her, though, and how much she needed to earn to break even for the year. With most of that income coming in during the warmer months, she could ill afford to be at war with the neighbours.

Max passed her the cup. "Here."

"Thanks," she said, wrapping her hands around it and instinctively blowing on it before taking a sip. The liquid hit sharply, the heat and bitterness lingering on her tongue.

"That's good," she said, giving her neighbour a smile of approval as she placed the cup on the worktop. "I just hope I can make enough to cover my expenses. I'm not expecting to get rich. This was never about becoming a millionaire. It's a lifestyle choice. A way out of the corporate grind, of feeling stuck and—"

"Unfulfilled?" Max suggested.

A faint smile touched her lips that he seemed to understand.

"Most of us are, aren't we?" he continued. "All trying to find something that feels more like living?"

Clem nodded, cursing her naivety for thinking that everything would be easy. Just because life was challenging and unfulfilling, it didn't automatically mean change fixed everything. New beginnings came with their own trials: uncertainty, hard graft, and moments like these where optimism felt foolish. She'd wanted a fresh start, not a fresh set of problems dressed up as opportunity.

Victoria stood in the cobbled courtyard, cold and dripping wet. Every instinct told her to move; to act. Instead, she stood frozen by shock and disbelief. She couldn't enter the building like this, soaked through and stinking, but what now?

People were beginning to stop and stare. She rubbed her arms as waves of shivers ran through her, only to realise her cashmere jumper was missing and likely at the bottom of the canal. It had been one of her favourites, too.

"Vic!" Jasper shouted, striding towards her. "Get in the car."

The lights of his white Audi blinked at the far end of the courtyard.

"Where are we going?" she asked as he reached her side.

"I'm taking you home, of course. What the hell happened? A visitor said two women had fallen in the canal. I came to your office to see if you were in yet, only to see you being dragged out of the water through the window. Who fell in with you?"

"Her," Victoria growled.

"Her?"

Victoria wanted to reply, *That infuriating, high-ponytailed woman with the strangely captivating smile who's doing her best to put me out of business.* Instead, she said, "Clem," as she opened the passenger door.

Jasper reached behind the driver's seat and pulled out a plastic shopping bag. "Here, sit on this."

Victoria settled onto the rustling bag. The soggy fabric of her clothes stuck to her, sending a wave of cold through her trembling body with every movement.

Jasper flicked on the heated seat and nudged the climate control up a few degrees. "Maybe it'll stave off hypothermia. At the very least, it might calm your nipples down." He nodded towards Victoria's chest as he pulled out of the car park.

They had caught Clem's eye, too; she appeared to have been enjoying herself until Victoria felt compelled to interrupt her ogling. If she hadn't been dripping wet and freezing cold — and if it hadn't been Clem — she might have enjoyed the attention herself. It had been a long time since an attractive person had cast an eye over her like that. A voice in Victoria's head snapped: *Oh, shut up. She isn't attractive. She's infuriating.* Worse still, Clem threatened to bring about her downfall if something wasn't done about her competing business, and soon.

"Thanks for rescuing me," Victoria said to Jasper as they idled at a crossing. "I was at a loss for what to do back there."

"I noticed. So, what happened?"

"She copied our café offer and put her sign in front of ours."

"And how did that end up with you both going for a swim in the canal?"

"I moved her sign, and we sort of tussled over it," Victoria muttered with an exasperated sigh. "She lost her balance and grabbed my arm to steady herself, pulling me in with her."

A smile tugged at the corner of Jasper's mouth. "You… *tussled*?"

Victoria pursed her lips, unsure where the amusement lay in what she'd just endured.

"Did you push her?" Jasper asked.

Victoria's stomach lurched. Had she pushed Clem? She didn't think so, but everything had happened so fast, she couldn't be sure. All she could remember was that final moment, when they'd lost to gravity and Clem's eyes had locked with hers in a mutual panic. They were a deep brown, matching the colour of her hair, and the way they'd fixed on her with such a strange intensity made Victoria's stomach twist.

"Why didn't you just move our sign elsewhere?"

"I didn't really get the chance; plus, that's the best spot. We can't obstruct the path with signage, and I couldn't move it further forward as hers was almost on the towpath," Victoria replied firmly, recalling the strict rules Mr Armitage enforced to allow them access across the bridge.

"Well, it might've saved me from taking you home reeking of canal water," Jasper muttered, rolling down the window.

"I could have walked."

"No, you couldn't."

He was right. Her brain had stopped working properly, what with the shock and cold setting in.

"What was our sign doing there, anyway, to make her want to block it?" Jasper demanded.

Victoria stared at the hedgerows whizzing by, trying to think of a way to get out of explaining. She couldn't.

"I told Christine to put a sign out," she admitted.

She'd hoped Clem would realise she couldn't compete and leave. To find her still there, and the wharf's sign blocked with one offering an identical deal, had boiled her blood and, apparently, her brain.

"I didn't tell her to put it near Clem's sign. That was all Christine's doing," she quickly clarified.

Jasper shook his head. His silence was more unsettling than anything he could have said.

A few minutes later, they pulled into the driveway of Victoria's house.

"Did your handbag get wet?" Jasper asked as they stepped out of the car.

"No, thankfully I dropped it," Victoria replied, grateful for small mercies as she fumbled through her bag for her keys.

"In the tussle?" Jasper asked dryly, covering his smirking lips with his hand.

"Yes," Victoria hissed, not bothering to meet his gaze as she pushed open the front door.

"Well, if a shower doesn't get the smell out, at least the spa tomorrow will help clean your pores — if they let you in. I've been looking forward to it for weeks, and I'm prepared to go in alone, even if it is your birthday present."

Victoria glared at Jasper as he made his way inside.

"You'd do the same," he teased, grinning back at her.

"Make yourself useful and fix me something hot to drink," Victoria instructed as she slipped out of her wet trainers, leaving them on the doorstep.

"Tea, I think," Jasper said, disappearing into the kitchen.

Victoria gave a hum of agreement as she made her way to the boot room. Stripping off everything but her underwear, she shoved it all in the washing machine, trying not to gag at the stench.

Fifteen minutes later, washed and clothed, she joined Jasper by the large conservatory window, collecting a mug of tea from beside the kettle.

"Better?" Jasper asked.

"Much," she replied, taking a sip of the warm liquid before noticing a sweet taste. Jasper must have added sugar for the shock.

"Have I told you how much I adore the view from here?" he said as he gazed out at her garden.

"Wait until this afternoon when an orange boat turns up to ruin it." Victoria groaned.

Jasper turned sharply to look at her. "Seriously? Clem's boat?"

"The one and only. Her parents own the house next door."

His jaw worked silently for a few seconds. "Can you just moor a narrowboat at the end of your garden?"

"Yes," Victoria confirmed with a nod. "It's a private mooring. You need permission, but plenty of people have them. Apparently, she's not content with mooring outside my office window; I must tolerate it at home, too. It's beyond the pale." She huffed and then gulped the rest of her tea. "We should get back."

By the time they returned to the wharf, the news had already spread amongst the staff. Christine was the first to appear in her office.

"Did you block Clem's sign with ours?" Victoria immediately demanded.

Christine's eyes darted around the room. "How was I to know it would start World War III?"

"What did you think would happen? I asked you to come up with an offer and put a board on the towpath. Not block the competition," Victoria snapped.

"It kind of worked," Christine reasoned. "We were busy early on, but then it died off."

"Because she retaliated and did the same to us," Victoria shot back. "We have no legal standing to move her. Assuming she has the correct permits, then she has every right to be there. We need to come up with some other tactics to win back business."

Christine's eyes lit up. "Leave it with me. I might have an idea."

"It had better be an improvement on your last one!" Victoria yelled.

It didn't matter. Her catering manager had already waltzed from the office.

# CHAPTER 6

*S*aturday passed for Clem without the drama of the previous day. No one had fallen in the canal, the wharf's A-board had vanished, and the angry boss lady was nowhere in sight. This was suspicious. Clem didn't know the woman, but first impressions counted for something, and Victoria Hargreaves didn't strike her as the type to back down quietly or let things go without a fight.

Another meeting wasn't far off the horizon. Max had spotted the woman's jumper floating past when he'd returned to his boat. Clem retrieved it with her barge pole and now returning it felt unavoidable. It looked expensive, so she left it soaking in the bathroom sink until her parents arrived; her mum would know how to revive it.

The day was wet and blustery, a sharp contrast to the sunshine of the day before. The usual stream of cake-happy customers had vanished, replaced by a slow trickle of soggy dogs and their equally damp humans, huddled beneath umbrellas and desperate for something hot to drink. Clem passed steaming cups through the hatch to grateful hands until the wet boots and muddy paws finally pattered away, leaving only the steady drumming of rain on Florence's roof for company.

Using the quiet moments to her advantage, Clem tapped out upbeat and thoughtful replies to a handful of foodie reviewers, including two popular YouTubers who'd promised to swing by in the coming weeks. Their visits could make all the difference to her business, especially now, with footfall unpredictable and word of mouth more powerful than ever. She needed eyes on Florence, and more importantly, she needed people to care enough to either return or tell their friends.

With the afternoon dragging on, she decided to close a little earlier than usual. After setting aside a slice of carrot cake for her mum and a square of rocky road for her dad, she took the opportunity to meet some of her fellow traders. Armed with the last slices of cake, she handed them out to warm smiles, delighted groans, and generous praise. She then returned to Florence, hopeful that a little goodwill might bring in some new custom from her neighbours.

After turning Florence around, she disposed of the day's rubbish and refilled her water tank before heading home. She still needed to get Florence clean and shipshape before her parents arrived. A flurry of nerves caught her off guard. *It's just a boat*, she told herself, but another voice argued, *Not just any boat — it's* Florence. There was an underlying excitement beneath it all: Soon she would see her mum's reaction.

She moored along the towpath on the opposite bank from her parents' house, a little further down from the bridge. The jetty she left free for them to use, knowing they'd need easy access to the house over the weekend.

Once Florence was spick and span, Clem kicked off her shoes and lay back on her bed. Opening her laptop, she checked her socials and then tracked the day's engagement. Measurable marketing was the best form of marketing, and the QR code on her cups was working well. It took customers to a webpage with links to all her social media handles and words of encouragement to follow her. There were fifty-nine hits on the page and seventy-six new Instagram followers that week, which meant seventeen of those new followers must have been organic.

Having responded to the handful of comments with thanks and gentle nudges to leave her a Google review, she opened a new tab and searched for information on Otterford Wharf. A staff page proved Max to be correct. Lemon Drizzle's real name was Victoria Hargreaves, director, and Coffee and Walnut was Jasper Sinclair, the museum's curator — a name that suddenly felt familiar. The catering manager was a rather stern-looking woman named Christine Baxter. Her expression in the photo was like a collapsed soufflé, deflated and utterly joyless. Clem sniggered, remembering Max's comment about the terrible cakes.

A quick trip to Instagram confirmed why Jasper Sinclair felt familiar: He was one of her new followers. How would Lemon Drizzle feel about that? The thought made Clem smile until she realised he may have been asked to spy on her.

Her gaze drifted to Victoria's image on the wharf's website. She looked sultry in that effortless way that made people turn their heads without knowing why. There was a depth to her beauty, something you didn't notice all at once. Her mousy blonde hair fell in a soft wave over one eye, not quite styled yet somehow perfect. Clem's chest gave a traitorous flutter as she recalled yesterday's soaked, see-through shirt. Taking a deep breath, she forced the image away. Getting gooey-eyed over Lemon Drizzle was not in any recipe for success, and anyway, she was far too sour for Clem's taste.

A nose around the website showed the wharf was rich in potential but clearly underutilised. Its social media pages confirmed it. Although they existed, they were severely neglected. With the right marketing, there was so much that could be done to improve things. The thought sent a thrill through Clem as ideas sparked in her brain like wildfire. They would have to wait, though, as a text from her mum to say they'd moored up at Gram's jetty had her heading up to the house to greet them.

"Where's your boat?" her mum asked, immediately pulling her into a hug on the doorstep.

"On the other side of the bridge," Clem replied.

Her dad appeared in the doorway, so she stepped back from her mum's hug and embraced him.

"Let's see it," her mum said, practically pushing them both out the door and slamming it shut. "I can't wait to see how you fitted everything in."

Her dad shot an amused eye roll at Clem. She smiled as she linked her arm through his and they obediently followed her mum, who was already marching off down the lane.

"The builders seem to be cracking on," Clem said to her dad. "I've checked in a few times, but they seem to know exactly what they are doing."

"That's because your mum doesn't stop ringing them," he whispered in her ear.

Clem laughed. "Poor Billy."

"It suits me fine," he chuckled. "If she's nagging him, then she's not nagging me to fix this or that."

"I heard that, Tom," her mum shot back.

Clem caught her dad's eye, and they grinned. Getting a ticking-off from her mum had become a badge of honour.

As they approached the bridge, Clem quickened her pace to catch up with her mum. She reached her as she came to a halt and gazed down the canal.

"Florence?" Her mum read the livery, then turned to Clem. "You named her after my first boat?"

"No. Well… yes, but it's not simply her name. She *is* Florence. Your Florence."

"It can't be *my* Florence!" her mum scoffed.

"Why not?

"She must have gone to the scrapyard years ago."

"Lots of old boats get restored."

"Well, this…" Her mum trailed off, then looked at Clem in confusion. "It can't be?"

"It is."

As her dad caught up to them, her mum turned to him. "Tom, Clem says it's Florence. *Our* Florence."

He nodded. "That she is."

"You knew?" she demanded, hands resting on her hips.

"Of course. I sorted all her licences, didn't I? There aren't many 1974 Hancock & Lane cruisers about."

"I managed to find flecks of paint under all the layers and repainted her in the same colour." Clem beamed, remembering the thrill of her discovery. "At least I hope it's right. I don't think any other period in history would produce orange boats."

"It looks spot on to me," her dad remarked, "but it's been about thirty-five years since we sold her."

"She's truly clementine," her mum remarked.

"Clementine?" Clem questioned.

"Yes. It was the name of the original paint colour. Didn't you realise you were named after Florence?"

Clem couldn't help the soft smile that tugged at her

lips. "You let me think I was named after an orange when all along you named me after her."

Her mum shrugged. "Well, now you know. Is she the same inside?" she added cautiously.

"Nowhere near, I'm afraid. I have installed a professional kitchen, remember. Come and look inside."

Her mum remained silent until she stepped on board and turned to her daughter.

"Oh, Clem," she murmured, shaking her head. "I can't believe it's her."

"No? Then look at the tiller."

Her mum traced the carved initials — CW, BW, and TW — on the wooden tiller, smiling as her fingers brushed over them.

"It really is her," her mum sniffed as her dad squeezed her shoulders.

"She still has her original stove, too. She underwent restoration in the late nineties. They reversed her layout then, so you'll find she's a bit different inside. Go in."

Clem slowly descended the steps behind her mum, giving her space to take it all in.

"Oh, this is a much better layout!" she enthused. "It never made sense to me why bedrooms were next to the stern. You'd have to traipse through to get to the galley or walk around the outside to make a cuppa."

"It was useful, though, when you were little, Clem," her dad added, looking around. "We'd shut the bedroom door, and you'd play safely in here whilst we watched from the tiller." He hummed. "Takes me back. All the orange pine tongue-and-groove panelling has gone, though."

"There's still some left in the bedroom, but it's painted thankfully," Clem confirmed.

She glanced at her dad, but he seemed lost in thought.

"When you got too big, we had to sell her. It was for the best," he said at last, meeting her eyes with a smile.

Her mum chimed in, her voice gentle. "You needed more space than Florence could give you, and we didn't want her to feel like a prison."

Clem found herself nodding, offering her parents the reassurance they seemed to need — that they'd made the right choice all those years ago. And they had. She couldn't imagine growing up aboard Florence, the three of them crammed into such a tiny space.

Still, part of her ached at what they'd given up for her. Although she couldn't remember much of that time, looking through the old photographs made her realise there had been a kind of magic to those early years.

"The kitchen is perfect," her mum said, breaking the silence as she inspected everything.

"Well, I had a little help on the layout," Clem said, giving her mum a nudge. "Thanks for the suggestions. The appliances do work best being on one side, just like you said."

Her mum opened a small cupboard that separated the hot and cold appliances and peered inside. "Galleys happen to be my forte," she added with a smile. "I've spent enough years in them. Keeping doors that you open regularly to one side works wonders for efficiency."

She stepped inside the bathroom next. "What's this?" she asked, poking at the sopping sweater in the sink.

"I was hoping you could help me bring it back to life," Clem admitted sheepishly. "It kind of fell in the canal. I've rinsed it several times and left it to soak. I wasn't sure what to do to get the smell out."

Screwing her face up, her mum plunged her hands into the sink, feeling the jumper. "Not letting it soak for too long would be a start. This is cashmere." She drained the basin, then pressed the jumper gently to squeeze the excess water out. "I'll see what I can do with it."

"Thanks," Clem said, relieved it was one less item on her to-do list.

"Now let me see the rest," her mum said, drying her hands on a towel.

Clem led them down to the bedroom.

Her mum pointed to the bed. "We used to have a sofa there, facing this stove." Her fingers traced along the appliance, stopping and circling an area on its top. "That's definitely the original stove. I recognise this dent. Your dad dropped a hammer on it."

"That's right," he said, a smile forming at the memory. "It just missed my foot."

"It was Florence that brought us together," her mum said, smiling at her dad. "You came out to fix her engine for me."

"Yes, and I only charged you for parts because you were upset at your boss getting handsy."

"Mmm. It came with the territory as a secretary in those days."

"Probably still does." Clem groaned.

"But your dad turned the day around for me." She rubbed her hands together and then squeezed Clem's cheeks. "I'm so glad you've brought her home. I can't believe you managed to keep it from me all this time."

Clem couldn't help feeling a little smug at how well her plan had come together. "I'm not you, Mum, and it's only been six months. To be honest, it didn't feel real until I moored her at Gram's. When I collected her, it felt like I was hiring her for a couple of weeks, and then someone would demand I return her."

Her mum wiped her cheeks. "Oh, get me a tissue for

my eyes and a bag for that jumper, will you? It's time I got dinner in the oven."

Clem looked to her dad, who was still grinning. They both knew her mum well enough to know she couldn't cope with anything too soppy and didn't like to show emotion very often — if ever.

After a dinner of exquisite lasagna aboard *The Kingfisher's Rest*, Clem insisted on helping her mum with clearing up the galley, mainly as an excuse to question her about their impending retirement.

"Are you sure you're ready to hang up your apron and sell up?" she asked.

"It makes sense," her mum said with a shrug. "Everything has happened at the right time, at least for your father. I'm not sure I'm as ready as he is. I just feel like I'm losing a part of myself, along with my home. What am I going to do all day if I don't have the *Kingfisher*?"

"Find a hobby?" Clem suggested, then added, "It is retirement. It's supposed to have a different pace. You could take up gardening, grow some veg."

"Gardening?" Her mum scoffed. "I never had much luck making anything grow except you when we lived on land."

"There's a golf course near here. You could try that. You might even meet some local people, make some friends."

"Golf! I don't think so. The clothes would be terrible for my figure."

Clem sniffed out a laugh. "All right. What about a job?"

"Who would hire me at my age?"

Clem prayed she wasn't looking for an answer and busied herself with packing the dishwasher.

"Anyway," her mum went on, much to Clem's relief, "most women my age are busy with their grandchildren."

Well. There went her short-lived relief.

"I can only apologise for not having had children to keep you busy in your old age. How remiss of me," Clem said sharply.

Her mum pulled a face. "You know what I mean. Your life is what it is. I accept that. If children aren't on the cards, then they aren't on the cards."

"I've never said they weren't."

Her mum pulled a face. "It would be a bit of a challenge, wouldn't it?"

"Because I'm a lesbian?" Clem shot back, wringing a tea towel in her hands.

"No — well, yes — but mainly because you're single."

"Plenty of single women have children."

Her mum heaved a sigh. "Children are challenging enough with two parents; I wouldn't recommend doing it alone. I assume there's no love interest on the horizon?"

"No," Clem groaned, bracing for the inevitable deep dive into her love life — or lack thereof.

"You're unlikely to attract anyone living on a boat," her mum continued, aggressively squirting the worktop with antibacterial spray.

"You managed it with Dad."

"He was a single man with a boat, too. The chances of meeting another single lesbian living the narrowboat life are slim, I'd assume."

"There's more to it than coming across another lesbian with a boat, Mum," Clem grumbled. "There is such a thing as chemistry. We don't simply shack up with the nearest one, you know."

Her dad appeared in the doorway suddenly, much to Clem's relief. "Have you met that woman from next door yet?"

"Victoria Hargreaves? Yes," Clem groaned. "I had a bit of a run-in with her, which resulted in the pair of us ending up in the canal."

Her mum recoiled in horror. "What?"

"The jumper is hers. She lost it in the canal, and I fished it out."

"I just hand-washed *that* woman's jumper?" her mum screeched.

"Yes."

Her mouth opened and closed several times before finally managing, "Why?"

Clem wasn't entirely sure she had an answer. It felt like the right thing to do. Neighbourly. "I feel responsible for her ending up there. The least I can do is return her jumper."

If they were going to be seeing each other regularly, in one location or another, Clem figured they might as well try to get along. One thing she couldn't stand was animosity; it was far too uncomfortable for her liking. And, if she was honest, a part of her wanted to see Victoria again — if only to apologise, of course.

"You should've left it there," her mum said, folding her arms. "Along with her."

"That's a bit harsh," Clem replied.

"Gram often complained to us about her. It took a year to renovate that house next door — noise morning, noon, and night. Now it's our turn. I told Billy not to worry about the disruption. I said there was no one living next door."

"Mum! I can't believe—"

"How exactly did you end up in the canal?" her dad butted in.

"She runs the wharf opposite. She wasn't happy with me competing against their café. We ended up having a bit of a disagreement over a sign, and in we went."

"Ha!" Her mum chuckled. "You give her a run for her money."

Clem had to grin at that. "I intend to."

"Which days are you working?" her dad asked.

"Every day at the moment."

He nodded in understanding but added, "Don't you work yourself into the ground. You need a couple of days off a week."

"I'm not sure I can afford to, not now that I work for myself."

"If you will quit a well-paid job," her mum sniped.

"Well paid but not fulfilling, Mum. I keep telling you that," Clem said through gritted teeth.

"Money isn't everything," her dad added.

"Exactly, but enough to cover my bills would be nice." The week had been relentless. Clem felt the tiredness in her bones, but the exhilaration kept her going, canal dunking aside. "Anyway, I need to get a feel for the footfall, work out which days are busier and when I can afford to close. I've learnt today that opening on rainy days is best avoided."

"Well, you have to make a success of it now," her mum said matter-of-factly.

"Why?"

"I can't have you selling Florence. Not when we've just got her back."

"No pressure then," Clem mumbled to herself, fully aware there was no turning back.

"Even more reason now, if it upsets that woman," her mum added.

Clem took this as her cue. "I'd best head off. It looks like the sun will be back out tomorrow, so I've got a lot of baking to do. Thanks for dinner, Mum."

Thrusting a container at her, her mum said, "Don't forget the leftovers, and *this*." She put the jumper on top. She then allowed herself to break into a momentary smile. "I'm so pleased you've got Florence, Clem. Next time we see you, we'll have to go for a jaunt in her, see if she still feels the same."

Heading up the garden a few minutes later, Clem felt a tightness gripping her chest. A worry had been building inside her all week, making her question her choices. Was this all a huge mistake? She'd thrown everything into this new life, but the uncertainty was gnawing at her. *What if I made the wrong decision? What if I can't make it work? What then?*

A light flicked off in the downstairs window next door, catching her attention and dragging her thoughts back to Victoria. There was something about her, something Clem couldn't put her finger on, that had lingered since their clash.

As Clem reached the lane, an upstairs light in the house came on, illuminating the darkness. A man, presumably Victoria's husband — Clem hadn't missed the ring Victoria was wearing when she'd gripped the A-board — stood at the window. His arm reached out to draw the curtain, but a second figure appeared beside him.

Clem was about to turn away when she noticed the woman's hair was short, like it was styled in a pixie cut. She wasn't well versed in Victoria's shape, but the last time she'd seen her, she'd had shoulder-length hair. The mystery woman leaned in and kissed the man's neck as he closed the curtains.

As the light dimmed, Clem glanced at the driveway. The green Jaguar E-Type she'd spotted Victoria leaving in early that morning when her groceries had arrived was gone. In its place sat a black Porsche 911 GT3. A shiver ran through her. Whether from the cold air or whatever domestic infidelity she was witnessing, she wasn't sure.

What exactly was she supposed to do with this information? Keep it to herself? Tell Victoria? First, she needed to be sure Victoria hadn't had a drastic haircut.

Reaching Florence, Clem pondered keeping her nose out of her neighbour's business. After all, no good deed went unpunished. But something inside pressed on her, and she knew she would have to tell her. She didn't have anything to lose; only Victoria did — if she hadn't already lost it.

# CHAPTER 7

*V*ictoria clicked the end of her Parker pen in and out repeatedly. The spa weekend with Jasper had left her feeling temporarily rejuvenated, but she was no less troubled by her problems. A bit of steam and a massage were mere plasters covering cracks in her skin; some ran so deep they stung to her core.

Being jolted awake by the builders banging away next door at a ridiculous hour had only increased her stress levels that morning. When she popped her head in before work to ask for a little consideration, they said their boss had told them no one was living next door, so they needn't worry about the noise. Victoria had growled inwardly at that. No doubt Clem had found it amusing to misinform them.

It wasn't only the early wake-up call that was making her feel uneasy. As much as she didn't appreciate her dunking in that green swamp, what gnawed at her most was embarrassment over how she'd acted out. If she'd just taken a breath and spoken to Clem calmly, she might not have wasted so much time googling 'canal-borne diseases' during her spa weekend.

The fact that she was turning fifty on Saturday hadn't escaped her notice either. She'd tried to ignore it, but the looming party — a joint celebration for her birthday and the wharf's first anniversary — made it impossible. The last thing she felt like now was a party, but regardless of her feelings about reaching fifty, the wharf's first birthday *did* need to be feted.

Christine had ordered all the food from their supplier, and it was due in with their usual Friday delivery. The decorations and drinks were in Jasper's office. With him away at a conference Thursday and Friday — and not returning until after lunch on Saturday — he was in charge of decorating the café as soon as he returned, so that it would be ready for the party at seven.

Spinning her chair around, her gaze fell on the orange blob of a boat directly opposite her office window, a grisly reminder that there might not be a second birthday to celebrate. Through the small, rectangular windows, she could make out a figure moving inside the boat. When she squinted, she caught sight of a swaying ponytail. It had to be Clem. She was unlikely to have staff on such a small narrowboat, even if she could afford them. It was too small for one person, let alone two.

Victoria had only been on a narrowboat once, for a girls' holiday at university, and it had been the longest, most uncomfortable week of her life. What possessed them to think cramming six women into a sardine can was a good idea, she couldn't recall. The feeling of being unable to breathe, however, had stayed with her, not helped by a particular friend who also took her breath away. In the end, she spent most of the trip perched on the stern or stretched out sunbathing on the roof, pretending she was anywhere else.

Still, the experience had proved worthwhile in that it confirmed confined spaces weren't for her. It also reinforced her architectural education, teaching her the value of flow — specifically, how people moved through a space, how light shifted during the day, and how too much clutter could choke the life out of even the most beautiful design. Whenever she reimagined a period home or transformed neglected buildings, she always began with air, light, and movement.

Noticing Clem was no longer bobbing back and forth inside the boat, Victoria found herself scanning the windows, then the stern, waiting for her to reappear. There was something about the woman that pulled at her. She was intriguing, no question. Curiosity whirred inside Victoria, a need to understand her new neighbour despite the stress she'd brought to her door.

She considered going over and clearing the air. Acting in haste and lashing out weren't typical for her. She was someone who took her time, weighing options, analysing outcomes, and visualising the bigger picture. These were, after all, the skills of an architect.

What had come over her on Friday? Was it the unfamiliar sensation of feeling under threat that had kicked her survival instincts into gear? Touching someone else's property, let alone engaging in a tug of war over it, had been a bad idea, and she knew it.

She yawned and rubbed her eyes. One thing she felt for certain was her growing discomfort at the thought of Clem perceiving her in this way. With every passing minute, that impression was likely solidifying, and the very thought made her uncomfortable. Confrontation wasn't something she gravitated towards. It was the part of her job she loathed the most, handling staff issues and awkward conversations, but with Clem, it felt suddenly necessary to have a proper conversation. A chance to apologise, to sit down and work things out.

Her defence mechanisms kicked into gear. What was there to work out? Clem was a threat, and threats needed eliminating. A sharp, frustrated huff escaped her lungs. If she couldn't even get her thoughts to align, how on earth was she going to deal with the situation?

A fast-moving figure on the bridge caught her eye — Clem. Victoria sat bolt upright, watching her as she strode towards the wharf, only to stop abruptly, turn around, and head back towards the towpath.

*What is she doing?*

Clem halted again, turned once more, and retraced her steps back across the bridge to the wharf, eventually vanishing from view.

Victoria whipped a compact mirror from her top drawer and gave her face a once-over, only to toss it back in the drawer.

*What am* I *doing?*

Clem was unlikely to be coming to see her. More likely, she was doing exactly what she and Jasper had done: checking out the competition. Victoria could have told Clem herself: The wharf's cakes were no match for hers.

Pushing away the urge to spy any further, Victoria picked up her pen, determined to focus on her work and put the woman out of her mind. She dropped it not two minutes later as a knock at the door made her jump.

"Come in."

The door opened, revealing Clem.

She hovered in the doorway, shoulders slightly hunched, eyes scanning the room. A faint crease formed between her eyebrows.

"Clem."

"Victoria."

The use of her name took Victoria by surprise. Clem must have done her research.

"The woman at the reception desk told me where I could find you," she said. "I hope I'm not interrupting?"

"No, not at all," Victoria replied with a smile, instantly regretting her level of enthusiasm. She was relieved to be on her own turf and nowhere near the canal whilst talking to the newcomer.

"I found your jumper in the canal," Clem said, stepping forward to hand it over the desk before moving back again. "I hooked it out for you and washed it — hand-washed it," she added quickly.

Victoria caressed its softness between her fingers. The jumper felt better than it had before it went in. She pressed it to her nose, inhaling a lavender scent that was far more pleasant than the smell of canal water she'd expected.

"Thank you," she said softly, surprised but touched by Clem's efforts.

Clem fidgeted, her hands twisting together as if she wanted to say something but struggled to. Finally, she spoke, her voice quiet, almost reluctant. "I'm sorry about the whole dragging you in the canal thing. I was hoping to regain my balance."

Victoria arched an eyebrow and smiled. "Well, perhaps we did get off on the wrong foot — quite literally."

Clem smiled back, and Victoria noticed how it shifted the whole geometry of her face, making something flutter inside her in the process.

"I hope you managed to get the smell off you," Clem said.

"I happened to be at the spa this weekend, so I think I

was successful. I've not had any complaints so far. Perhaps I should send you the bill."

She hoped her attempt at humour would ease the tension, but Clem shuffled uneasily and looked down, plunging her hands into her pockets.

"All weekend?"

"Yes, Saturday and Sunday," Victoria confirmed, unsure why it was any of Clem's business. She took a deep breath to calm the exasperation rising within her and studied Clem as she looked around the room again.

"So, the wharf seems like a great place," Clem said, finally making eye contact.

"Thank you," Victoria replied, feeling slightly fidgety at all the small talk.

"Great reuse of a building."

Victoria inclined her head. "Thank you, again."

"Was it your idea, then?"

"Yes, from a derelict building to this. All me."

Why was she bragging? It wasn't all her; she had a team of people who had helped make it happen.

"I bet you have big plans for it."

"Mmm," Victoria murmured, unsure exactly which part of the wharf's set-up wasn't meeting Clem's requirements already and what more she expected from it.

Another awkward pause hung in the air until Clem broke it.

"My parents were here for the weekend."

"Oh," Victoria replied, somewhat puzzled as to why Clem was sharing that.

"We had dinner on their boat."

"Well, I expect it will be some time before the house is ready. How long do they think it will take?" she probed, taking the opportunity for a bit of fact-finding.

"Erm, a few months." Clem blinked as if she had lost

her train of thought. "They retire at the end of the summer, so it needs to be ready to move in to then."

Victoria nodded. "Oh, right." She desperately wanted to raise the noise issue but worried it might pour water on a situation that felt like it was only just beginning to dry out.

"It's just," Clem ventured, "that night… when I left my parents to go back to Florence — erm, my boat — I saw a man in your house."

"My husband, at a guess," Victoria said, her nerves twitching at the randomness of the remark. Noticing the door was ajar and unsure where the conversation was going, she got up to close it.

Clem meanwhile forged ahead. "There was someone else there with him. A woman."

Victoria's heart skipped a beat. She forced a smile, casually replying, "He probably invited a friend to dinner."

"Upstairs?"

Her smile faltered as she sat back down. "Maybe he was showing her around."

"While she kissed his neck?"

Victoria blinked, her mouth suddenly dry. A sharp pulse throbbed behind her eyes, but she kept her tone even.

"Are you sure that's what you saw?" she asked calmly, though the weight in her chest told her she already knew the answer.

Clem nodded. "Yes. I saw enough to know. She had short hair. Like a pixie cut, if that helps?"

"How would that help exactly?" Victoria barked, suddenly unable to contain her rising anger.

It did help, but she wasn't about to reveal that her husband's secretary, Hannah, had a pixie cut. It was none of Clem's business anyway, and it had been some time since Victoria cared what Drew got up to.

Clem stared blankly at her, making Victoria bite her lip. This wasn't Clem's fault; she was doing what she thought was right, even if it did leave Victoria feeling naked, shaky, and nauseous.

"Believe me or don't." Clem shrugged. "It's no skin off my nose. I don't like seeing other women get shat on, that's all. I should have made an exception… for you."

Victoria groaned internally at the fact that once again their conversation was spiralling.

"I came to apologise, which I've done," Clem continued, her voice clipped, previous agitation gone. "I'll leave you to mull it over. But I know what I saw," she added, heading towards the door.

Anger surged through Victoria, more at herself than anyone else. "You can tell those builders to keep the noise down," she snapped, her words sharper than she'd intended.

Clem opened the door and turned back. "Suck it up. My great-aunt put up with your renovations for a year."

Jasper appeared, fist ready to knock when Clem swept past him. She looked back and winked at him.

"Everything okay? You two aren't off for another swim, are you?" he asked Victoria, his mouth quirking as though the idea amused him more than it should.

A mixture of embarrassment and uncertainty kept her from speaking the truth. She'd never told anyone about her marital arrangements before, and she wasn't about to start now — not even with Jasper.

"No," she said, forcing a smile. "Everything is fine. She returned my jumper. Why did she wink at you?"

"She must have recognised me from the other day."

Victoria raised an eyebrow. "She recognised you from one visit?"

Jasper squirmed. "Perhaps she has an amazing memory?"

She pressed onwards. "Jasper?"

He let out a long breath as his shoulders slumped. "Okay. I've been over there a few times. Her cakes are *so* much better than ours. I can't help it. I'm an addict; I freely admit it."

Victoria glared at him. "If we can't even get loyalty from the staff, we're fucked!"

Jasper drew back and winced. "Sorry."

"It at least explains your eagerness to get over there and sample her cake. You sat there eating it like it was your first time. You'd make a great actor, you know."

"I would." He grinned.

Victoria sighed and spun her chair around to the window. "I can't stop thinking about her lemon drizzle either."

"Ha! See?"

She levelled a sceptical brow at him. "Not enough to go over every day. I have some restraint, even if others don't."

Jasper bit his lip and joined her by the window. Clem was crossing the bridge, and Victoria's eyes tracked her automatically.

"I like her," Jasper said, his eyes following her, too, "even if she is causing us grief."

"There's something about her," Victoria murmured.

"What?"

"Oh, nothing," she replied, realising she'd spoken the words aloud.

"We should get her to bake for us. Stop Christine buying that rubbery, plastic shit."

"Don't be ridiculous," Victoria said before realising it

was a good idea, albeit an impossible one. "What did you want, anyway?"

"I came to see if you wanted to go out for lunch today."

She did, but she had too much on her mind to enjoy it. "Not today. I'm a little snowed under. I think I'll work through it."

"Okay, but make sure you eat something."

She acknowledged him with a vague 'mmm', her eyes still fixed on the boat.

"You should follow her on Instagram," Jasper quipped, heading for the door. "She puts a post up at the end of the day with a discount on any leftover cake. You might be able to bag that lemon drizzle at fifty per cent off!"

She turned, narrowed her eyes, and chucked her pen at him. Jasper skipped out the door, laughing.

Even so, Victoria thought, following Clem on her socials might not be such a bad idea. It was another way to monitor the competition, and she might even steal some of her marketing tactics. Clem clearly had a few up her sleeve.

The room felt suddenly empty, as did Victoria. Empty and frustrated. Why couldn't she and Clem hold an adult conversation without sparks flying? Why did it have to be Clem who was lurking around her house at night to witness such things?

She pressed her hands to her stomach and swivelled her chair back to the window to watch the wharf's comings and goings.

At least she had her jumper back; that was a small win. Still, she couldn't help but wonder if it had been meant to soften the blow: *Here's your jumper back, and, by the way, your husband is having an affair.* If so, it wasn't necessary. She was no stranger to Drew's antics; she just preferred not to think about them, let alone have someone shove them in her face uninvited. It at least explained Clem's restless manner when she had arrived. It couldn't have been easy to come over to her office and tell a relative stranger such news.

Drew hadn't mentioned he'd be staying at the house whilst she was at the spa. She realised she shouldn't have told him she'd be away. The rules had been clear: No one else was to come to the house. That had been non-negotiable.

They got on well enough — were cordial, even — but she wasn't foolish enough to believe she and her husband still loved each other. Not in the way they had when their lives were full of hope and ambition. A divorce would have made more sense, but with neither of them suggesting it, their marriage had settled into something more like a financial arrangement.

The rot solidified when he refused to relocate with her, saying he needed to be permanently based in London for work. Renovating the house was her domain, and he'd shown little interest in the wharf either once the apartments were finished and sold off. When he asked for an open marriage — logical, he'd said, given how much time they spent apart — she'd known their romantic relationship was over.

She suspected the only reason he hadn't already filled the ground floor with apartments and sold them off, even with the lack of profit, was because it kept her out of London — out of the way so he could do whatever he wanted. So, she was sceptical about his threats, but she couldn't rest on her laurels and potentially lose the place.

The wharf meant everything to her and to Jasper. It wasn't simply a business; it was a dream they'd built from nothing but hope and a shared vision. She couldn't imagine not working with him anymore. He was the only person who understood her mission to create something lasting. He'd worked tirelessly alongside her to bring it to life.

Movement on the stern of Clem's boat pulled Victoria from her thoughts. Clem was tying up a rubbish bag. She glanced towards the wharf, and their eyes seemed to meet. Victoria froze, hoping Clem was merely looking in her direction, not directly at her. Getting caught spying from the window wasn't on her to-do list for the day, but the deliberate twist of Clem's head and the intensity of her stare before turning back to the bin confirmed it: She'd been spotted.

Could this day get any worse?

Thankfully, it remained uneventful, and by the time Victoria arrived home later that afternoon, she mustered enough energy to scrub all surfaces, strip the sheets, and wash every glass like she was exorcising something.

She opened a bottle of wine and filled a glass, sinking into her chair. The calm they both brought her was much needed, but the moment she looked out her window, she remembered: Her view was now compromised, shifted by the arrival of a stranger; a woman who'd been in her life for less than a week and had already upended everything.

 lem lifted a banana loaf out of the oven, followed by a ginger cake. Both felt heavier than usual. A restless night — courtesy of her run-in with Victoria the previous day — had left her mind whirring and her body achy. This morning, she felt well and truly pissed off with the world.

The galley wasn't improving her mood either. The kitchen in her old flat hadn't been large, but at least it was square, allowing her room to move. Florence offered no such luxury. Clem couldn't even look in the oven head-on; it was all swivelling hips and shuffling, which had resulted in her bashing her elbow against the worktop. Despite trying hard to convince herself that there was plenty of space and that the whole idea hadn't been a mistake, worry coursed through her.

Her gaze drifted to Victoria's office window directly opposite — another worry. Why did every conversation with that woman feel like it was destined to escalate? Victoria was infuriating. *Infuriating but also hot,* a little voice in the back of her head teased. The thought only unsettled her further. As much as she wanted to push it away, the more the tingling in her gut pulled her towards it. As Clem restocked the paper cups and plastic lids beside the espresso machine, she decided a woman could be both attractive and infuriating.

Telling Victoria what she'd witnessed had brought her no peace. It stewed inside her and even made her feel sorry for her despite Victoria's reaction. But really, what had Clem expected? Of course the woman was going to be defensive. It couldn't have been easy hearing something like that from a stranger, especially not from one you'd already fought with. Still, something about Victoria's reaction suggested the news hadn't come as a complete surprise. Did she already suspect it?

Despite the aches, the gloom, and an anxious undertow holding her hostage, Clem soldiered on. She lifted the loaves out of their tins onto the cooling rack, untied her apron, and picked up her phone. It was time to do her usual checks on social media, post some cake photos, and look for any new reviews. The last item on her to-do list usually gave her a lift, so she started there. Three new written reviews popped up, making her feel better — until she saw they were all one-star. Her heart pounded as she began to read.

*"Overrated and overpriced. Dry sponge and coffee that tastes like dishwater! No, thanks!" —Karen C.*

*"Stopped by on a rainy afternoon, hoping for a coffee and a good slice of cake. Got a bitter Americano and an overpriced sliver of cake with gritty icing. The owner looked annoyed that I was even there. Don't waste your time or money here!" — Bob H.*

*"I really wanted to like this place, but unfortunately, it missed*

*the mark. The coffee was weak and bitter, and the 'freshly baked'
cakes tasted like they'd been sitting out for days. I heard the café
in the nearby wharf has much more to offer. Go there instead!"*
      *— Lee W.*

"What the actual fuck? 'Go there instead!'" Clem
hissed. This was all she needed. Taking deep breaths, she
tried to convince herself they didn't matter, that they
wouldn't affect her. She had so many five-star reviews,
these barely made a dent in her overall rating. Still.

Then she noticed something odd: All three reviews had
been posted around the same time last night. Suspicion
took root. Could it be? Would Victoria really stoop low
enough to post shitty reviews about her competitor's
business? *Yes,* was Clem's immediate thought. She
wouldn't put it past the woman, not after her
underhanded stunt with the signage.

Clem set the phone down on the worktop and stepped
away from it. What she needed now was a moment of
calm. She headed to the bow, sat down, propped her feet
on the gunwale, and closed her eyes. *Gritty icing.* She
sieved her icing sugar meticulously, and her cakes didn't
sit around for days. Ever.

These were genuine fake reviews. The question was:
What was she going to do about it? She could report
them, but it was unlikely to get her anywhere. Would
confronting Victoria about them just lead to another
slanging match? Then again, did she even care if
it did?

Her phone rang from inside Florence. Straining to catch
the ringtone, she recognised it as the one she'd assigned to
her dad. Clem sprang up from the chair and ran inside to
retrieve it.

WHACK!

Her knee collided with the edge of the bed, sending pain shooting through her leg.

"Fuck!"

Hobbling down the narrow corridor to the kitchen, she seethed — at the reviews, at Victoria, at her bad luck. With her level of spatial awareness, what the hell had she been thinking of buying a narrowboat?

"Hi, Dad. Is everything okay?" she asked quickly, her voice tight as she silently panted through the pain.

"Oh yes, we're making good progress. It's just… I've had a call. You know how I sorted all your permissions for trading at the wharf? Well, I forgot to mention that I went to school with the landowner."

"*Forgot* to mention." Clem groaned, leaning over to rub her knee. "Is that how I managed to get the best spot?"

"That's not important right now."

She was about to argue that nepotism was important when he added, "Someone asked him to revoke your mooring agreement."

She shot upright. "What? Why? *Who*?"

"They wouldn't give him their name, but they told him that you were being physically violent and causing a health and safety hazard — something about your sign blocking the towpath."

"What?"

"He sent them packing," her dad added quickly.

Clem exhaled with relief. She didn't need a name; she knew who was behind this.

"Victoria," she muttered, her eyes drifting towards the woman's office window.

"You think it has something to do with her?" her dad asked. "I'll be having words when I see her next."

"Seriously, Dad? I'm forty. I've never needed you to fight my battles."

"You did at school when that boy nicked your pencil case."

"I was six! And for the record, I didn't need your help. I kicked him in the shins, and he never bothered me again."

Her mum's voice cut in through her dad's fading chuckles. "That woman needs putting in her place."

"It's fine, Mum. I'll handle it."

"Just wait till I see her again," her mum snapped. "She'll be getting a piece of my mind for messing with my daughter."

"I can handle Victoria Hargreaves," Clem stated. "In fact, I'll do it now."

"Well, you give her what for."

"I will, Mum."

Clem hung up and squinted across at Victoria's window, trying to see if she was in her office. Right on cue, Victoria spun her chair around, putting her straight in Clem's eye line. Clem quickly stepped back. She had caught Victoria nosing at her the day before, and she wasn't about to get spotted doing the same.

She removed her apron and stepped outside. Max was sitting on his chair, so she called over to him.

"I'm going to be a bit late opening. Could you keep an eye out for any customers, please? Let them know I'll be back soon."

He jumped to his feet. "Better still, I can open up for you."

Grabbing a sign propped against a plant pot on the top of his boat — *Vinyl Bought* — he flipped it and placed it on his chair. The reverse read, *Pay at Clem's Coffee & Cakes*, with an arrow pointing her way. He picked up his card reader from a nearby table and was beside her in a shot.

Clem blinked, taken aback by how prepared he was.

"What? I miss making coffee." He squinted at her, giving her a once-over. "Are you okay?"

Clem clenched her jaw and rolled her eyes. How was she supposed to answer that?

"What's she done now?" Max tutted, resting his hands on his hips.

"Who?"

Max tilted his head towards the wharf. "Madame Corset."

"How did you—?"

He lifted an eyebrow. "I can see the steam coming out of your ears, and you're physically shaking. Only one person has been causing these emotions in you since you got here."

Shit, he was right. She was shaking.

"She left some bad reviews and tried to get me kicked off my pitch," Clem admitted.

"Ouch! What a bitch. Blocking your sign is one thing, but bad-mouthing you and trying to get you moved? That's harsh. Go kick her pert butt."

Clem's eyebrows shot up.

Max shrugged. "I might be gay, but I'm not blind. She has a great arse."

A laugh escaped Clem before she could stop it. It bubbled up through the thick layer of her anger despite her attempts to hold it back. She shook her head at him, trying to look disapproving but failing.

"What?" he called out. "Don't tell me you haven't noticed."

Clem ignored him and strode across the bridge, annoyed at Max for making her laugh and even more so at herself for thinking about Victoria's bum. Damn Max for putting that image in her mind. She clenched her fist, trying to summon her anger back. It came easily. The woman was completely out of order, and this was the final straw.

She followed the route she had taken yesterday, giving a polite nod to the woman at the reception desk but not stopping. She knew exactly where she was going. As she passed through the café, she couldn't help admiring it again; it was such a charming, inviting space. She could think of so many uses for it. Shame it belonged to someone so determined to make herself unlikeable.

Victoria's door was ajar. Clem didn't hesitate before marching straight in. If the door hadn't been, she would have thrown it open. Or kicked it, the same way she'd kicked that boy's shin at school.

"Clem, how can I help you?" Victoria said, drawing herself upright in her chair.

"Help me?" Clem growled. "You've done enough of that already — like helping me get moved off my trading spot. You do realise you don't own the waterways, right? The towpath and traders have nothing to do with you or your precious wharf."

Victoria just blinked at her, so Clem decided to carry on whilst she had steam behind her.

"How dare you. I'm trying to make a living. I can't help it if people prefer my cakes to yours. If you want to compete, then compete, but play fair. Don't stoop to underhanded tactics to get me moved on. And those bad reviews—" She shook her head, seething. "This is how you repay me for warning you about your sleazy husband? I wish I hadn't bothered."

Victoria's eyebrows arched. Without a word, she stood, walked around her desk, and shut the door. Clem stiffened, instinctively taking a step back.

Victoria pulled the visitor chair out. "Sit."

Clem stared at her, unsure what was coming next.

"Now," Victoria said — not loudly, but with a quiet authority that had Clem sitting before she knew she had done.

"Would you like to start again?" Victoria asked, returning to her own chair. "More calmly this time, so I can establish exactly what I'm being accused of."

Victoria's tone was different to what Clem had been expecting, more composed. She'd prepared herself for another shouting match, but something had changed. It was unnerving.

Clem drew in a deep breath, realising she was still shaking. "You tried to put me out of business."

"Hardly, it was just a bit of free cake."

*Just a bit of free cake!* Clem's jaw tightened. *How dare she trivialise it.*

Victoria continued before she could respond. "For what it's worth, I don't want to put you out of business. I think you have a great one. I just wish you would conduct it elsewhere, so I don't have to keep looking at you."

Clem's eyes narrowed. "No one's forcing you to keep looking."

Victoria's gaze flicked away, and her cheeks tinged pink. She stood abruptly and began pacing the room.

"We are all desperately trying to keep our businesses afloat. You aren't unique in that. The wharf has to make a profit, too, or it'll close."

The comment knocked Clem back in her seat. "What?"

The wharf was also struggling. How? It was an amazing place except for the supposed shit cakes. But then, shit cakes alone were unlikely to bring down an entire business. Except maybe her own.

"Yes, we are struggling, and you haven't helped," Victoria said, holding up her hands, "but I'm not one for underhanded tactics."

Clem opened her mouth to argue, but Victoria's unexpected honesty held her back.

"Having you moved on has nothing to do with me, I assure you. I admit the free drink offer was my idea, but the execution had nothing to do with me either. I suspect I have a wayward catering manager, who likely blocked your sign, too." Victoria let out a breath. "I will deal with her."

"And the reviews?"

"Not me either. I will investigate it, and *if* we are responsible, I will do everything I can to have them removed. I promise."

Clem's mind drifted as she watched Victoria — the sway of her hair, the animated movement of her arms — her words passing by unheard. Her stomach betrayed her with that familiar tingle, the one that said, *We know you hate her, but you're wrong, and we feel something else entirely. Suck it up.*

She sighed, realising her body was winning this one. Victoria turned and glared at her with a look so icy it made Clem shiver. It was then she realised she'd sighed aloud.

"I'm sorry if my apology is boring you," Victoria snapped.

"No — shit — sorry. I wasn't—" *Wait, she apologised? Why wasn't I paying attention?* "I didn't mean to—"

*Fuck.*

The shift in atmosphere was enough to put Clem on her feet. It was time to leave, before things escalated again. She'd said everything she needed to, and Victoria, well, she had been nothing but calm until a moment ago. Annoyingly so. Clem wanted to blow off steam at her, not be lightly pricked with a pin so she could quietly deflate in her chair.

"I should get back."

Victoria rolled her eyes and gestured towards the door. As Clem reached it, her voice came, soft and insistent.

"Clem, I will sort this out. This isn't me."

All Clem could do was nod and leave, flushed with embarrassment and angry at herself. If Victoria was telling the truth, then she'd done little more than advertise some free shit cake, which was likely hurting her business as much as it was Clem's. It wasn't sustainable for either of them, and she decided she would remove the offer, regardless of whether Victoria did or not. She needed to stop reacting, but she couldn't help it. The woman got under her skin.

The day had barely begun, and already she wanted it to be over. Back on the towpath, it was so busy that Max had to rush off to his own customers, and Clem hit the ground running with her own. She didn't even get a chance to tell him what had happened.

By the time the day ended, she was completely drained and even more disappointed at herself after dropping half the banana loaf on the floor. With poor weather forecasted for Wednesday and Thursday, it was the perfect time to take a break and gather herself. She craved a lie-in and the chance to catch up on sleep. Maybe she would take a quiet cruise down the canal for a change of scenery. Anything to clear her head of Victoria Hargreaves.

She fired off a text to Max to thank him for his help and say she'd see him Friday. Heading back to her jetty, she vowed to stay well away from the woman at the wharf in future.

# CHAPTER 9

*V*ictoria strolled along the towpath later than normal, having decided to start work from home. The air was damp and oppressive, but the pops of colour from the bluebells coming into bloom brought a smile to her face. Soon, the woods alongside the canal would be a carpet of rich purple.

She adored flowers. Drew used to buy them for her every week — until they found out he was infertile. Then the flowers stopped. She never questioned why, just let the habit die alongside her hope. Maybe he couldn't bear the reminder of beauty when something fundamental inside him was broken. Now, with more time to spend in her office, she decided to buy them herself. She didn't need to wait for someone else. Drew certainly wouldn't be buying her more, and no one else would either.

The familiar hum of a narrowboat echoed along the cut. She didn't turn — narrowboats passed her all the time — but as the chugging grew louder, something urged her to glance behind. The bright orange bow told her immediately it was Florence. A groan escaped her as she realised she was on first-name terms with a boat. At the stern was Clem, her head poking over the top.

Wondering if Clem was watching her, scrutinising her every move, Victoria's heart began to throb — not faster but harder. Her ankles wobbled slightly as she reached up to check her hair. The best course of action was to keep her eyes straight ahead and focus on not tripping over something.

Picking up her pace slightly, she groaned at herself. What was she doing? Narrowboats were slow, but she couldn't outpace one. Why was she even trying to? She slowed her stride again, hoping it would go unnoticed.

As the bow came into her peripheral vision, her eyes drifted to it. She cursed them. Her stomach twisted into knots, and her heart hammered even harder with every window that slid past. Any second now, Clem would be level with her. What should she do? Ignore her? That would be impolite. Smile? Too much, perhaps. She decided finally that at least looking Clem's way to acknowledge her presence was best, so she turned. Their eyes locked.

Clem's gaze held steady until, with the faintest smile, she turned away. Victoria flashed one back, only to realise she probably hadn't seen it. As Clem and the noise disappeared into the distance, Victoria was left feeling she'd been rude after all.

Inhaling deeply, she tried to quieten her pounding heart. But why was it even racing? Fear of another confrontation across a body of water? She wasn't sure what she'd expected, but Clem flashing her a smile and not giving her the finger felt like a good sign.

She'd done so well the day before, keeping calm while Clem accused her of writing fake reviews and trying to get her moved from her pitch. She'd bitten her tongue, stayed composed. But then, mid-apology for her part in the altercation over the sign, Clem had audibly groaned. That had been the final straw. Her temper had slipped, and she'd snapped — something she regretted the moment the words left her mouth. But the damage was done; it had been enough to make Clem want to leave. She knew she should have handled it better. With a sigh Victoria pressed her fingers to her temples. Her head throbbed, fuelled by replaying conversations and overthinking everything she'd said.

By the time she reached the wharf, Florence was nowhere in sight. Her mooring spot sat empty. A thought gripped her chest: Had Clem left? Had she driven her away? An initial moment of joy that at least one of her problems might have resolved melted into a strange sense of loss.

Victoria was growing strangely accustomed to the orange boat outside her window, and the thought of never tasting Clem's lemon drizzle again left an unexpected ache inside her. But it wasn't the cake. It was the thought of never seeing Clem again that made her palms sweat and her heart lurch.

Why? What was it about the woman that had gotten so deep under her skin? Why had she forced herself to stay calm the day before — well, up to a point — and then promised to sort things out? She'd always had a strong sense of justice, and Clem had been so distraught that it was only natural for Victoria to want to help, even if it meant facing an awkward conversation with Christine this morning.

The usual sense of peace the wharf offered failed to materialise as she entered its front doors. Victoria's stomach rumbled — whether from nerves or hunger, she couldn't tell. She stopped at the counter in the café for a croissant and a peppermint tea, hoping to soothe any queasiness bubbling there. As she queued, she glanced around the room. It was a little busier today, no doubt helped by Clem's absence and the rain beginning to drizzle outside.

She remembered the first time she had stepped inside the old factory. Water had trickled down the walls and pooled across the floor, each drip from the ceiling echoing eerily through the cavernous rooms. Glass crunched beneath her feet from the shattered windows, the gaps allowing a low whistle of the wind to snake through. Old machinery sat abandoned, covered in cobwebs and flaking paint, relics of a bygone era.

The upper floors had been the worst. Holes in the roof let in rain and pigeons, which nested in the strangest places. Warped, rotten floorboards creaked with every step, as though the building resented the intrusion. A damp, musty odour lingered throughout the entire building.

Despite the decay, Victoria found the old factory mesmerising and immediately began restructuring it in her mind. She'd even managed to rescue some of the old machines despite Drew's attempts to dispose of them all. To him, they held no value, but she knew they would prove useful in the museum — some of the smaller pieces, at least. Jasper had been ecstatic to find them in the outbuilding and decided to restore a sewing machine to working condition so visitors could try their hand at it.

By the time Victoria reached her office in the now thoroughly intact building, rain was pelting at the windows. She'd been praying for a downpour, hoping it would steer weary travellers towards the shelter of the wharf rather than to a long queue outside a damp narrowboat. It was having that effect now as rain-soaked people and dripping pushchairs hurried across the bridge towards the warmth of the café.

A lightness bloomed in her chest that there was no competition today, but it only served to remind her of Clem's absence. Had she checked the forecast and cleverly chosen to skip trading today? Realising how much she was hoping that Clem would return tomorrow, Victoria forced her attention back to her work, only to find it drifting inevitably to Clem's reviews.

Christine had been on annual leave the day before, meaning Victoria couldn't tackle the issue immediately. What she'd hoped would be an opportunity to mull things over had instead given her too much time to stew and grow angrier at the injustice Clem was being dealt.

"Knock, knock."

"Jasper," Victoria greeted him. The relief in her tone at a welcome distraction was as obvious to her as it was to him.

"What's up?" he asked, coming in to perch on the edge of her desk.

Victoria swivelled her laptop so he could see the one-star reviews. His eyes skimmed the screen.

"Golly. They are a bit out of line, not to mention patently false."

Victoria hummed. "And Clem's accused me of posting them."

Jasper's eyes shot to hers. "Seriously? Like you'd do such a thing." His lips tightened. "Even though you *did* want to sink her boat not long ago."

"Oh, come on. I wasn't serious." Victoria huffed, crossing her arms.

"I could tell her it's not you if you think it would help."

"Don't waste your time. I've already told her. Whether she believes me or not, I've no idea."

"Who do you think left them?"

They looked at each other again, and as if reading her mind, Jasper answered his own question. "Christine?"

"It's likely." She glanced at the clock. "She's due in any minute."

"What will you do?"

Victoria twitched her shoulders. "I've never gelled with the woman, but she is efficient."

"But could someone else be more efficient?"

She hadn't considered it from that angle before. She didn't want to lose Christine — she did a good enough job — but would someone else do it better?

"What would you do?" she asked.

"Sack her," Jasper answered without hesitation.

"Really?"

"Yes. I've never liked her."

"Why didn't you mention that when we hired her?" Victoria demanded, leaning back into her chair.

"*You* hired her. We agreed I'd run the museum, and everything else was your domain, including the hiring and firing."

"You are welcome to give your input, you know."

Jasper shrugged. "Well, I have now."

"You know disliking someone isn't a reason to sack them," she said — as much as Victoria wanted it to be. She hadn't liked her much either, but Drew had suggested Christine would be the most qualified candidate when he'd sat in on the interview. She would have preferred one of the more personable applicants.

"So get her to admit it," he said, "and then sack her for gross misconduct."

At the sound of the café door opening in the corridor, Victoria's gaze shot to Jasper.

He raised his eyebrows. "If that's her, then there's no time like the present."

Spotting her catering manager passing by her door, she nodded at Jasper to confirm his suspicions.

"Oh, Christine," the curator sang out. He flashed a grin at Victoria as he got up. "Good luck," he whispered, then added in a louder voice, "Let's do lunch," as he squeezed past Christine in the doorway.

Victoria shot him a look — half scathing, half pleading — but he simply winked in response and vanished down the corridor.

"Yes?" Christine said abruptly.

"Come in and close the door, please," Victoria said, resisting the urge to stand and pace. She shifted in her chair.

With a cautious eye on her boss, Christine shut the door and helped herself to the seat opposite.

"I'll get straight to the point," Victoria said, interlacing her fidgety fingers. "Did you post some bad reviews about Clem's business?"

Christine's forehead creased. "Clem now, is it?"

"Yes, it's her name."

"I was only doing what I thought best to help *this* business," she answered, folding her arms.

"By writing fake reviews?" Victoria questioned.

"You gave me free rein for my ideas."

"I did not. I stipulated it should be better than the last one, and it has not been! That was underhanded, and so was this. What on earth possessed you to escalate things and try to get her removed from her mooring? I assume that was you, too?"

Christine turned her head away, fixing her gaze on the ceiling instead.

Victoria took a deep breath as silently as possible, then murmured, "I never agreed to any of it."

"That offer idea was yours, remember," Christine accused.

"It was. A bit of competition is healthy, but I fight fair, not dirty, like you."

"Dirty!" Christine protested. "It's your business at stake, not mine."

"What exactly did you do?" Victoria demanded, hoping to get to the truth of the matter.

"I rang the landowner," Christine admitted. "Said she was blocking the towpath and picking fights with neighbours."

"She only fought back as you gave her something to fight against — by blocking her sign in the first place! What was she supposed to do?"

Victoria tried to suppress her creeping sense of guilt. Her initial instinct had been to retaliate, too, and block Clem's sign with the wharfs, but she'd been angry. She didn't intend to do it. At most she had tried to move Clem's to one side. Then one thing led to another, and they had tussled over it.

"How did she find out it was us, anyway?"

"You, Christine, not us," Victoria said wearily. "I don't know. She didn't share the particulars during her tirade. You have put me in an extremely difficult position, spreading lies that trace back to my business — and to me."

"Well, if you want to sit around here and watch her take all our customers, that's up to you, but I'm not going to. Anyone would think you *like* having her out there."

*Did she?* Victoria wondered.

*Yes,* a voice answered instantly.

"And don't bother firing me. I resign. Effective immediately," Christine said, getting to her feet.

"What?" Victoria blinked. She hadn't expected that. "Well, you're already fired anyway," she snapped back.

Christine narrowed her eyes. "You need to get your priorities straight or you'll lose this place. Shame. It has so much potential — just needs a real leader."

Victoria scoffed, but the sound caught in her throat. *A real leader.* As if she wasn't trying.

As Christine swept out of the room, Victoria shouted after her, "You'd better take those reviews down or you won't get paid!"

She knew she couldn't withhold her final wages, but it was worth a try.

What had Christine meant by *so much potential*? The phrase echoed Clem's words to Victoria, that she must have big plans for the place. But what more did people want? She'd created something remarkable. The café was versatile and inviting — except for the chemical cakes — and Jasper had worked wonders with the museum.

What was she missing? She may have brought the building to a position where it could be something, but was the rest pure fantasy? Would everyone be better off if she brought someone else in to run it whilst she returned to what she was actually good at? The wharf needed a manager who could hire and keep good staff, who could implement changes — *a real leader.*

Reality hit her hard. She was now without a catering manager, and there was the wharf's birthday party to cater in three days. Victoria slumped in her chair and instinctively swivelled it to face the window. The vacant mooring before her was a stark reminder that Clem was missing — perhaps never to return.

A pinch in her chest took her by surprise. Why was she so concerned about the café boat owner's whereabouts, and why did she feel like a truck had hit her ever since she got pulled out of the canal?

# CHAPTER 10

*C*lem stretched back in her chair, propping her feet on the gunwale and tilting her face towards the welcome warmth of the sunshine. After two days off, she felt mildly refreshed, even if it had been a long and busy Friday. The lunchtime rush had become so frantic that Max popped his head in to ask if she needed help. She had promptly set him to work on the espresso machine. Now she was looking forward to the scrumpy he'd promised to bring over once he closed up.

The break had given her space to breathe and reflect on how things were going. She'd realised she could use a backup traybake for later in the afternoons. Customers had been asking for something savoury around lunchtime, so she'd added sausage rolls and cheese scones to the menu. They'd sold out in fifty minutes flat. It was amazing what ideas came to mind with a bit of downtime.

The relaxing cruise she'd planned on the first day of her break had been a complete washout. The heavy rain that had been forecast for late morning had arrived early, so she'd turned around and gone home. Standing at the tiller in the pouring rain wasn't her idea of relaxation. It only served to reinforce the nagging feeling that maybe she wasn't cut out for boating life. Had she grown up with some nostalgic, rose-tinted view of it?

She'd only lived on a boat until she was five and remembered little of it, but she'd spent plenty of time aboard *The Kingfisher's Rest*, which she'd thoroughly enjoyed. Of course, that had felt more like a holiday, with her mum handling the meals and her dad doing the heavy work. Her own contributions were limited to the occasional bit of piloting and opening a few locks.

*The Kingfisher's Rest* was also luxurious, and although Florence had been newly refurbished, she couldn't compete with the space and comfort of a twelve-foot widebeam. Living in your workplace, she was discovering, also made quite a difference.

The weather wasn't the only reason she regretted leaving the jetty that morning. It had resulted in an awkward encounter with Victoria. Less than twenty-four hours after vowing to avoid her, she'd spotted Victoria on the towpath. There was no getting past her unseen. On foot, one could turn around and slip away unnoticed. Gliding along a thin stretch of water on a bright orange narrowboat, there was no escape.

Sailing past her at a glacial pace, she had felt compelled to acknowledge the woman. What was intended to be a brief nod instead became a long stare. Victoria had that older-woman sexiness wrapped up in confidence, and it made Clem's brain stall for a moment. It might have been the cause of the inane smile on her face as she cruised away. Hopefully, Victoria hadn't noticed from so far away.

On her second day off, she'd struggled to keep her mind off the woman and ended up deep-cleaning Florence before beginning her evening bake. Cleaning was good for the soul, not to mention a welcome break from a relentless queue of customers.

She'd done her best to move on from the awkward encounters with Victoria and had avoided checking her ratings since. But now, pulling out her phone, Clem decided it was time. As much as it grated her to not have the full five stars, it was probably best for business. It was unrealistic to be that perfect, and it stank of paid reviews. Bad feedback was always useful — if it was genuine, anyway. It often pointed to areas that needed improvement.

Victoria had added a comment to the one-star reviews. She'd stated that as the director of Otterford Wharf, she suspected they were the work of a disgruntled former employee, adding, *I would encourage anyone to try Clem's Coffee & Cakes for delightful cakes and friendly service from an even more delightful Clem.*

Clem blinked and reread the last bit. *An even more delightful Clem.* Seriously? Victoria had written that. Her stomach fizzed, and goosebumps prickled along her arms. And *former employee*? Had Victoria sacked her catering manager?

At that moment, Max climbed onto Florence's bow with a bottle and two small glasses in tow.

"I do have glasses, you know." Clem smirked.

He shrugged, handed her one, and filled it halfway with scrumpy.

"Thanks," she said. "I appreciate you helping today. I was struggling to keep up."

"No problem. I enjoyed it," he said, taking the seat beside her.

"I am going to pay you for all the hours you've worked."

Max opened his mouth.

Pretty sure he was going to protest, Clem cut in. "I insist. And it will only be minimum wage. I can't afford any more than that."

"I could certainly use the money, so thanks. Now, tell me what happened the other day with Victoria and those bad reviews."

Eager for Max's opinion, Clem handed over her phone to show him Victoria's replies.

His eyes scanned the screen, jaw dropping as he read. Passing the phone back, he asked, "So she wasn't the one who left them?"

"No. She seemed to think it was her catering manager. Christine, I think her name was. So it was likely she who made a complaint to the landowner, too."

"How sure is Victoria?"

Clem shrugged. "I don't think it could be anyone else. The curator, Jasper Sinclair, had no complaints. He was coming most days for coffee and walnut cake."

Max fidgeted in his seat and said far too casually, "Oh, was he?" He failed miserably to hide the grin tugging at his lips, which suggested he might have noticed.

Clem narrowed her eyes. "Yes... what's this about?" She waved her finger at him. "You were grinning like this the last time I mentioned him, too."

"Oh, nothing," Max said, his eyes softening. "I think he's fit, that's all."

"Is he gay?" Clem asked, though she felt she already knew the answer.

"No straight man dresses that well, trust me. His waistcoat collection? Adorable."

Clem chuckled. "If you say so."

"But I'm in my thirties, and he must be in his late forties, maybe older."

"What's age got to do with anything?"

Max shrugged and took a sip from his glass. "Nothing, I guess."

"Have you ever spoken to him?"

"No, I did a guided tour around the museum once. Did you know he's the UK's leading expert in corsetry? He's been on television talking about it, and he's written books. I think he even lectures at Oxford."

"Oh, wow! You've *really* done your research."

Max pinked.

"Was the tour interesting?" Clem asked, genuinely interested.

"I don't think I took in a single word he said."

"Too busy drooling?"

"Something like that." Max smiled.

Clem chuckled. "You should take him a slice of coffee and walnut. Chat him up."

Max squirmed. "Oh no, I couldn't. I'm rubbish at that sort of thing."

A fast-moving figure crossing the bridge caught Clem's attention — Victoria. She slumped in her chair, hopeful the woman would walk on by. She didn't. Instead, she approached the bow, and Clem braced herself for another conversation.

Victoria held up her hands where she stood on the bank. "I come in peace; I promise."

There was a dampness on her forehead and a tremble in her voice when she spoke. Her blue eyes were unreadable, like she was half there, half tangled in deep thought. There was something so magnetic about her that Clem pushed her buzzing thoughts aside. Something was wrong, and her heart squeezed with concern.

"Are you okay?" Clem asked, brushing her hair from her shoulders.

"No, not really," Victoria admitted. "I'm a catering

manager down, and I'm hosting a party of fifty tomorrow afternoon, which I need to cater. Christine's parting gift was cancelling the entire food order. To top it off, a couple of members of staff left with her."

"Shit."

"Precisely," Victoria said with a heavy breath. "Look… can we start again?"

"I'd like that," Clem said, unable to prevent the smile that was forming on her lips.

She stood and offered her hand, gesturing with her head to the boat. Victoria blinked; then, as if noticing she was being invited aboard, she stepped onto the gunwale and took Clem's hand. Her skin was soft, softer than Clem had expected, and her grip was vice-like as she descended into the bow.

"Thank you."

Clem gestured to her empty chair. "Sit." When Victoria hesitated, she added, "Now." She smiled, realising she was echoing Victoria's exact words from earlier in the week. Why had she remembered them so precisely?

Victoria smiled, too, as if she was having the same thought, and lowered herself into the seat.

Max jumped up and offered his chair to Clem, then perched on the gunwale with his glass.

"Thanks," Clem said, turning the chair to face Victoria better, still unsure what exactly she was doing here. "Victoria, this is Max, he owns the neighbouring boat."

Victoria gave him a nod. "Hi." She turned her attention to the bottle on the small table. What's that?"

"Scrumpy," Max said. "Want a glass?"

Clem noticed a slight tremble in Victoria's hands. The scrumpy was pretty good at settling any anxiety, but something told her Victoria might need an entire vat of it.

Victoria nodded. "Please."

Clem turned to Max. "Could you grab—" Before she could ask him to grab a glass from inside, Victoria had picked up Clem's half-full glass and downed it in one go.

She coughed, eyes watering, then wiped away the alcohol-induced tears. "Wow, that has a kick."

"Max brews it," Clem said with a grin.

Victoria gave him a nod of acknowledgement. "Don't let my curator, Jasper, find out. He has a thing for cider — the stronger, the better."

Clem shot a smirk and a wink at a grinning Max.

Victoria shifted in her seat. "I know I have no right to ask for your help, but here I am. I'll cut to the chase. I need cake, and I need it tomorrow. Can you help?"

"Oh, erm — what exactly do you need?"

Victoria twisted her lips and looked down. "Could you manage four Victoria sponges? I think that should be enough for fifty people."

"Yes. I can manage that," Clem answered immediately. Victoria sponges weren't exactly a challenge — eight sponges, some whipped cream, strawberry jam, and a few strawberries to decorate.

Victoria sat back and exhaled. "Thank you."

"What time do you need them?"

"The party starts at seven."

"I'll need to start early in the morning. I'll have my own baking to do, too. Do you have somewhere to store them?"

"Yes, plenty of fridge space. You're welcome to use the wharf's kitchen. I can open as early as you want, and you're welcome to make anything you need for yourself there, too, if it helps you."

That wasn't a bad suggestion. With more space to move around and bigger work surfaces, she'd work faster and more efficiently.

"Sure," Clem said. "Only one problem: I'll need some ingredients. I keep a certain amount of stock on board but not enough for all that. And I'll need fresh strawberries."

Victoria pulled out her phone and fiddled with it. Offering it to Clem, she said, "Here, write me a list. You'll have everything you need. I have to go to the supermarket now anyway."

Catching the strain in her voice, Clem raised her hand, refusing the phone. "I'll do you one better," she said. "I'll come with you."

Relief flickered across Victoria's face. "Thank you."

"I will take your number, though," Clem added casually.

Victoria's head tilted in question.

"You know, in case I need to contact you about tomorrow."

"Oh," Victoria said, her voice hitching slightly. "Yes. Of course."

Her cheeks flushed a little, and Clem couldn't help but wonder what Victoria thought she meant. Was she hoping Clem meant it in the traditional sense? But what was Clem thinking? The woman had a husband — a lying, cheating husband, yes, but a husband, nonetheless — and there was no reason to believe Victoria appreciated women the way Clem did. She noticed everything: the way a woman's hair caught the late-afternoon light, the dip of her neck, the gentle curve of her waist. There was a quiet beauty in the female form, an elegance in every movement, and she had always been attuned to it.

"Clem?"

Victoria's gentle voice snapped her from her thoughts. Realising those thoughts were all about Victoria caused the warmth in Clem's cheeks to deepen.

"Yes," she replied, hoping it wasn't noticeable.

"Type your number in."

Taking the phone Victoria held out, she entered her number and handed it back. A second later, her own phone vibrated on the table as Victoria rang it.

"There. Now you won't have to come to my office the next time you want to reprimand me."

The small dig pulled a smile from Clem as their eyes locked. "Behave and I won't have to," she said, tucking a stray strand of hair behind her ear.

Victoria's right eyebrow arched as the corners of her mouth lifted. "I should get back to work. I have a shopping list to finish. I drove in today, so my car is at the wharf. Shall I meet you there at five? It's the—"

"Green Jag. Yes, I know."

Victoria gave a nod.

Max jumped onto the gunwale and hopped across to the towpath, offering Victoria a hand up. She took it with a smile.

"Victoria?" Clem called.

"Yes?"

"Have a coffee, won't you? Make sure that cider's fully worn off before you drive."

Victoria flashed her a warm smile, making Clem's chest tighten. "Of course." She turned and walked away.

Clem watched her cross the bridge, still feeling the echo of that smile, as Max dropped into the chair beside her.

"That was a bit flirty," he teased.

"What?" Clem scoffed. "No, it wasn't."

"'Behave and I won't have to'?" Max mimicked. "Come on. That was *majorly* flirty."

"Well, it wasn't my intention."

"If you say so." He shrugged in a way that suggested

he didn't quite believe it. "I can read body language as well as you. I saw the way you looked at her."

"What way?" Clem asked defensively.

"Your eyes went all glassy. You couldn't take them off her. And touching your hair? A classic tell. When you sat down, you turned your whole body to face her."

"I was simply giving her my full attention."

Max raised an eyebrow. "She's a bit older than you, right?"

Clem shrugged. "I guess."

"And there you were, defending age gaps not ten minutes ago. Now I know why."

"She's married," Clem protested.

"But you're not denying your attraction to her."

She shook her head. "We're not going there."

"Well, I would have told her to get lost, not offered to go shopping with her. You're too soft."

Clem had to laugh at his comment. There was a time she might have done just that, but today she was applying a different tactic to see if it would change the outcome. So far, it had. She was now in possession of Victoria's phone number and would soon be zooming into town with her in her cute classic sports car.

When Max seemed to be awaiting a rebuttal to his comment that she was too soft, Clem replied, "Says the man who gave her a hand off Florence."

"I was being courteous and neighbourly!" he said. "It's not my battle."

Clem narrowed her eyes at him and scrunched her face. "Anyway, I'm not soft. I just have a heart."

"Same thing. More scrumpy?"

"More? I haven't had any yet. Victoria skulled mine, remember? But no, thanks. I'd best keep a clear head for later. Oh! Which reminds me: I've written you a marketing plan."

Max's brow furrowed. "Okaaaay."

"Don't worry. It shouldn't take you more than about fifteen minutes a day. You'll get quicker at it once you know what you're doing, and your confidence grows. You just need to find your marketing voice."

Clem went inside to retrieve her laptop from her bed and opened it on the table in front of him. With a few taps, she turned it towards him.

"Type in your email address and I'll send it over."

He typed with one finger, making Clem wonder if he was up to the task ahead. Maybe he was better on his phone. Eventually taking the laptop back, she opened the document and proceeded to walk him through each step of her plan over the next forty-five minutes.

"If you forget how to do something, just shout," Clem urged her neighbour as they reached the bottom of it.

Max gave her a tight smile. "Thanks. I'll do my best with it all." He glanced at the screen again and took a deep breath.

"That's all you can do. It will become second nature in no time," Clem said gently, noticing the flicker of panic in his eyes.

"Right, I'd better get my skates on. Madam will be waiting."

"Good luck. You'll need it," Max replied, already getting to his feet.

He left Florence with a speed that made Clem wince. A knot of guilt tightened her stomach. Maybe she'd thrown too much at him too soon. Whether he sank or swam was a worry for another day. Victoria's problems were more pressing, and if Clem could help the woman, then nothing was going to stop her.

# CHAPTER 11

*V*ictoria grabbed her bag and left her office. Work was done, and all she wanted now was to go home and zone out — but the supermarket beckoned.

*Damn Christine!*

She wouldn't be in this mess if it weren't for her former catering manager's festering bitterness. If she'd realised just how deep it ran, she might've thought to double-check the order.

On the positive side, she was getting to spend time with someone who was… what, exactly? What was Clem to her, and why was there a bubbling excitement inside her at the thought of spending time together? She'd spent the last forty-eight hours worrying Clem wouldn't be returning to her trading spot, and now she'd agreed to bake cakes for the party and help her at the supermarket. Having half-braced herself to be dragged into the canal again, Clem had turned out to be surprisingly agreeable.

Victoria had nearly cancelled the party when she discovered the entire food order was missing from their delivery. But deep down, she wasn't ready to give up. Some things were worth the effort, and the wharf was one of them.

As she stepped into the courtyard, she spotted Clem checking out her car, holding what looked like a cake box. Was that a gift for her? Her mouth watered.

As she reached the car, Clem held it out to her. "Here. Lemon drizzle."

Victoria's cheeks bulged as she tried — unsuccessfully — to contain her happiness over what was, essentially, just a slice of cake.

"Thank you. That's my favourite."

"Really? Lucky guess on my part," Clem said with a smug little shrug.

Unlocking the car and pulling her seat forward, Victoria carefully placed the box on the tiny seat behind it. Climbing in — with the usual groan from her body at how low down it was — she noticed Clem admiring the interior.

"You like?" Victoria asked, clicking on her seat belt.

"Yes, it's lovely. You don't see many of these around, not in this condition. How long have you owned it?"

"About ten years. It was a fortieth birthday present, from Drew — my husband."

A sudden silence made Victoria regret mentioning his name.

"Wow, great gift, and I wouldn't have put you at fifty," Clem said, dissipating the awkwardness but leaving a burning in Victoria's cheeks.

Having expected a comment about her wayward husband, this comment on her age caught her off guard in the best possible way. That Clem had looked at her and thought she was younger made her heart skip a beat.

"Well, I'm not quite fifty yet." *Give it a few hours.*

Victoria started the car, then drove across the cobbles and out onto the road.

"Did you have that coffee?" Clem asked.

"I did; it helped, I think. That scrumpy certainly hit the right spot."

"It doesn't take much."

"Your friend Max seems nice," Victoria said, hoping to get some clarification on what exactly Max was to Clem. Not that it mattered, of course; she was simply wondering.

"He is."

Well, that seemed to confirm they were only friends.

"Jasper will be all over him when he finds out he brews it," she said.

"Is he seeing anyone?" Clem asked.

"Jasper? Not that I know of, but if you're interested, I hate to break it to you: He's as gay as Eurovision."

"Not for me." Clem chuckled. "Men are *not* my thing. Never found a need for them."

"Oh." *Oh — why did she say that?* What was someone meant to say to that? Victoria suddenly felt jittery, like adrenaline was coursing through her. She was beginning to regret mixing scrumpy with coffee.

"I was asking for Max," Clem explained. "He's had eyes for Jasper for a long time, apparently."

"Then he already holds the key to Jasper's heart," Victoria said, trying to focus and forget about Clem's sexuality. It didn't matter to her that Clem liked women. "He needs a man. He's been single too long."

"Where is Jasper, anyway? Can't he help you prepare for tomorrow?"

"He's at a conference in London, not back until tomorrow afternoon. I've put him in charge of decorating the café and setting everything up."

They lapsed into a comfortable silence. The fields rolled

past, soon giving way to buildings as they crossed a bridge over the canal leading into town. The nearest supermarket was on the far side, and rush hour had them queuing in traffic. The stillness, though it served to calm her, was beginning to feel a little awkward, so Victoria decided to break it.

"Where do you get all your supplies from?"

"I get deliveries to my parents' house."

"Oh, of course," Victoria said. She'd noticed the van but assumed it was just general groceries for Clem. "Makes sense." Not wanting the conversation to fizzle out, she added, "Can I ask how you knew it was us — Christine, I should say — who tried to get you moved?"

"It seems my dad is friends with the landowner, who also seems to own that stretch of the canal."

"Ah. Mr Armitage," Victoria said as the traffic moved.

"Yes. He was straight on the phone to my dad and quite happy to spill the beans."

"Is that how you got yourself the best trading spot?" Victoria asked, glancing at Clem as her mouth opened in mock offence.

"I wouldn't know anything about that — or what *is* the best spot."

Victoria grinned. "Okay, I believe you."

"But, for what it's worth, I am sorry about Christine. If I had any part in her firing."

"Thank you, but it's no real loss. Yes, she's put me in a difficult position with what she did to you, but she's been a pain in my backside for a while. Her departure would have happened sooner or later. I insisted she remove those reviews, but you might have noticed she hasn't. I did add a comment, though. I hope it helps."

"I saw. Thank you; it means a lot."

Victoria smiled as she reversed into a parking space. "It was the least I could do."

As she applied the handbrake, Clem fidgeted in her seat and then turned to face her. "For what it's worth, my mum told the builders no one was living next door."

"I should have known," Victoria said with a roll of her eyes.

"Sorry. My parents can be a bit full-on sometimes."

"Don't worry about it. I was having a bad start to the day when I met them. I may have been a bit abrupt."

"We all have bad days," Clem said gently.

A soft smile followed. It was light, kind, and entirely disarming, and it hit Victoria square in the chest. Her heart squeezed, causing a warmth to rush through her. Why did Clem make her feel such things?

"I'll grab a trolley," Clem said, suddenly reaching for the door. "Meet you in there."

"Thanks," Victoria replied, grateful to have a moment alone to collect herself as she exited and headed into the store.

Clem joined her a few minutes later as she was rummaging through the cucumbers, trying to find the freshest ones for the salmon and cucumber sandwiches. Noticing her companion squirming and biting her lips together, Victoria pointed one of the long, green vegetables at her.

"If you're thinking of making a cucumber joke, so help me, I'll—" She waved the cucumber menacingly.

Clem raised her hands in mock innocence. "Hadn't even crossed my mind."

Victoria smiled. "Now, have you got a list?"

"All in here," Clem said, tapping the side of her head. "Baking is second nature. You know, this place sells cakes.

It would've saved you the trouble of begging me to bake. They're not as shit as yours either."

Victoria's jaw dropped. "I did *not* beg. And how did you know about our shit cakes? Been checking out the competition, have we?"

"No. Max told me how awful they were. Anyway, I'm not the one sending my curator to fetch me lemon drizzle and then sitting on the towpath practically inhaling it."

"I did not inhale it!" Victoria protested, but spying Clem's overly pleased with herself grin, she added, "Okay, maybe I did."

Clem winked. "And *that's* how I know you like lemon drizzle."

"Hmm," Victoria said, lips pressed together. "There is no harm in keeping an eye on competitors. Anyway, I don't want shop-bought. This is the wharf's first birthday. I need the bes—"

"Oh, I see. I'm the best, am I?" Clem said, her face creasing with amusement.

Victoria narrowed her eyes. "You know what I mean."

"Do I?" Clem teased, rubbing her chin.

"Oh, shush. You know you are. Your lemon drizzle is divine."

"Yeah. I do know." Clem smirked, bumping her shoulder gently into Victoria's and sending tingles shooting straight through her in the process.

Was Clem being flirtatious, or was Victoria overthinking? She didn't know Clem well enough to know all her sides, but she was pretty sure the pissed-off version she'd seen so much of couldn't be the *real* Clem.

"The best cake maker — *and* modest too. You really are the complete woman," Victoria drawled.

"I like to think so," Clem said, leaning on the trolley. "So, what's on your list?"

"Scones."

"Scones? You're *buying* scones."

"Yes. What else do you suggest I do? Find a magic lamp and rub it?"

"You could rub me." Clem bit her lip, eyes widening. "Oh — I don't mean. Oh, erm. I just meant I can bake you some scones."

Victoria raised an eyebrow, hoping the heat prickling her cheeks wasn't visible. "You can?"

"Of course. They're hardly difficult."

"I wasn't suggesting you *couldn't*, merely questioning whether you were offering to make them. At least I *think* you were offering."

"I was," Clem said, resting a hand on Victoria's arm. "I am."

"Thank you."

Their eyes met, lingering just long enough for Victoria to register the warmth of Clem's hand through her sleeve. It stirred something she hadn't felt in a long time, the feeling of comfort and connection. She'd almost forgotten how grounding it could be to feel someone else's touch. Realising how much she missed the feeling and how rare it had become in her life made her heart feel heavy.

"We should get on," Victoria said, desperate to stop her thoughts.

"Yes, of course."

Half an hour later, with everything packed tightly into the small car, Victoria turned to Clem, who was wedged in the passenger seat beside her.

"Are you sure you're okay?"

A muffled 'yes' came from behind a pile of carrier bags.

Victoria winced. She didn't sound okay. "It's not far," she tried to reassure Clem. "I didn't realise how much I would need — or just how small the luggage compartment is."

"It's fine. We got it in… just. As long as we don't crash or I need to breathe for the next ten minutes, I'll survive."

Victoria laughed. "Sorry." Relieved to hear a quiet chuckle beside her, she drove out of the car park.

Bags rustled behind their seats as the car turned a corner. Maybe she should be thanking Christine after all. She and Clem had enjoyed a perfect outing — no shouting, no swearing, no storming off — and she'd had the most enjoyable trip to the supermarket she could recall.

With rush hour traffic long gone, the drive back to the wharf was relatively quick. Victoria reversed up to the main entrance between the picnic benches, sparing herself the effort of lugging everything across the courtyard. She made her way around to the passenger side of her car and freed Clem from beneath the pile of bags.

"You should head off. I can get all this inside," she said, lifting the bags from her lap.

Clem got out and stepped towards Victoria. She was so close — the kind of close that made Victoria's breath hitch.

"Let me help." Clem's fingers brushed Victoria's as she reached for the bags.

It was the lightest of touches but still sent a tingle through Victoria's hand.

She tried to shake Clem off. "No, honestly. I can manage."

"It's fine. I'm happy to help," Clem said, giving the bags a gentle tug.

Victoria pulled back. "I've taken up enough of your time already."

A knowing grin spread across Clem's face. "Do you not remember how our previous tug of war ended?"

Victoria huffed out a laugh and released her grip. "Okay. You can help."

After several trips back and forth, they wrangled all the shopping into the wharf's kitchen. Victoria locked up and returned to Clem, where she lingered by the Jag.

"Well, thanks for your help," Victoria began. "It was kind of you to offer."

"Anytime," Clem replied, digging her toes into the gaps between the cobbles.

"So, I'll see you here in the morning?"

"Yes." Clem looked up. "Is six, okay? Or too early?"

"Six is perfect." It wasn't. It was way too early, and with the party likely leading to a late night, tomorrow was going to be a very long day. Too long for her liking.

Clem gave a firm nod and backed away, hands tucked in her pockets. "See you then."

"And thanks for the cake," Victoria called after her. "Can't wait to dig in."

With a wink, Clem turned and strode across the courtyard towards the bridge.

Victoria leaned against her car for balance, feeling like all the blood in her body had rushed to her head. Heat rushed under her skin as her knees threatened to give way. Damn the woman for making her feel like this. It wasn't helpful. She didn't need to be having knee-weakening feelings — not now, not ever. She'd put herself out to pasture a long time ago, and she wasn't looking to rejoin the herd. She'd moved on from all that.

With Clem out of sight, Victoria checked her watch. It was late. She needed dinner and her bed. Without Christine, she'd be stuck doing all the food prep for the party herself. Poor Emma would have to manage the café alone. Even with lunches off the menu, thanks to staff shortages, it was still a lot to ask of her.

Victoria got in the car and drove home. As the road wended before her, her thoughts immediately fell back to Clem. The woman made her laugh, and in her company, Victoria felt lighter, as though some of the weight she'd grown used to carrying was beginning to lift. It was a strange feeling, considering Clem's presence was also part of what made everything feel so heavy.

Still, she hoped they'd find a way through. If they could work together, they might even find a way to make both of their businesses thrive. If she made some tweaks to the café and they could agree on some operational boundaries, they would have no reason to be anything but neighbourly.

As for the odd feelings Clem stirred in her... Well, Victoria decided she needed to get a grip. She was married and would remain so, if only for the sake of the business. Unlike her husband, she wouldn't stray from a contract. Not even at the wink of a beautiful woman.

# CHAPTER 12

*C*lem surveyed the ingredients laid out across the stainless steel worktop in the wharf's kitchen. There was a lot to get through in a few hours, even less time than planned thanks to Victoria running late. With two cups of coffee inside her, though, Clem felt up to the task.

She'd politely declined Victoria's offer to assist; the half-covered yawns and heavy-lidded eyes suggested she'd be more of a hindrance than a help. So Victoria headed off to her office, giving Clem space to focus on the task ahead, without distractions. Because that's exactly what Victoria was: a distraction. Clem still couldn't believe she'd winked at her the previous afternoon. It had just happened, in an instinctive, automatic way. She'd briefly caught her reaction and could've sworn she saw Victoria leaning against the car as if her legs had stopped cooperating. Perhaps she had stumbled, though, or was simply tired from her stressful day. What else could it be?

Clem opened a bag of flour and began weighing it. Victoria's words — that she needed the 'best' —

unhelpfully drifted into her mind. Clem smiled as she closed the bag, the words dancing inside her. Of all the compliments she'd received about her cakes, this one felt different, more personal and therefore more poignant.

She'd even come out to Victoria, and after a brief 'Oh', the conversation had moved on. There wasn't a flicker of awkwardness. It clearly hadn't bothered her. And why would it? Victoria didn't strike her as ignorant or narrow-minded; she appeared to be open and educated.

Having mixed the batter and distributed it evenly in the cake tins she'd brought with her, Clem left the Victoria sponges to bake. She mixed the ingredients for scones by hand with the lightest of touches; no one would want them dry and airless. Once they were in the large oven, she left the sponges to cool, turning her attention next to a banana loaf and a cherry Madeira. Florence needed supplies for the day's trading, and both were quick and reliable options. As they baked and the scones cooled, Clem whipped cream in an industrial-sized whisker, giving the machine an envious eye as she did.

The whole kitchen stirred jealousy inside her. It offered so much open, flexible working space compared to Florence's cramped galley, and there was little chance of knocking into anything. The machinery was second to none as well, the oven being triple the size of her own. Being able to mix all the batter at once saved a significant amount of time. She could far too easily get used to this.

Pleased with her productivity, Clem found it was soon time to track down Victoria. She left the kitchen and headed to the office, where she found the door ajar. Poking her head around it, she spotted Victoria curled up on a sofa in the corner, fast asleep.

Clem hesitated, not wanting to disturb her but knowing she must. Victoria's gentle breathing and the slow rise and fall of her shoulder made her look so peaceful. Clem stepped closer. A stray strand of hair had fallen across Victoria's face, adding to her quiet charm.

Crouching beside her, Clem brushed it from her cheek. "Victoria," she whispered.

Victoria's eyelids fluttered until her blue eyes finally settled on Clem with a smile.

"Sorry. I didn't want to wake you, but—"

"No. No, it's fine," Victoria replied, getting up so quickly Clem was sure the blood would rush from her head. "I could've slept for a week, so I'm grateful you did. I've got a lot to do today."

"I need to know where you want everything stored."

"You've made everything already?"

"Yes," Clem said, taking the slight tone of surprise in Victoria's tone as a compliment. "Come and see."

She held the door open for her, admiring just how shapely her figure was cut in the cute, navy, corduroy pinafore dress. How did she miss that earlier this morning? As she passed, the air stirred, and Clem caught a pleasant scent of jasmine that she now associated with Victoria. It had lingered in the close confines of the Jag.

As they arrived in the kitchen, Victoria's face lit up at the sight of the cakes.

"Oh, my. These look wonderful." Turning to the scones, she added, "And these — they're so small and cute!"

"Intentionally so," Clem replied. "Scones aren't the easiest to eat while chatting at a party, so I figured bite-sized might be preferable. With cake on offer, too, not everyone will want a big one. Those who do can have two. I've made plenty."

"Brilliant," Victoria said, turning around, her hands clasped in front of her. "You're brilliant. I wouldn't have thought of that. Thank you for all this."

Clem's cheeks warmed at the praise.

"Anytime. Although a bit more notice next time wouldn't hurt."

Victoria laughed. "I don't plan on making a habit of losing catering managers. Be sure to send me an invoice, won't you?"

"You bought all the ingredients, and we can call my time an apology for taking you for that swim."

"Oh…" Victoria's face seemed to fall in that moment. "Are you sure?"

"I am," Clem said firmly, hoping she wouldn't put up a fight.

"Well then, thank you again," Victoria replied, her smile so soft and endearing it made Clem's hectic morning feel worthwhile. "Right, I'd better crack on. I have a mountain of sandwiches and sausage rolls to make. Salads to prep…"

"Alone?" Clem's voice lifted, more sharply than she'd intended.

"Yes." Victoria arched a friendly eyebrow at her. "Might I remind you I'm short-staffed because I sided with you."

Clem grinned. "Remind me again why you did that?"

"Christine was out of order. A bit of competition is fine, but I draw the line at dirty tricks. Those reviews were unjustified."

Clem felt a pang of disappointment that it wasn't for any reason beyond standing up for what was right, even though that was a fair justification. Before she could dwell on it, a young woman appeared at the kitchen hatch. Clem recognised her: Blueberry Muffin, another of her wharf regulars.

"Morning, Victoria."

"Morning, Emma. This is Clem. She's made all this for

the party," Victoria said, smiling broadly and gesturing towards the centre island.

"Oh, hi — Clem," Emma said, biting her lip. Her eyes bulged at the cakes as she tied her hair back in a ponytail. "Wow. They look amazing. I can't wait to try them later. They look way better than the sh—"

"Yes, thank you, Emma," Victoria cut in quickly.

Emma grinned and vanished, leaving Clem to stifle a laugh — only to fail miserably.

"Yes, even the staff despised them," Victoria acknowledged with a huff.

"Oh, I know. She comes to me every morning for a blueberry muffin."

Victoria rolled her eyes. "Why does that not surprise me? It seems Jasper's addicted to your coffee and walnut cake."

She was about to reply that she knew that, too, when she noticed that Victoria was frowning and rubbing her chin.

"Maybe I should close the café earlier today. Not that I can afford to, but poor Emma's having to cope out there alone."

Clem reached out and gently squeezed Victoria's arm. "I could stay and help."

Victoria looked down at her hand. "I wasn't trying to guilt-trip you."

"It was a genuine offer," Clem asserted, drawing her hand back. She'd only meant to offer comfort; now she was left feeling like she'd overstepped.

"What about Florence?"

"Max would probably look after her."

"All day?"

Clem made a quick calculation in her head. "With the two of us, the rest of the food will take half the time. Why don't I come back after the lunch rush? You'll be free to help Emma until then."

A flicker of relief crossed Victoria's face as her shoulders relaxed. "Are you sure?"

"Yes," Clem said, trying not to sound too eager at the prospect of spending more time with her. "As you pointed out, it's my fault you're in this mess," she snarked.

"I took particular pains *not* to say it like that."

"Victoria, I'm teasing you," Clem said, nudging her gently.

"Oh." A sheepish smile crossed Victoria's lips as her gaze dropped.

"We need to stop reacting off each other; we're not enemies. I don't get up at six a.m. to bake for someone I don't like. At most, we are adversaries. Or maybe... competitive friends. For what it's worth, I don't want this place to fail. I think it's great. I'm sorry it's not thriving — and if I've made things harder. I seem to cause you nothing but problems."

"I don't blame you. Even if my ex-catering manager does," Victoria added with a wry smile. "Our problems go deeper than a bit of competition. You're just the tipping point, it seems. A mix of bad winter weather and fading novelty with the locals haven't left us in a great position. I should have been working here full-time when we opened."

"Why weren't you?" Clem asked, intrigued to know a little more about Victoria.

"I had big projects in London I couldn't abandon. Some of them take years to complete, and I couldn't walk away. I guess I've taken my eye off the ball. Or it was never on it to begin with."

"But you're here full-time now," Clem said

reassuringly, knowing that showing up was a vital part of any successful business.

"Yes."

"Then it's onwards and upwards. You can't change the past, but the future's up for grabs. And you know, the novelty wearing off isn't necessarily a bad thing."

"How so?"

"It means they *know* you exist. Now you need to find a way to lure them back."

"That's the problem," Victoria sighed. "I don't know how. I'm not a marketing whizz."

"Well, that's where you're in luck — I am," Clem said, her tone light but steady. "It's not as daunting as it seems. You've already laid the groundwork; now you just need a few gentle nudges in the right direction."

"I'd really appreciate that. I need bums on seats — and fast."

Clem caught Victoria's eye. "You have ideas when it comes to taking down the competition. At least, I assume the free hot drink offer was yours."

Victoria looked away, but a smile edged her lips. "It was."

"See? We'll make a marketeer of you yet. If the winter season caused you problems, you need to take advantage of it next time — it'll be here before you know it. Host a fireworks night or a Christmas market. The courtyard would be great for that. Don't limit yourself to what's already here. You're more than a museum and a café. Think big! Honestly, Victoria, there's *so* much potential here. Utilise the café space. You've got room to section off an area for groups. Encourage knitting circles, puzzle clubs, and the local WI. Get a book club in after hours, hold a quiz. I assume you have an alcohol license, so hire the place out. That large car park on the other side of the building, is it only for the apartment owners?"

"No. They have reserved spaces, but the rest is for our visitors. And yes, we have a license," Victoria confirmed.

"Then you're set for meetings, parties, wakes, and even weddings. Collect email addresses in exchange for a free hot drink and start a newsletter. Offer loyalty cards. Get the kids in during the holidays with fun activities." She drummed her fingers on the worktop before adding, "More urgently, you need to sort your social media out."

Victoria nodded, brow furrowed in thought.

"The museum must be popular with schools," Clem continued, finding herself in a flow of ideas she couldn't — or didn't want to, if she were honest — put the brakes on. "It's a perfect place to combine the social history of corsetry with the industrial machine. How many groups visit? Have the University of the Third Age been? Retired people love somewhere to walk to, so *become* that destination. Offer lunchtime deals, especially on pension day. If you don't give people a reason to come—"

"—then they won't come," Victoria finished with a nod.

"Exactly," Clem said, almost out of breath but relieved Victoria was finally grasping the underlying issues here.

A small part of her was a little jealous of everything there was to do. She loved a project, particularly a marketing one, and the wharf was a worthwhile venture, bursting with potential.

"Is this your way of telling me I need more than a few corsets and cake to survive?" Victoria said, raising an eyebrow.

"Yes, it is," Clem replied without hesitation. "And this may not be the right time to say it, but… I've started serving sausage rolls and cheese scones. Sorry."

Victoria shrugged. "It's a free world. That I do believe in. And you've given me food for thought on what I need to do — pun fully intended."

Clem's chest tightened as Victoria's expression hovered between amusement and worry. She wanted to lift the burden from her shoulder, not pile more on.

"And there was me thinking you were just a baker," Victoria said.

"I'm a marketing guru at heart, and I'm very particular about what I market these days."

Clem took the gentle tilt of Victoria's head as a sign she wanted to hear more.

"I worked in fast food until recently. Not only was the daily grind getting me down, but the ethics were, too. Or lack of. I couldn't keep pushing people towards food I don't believe in, food that's engineered to be addictive and nutritionally empty." She stopped for a breath, then added, "I wanted to feel proud of the message behind a campaign, not cringe every time I saw it."

"I can understand that. I can't believe what's in the cakes we were serving to people. I won't be buying them, that's for certain."

"Good."

"So, how did you wind up where you are now?" Victoria questioned.

"When they dangled a big promotion in front of me, I walked away. I used my inheritance from Gram to start over. Sometimes I wonder if she knew I'd lost my way and left it for that reason, to help me change course. And who knows if I even made the right change, if I'm on the right course now." She swallowed hard and took a deep breath. "It pains me that it took her death to make any of it possible."

"If she did," Victoria said softly, "then I'm sure it

brought her comfort knowing that she could help you in the future. Even if she wasn't around to see it."

Clem nodded, her throat tightening as her eyes moistened. The pain of Gram's absence was as raw as ever. She looked away and wiped them quickly, hoping Victoria hadn't noticed. "Let's get this lot put away. It's about time I opened Florence up."

Victoria reached for some disposable plastic containers on a high shelf.

"These should do for the cakes," she said. "I've got platters to serve everything else on."

Clem suspected they had once contained chemical cakes.

"Great." She began filling the containers with scones, which were now cool to the touch. "Aren't you glad you didn't get rid of me?"

"The thought never crossed my mind," Victoria said with a mock-scandalised tone.

Clem chuckled. "If you say so."

# CHAPTER 13

Following a later-than-planned start and a relentless lunchtime rush assisting Emma in the café, Victoria seized a quiet lull to begin prepping the party food. As she bent to retrieve chopping boards and baking trays from under the island, her body protested. If she could snatch another half hour's nap before the party began, it might just take the edge off her aches.

It had been a struggle to keep her eyes open since she'd woken a little later than planned, which had in turn put her behind schedule to open the wharf for Clem. It wasn't a great look, turning up fifteen minutes late while someone was doing you a favour. When Clem insisted that she would crack on alone, Victoria hadn't argued. Exhaustion pulled her to the sofa in her office, where she'd fallen asleep instantly.

Waking to find Clem only inches from her face had felt oddly comforting. For a brief, dazed moment she'd believed she was dreaming. The idea that Clem wasn't real had gripped her chest with a strange ache. Then, once she realised Clem really was there, she'd immediately felt vulnerable and exposed. Embarrassment nagged at her hours later despite her attempts to brush it off. It was just sleep, after all; nothing worth feeling awkward about.

Clem's mouthwatering creations had lingered in Victoria's mind all morning, too, but at least both thoughts, the embarrassing and the tantalising, had proved a welcome distraction from having turned fifty. Despite her underlying nerves about the party, Victoria was counting down the hours until she could finally sink her teeth into a slice of cake.

A glance at her watch made her heart jolt — it was two p.m. Only five hours until the party started, and she would need to get home to shower and change before then. Would Clem even come back like she'd promised? Victoria's hand slid to her arm, where Clem had squeezed it earlier. Strangely, she could still feel her there, like she'd left a trace of herself behind. Was it simply tiredness playing tricks on her? She flexed her fingers around the spot, hopeful it might disperse the feeling. It didn't. Maybe the feeling sat deeper inside her.

"Hey. Emma said to come through."

Victoria startled at the sound of Clem's voice. "Hi. I'm relieved to see you."

"Did you think I'd change my mind?" Clem asked, smiling smugly.

"Perhaps," Victoria admitted.

"I don't break a promise. Now, where do we start?" Clem asked, rolling up her sleeves and washing her hands in the sink. "Shall I do the sausage rolls whilst you butter the bread? Then I can help you fill the sandwiches."

"Sounds like a plan," Victoria said, heading to the fridge. She opened the door, giving the cakes a loving look, then extracted the sausage meat and ready-to-roll pastry. As she turned to place them on the worktop, she bumped straight into Clem. "Oh. Sorry," she muttered, dying a little inside from the fresh wave of embarrassment.

"No problem. Let me take those." Clem reached for the items.

"Thanks," Victoria replied, her heartbeat growing stronger, as though it knew something she didn't.

"I have a confession to make," Clem said, arranging everything on the worktop.

Victoria braced herself as she stacked slices of bread, ready to butter. "Confess away."

"It was my mum who washed your jumper."

That she wasn't expecting. Although thinking about it, Clem didn't strike her as the type of woman who knew the intricacies of caring for cashmere.

"Ah, I see. Won't break a promise but will steal credit for someone else's handiwork. I'm on to you," Victoria said, prodding Clem with a cucumber.

"Hey," Clem laughed, squirming away as she tried to open a packet of pastry. "Give me *some* credit. I fished it out of the canal, and I endured the stench whilst it soaked in my bathroom sink."

"Then thank you. I will have to remember to thank your mum one day, too," Victoria said, handing her a rolling pin.

"Mmm. Maybe shout it at her from a distance."

Victoria chuckled as she peeled a layer of butter away from its container with her knife. "I gather your parents aren't my biggest fans. Can I assume that's due to me asking them to stop blocking the road?"

"That and they know why your jumper was in the canal. They might still be under the impression that you were the one who tried to get me moved on. I should set them right."

"Yes, please let them know I had nothing to do with it. If we're going to be neighbours, I'd rather they didn't believe I'm the she-devil who tried to sabotage their daughter's business."

"Even if I tell them, I can't guarantee they'll believe me," Clem said, chuckling as she began rolling the pastry.

"I only wanted to get to work, but their van was in the way. Then I tried to make polite conversation." Victoria snorted. "Big mistake."

Clem's amusement eased some of her discomfort with the situation. If she was laughing at her parents' reaction to Victoria, then it couldn't be all bad. Victoria was unlikely to see her neighbours often, so it hardly mattered.

They fell into a brief silence, busying themselves with their duties and instinctively working around each other. When Victoria found the silence too awkward, she broke it.

"So, are you going to tell me why your cakes are so good?"

"You expect me to divulge my secret recipes?" Clem asked, tilting her head playfully. "Planning to poach them, are you?"

Victoria recoiled in faux horror as she opened a packet of ham. "I wouldn't dream of it. Baking is not my forte, so fear not, your secrets are safe with me."

"Okay," Clem relented, laying the sausage meat in long lines along the pastry. "Between you and me, the key is to keep it simple. Blend key flavours. People like their cake traditional, so don't mess with it. Once you add the flour, don't over-beat the mixture, and always weigh it into the pans before they go in the oven. Basic things, really, but they make all the difference. Oh, and I use Jersey butter where I can because it makes the cakes taste amazing and has a nice yellow colour. I think you noticed that." Clem's eyes sparkled with mischief.

"I might have," Victoria admitted, biting her lip as she tried and failed to keep a straight face. "Where did your passion for baking come from?"

"Gram. My grandparents both died when my mum was young, so her aunt and uncle adopted her. I spent a lot of time with them when I was growing up. Gram loved to bake, and I loved cake, so we were a perfect match. She taught me everything I know."

Clem fell into silence, her gaze drifting off into the distance. Victoria scrambled for the right words to respond with. As Clem began rolling the pastry around the sausage meat, something came to mind.

"It's strange to think of you spending so much time next door another lifetime ago." Feeling immediately foolish for saying aloud what should have been a private thought, she added, "Sorry. That sounded weird."

Clem flashed her a warm smile as she cut the pastry into individual sausage rolls. "It wasn't exactly a lifetime ago, but since I left university, work kept me away more than I would have liked. In recent years, after my great-uncle died, Mum and Dad would pick up Gram on their boat. We'd spend time pottering around the canals. They have a much bigger one than Florence and run it as a hotel. I think it was the only time she left the house in the last few years."

"I never saw much of her. Renovating the house and the wharf kept me fairly occupied."

Clem pulled a wry face. "Shame. She was the best."

"I'm sorry I didn't get to know her," Victoria mused. She tucked that regret away alongside so many others.

With the sausage rolls in the oven, Victoria set Clem to work layering egg mayonnaise onto the bread.

"This party seems pretty important to you," Clem said softly.

"It is. It's the wharf's first birthday. Everything has to go well. At this rate, it could be a farewell party rather than a celebration."

"Are things really that bad?"

"Yes," Victoria said, exhaling. "Drew's development company owns the wharf. Well, the individual apartments are sold off, but he owns the building itself and the entire ground floor. He'll turn that into apartments, too, if we don't start making money."

"I'm sorry."

Victoria flashed her a flat smile.

"You said once that this was all you," Clem continued.

"Yes," Victoria confirmed, amazed Clem had remembered. "I was an architect. Redesigning this entire building was my biggest project."

"*Was* an architect? I'm pretty sure you still are. You don't just stop being one, do you? It's not like you hand your pencil and ruler back in."

A smile tugged at Victoria's lips. She hadn't thought of it like that. "No. I don't suppose you do."

"So, how did you come by the wharf?"

"There was a time in my life when I needed a distraction from" — Victoria paused, searching for the right word — "everything. I began looking into my family history and discovered my three-times-great-grandfather was a corset manufacturer."

"Ahh."

"My research led me here, to his factory, and I immediately felt a connection to it. An overwhelming urge to save it."

"Understandable."

A familiar pang of worry settled in Victoria's chest as it often did. So often, in fact, she wondered if it was making itself at home. Had she saved the factory? Was she still saving it? When would she know if she'd saved it?

"Where does Jasper come into it?" Clem asked, interrupting Victoria's spiralling thoughts. "Max said he's the country's leading expert on corsets."

Victoria lifted an eyebrow and turned to Clem. "Max has done his homework."

"Oh, he has. Probably a little more than is healthy." Clem chuckled.

Victoria grinned as she began slicing the sandwiches. "I had the idea to create a sort of homage to corsetry, which led me to Jasper. We hit it off straight away. I couldn't have done all this without him. He showed interest in my ideas and was passionate about my vision; he was someone I could bounce ideas off — unlike Drew, who showed no interest. He was all about money. Still is." She paused, took a deep breath, and continued. "So Jasper and I decided to set up the museum to bring years of research and history together in one collection. It's another reason I can't let it fail. I'd be failing Jasper."

"You will fail no one as long as you try your best," Clem reassured her. "That's all anyone can ask of you."

"What if my best isn't good enough?" Victoria asked, the words catching slightly in her throat. "My skills lie in developing sites for use. I'm not proficient in generating a profit from them. Once I finished the wharf, I had no idea what I was doing."

"I'd say you've done a pretty fine job getting it to where it is today. You might need a little help taking it to the next stage, but there's no shame in that. Even the best entrepreneurs know when to call in the experts. You asked me when you needed cake. Delegate more often."

Victoria nodded. It made sense, where she could afford it, but it didn't stop her feeling inadequate, especially when it came to the simpler task of baking. Her mum had been so convinced that she was destined for academic greatness that her education in domestic duties fell by the wayside.

"So where is this husband of yours?" Clem asked, scraping the last of the egg mayonnaise from its tub.

Victoria's cheeks burned at the directness of the question. She felt stupid for mentioning Drew. Clem had likely taken it as an invitation to talk about him. Since they were growing closer, Victoria supposed it was inevitable the subject would resurface, no matter how much she wanted it to stay buried.

With reluctance, she said, "You might have already guessed we don't exactly have a… conventional marriage. But he'll be here. He promised." Not that his promises were worth much.

"And so he should be. One year is something to celebrate."

"Well — fifty, actually," Victoria mumbled.

"What?" Clem paused, then set down her spatula.

"It's my birthday today," she confessed.

"What! Are you serious? Happy birthday!"

Before Victoria knew it, Clem was hugging her. She couldn't even reciprocate easily because of the knife she was holding, but she tried.

Clem stepped back and gave her a playful nudge with her shoulder, a nudge that made Victoria's breath hitch.

"That comment yesterday about you not quite being fifty: total failure on your part to mention it was only a few hours away."

Victoria shrugged. "I try not to dwell on it." She picked up some cut sandwiches and took them to the other side of the island to arrange them on a platter.

"What? It's something to celebrate! Fifty is a huge milestone. A whole half-century," Clem teased.

"Yes! Thank you for the reminder," Victoria said dryly.

At that, Clem fell into silence, but Victoria noticed something shift in her face, a flicker in her eyes. Her mouth was poised to say something, but she didn't speak. Victoria had seen it before.

"What do you want to say?" she prompted.

Clem looked up. "Oh, erm, just that… I won't tell anyone. In case you worried that I would. You know, about what I saw."

Victoria paused. It hadn't occurred to her that Clem would say anything, and anyway, who would she tell?

"I wasn't worried."

"Oh, good," Clem said, relief audible in her tone. "So… do you have family coming?"

"Family!" Victoria let out a long breath. "No. My brother emigrated to Canada, and my parents live in the Lake District. We all lead very separate lives."

"That's sad."

Victoria twitched her shoulders. "Is it?"

She'd made peace with her solitude a long time ago. When it came down to it, Jasper was the only person in her corner, not Drew. A long time had passed since he had been that to her — or since she had thought he was. All he did now was make her feel more alone.

"Yes, it is," Clem insisted. "My parents annoy me sometimes — well, Mum mostly — but I wouldn't be without her. Did you have a falling-out?"

"No, not exactly. I grew weary of carrying the weight

of other people's expectations. As I got older, I realised I didn't have to."

"Oh."

Concerned that Clem's intense gaze might coax more out than she was ready to give, Victoria turned her attention back to the last sandwich and asked, "Have you eaten?"

"I had some banana bread before I opened up."

"You can't live off cake," Victoria chided, "as tempting as it might be. Here." She cut the ham sandwich in two and handed Clem one half. "I don't want you passing out on me."

Clem gave a small smile as she accepted the offering. "Thanks."

Victoria tucked into the other half and watched as Clem attacked hers like a feral goat — albeit a rather charming one.

With energy levels restored and everything laid out on silver platters, wrapped in cling film, and packed into the fridge, their work was complete.

"Is Max looking after Florence for you?"

Clem nodded. "He's a lifesaver. He'll close up as soon as things quieten down."

"Thank him from me. And thank you, again, for swooping in and rescuing me. I'm not sure what I would've done without you — or if I really deserve it."

Clem tilted her head, a faint smile playing at the corners of her mouth. "Help often comes from the places we least expect."

"It seems so." Victoria met her gaze, the hint of a blush rising to her cheeks.

"And for the record," Clem said, leaning in slightly, her voice lower, "I only swoop when the cause is absolutely necessary and deserving."

Victoria wasn't sure how to respond to that or to Clem's soft, disarming smile. She matched it as best she could. "If you are out of pocket at all, you must let me cover everything."

She was all too aware of how much Clem had given her already in time, effort, and kindness. The last thing she wanted was for her to be financially burdened.

"It's fine," Clem said, shaking her head. "It's nice to get a break and do something different."

"You mean make sausage rolls within four different walls?"

"Something like that." Clem chuckled. "Florence can get a little claustrophobic."

"You don't need to tell me. I went inside one of those things many years ago. I'm not in a hurry to repeat the experience."

Clem pulled a wry moue. "Noted."

"But I am going to insist on repaying you for today by cooking you dinner one evening."

"That would be lovely," Clem said, her expression brightening into one of her enormous smiles. "After spending all day in the kitchen, the last thing I feel like is cooking."

"That's a date then. I mean an, erm..." Victoria grew flustered, heat rising in her cheek as she battled her brain for help rephrasing the sentence. She soon gave up. "Oh, you know what I mean."

"I do." Clem smiled. "And I'm looking forward to it — not just for a peek inside of your house."

"Noted," Victoria returned. Emboldened by their easy conversation and newly formed truce, she added, "Whilst I'm already pushing my luck..."

Clem raised a perfectly timed eyebrow. "Yes?"

"Were you serious this morning when you said 'anytime'?"

"Erm. I guess. Why?"

Though she was tempted to backtrack based on Clem's suddenly uncertain tone, desperation spurred Victoria on.

"I don't suppose I could impose upon you to supply me regularly with cakes. Just until I sort out a new catering manager?"

Clem's forehead creased in mock offence. "You'd go back to your shitty cakes then, would you?"

"Ideally not." Victoria laughed. "I will definitely be voting to keep them."

Victoria watched Clem's face twitch.

"I'd need orders in advance," she finally said. "No dropping panic bakes on me."

"Everything would come through Emma," Victoria reassured her. "She could give you forty-eight hours' notice. Would that be enough?"

Clem gave a firm nod. "It would."

"Thank you," Victoria said with relief, feeling lighter at the prospect of one problem finding a resolution.

"I haven't told you my terms yet," Clem said, hands resting firmly on her hips.

"Go on," Victoria said, drawing in a breath.

"I will supply you at twenty per cent under my retail price — on one condition: You don't undercut me. I rely on passing trade, and you have something to attract people, so I don't want to see any of your special offers. Okay?"

Victoria thrust out her hand. "Deal."

Clem took it. Her grip was firm and warm, like her eyes. Victoria held on, meeting Clem's gaze and mirroring her smile. The warm, tingling sensation spreading through her body made Victoria reluctant to let go.

The kitchen door burst open then, and they jumped

apart like teenagers caught doing something they shouldn't.

"I'm here! Don't panic!" Jasper hollered as he strode in, arms raised like a Roman emperor greeting his subjects, a packet of balloons in one hand. His eyes landed on Clem, then flicked between them both. "Clem! Very nice to see you. I hope I'm not interrupting anything."

"No, not at all," Victoria replied, her voice a little too high to sound convincing. She hoped Jasper hadn't noticed and flashed him a smile. The faint twitch at the corner of his mouth suggested otherwise. "Clem's been assisting me with the food, and she's made us some rather lovely cakes. Everything's in the fridge, ready for later."

Jasper headed over for a look. "What a feast!" he said, eyes wide as he took it all in. "You're a marvel, Clem. Thank you."

"You're welcome. There's no coffee and walnut, I'm afraid."

"Well, aren't you the party pooper," Jasper deadpanned, giving her a wink as he closed the fridge door. He stepped towards Victoria, pulling her into a hug. "Happy birthday to you."

"Thank you," she replied, returning Jasper's squeeze. The warmth of it brought Clem's embrace to mind. As Jasper pulled away, she found herself wishing it had been Clem's arms around her again. Something about the woman made Victoria feel lighter, as though her problems weren't quite so big. *Safe*, she realised. She felt safe.

"Now if you'll excuse me," Jasper said, cutting through her thoughts. "I have fifty-odd balloons to blow up."

He took a balloon from the packet and started stretching it. As he reached the door, it opened; Max strode in, bumping straight into Jasper.

"Oh!" Max blustered as he turned a deep shade of pink. "Sorry."

"Entirely my fault, old chap," Jasper reassured him. "What can we do for you?"

"Erm, the woman at the counter said to come through." His eyes were wide, like a deer caught in headlights, until he spotted Clem. "I've locked up Florence for you, Clem."

"Thanks. I really appreciate it."

Jasper stood back, rested his hands on his hips, and gave Max an appraising glance. "You look like the kind of man who can blow well."

Max stuttered and then said with a cheeky smile, "I've had no complaints so far."

"Oh, really?" Jasper's eyes widened. "Can I borrow you? I can't promise to give you back."

"Fine by me." Max shrugged.

He threw the keys at Clem, who barely caught them, and looked about as startled as Victoria felt at the men's banter.

Jasper linked his arm through Max's. "Marvellous. Now, you ladies shoo. Go make yourselves look even more beautiful for the party. Leave the rest to us."

"Um, I'm not..." Clem began but then busied herself giving the worktop another wipe.

Jasper raised an eyebrow at Victoria, shooting her a pointed glare. She knew exactly what he was suggesting. How the idea hadn't come to her independently was frustrating to consider.

"Toodle-pip!" Jasper called, leading Max from the kitchen.

Once they were alone again, Victoria idly realised she hadn't thanked Max for freeing Clem up. There would be another time, though; right now, she needed to focus on settling the flutter of nerves in her stomach. She turned to Clem.

"Would you come to the party?"

The smile tugging at Clem's lips told Victoria she'd asked the right question.

"I'd love to, but there's just one problem."

Victoria's smile faltered. Of course there would be a problem.

"I'm not sure there's enough food," Clem teased.

"How much do you intend on eating?" Victoria goggled.

"Well, I heard that the cakes and scones were the creation of the 'best' baker in town, so I'm going to struggle to hold myself back."

"Ha. You're never going to let me forget that, are you?"

"Nope," Clem said with a firm shake of the head.

"Come on. I'll see you out. I need a breath of fresh air."

Victoria led them into the courtyard, which was quiet except for the babble of the fountain. The warm afternoon sun was casting long shadows over the uneven cobbles. She often imagined how it must have felt to stand here one hundred and fifty years ago, when the factory was busy with industry. The air would have been heavy with coal smoke and oil, the clatter of machines spilling from the windows. Horse-drawn carts would have rattled over the cobbles, ferrying crates of finished corsets to waiting boats as foremen shouted orders. It would have been alive — unlike now.

"Thanks again," she said softly, turning to Clem. "For everything."

"I was happy I could help. I'll see you later."

"You most certainly will," Victoria said with a smile as Clem backed away.

Disappointment hit her as she then turned and crossed

the courtyard. What had she expected? Another wink? A glance back? The absence of both made Victoria feel strangely hollow.

As she drove home, she had to remind herself it was her fiftieth birthday — a milestone, as Clem had said, and one she'd dreaded for a long time. All she could think about now was the woman who'd turned up to help and made sure everything ran smoothly. Clem hadn't known it was her birthday or just how important the party really was to her; regardless, she'd shown up. That stirred something in Victoria she hadn't expected, a feeling she wasn't sure she wanted to let go of.

# CHAPTER 14

Victoria checked her watch for the umpteenth time. Where the hell was Drew? Her phone buzzed on the arm of her chair, and she lunged for it.

*Running late, meet you there.*

She threw it back down. Not even an apology or so much as a 'happy birthday'. *Arsehole.* How much effort did it take to at least pretend you gave a shit? Not that pretending would make her feel any better, but it would have been better than ignoring her.

What was she supposed to do now? Walk in heels? Call a taxi? That would take forever on a Saturday night. She could drive and get a lift back with Drew... if he ever showed up.

Her eye landed on Florence next door. Victoria had noticed the narrowboat still moored in her trading spot just before she left the wharf, so she'd assumed Clem would stay there for the party. Now that she saw the boat just beyond her back garden, she wondered — Could she catch a ride with Clem?

The thought struck then that Clem might have decided

against going. It hit Victoria harder than she liked. She realised she was counting on seeing Clem again. Spending most of the day with her didn't feel like enough. She was light and funny — the complete opposite of how heavy and serious everything else in Victoria's life had felt lately.

Maybe Clem had left Florence and walked to the wharf. In which case, there'd be no chance at a lift. Victoria rolled her eyes at all the possibilities buzzing around in her head. There was only one way to find out. She picked her phone back up and slipped it into her purse. Giving one last glance at the mirror to check her hair and makeup, she headed next door, where she took the side path of the neighbouring house through the garden and out the gate at the bottom, which led onto the jetty.

"Clem! Are you there?" she called towards the narrowboat

A bang, followed by a "Fuck!" gave Victoria her answer.

Clem emerged onto Florence's stern, clutching her head. Her eyes widened immediately. "Wow! You look... stunning."

Victoria looked down at her black, knee-length sheath dress and tightened her champagne-coloured blazer around it. She had bought the outfit especially for tonight.

"Thank you. So do you," Victoria replied, taking in Clem's white maxi dress and denim jacket. Having only seen her in jeans and jumpers, it threw her for a moment. The feminine look suited her. "Are you okay?"

"I'll live. Whether on a narrowboat or not, time will tell. I'm not very spatially aware," Clem said with a rueful smile as she rubbed her head. "It's nothing that won't mend — like the rest of my bumps and bruises."

Victoria gave her a sympathetic smile. "Are you heading to the wharf?"

"Yes. You invited me to a party, remember?"

"Oh, yes… I just meant—"

"You thought I'd change my mind?" Clem asked, arching an eyebrow.

"Ha," Victoria replied, recalling those as Clem's exact words from earlier, when she'd been fretting she wouldn't show up to help. She should start trusting the woman a little more. "I find myself in need of a lift."

"Then climb aboard. I was about to leave."

Victoria took the hand Clem offered and stepped onto the boat.

"How come I have the pleasure of escorting you?" Clem asked.

"Drew was due to pick me up. He's travelling from London today, but he's running late."

Clem huffed. "It's your birthday. Your fiftieth. I wouldn't let you out of my sight all day if you were married to me."

The comment caught Victoria off guard. Clem wasn't married to her, but it felt like she hadn't let her out of her sight all day. She flashed an appreciative smile and decided it was best to change the subject.

"I keep meaning to apologise for being rude about your boat, though I stand by what I said."

"You apologise but stand by your words? Bold move," Clem said, her lips thinning into a sardonic smile even as she gave a gentle nod.

"She *is* garish," Victoria said with a shrug, "but I could have put it more politely."

Clem smiled. "She's not my favourite colour, but I wanted to restore her to the original. She used to belong to my mum. I was born inside her."

"Oh — wow. I wasn't expecting that."

"They sold her years ago, and I managed to find her. So yes, be mindful of what you say. She's family."

Victoria laughed. "I will."

"Now, we should get a move on. We don't want Cinderella to be late for her ball."

"I'm already late," Victoria sighed. "Anyway, isn't it fashionable to arrive a little late to your own party?"

Clem checked her watch and started Florence's engine. "Perhaps not half an hour late. Sit inside if you like. Make yourself at home."

"I'd much rather be out here—" Victoria cut herself off before *with you* could slip out.

"Well, if you insist." Clem opened a cupboard just inside the door and extracted a blanket. "Here. It will keep the chill off as we move."

Victoria accepted it gratefully. The cool evening air was swirling around her bare ankles, and her thin blazer was doing little to help. Wrapping herself up, she leaned against the railing and watched as Clem expertly guided Florence down the canal.

This certainly wasn't how she'd envisioned arriving at her fiftieth birthday party. It couldn't have been further from the plan. And yet, deep down, it felt oddly perfect despite her complicated feelings about canal boats.

She watched the wind tug at Clem's dress, then catch her hair, sending it streaming behind her like something from an old movie. It was nice to just be in her presence, peacefully and without tension. Most of their encounters so far had been full of chaos — arguments, accidents, unexpected collisions.

For the first time, Victoria had the space to see Clem. On the surface, she was unremarkable — average height, average build — but nothing about her was forgettable. She carried herself with quiet resilience, stood her ground without arrogance, and offered help instinctively, all without making a performance of it.

Victoria had always felt there was something undeniably attractive about the shape of a woman, so understated compared to the blunt geometry of men. Feminine allure came from a subtle, authentic grace that didn't demand attention; it simply deserved it. It held power the way some women did: naturally, without effort, without apology.

Realising the boat was slowing, Victoria looked up to see the wharf ahead. Where had the time gone? She'd been so deep in thought she could barely recall any of the journey. She only hoped she hadn't been staring at Clem the whole time, lost as she was in her own world.

They disembarked and walked quietly together over the bridge, which was lit by a string of hanging bulbs. The cascading light gave off a romantic hue. Part of her wanted to stop Clem, return to the boat, sit on the bow wrapped in blankets, and pass the time. She didn't want to face a waiting crowd of people she hardly knew and be reminded of how few friends she had. She knew it was the quality that counted, though, not the number. Over the years, she'd come to realise that most people were, generally, overrated.

The cobbles reminded her she was wearing heels, her ankles wobbling as she focused on picking her way up the path. It must have shown as Clem linked her arm through Victoria's, steadying her as they continued to the main entrance. As they entered, Victoria gently pulled away.

"Thank you for getting me here in one piece," she said.

Clem beamed. "Anytime."

There it was again — *anytime*. Victoria wondered whether Clem said it to everyone or just to her. She wanted to believe the latter but knew it was probably the former. Letting the thought go, she headed into the café.

The room was pulsing — a blur of voices, echoes, and low background music. Gold and silver balloons hung from the steel beams while guests mingled in loose clusters beneath them. As Victoria passed the café counter, heads turned and applause followed, heating her cheeks in an instant.

A thought struck her: She was making an entrance with Clem, not her husband. Would that look strange? Most of the people here were his contacts, his acquaintances. Did it matter? She and Clem were just friends.

The thought sat inside her — a warmth blooming in her chest accompanied by a twist of nausea in her stomach. The truth was, what she felt towards Clem, she'd never felt towards someone she considered just a friend before. She couldn't recall feeling it as deeply as this with Drew — not even when they first met.

A hand on her back urged her forward. It was Clem's, reassuring and encouraging. With a deep breath and a forced smile, she pushed herself onwards.

As the clapping subsided, Jasper emerged from the crowd holding two glasses of champagne. He handed one to her and air-kissed both cheeks.

"Happy first birthday to us." He clinked his glass against hers, then stepped back. "Vic, you look stunning." He turned to Clem. "As… do… you!"

The two exchanged a warm smile. Then, returning his attention to Victoria, Jasper took her free hand and gave it a playful tug, coaxing her into a twirl. She spun, half laughing, and caught the way Clem's eyes followed her — a look that sent her stomach into a dizzying somersault. As she came to a stop, she looked Jasper over.

"You're looking dapper as always. Is that another new waistcoat?"

With a dramatic flourish, Jasper slipped his suit jacket off one shoulder to reveal a crisp, white waistcoat. The back was in the style of a corset, with black satin ribbon laced through silver-rimmed eyelets.

"I brought it back from London — Liberty's, in fact. It's part of the new range I'm working on with them. The idea is to blend the elegance of corsetry into contemporary menswear."

A gentle pressure on her elbow drew her attention. The clean scent of washing powder drifted beneath her nose. Clem leaned in, her breath grazing Victoria's neck.

"I'll leave you two to it," she said with a nod towards the buffet table. "I've got my eye on those Victoria sponges. I think I'll do a bit of quality control... see how *moist* they are."

Victoria gave her a nod and a smile, appreciating that the woman was probably starving. As Clem walked away, she fanned herself with her hand. Was it hot in here, or was it just her?

Jasper sidled up beside Victoria as soon as Clem was out of earshot. "Where on earth is Drew?" he hissed. "I thought he was picking you up."

"He got held up or something," she said with a shrug. "I got a lift on Florence," she added, her tone lighter, unable to stop the smile that was creeping in as she remembered the trip up the canal. It was far better than sitting in the frigid silence of a car shared with Drew.

Before Jasper could say anything, the chatter in the room fell sharply. All eyes turned to the café door. A tall man with a flawlessly classic side parting strode in, his brown hair perfectly in place. His tailored, navy blue, Savile Row suit shimmered, and his brown John Lobb shoes shone with a high polish. Victoria scowled. Of course, Drew had to make an entrance like that.

Without so much as a glance around the room for her, he moved through the crowd towards the bar, offering firm, two-handed handshakes that had always turned her stomach. Over-sincerity had always read as insincerity to her, especially when it came from her husband.

She turned to Jasper, noticing his full-body shudder as his gaze fixed on Drew. A flush of embarrassment crept up her neck.

"You've done a great job with the decorations and laying the food out," she said to him, in need of a distraction. Her eyes scanned the room for Clem. She spotted her at the bar along with a new but familiar face. "I see you roped Max in to help on the bar," Victoria added, nodding towards him. "He seems like a nice *young* man."

"Would you like to emphasise *young* any further?" Jasper intoned.

"What?"

"He's not that much younger — and he's very eager to please," Jasper said, his grin unmistakably suggestive.

"I bet he is. But be gentle with him, Jasper."

His eyes shimmered with mischief. "Oh, I intend to be."

She rolled her eyes. Just then, Drew's voice came low and steady behind her.

"Victoria, there you are. Happy birthday."

"Thank you," she said as she turned to her husband, resisting the urge to point out it was now almost the day after.

"We must mingle," Drew said, taking a sip of champagne. "There are a lot of important people here."

He gave a cursory nod in Jasper's direction, then took

Victoria's arm and began leading her away. She wanted to tell him, *They're not important to me.* There were few who were. She glanced over her shoulder towards the bar and spotted Clem. Their eyes met, and something in Clem's face shifted, pinching into tension. She looked away, leaving Victoria to wonder what was going through her mind.

As Drew introduced her to a couple nearby, Victoria kept one eye on Clem, who was now stepping behind the busy bar and slipping off her denim jacket. Did that woman ever stop working?

She had the sudden urge to pull her to her side, but mindful that Clem didn't know many people, she resisted. She likely felt a little out of place, and knowing Clem, she probably wanted to help a friend. That seemed to be her way, Victoria thought with a smile.

"Are you sure you don't mind helping? These people drink like fishes," Max said, teasing the cork from a bottle of champagne. "I can't keep up with filling the glasses. Emma has gone to wash some up in the kitchen."

"Of course not. You've come to my rescue enough times. Plus, I don't know anyone here, and Victoria's tied up with… I assume her husband."

She nodded in their direction as she covered a yawn.

"He's a looker — if you like Ken dolls."

"What are *you* doing here, anyway?" Clem sniggered, placing her jacket on a table behind them. "I thought Jasper seconded you to blow up some balloons."

"He did. Then I stayed to help him set up. He asked if I would man the bar and promised me payment beyond my wildest dreams." He wiggled his eyebrows, then turned away with a grin.

Clem followed Max's gaze to where Jasper was standing. He gave Max a wink. Clem rolled her eyes at the pair of them.

"Sounds like a very professional arrangement. What is it with gay men admitting they're attracted to each other immediately?"

"Hormones."

"Hmm. I have *plenty* of those, but it can still take me six months to even ask a woman out."

"Any woman in particular?" Max teased, nodding at Victoria. "She's looking stunning tonight."

"Married," Clem shot back a little too quickly.

"Again — not denying it."

"I can't deny it," Clem admitted with an exasperated breath, her tongue looser than she'd like after drinking a glass of wine whilst getting ready for the party.

"Tell me more," Max demanded.

"There is nothing to tell. As you said, she's stunning… She's beautiful."

"Makes your little heart scream, does she?"

Clem chuckled. "Something like that."

"Ha! Knew it. It wasn't five minutes ago that she was boiling your blood."

"In the past," Clem retorted. Then, changing the subject, she added, "You own a tuxedo?"

"You own a dress," he retorted.

Clem narrowed her eyes at him.

Max looked down at himself. "Jasper lent me his old one. It's a little big around the waist, but the belt's holding up well. His apartment is amazing."

"You've been in his apartment!" she enthused. "Fast work indeed."

"Just to change!"

"You've been almost naked in his apartment."

It was Max's turn to narrow his eyes. "Very funny. But yes, partially. I'm hoping I'll be back in it by the end of the evening."

Clem shook her head in mock disbelief.

He nodded towards the buffet table. "You two did a great job with the food — you make a good team. Everyone has been complimenting your Victoria sponge."

She had to admit they did, and she admired the table as Max turned his attention to a thirsty guest. A relentless day's work that had left her exhausted had rewarded her with Victoria's appearance on the jetty — even if it had resulted in a bump to the head when she'd been so quick to exit Florence. She'd only nipped back to the house after realising she had nothing suitable aboard to wear to the party. When she pulled a few items of clothing from the suitcase she'd left in her parents' garage — half expecting them to smell musty — she was surprised to find they still carried the faint scent of washing powder.

Sharing the quiet of the canal in the early evening with someone she admired — a little too much, if she was honest — had brought a sense of unexpected peace. Neither of them had spoken, but nothing needed saying. When they reached the wharf, she sensed Victoria was reluctant to step off Florence. Clem was, too. She was itching to kidnap her and float off down the canal for the rest of the evening.

She'd felt a little awkward arriving with Victoria. All eyes had been on them — her especially, when they were likely expecting to see Drew. Then Victoria and Jasper had shared a celebratory moment, making her feel even more like a spare part, so she excused herself in favour of the buffet table.

Two men appeared at the bar. With Max busy attending to other guests, she handed them a bottle of beer each. Max and Jasper made a great team, too. They had transformed the room into a celebratory hall, proving her point that the café held more potential than it was currently being utilised for.

A long stream of thirsty guests followed behind, keeping them busy for almost an hour. With a brief lull in demands for drinks, Clem scanned the room for Victoria. She was unable to spot her among the crowd of bodies, so her eyes filtered for Drew, given his impressive height. She was now sure the man in the overpriced suit with the French cuffs and flashy Rolex was him. The rigidity that had seemed to take hold of Victoria's body since he arrived was telling enough.

Clem finally spotted him with Victoria hanging off his arm, possessively parading her like nothing was wrong in their relationship. Pretending he hadn't let her down being late, wasn't seeing someone else, and, in short, wasn't the arsehole Clem knew him to be. Her chest tightened at the sight of them together, forcing her mouth open to gasp for breath.

She watched as they joined a group in the corner, where his gestures turned exaggerated and theatrical. People laughed too easily, charmed by whatever story he was sharing. Clem's shoulders twitched as she ground her teeth.

Victoria was smiling, though not really. Clem knew her real smile by now — the way it reached her eyes, making them glow, and lifted her whole face. This smile was too polished, too rigid and still.

Victoria's gaze shifted, drifting across the room until it landed on her. In an instant, the smile changed, softened into something honest. It simmered some of Clem's anger off, even if it made the heat in her chest burn hotter.

Jasper appeared in her eye line, partially blocking the view she was enjoying of Victoria.

"A glass of champagne, please, Clem." His gaze drifted to where Clem's had been so engaged. "Beautiful, isn't she?"

What was it with everyone pointing out how beautiful Victoria was? Like anyone could miss it — except perhaps Drew. His eyes had barely left *her* all evening. Clem could feel them, heavy and constant as she tended bar, and she fought the urge to give him a piece of her mind. But she wouldn't. It wasn't her place. And if he couldn't see what he was missing in his wife, that was his loss.

"Yes," she answered softly. "She's enchanting."

"The best friend a guy could have. I can't thank you enough for getting us out of a hole today. I hated leaving her in the lurch."

"It was nice to be able to help for a change. I gather I've become a bit of a nuisance."

"I wouldn't go that far." He smirked.

"She might." Clem nodded, eyebrows raised, in Victoria's direction. Jasper turned to look again.

His friend fixed the pair of them with a steady stare.

"She was a pleasure to work with," Clem added.

"That much I do know. I was festering in a broom cupboard in an Oxford college until she knocked on the door one day — full of excitement, questions, and plans."

"Do you still teach?"

Jasper nodded. "On occasion. I have a few DPhil students."

"So should I call you 'Doctor Sinclair'?"

"You could, if you really have to."

The smug grin on his face suggested he wasn't opposed.

"I must say you are brave, living on one of those things." He gestured out the window to the canal. "Dear Max showed me around his place earlier. There isn't much room to breathe, is there? I thought I'd pass out."

"Well, I'm sure Max would have eagerly resuscitated you."

Jasper gave her a smug smile. "Oh, no doubt."

"Honestly, some days I don't think they're for anyone," Clem admitted. "It's relentless. Filling up water every few days, rubbish piling up in about five minutes, always stressing about power, safety, and gas. And don't get me started on running a kitchen in a space the size of a cupboard. I miss long, hot showers — and not wondering if I'll blow a fuse every time I turn on the kettle."

"Wow, you're really selling it," Jasper snarked. "Definitely avoid narrowboat sales as a future career."

"I'll bear it in mind," Clem chuckled.

A looming figure appeared behind Jasper. As if sensing it, he turned his head slightly, then took the glass of champagne Clem handed him.

"It's been a pleasure, Clem, as always." Turning, his voice tightened. "Drew."

"Jasper. Nice to see you." Drew's voice was smooth, but his jaw tightened, betraying the truth of his feelings.

"Yes, I expect it is," Jasper said dryly.

Clem struggled to contain her amusement. So, Jasper wasn't a fan of Drew either.

She felt a sudden nervousness at meeting Victoria's husband face to face, but as Jasper walked off and Drew stepped forward, there was no escaping it.

"Two glasses of champagne."

"Please."

Drew frowned. "Sorry?"

"Apology accepted," Clem said with a flat smile.

"What? Do you know who I am? I paid for all this," Drew hissed.

"I don't care who you are or if you paid for it. I am serving it and therefore I expect a please. It's called being polite. I guess you missed that particular lesson in" — she looked him up and down — "business school. Whatever status you have applied to yourself means nothing to me. If a child can manage it, I'm sure you can, too."

He shifted, then smirked. "You play hard. I like that."

Clem rolled her eyes. Typical arsehole response, thinking she was playing hard to get.

"Am I supposed to feel flattered? Whatever cheesy lines you have stored up your overpriced sleeve, I'm not buying it. You're not even shopping in the right market."

"Oh, is that right? Maybe you just haven't met the right man yet."

Clem planted her hands on her hips and levelled a look at him. "Seriously? A woman tells you she's not interested, and your response is to mansplain her sexuality back to her?" She let out a short laugh. "Trust me, I've met plenty of men. That's one of the reasons I'm happy to be a lesbian." Her gaze swept him up and down again. "It's preferable to walking clichés like you — all style over substance. The danger with men like you is no one sees the cracks until they've already fallen through them."

He seemed more entertained than offended by the idea he could be a threat, which only proved her point. Not wanting to spend another minute with him, she decided to forgo waiting for a please. She filled two glasses with champagne and passed them to him.

"Here. Now, why don't you run along and pay a

compliment to your beautiful — and yet invisible — wife? If you can even remember what she looks like."

Drew raised an eyebrow at her. Clem raised one back and glared at him.

~

"Vic!"

"Oh, sorry," Victoria replied, turning to find Jasper beside her. "I was miles away."

"So it seems. Here, hold my glass. I'm going to grab some cake. Want any?"

Victoria shook her head, hardly hearing him. Her attention was on Drew and Clem at the bar. She had hoped they wouldn't meet. Part of her feared Clem might say something about the dalliance she'd spotted in their upstairs window, but then she had promised not to say anything to anyone. Did that include Drew? Her earlier nausea was rising again. She took a swig from the glass, then another, watching Clem, who had her hands firmly on her hips. Should she go over?

Jasper reappeared beside her and took his glass back. "Did you just drink all that?"

Victoria looked at the empty glass. "Oh, sorry." She didn't even remember draining it.

"Never mind. I should keep a clear head for later anyway," Jasper said, looking over to the bar. "Clem scrubs up well, don't you think?"

Victoria followed his gaze. "Indeed."

"I'm not sure which of you has been unable to keep their eyes off Clem more, you or Drew."

"What?" Victoria snapped, turning to look at Jasper.

Jasper shrugged. "Simply saying what I see."

What on earth was he insinuating? He had no idea she

was attracted to women. Or did he? Maybe, being gay, he picked up on things or noticed body language that she didn't realise she was exuding. To her, people were all the same.

"Come on, Vic, I'm not blind. You and Drew are hardly Kate and Wills. Clem's put a spring in your step that I haven't seen since you were working on this place. What did I walk in on earlier in the kitchen? Your faces were a picture," Jasper said with a playful smirk. "I don't think I've ever seen you smiling like that."

Victoria shrugged, hoping to steer him off course. "She just agreed to bake for us, that's all. I like her energy."

"So do I. And that's great that she's going to help us."

"She was also full of ideas about the wharf," Victoria relayed with excitement.

"Ideas?"

"Yes. Turns out she's a marketing guru. She gave me a whole list of things we could try."

"Is she now?" Jasper mused, rubbing his chin. "Just what we need."

"She was high up in the fast-food industry, I understand. Or was about to be; then she jacked it all in."

"For a narrowboat?"

Victoria nodded.

Jasper raised his eyebrow. "Wow. She's got some guts."

"Mmm. She might have given me all these ideas, but I have no idea how to implement any of them. So, I was thinking about asking her to work for us. Only part-time, to fit around her business."

"She'd be fun to have around the place. Might even make you smile a bit more," he teased.

"Ha!" Victoria said, forcing a grin. "Anyway, what were you and Clem talking about over there?"

"I was thanking her for helping today. She was telling

me how much she enjoyed spending time with you. She even called you enchanting."

A wave of adrenaline rushed through Victoria as she examined him for a hint of teasing, but his gaze had flitted to Max.

He looked back at her with a smile. "So, who knows? You two might be the dream team to bring this place back from the brink."

"Hmm." She was about to move the subject away from Clem when she noticed Drew heading their way, carrying two glasses of champagne.

"I might need that refill after all," Jasper said, looking at his empty glass, then whizzing off so fast he created a breeze.

Drew approached, all smiles while he glanced back at Clem. Of course a man like Drew would notice her. She was exquisite.

"Who's that?" he asked, his eyes fixed on Clem as he held out a glass to Victoria.

She didn't want to tell him. She didn't want him to know anything about her. She was... She stopped the thought before she finished it, but the word *hers* was already resounding in her head. Clem wasn't hers and never could be.

"Clem," she answered lightly, taking the glass. "One of the narrowboat traders; she helped me out today with the food. I couldn't have done it without her since Christine walked out without giving any notice."

"Well, what do you expect when you hire someone like her?"

"*You* suggested she was the most qualified candidate," Victoria said, trying to keep calm for more reasons than she could count.

"Yes, out of those available. It doesn't mean you should

have stopped looking for the right one. Really, Vic, are you sure you're cut out for business?" Drew scoffed.

She was becoming increasingly aware that perhaps she wasn't.

"It's not all about qualifications," he chortled. "Sometimes you have to use your instinct. Make sure they have a personality."

Victoria was about to say that was exactly what she had intended on doing at the time, but Drew continued.

"If you're going to be stuck working with the underlings, make sure you can stand their company." He pulled himself up and surveyed the room.

Biting her lips together, she remained silent. She valued all her employees. At least now she knew her instincts weren't so far off after all when it came to employing people; she just needed to trust them more.

Noticing his eyes were on the bar again and particularly on Clem, she sniffed with amusement, "You're wasting your time there."

"Yeah, she said she was a lesbian." He pulled his phone out. "I told her she hadn't met the right bloke yet."

"Please tell me you didn't," Victoria hissed, recoiling as her expression froze somewhere between shock and second-hand embarrassment.

He shrugged. "What? It was a joke."

"It wasn't funny. You keep away from her," Victoria growled, not realising her voice had grown so loud and people were beginning to look in their direction.

He shoved his phone back in his jacket pocket. "Okay, *Clem* is off-limits. I have to head off anyway."

Her eyebrows shot up. "You just got here."

She questioned why she was so surprised. It was predictable for Drew to be absent from her life; she'd feel more relaxed without him around anyway.

Avoiding giving any details, he said, "I'm sure you can catch a lift back to the house or get a taxi." Looking at his watch and then around the room, he added, "I'll see you in a couple of weeks for the business awards," and walked away.

Victoria huffed. He'd done everything necessary, making sure to show his face and shake a few hands. That was the only reason he'd come, it seemed. It certainly wasn't to compliment her on how she looked; he hadn't bothered — unlike Clem. She couldn't seem to get her jaw off the floor when she emerged from Florence.

"Hey," a kind voice said from behind her. "Having a nice evening?"

"Emma. Hmm, yes, wonderful, thank you," Victoria lied. She reached out and placed a hand on Emma's arm. "Thank you for today, and for the last few days. I appreciate the effort you've put in since Christine left."

Emma's lips twisted into something close to a smile. "I know it's probably not the right time, but I wanted to say — well, ask — if you would consider me to replace Christine."

"You?" Victoria asked, gently withdrawing her hand.

"Who looked after everything when she was on holiday?" Emma pleaded. "I can do all the ordering. I've been here from the start. I know how everything works. I've never missed a day of work. I love my job, and I love the wharf."

Victoria blinked. "Golly."

"I get that a lot needs to change around here. Particularly in the café. Starting with the cake, and then the coffee."

Victoria drank in Emma's enthusiasm. She was practically vibrating with anticipation. Her lips were parted, poised for a positive response. Now was the time to trust her instincts.

"How about I give you a two-week trial? Does that sound fair?"

Emma's face lit up. "More than fair. Thank you." Before Victoria knew it, Emma had leapt forward and hugged her. "I won't let you down."

"And I think I have solved our cake problem," Victoria added. "Clem has agreed to bake for us."

"That's amazing," Emma said, eyes wide as she pulled back. "I heard her cakes were really tasty."

Victoria tried not to laugh at Emma's attempt to make out she didn't know firsthand how good Clem's baking was. She couldn't blame her for the little white lie; it seemed they all had a soft spot for Clem's cakes.

"Oh, and happy birthday." Emma squished her face. "Jasper told me."

"It's not a secret," Victoria allowed. "I wanted to focus our efforts on the wharf today."

That was true, but she also knew if she didn't agree to combining the celebrations for both occasions, then Jasper would want to celebrate her birthday in some other no doubt exuberant way. Knowing him, he would organise a ghastly surprise party. Their quiet spa weekend was enough *celebration* for her.

"If it's any consolation, you don't look a day over forty," Emma said before skipping off.

*Any consolation?*

Victoria sniffed with amusement as Emma joined their receptionist, Rachel. They were fawning over Clem's Victoria sponges. It brought a smile to her lips, as did Emma's comment, even if she knew it wasn't true. She knew ageing was inevitable, fixed yearly by the candles on a cake and the gradual loosening of skin around her eyes.

Somewhere along the way, the lines on her face would have to stop being a battle to fight, and she would need to accept them for what they were, a record of endurance. For the moment, they were another thing she was trying to ignore — like her marriage.

Fifty probably felt a lifetime away to someone like Emma, but it was waiting around the corner for her, ready to pounce. And now that Victoria had hit it — the so-called halfway point — she didn't feel any different. Perhaps just a quiet sense of relief that she was on the other side of it. It wasn't such a frightening place after all. One less thing to dread for a few years. She'd leave sixty for future Victoria to worry about.

Wandering over to the bar, she felt in need of something only Clem could give her, not that she knew what that something was. When she noticed she wasn't there, her heart began to pulse.

"Where's Clem?" she called over to Max, who was filling two glasses with red wine.

"She left."

Victoria felt her heart sink in her chest as Jasper appeared by her side. "Already?"

"She was pretty done in. Early start and all," Max replied as he turned his attention back to a guest.

"Drew didn't hang around either," Jasper said, leading Victoria away from the bar.

"No, he just left," she said, her eyes scanning the room in case Clem was still milling about.

"I know. I saw him getting into his car. A woman was waiting in it."

*Seriously?* He couldn't even make the effort to even pretend for one day. And he'd likely made Clem so uncomfortable that she'd left. Victoria had been hoping to pull her away from the bar and spend some time getting to know her better. Now, all she wanted to do was climb into bed and hide under her duvet.

She sensed Jasper eyeing her.

"I'll fetch you another drink… and some cake."

With a nod of agreement from Victoria, he scurried off. She was grateful he didn't push for information. He must have worked it out by now or at least sensed something was off with their relationship. As she watched Jasper laughing with Max as he poured their drinks, a sense of utter loneliness gripped her. Even though Drew had managed to turn up, his presence was more business motivated than through any duty as a husband. Her best friend had a new love interest, and her new friend had abandoned her.

Her younger self would have expected her to be raising teenage children right about now — to be attending graduations, paying for driving lessons, meeting girlfriends or boyfriends. Instead, here she was, all alone.

# CHAPTER 15

Clem topped up her glass of wine and stifled a yawn. Leaning back, she propped her feet up on the gunwale. It felt like the longest day of her life. Her body begged for sleep, but her mind wouldn't let her rest, racing with thoughts she couldn't outrun: what Drew had said to her, the way he had paraded Victoria around like she was his property, and worse, how Victoria had let him. She was his abandoned goods, dragged out from the attic once a year like an old suitcase.

Clem hadn't been able to watch one more second of that insufferable charade. It was too painful. Drew didn't deserve a woman like Victoria, and the thought of their situation made Clem's blood boil. With the bar quiet and Max more than happy to carry on alone, she'd made her escape.

As she crossed the moonlit courtyard, she spotted Drew climbing into his car, where the woman with the sharp pixie cut sat waiting in the passenger seat. The sight of her being there, today of all days, sent more anger surging through her, propelling her forward. Although the urge to return to Victoria had tugged at her now that her odious husband had left, she didn't want to add her bitter mood to Victoria's evening.

Earlier in the day, when she'd tried to raise the subject of Drew, Victoria had been quick to change it, only remarking that their marriage wasn't conventional. Did she know about the other woman — or women? Allow it, even? It was beginning to feel that way. But why? Why would she put up with that? Clem intended to get to the bottom of it.

Gazing up at the stars as they began to vanish behind thickening clouds, her mind drifted back to their time together in the kitchen. How fun it had been, the ease between them, how good Victoria felt against her when they hugged. The thought made her stomach flip. She pressed her hand to it with a smile. She missed Victoria's presence when she wasn't around and found herself thinking about her all the time. A groan escaped before she could stop it. She was falling for Victoria. The unobtainable. Typical.

The woman seemed to have an uncanny knack for reading her. Whenever Clem struggled to say something awkward, Victoria somehow sensed it and gently coaxed the words from her. What did that mean? Was it that Victoria noticed things about her, or was she good at reading people in general —husbands and catering managers not included?

Clem found hollow victory in the fact that Victoria's loss on the catering front was her win. She'd be baking for the wharf now, and that came with a ready-made excuse to drop by more often and *bump* into her. If only her heart could stand it. Seeing someone regularly whom you admired — or, more truthfully, who you thought was an actual goddess — was bound to hurt. Still, the extra income would help.

The thought of her unpredictable future stole Clem's breath away. It reminded her that she hadn't baked this evening; she'd just accepted the invitation without thinking. That would mean an extra-early start tomorrow. The relentlessness of it all, she was sure, was fuelling her underlying anxiety. She kept telling herself that this was the price to pay for a different lifestyle, but then again, what was the point of freedom if all it did was leave you feeling overwhelmed? Were humans just programmed to worry about something and find fault with even their most recent dreams?

Clem rolled her shoulders back and tried to think practically. She'd work hard over the summer and save as much as she could. Worst case, she'd have to leave Florence tied to the jetty and move in with her parents over the winter, something that would feel like failure in her eyes. If she could make enough to get her through the colder months, she'd only have to work half the year. But to what end? To wind up bored, like her mum was likely to.

She could keep working through the colder months, hoping to break even while likely wondering if it was a total waste of time. Clem needed to be busy. Serving a handful of customers a few cups of coffee each day wasn't going to satisfy her. Maybe she should have thought about that before diving in. Had she been so swept up in the idea that she hadn't fully thought it through?

As she took a sip of wine, she spotted a figure crossing the bridge from the wharf. In the low glow of the hanging bulbs, she recognised Victoria. She must be walking home. Clem waited until she drew level with Florence's bow, then called out, "Victoria!"

She stopped in her tracks. Even in the dim light, Clem could see a wide smile lifting her cheeks.

"Can I get you a drink?" she added.

"Please," Victoria said, a hint of exasperation in her voice as she stepped onto the gunwale.

Clem offered her hand.

Victoria took it, leaning her weight into Clem as she stepped down with a sigh.

"Where were you heading?"

"I needed some fresh air, so I thought I'd wander into town and grab a taxi at the rank."

"Is the party over?"

"Almost. I'd had enough. There's nothing like others walking out on your celebrations to dampen one's mood."

"Oh... sorry," Clem said, regretting that her previous anger had kept her from returning to the party.

*Bloody Drew.*

"It's fine. I didn't even expect you to come, let alone stay, but I'm glad you did. It's been a long day for both of us."

As Victoria sat down, Clem checked her watch and then rested a hand on her shoulder. "It's still technically your birthday, and I'm here now."

Victoria smiled and, to Clem's surprise, patted her hand. "You are."

Clem slipped inside to fetch a glass, then returned a moment later, filling it with wine.

"Who else abandoned you?" Clem asked, settling back down in her own seat.

"Drew had to leave. Jasper disappeared with Max to his apartment with what looked like a bottle of scrumpy. He left Emma at the bar with only a handful of people lingering. Thanks for helping out, again; it was kind of you."

Clem gave a casual shrug. "I was feeling a bit like a spare part, and as you know, I can't bear to watch someone struggle."

"I can attest to that," Victoria said, shooting her a smile. "It was good of Max to take on the bar. The plan was that we'd all take a turn, so I was certainly grateful that Max spared me. I hope it wasn't an unenjoyable evening for you."

"No," Clem lied. "I thought it best to leave you with your friends."

"They aren't *my* friends; they're Drew's. I don't have any other than Jasper."

"Seriously?" Clem raised her eyebrows, disbelief colouring her voice. How could a woman like Victoria not attract people?

Victoria nodded as she picked up her glass. "I was friendly with a few colleagues from the architectural firm I used to work at. After I married Drew, he persuaded me to quit my job and go work directly for his business instead."

"Cut out the middleman," Clem put in.

"Exactly. Drew was the firm's biggest client, so my departure almost folded the place. Of course, I didn't know any of this until later. I bumped into an old colleague who told me she'd lost her job because of it. Drew must have known exactly what he was doing. Even if it made business sense for him, it didn't sit comfortably with me. People stopped talking to me after that."

Clem bit her tongue. She wanted to add something, but Victoria had just made her feelings clear that she didn't like what he'd done. Calling someone's husband an arsehole wasn't the best way to win over a new friend.

"After that, I found myself moving in Drew's circles, and rich men's wives are not my cup of tea." Victoria's eyes narrowed slightly. "Dare I ask what you thought of Drew?"

"I'm wondering when he's going to enter politics."

Victoria laughed, but her mirth quickly dissipated. "Drew told me what he said to you. I'm sorry."

Clem shrugged. "It's nothing I haven't heard before. Many times. You get used to it."

"You shouldn't have to," Victoria grumbled.

"No, I shouldn't. But arseholes are arseholes." Well, she'd said it, but Victoria didn't even flinch at the word.

"Most of the time, I count myself lucky that it's only words. Considering what some men do to women."

Victoria nodded.

"I noticed Jasper gave him a wide berth," Clem added.

The corner of Victoria's mouth twitched. "He's never been Drew's biggest fan. I assumed it was because they're two men at very different ends of the moral spectrum."

"Quite possibly." Clem suspected Jasper disliked Drew's treatment of Victoria as much as she did. Knowing she couldn't keep a lid on what she really wanted to say for much longer, she asked, "Can I tell you the truth?"

"Of course," Victoria answered with a tight frown. "I will put aside my annoyance that you haven't already."

Clem gave her an apologetic half smile. "The reason I left is that I couldn't watch the two of you any longer. All the fake smiles, the masquerade, it made me feel a bit sick. He left soon after me. I saw he had a passenger — the same one from your house. You know, the pixie."

Victoria nodded. "Jasper mentioned someone was waiting for him. I assumed it was Hannah."

"Hannah?"

"His secretary. He couldn't get away quick enough."

Clem turned to face her. "Why put up with it?"

"I agreed to it," she stated.

"What? You're kidding," Clem said, her heart sinking as she realised Victoria's situation was exactly as she feared. At Victoria's raised eyebrow, she hurried to add, "Sorry, of course you're not. Not sure why I said that."

"Mmm," Victoria muttered. "It's not something people joke about. We live apart. It's only natural."

Clem leaned back, shaking her head. "No, it's not. People can live on opposite sides of the world and still keep it in their pants if they want to. I get polyamory and open marriages where everyone is on the same page, but this sounds like an excuse for him to sleep with his secretary. Especially if you're not really on board with it, which I can tell you're not."

Victoria gave a nonchalant shrug and took a slow sip from her glass.

"Why did you even agree?" Clem asked quietly.

Setting her glass down, Victoria leaned back in her chair and let out a long breath. "I knew what he wanted… her. I didn't want her to be me, to take my place. I'm happy here. I love my house; I love the wharf. They are me, my visions, my creations. I don't want to lose them. It's a small price to pay to keep what means so much to me. If I can keep the wharf open, of course."

"Would he really close it?"

"I don't know. Selling up assets here would mean me living back with him, and I'm sure I would cramp his style. But it's not something I want to test. I want the wharf to succeed, to give it a new lease of life, so I can educate and feed people. What else have I got?" She paused, then added softly, "With him, I have everything I need."

Clem hesitated before asking, "What about love?"

"Love is overrated. It's a young person's game. They're

the only ones naive enough to believe in it. Sometimes convenience has to come first."

*Seriously?* Victoria had given up on love. Clem didn't even know how to respond to that. Victoria deserved to be fulfilled in every way. Damn it, Clem wanted to be the one to fulfil her. The thought made her insides ache. That arsehole treated her like shit, but she was still his, and she was loyal to him. Pain radiated from her clenched fists. She loosened them and took a quiet, deep breath.

"How long have you been together?"

"Fifteen years, married for almost twelve. We met when I was assigned to design his house in Primrose Hill, and later it became my home." Victoria fell into silence for a moment, then took a sip of wine and continued. "Historic architecture is my speciality, and Drew had plenty of other historic projects lined up around London, so they all came my way. I've worked on old police stations, train depots, chocolate factories, print works — you name it."

Clem's lips tightened into a smile at Victoria's sudden enthusiasm. It suited her.

"Impressive. Sounds like you were too busy to have kids. Probably a good thing, considering—"

"Drew is infertile."

"Shit. I'm sorry." *Fuck!*

Victoria gently shook her head. "You weren't to know. It broke him, and it became all about *him*. No one stopped to think how it impacted me. His family, I mean. No one ever asked me how *I* felt. It was all, 'Oh, you can't have kids. Poor Drew.'"

Clem's voice softened. "I guess, to them, you could still have kids."

"I could. But I couldn't. And I think he decided if he couldn't have a family, he was going to live young, free—"

"—and single?"

Victoria nodded, her eyes distant. "Looking back, yes. Over the last few years, I've felt like a bystander in our marriage. He went through a midlife crisis: sold the house I loved in a quiet, leafy area and moved us to a ghastly penthouse in Canary Wharf. He threw himself into work, and the business became more successful, taking up more of his time. Sports cars were being bought at a time when I'd hoped for pushchairs." Her voice cracked. "I stood on the sidelines, watching the life I'd dreamed of slip away."

"I'm sorry. That must have been…" Clem trailed off, unable to even find the right word to sum up how she must have felt.

Victoria shrugged. "I can't change anything now. It wasn't even his fault, but I would've liked a little consideration — you know, some understanding of how it might have affected me too. Especially from my in-laws."

Clem reached out and gently squeezed her arm.

"Did you consider adopting?"

"I wanted to, but he was having none of it. He wanted an heir, and he didn't see someone else's child as his heir." She paused for a moment. "And the more I couldn't have kids, the more I wanted them."

Clem nodded. "Makes sense."

"I distracted myself with my family history instead. My future might not have been working out as I had planned, but understanding my past grounded me somehow. It helped me come to terms with the fact I wouldn't be passing any part of me into the future."

*Ouch.* That hit home.

Victoria touched her face, but Clem saw it was a quick wipe of a tear. Without thinking, Clem squeezed her arm again, suddenly aware she hadn't let go.

With a sniff, Victoria looked up at the wharf. "Then I found this place. It was an escape from London — the memories, the hope I had there, the dreams… Drew." She twitched her shoulders. "Maybe I checked out first, made him look elsewhere. It was a time we should have been pulling together, but all we did was allow it to tear us apart."

Victoria wiped her face, this time not bothering to hide the tears. Clem fished a tissue from her pocket and passed it to her.

"Thanks."

"You should be proud of yourself."

Victoria sniffed from behind the tissue as she wiped her eyes. "Why?"

"Look up."

Lowering the tissue, Victoria followed Clem's gaze up to the wharf, where some of the apartment windows were illuminated.

"You did that. You lit it back up and gave it a new life. You made that happen — it was all you. And you will make a success of it. I'm sure if you put your full attention to it, you can make it thrive."

A smile flickered at Victoria's lips.

"Your parents must have been proud."

The exasperated sigh that followed told Clem that she might have put her foot in it again.

"They've never visited," Victoria answered softly, her fingers twisting the tissue in her hand.

"Not once?"

Victoria shook her head, slipping the tissue into her pocket. "This is my father's legacy right here, and it did spark their interest when I first told them about it. That was until they realised it was Drew buying it and I wasn't leaving him. Then it was radio silence. They never liked him. Mum said he had a wandering eye and that he would stray — and she was right, wasn't she?"

"Seems so."

She let out a faint breath. "They wanted grandchildren so desperately. My brother's a confirmed bachelor, so it all fell on me. And when Drew and I couldn't have a child, well, they told me to leave him. Infertility is no reason to abandon a marriage, is it? And I wanted to make it work; I really did. But I didn't know how it would change him."

"You couldn't have known," Clem said gently. "Have you spoken to them recently?"

Victoria closed her eyes and shook her head. "They don't seem to like the choices I make, so I gave up trying. I can only imagine what they would say about me giving up architecture. That was something they were proud of — probably the last thing, actually."

"I get that. My mum is always questioning my decisions, but wanting to prove your parents wrong isn't a good reason to stay in a bad relationship." Clem bit her lip, not realising what she'd said until it was out. She knew things were more complicated than that. When there were no reprisals from Victoria, she quietly added, "So, when did you last speak to them?"

"About five years ago. I sent them an invitation to the opening of the wharf last year out of reluctant politeness, but they didn't come. We exchange birthday and Christmas cards, but that's it."

"So they've never seen what you've achieved here? What you've created?"

Victoria shook her head. "No. And everything I did here was for me; it was about me. But, yet again, it all came back to Drew."

The injustice made Clem's jaw clench.

"Have you never thought about divorcing Drew?" she asked cautiously.

"Of course I have," Victoria said, her voice tightening, "but I'm not risking the house or the wharf. They're all I have left now."

"Have you tried talking to him? Expressed your concerns?"

"No."

"Things might not be as bad as you expect. He can't leave you with nothing."

"I know that, but I will lose control of what happens next if I do. He could sell the house and the wharf just to spite me. I don't trust him to act reasonably, and I've already lost too much." Victoria fidgeted in her seat and then continued, a little more sharply this time. "Everything needs to stay exactly as it is."

"With him cheating on you behind your back," Clem muttered.

Victoria's jaw tightened, and she snapped, "It's not behind my back."

Clem jumped out of her seat and pressed her palms into the side of her head "Argh! That doesn't make it any better, Victoria. It only makes it worse."

Victoria turned her head away, voice sharp with frustration. "You don't understand. It's complicated."

Itching with irritation she didn't want Victoria to see, Clem climbed onto the gunwale and jumped onto the towpath. Her chest tightened, breaths coming fast and shallow as she paced along the length of Florence.

"Clem, please come back," Victoria called out.

The soft plea stopped her. She paused, took a deep breath, and slowly turned back.

"These are my issues, not yours. Why are you so angry?" Victoria asked, her brow furrowing tightly.

"Why aren't you?" Clem pushed, breathless as she climbed back on board and sank onto her seat. "He treats you like shit, and you let him get away with it. You deserve better. You deserve to be happy."

Victoria rested her hand on Clem's leg. The warmth radiated through Clem's tense muscles, easing some of the tightness in her chest.

"I am happy," Victoria muttered.

"Bullshit," Clem shot back.

Victoria took a deep breath and let it out slowly. "I'm not a complete doormat. I set rules."

Clem desperately wanted to find out what they were, but she already felt she was overstepping.

*Fuck it!*

Victoria was a grown woman; she wasn't forcing her at gunpoint to reveal anything.

"What rules?" Clem pressed gently.

Victoria remained silent for a moment. Then, to Clem's relief, she spoke.

"He doesn't go near any of my friends."

"You don't have any other than Jasper, remember?" Clem replied flatly.

Although he'd had his eyes on her tonight. It made her wonder if Victoria noticed at all. And if she had, if she had said anything.

"He never takes anyone to the house."

"Failed," Clem retorted with a tilt of her head.

The comment made Victoria remove her hand from Clem's leg. Clem had been enjoying how it felt there, and she felt its absence, sharp and immediate.

When Victoria spoke again, her voice was slower, quieter. "That I and" — her jaw worked — "are never in the same room as each other."

Clem smirked. "Does the car park outside count?"

Noticing a pained expression on Victoria's face, she softened her tone. "You should be a main character in your own life, not an extra in Drew's."

"It doesn't change the fact that I *want* things to stay as they are. I'm an employee of his company. He owns the wharf, the house. Everything is in his name. I don't have anything, and who knows what I'll end up with in a divorce. I gave up the only job I was good at — for what? A calling?"

"I can relate to that. At least you didn't buy a boat and try to make a living off coffee and cakes to survive."

Victoria gave a faint laugh, easing Clem's tension for the briefest moment. "Hey, I've tasted your cakes. They're amazing."

"Do you still love him?" Clem asked, brushing past the compliment. She wasn't finished with her line of questioning.

Victoria hesitated. "We have a history together. We've built things."

"I'm not talking bricks and mortar, Victoria. I mean connection. Affection. Desire. The kind of love that lights you up."

"I fell out of love years ago," Victoria answered, her gaze drifting away. "We made a good team in business, just not romantically. I think it began to fizzle out as soon as the ring went on and the babies didn't come out. I miss what we were at the beginning."

Clem let out a humourless laugh. "If you're hanging around hoping to get that back, then I hate to break it to you, but you're dreaming. He's shown you who he is; how little he values you."

"Some things are too difficult to undo. Our lives are entwined even if our hearts aren't," Victoria said, her voice flat with the weariness of acceptance.

"There is nothing that can't be unpicked and something new sewn in its place — stronger. Sometimes it requires a leap of faith."

"I'm not religious," Victoria scoffed.

"I don't mean it like that," Clem groaned. "I mean trusting that the end of something isn't the end of *everything* but the start of something new. No matter how hard it is to begin again." Clem paused to soften her tone. "I've done it. I gave up a career, a guaranteed income, all because I knew deep down it wasn't what I wanted for my future. Who knows how it will turn out? I bake and sell relentlessly, and I still don't know if I can make it work." She tried to breathe, but the tightness in her chest returned. "If it doesn't, then I'll have to try and come up with a new plan. But whatever it is, it has to drive me out of bed in the morning. Something that lights my fire."

"You're braver than I am," Victoria murmured, quiet resignation threading through her voice.

"I took a risk… a risk that could see me homeless and jobless. And yeah, working in Florence wasn't quite how I pictured it, and I don't how long it'll last. I never saw myself doing it forever, but I knew I couldn't keep going as I was. I ran with an idea to escape. Then Florence came into it, and it became emotional." Clem sighed. "Now there's even more pressure to make it work because I could never sell her. It would break my mum's heart."

"Sounds like you are trapped," Victoria observed. "Risks are not so easily taken as they are spoken."

"You have an answer for everything," Clem said, frustration creeping in as she tried to ignore Victoria's comment. "Why hold so tightly to something that burns your fingers but not your heart?"

"Safety and security. I'm fifty," Victoria said, her words firm, almost defiant.

Clem softened. "And how do you think the next fifty years will play out turning a blind eye?"

Victoria's gaze hardened. "I can turn a blind eye to keep my life together."

Clem felt her anger rising again as her heart twisted. "He's in the wrong here. He's got plenty to lose, too — way more than you do, I expect." She paused, carefully choosing her words. "Why are you scared?"

"I don't want to be alone."

"It's better to be alone than unhappy. And honestly, I believe you already are alone."

Victoria folded her arms. "The wharf makes me happy. It sustains me… as much as I need."

"I'm not sure I believe that. What about your self-worth? Your dignity?"

Victoria looked away, her silence speaking louder than words.

"For what it's worth," Clem added gently, "I don't think you'd be alone for long."

Victoria gave a tired, humourless smile as she met Clem's gaze. "Don't be ridiculous. Who'd want me?"

Clem wanted to shake her and hold her all at once. To tell her *she* wanted her. Heat rose in her chest, but she kept her voice steady.

"Someone who sees what I see. You're smart, capable, not to mention beautiful. You're single-handedly running a business, holding it together while it feels like it's falling apart. That takes guts whether you believe it or not. You gave up a secure job to save the wharf. That's brave."

A fleeting smile tugged at the corner of Victoria's mouth, only to vanish again.

"You deserve to be loved, Victoria," Clem continued while she could. "Not tolerated. And not stuck in something because it's convenient. There's so much more waiting for you than this. You should be with someone you can talk to about your ideas, your challenges; who'll bat things back and forth with you and help you solve them. A person who will share a bottle of wine with you at the end of a long day."

She saw Victoria's eyes drift to the bottle of wine as her shoulders sagged.

"I'm not willing to risk it. It's not perfect, but it works. The truth is... I stayed because I couldn't bear what it would mean if I left. What it would say about me — that I didn't try hard enough. That *I* wasn't enough. That I was a failure."

Clem swallowed the ache rising in her throat; it felt like it was about to throttle her. She wanted to reach out to Victoria, to cradle her, to tell her everything would be okay, but she couldn't do it. She worried she'd pushed her too far already, and she didn't trust herself not to kiss the woman if she had the chance. She was vulnerable, raw with feelings she wasn't ready to face.

"I think you've spent so long keeping it together, you forgot you're allowed to fall apart — to start again."

Victoria didn't answer. She stared at the ground, shoulders beginning to shake. Clem's hand shot out to her leg, hoping to offer comfort as Victoria had done for her. She hadn't meant to make her cry, only to jolt her a little and get her to take a hard look at her life. Clearly, she already was. It didn't make it any easier to push that button and make the changes you knew you needed to make.

"I meant what I said, Victoria," Clem said, rubbing her leg. "You are incredibly beautiful. Not that beauty matters most in the grand scheme of things, just that—" Clem stopped, realising she wasn't saying what she was trying to convey. "I mean, there's so much more to you. You should remember that. And I see all of you."

Victoria looked up and wiped her eyes. No smile came, but something in her features shifted, the guardedness finally relenting.

Before Clem could reply, heavy blobs of rain splattered onto the table.

"And now it rains! The perfect end to the evening," Victoria said through a half laugh and tears.

Clem's heart broke at her woebegone laughter. "Come inside. You can't walk home in this. I'd give you a lift, but I've drunk way too much to steer — even at three miles per hour."

Victoria was close at her heels and collapsed straight onto the bed. "You don't mind, do you? I'm not sure I can stay upright any longer."

"It's fine. Make yourself comfortable. I'll get us some tea."

"Thanks."

Returning five minutes later, Clem found Victoria curled up on one side of the bed, fast asleep. She looked picture perfect, which drew a smile to Clem's lips. It seemed a shame to wake her and bundle her into a taxi.

Now Clem faced her only dilemma: climb into bed beside her or make up the other one. There was only one thing she wanted to do — but only one thing she could do. She threw a blanket over Victoria, turned the light out, and made her way back down the corridor.

# CHAPTER 16

$\mathcal{V}$ictoria opened one eye, then the other, squinting against the bright sunlight. Where was she? Fragments of memory from the previous night flickered back, pulling her upright — Florence. She'd fallen asleep on Clem's boat.

She checked her phone, but all she saw was her reflection in the dark glass. A faint clatter from the other end of the boat told her Clem must be busy in the galley. Scanning the bedroom for a mirror and finding nothing obvious, she noticed a line of books. Victoria examined them with interest, spotting *The Second Sex* by Simone de Beauvoir, *A Room of One's Own* by Virginia Woolf, *The Female Eunuch* by Germaine Greer, and *Want* by Gillian Anderson. Knowing Clem read these kinds of books made her smile. Weren't they the kind of books all women should read? A slight feeling of shame that she hadn't caught her off guard.

Taking another look around the room, she saw her purse peeking out from under the blanket. Clem must have covered her with it. Fishing out a compact, she did the best she could with what she had.

She spotted the chairs on the bow and recalled sitting there late into the evening. Clem had said something about being with someone you could enjoy a bottle of wine with at the end of the day. The words had stuck with her, much like Clem's company had. She was so easy to talk to. Well, not always easy. Clem had a knack for drawing out things Victoria didn't always mean to share. Things that were outright embarrassing, like how she didn't own a single thing in this world. But perhaps that at least gave Clem some idea of what she was up against — how hard it was for her to walk away.

As she tried to recall what else they had discussed, she remembered Clem had called her beautiful. That had hit her square in the chest. It had been a long time since someone had said that to her. They had also spoken of love. Victoria denied needing it, but that was a lie. She wanted that kind of love more than anything, and when Clem mentioned it, she hadn't thought of anyone else — just her and the way she made Victoria feel.

She wondered if Clem felt the same. She had caught Clem gazing in her direction enough times during the party, only to see her quickly look away. At any rate, Victoria had noticed, and it had made her feel wanted. Desired. Had she been doing the same to Clem? The thought caught in her chest. Jasper had certainly noticed her watching the other woman.

Their connection was undeniable — at least to her. It felt as though an invisible thread ran between them, weaving their lives together in ways Victoria hadn't expected. Clem's words echoed in her mind: I see all of you. What had she meant by that? And why had she gotten so angry over her situation? Victoria still wasn't sure. Clem hadn't explained, only pressed harder, asking why she wasn't angry. But Victoria had long since buried that anger. Time had dulled it. At least she thought it had, though she gave it a second thought as she recalled the tears that had fallen from her eyes. It had been late, and it had been a long day, she reasoned. She'd been tired.

She rubbed her eyes, still tired. None of it mattered anyway. She was a married woman, and unlike Drew, their vows still meant something to her. She wasn't like him — selfish, faithless. She had standards. Morals. Even if those morals sometimes felt like a cage of her own making.

Finding her shoes and grabbing her purse, she made her way down the corridor and opened the door at the end. The galley was alive with motion. Clem flitted among work surfaces, pulling things from cupboards. Cakes stood cooling on the side, filling the space with a sugary scent and stirring an unexpected hunger inside her. Clem must have been up for hours.

It suddenly struck her — where had Clem slept?

"Oh, morning," Clem said, finally spotting her. "How are you feeling?"

"Surprisingly rested, though a little hazy. Did you—" Victoria shook her head, stopping herself. It didn't matter if they had shared a bed or not.

"I made up the other bed. Don't worry, I'm not in the habit of corrupting straight, drunk women on my narrowboat. It's not exactly a den of iniquity."

"Sorry, I didn't mean to imply anything." Victoria scrunched her face, annoyed with herself. "For the record, I'm not straight, you know." The words slipped out before she could stop them. Why had she said that? Whatever her reason, relief flooded her, making her legs tingle and weaken. She had to lean on the worktop to steady herself.

"No? Oh! Sorry, I shouldn't have assumed." Clem

rubbed the back of her neck, her gaze flicking towards the floor for a moment until she looked up and smiled warmly. "But thank you for telling me. It's good to know."

Victoria tilted her head in question. "Is it?"

"Erm, err, yes," Clem stammered. "It's always good to know when you're in the *best* company. Coffee?"

"Please." Victoria was dying to know what she meant exactly. "I assume that's an upgrade from average company."

Clem chuckled, busying herself with the large espresso machine. "You know what I mean. There's something about being around other queer people." She paused, looking at Victoria. "Oh. Is it okay to say that? I know some older people struggle with the word."

Victoria raised an eyebrow. "Older... people?"

"Oh, sorry!" Clem replied, scrunching her face again. "I just don't want to offend."

"And yet you class me as an older person."

"Well, you kind of are." Clem smirked as she placed a paper cup under the spouts. "As am I — compared to the youngsters, anyway."

Victoria smirked at Clem, watching her dig a hole and try to climb out again. When she noticed that Clem had begun to fidget, she rested a hand on her arm.

"Clem, it's fine; use whatever words you want. What were you trying to say?"

"Oh, I just meant that when you're around other queer people, you know you're safe and they won't judge you. You're in your tribe — people who share similar experiences. Most of us know what some of us have been through — shame, isolation, fear, rejection, erasure, discrimination, inequality... The list is endless, isn't it? But they are the things that shape us into whatever form we end up in."

Victoria hummed her agreement. Even if she felt that being a closeted bisexual in a straight-presenting relationship had shielded her from some of it. She had still felt the fear. It still shaped her.

"It's such a different experience from straight people," Clem continued, turning to her with the paper cup full of coffee in hand. "They can never truly understand how we feel, even if they are allies.

"Most people don't even realise we have a different experience. They go blissfully through life, assuming we're all the same, that we've all had the same upbringing. And yet some still go out of their way to highlight our differences, with name-calling, controlling us, setting rules we have to live by, not seeing our relationships as equal."

Victoria nodded, trying to take it all in, but she found herself more caught up in the way Clem spoke, drawn in by her passion and the conviction in her voice.

Clem looked down at the cup she was still holding. "Oh, sorry. Espresso, right?" Her eyes twinkled as she handed the paper cup over. "I'm sure that's what you had with your lemon drizzle that first time."

"Correct. Thank you," Victoria said, taking it.

Their fingers brushed against each other. The touch was too brief to mean anything, but too deliberate not to. It was enough to send something light and electric skimming down her spine.

"Anyway, how are you finding it?" Clem asked. "The boat, I mean. You mentioned once you weren't a fan. In fact, I seem to remember you said something about vowing to never set foot inside one again."

"I believe I said I wasn't in a hurry to repeat the experience of being inside one, not that I wouldn't go inside one," Victoria corrected her matter-of-factly.

Clem smirked. "Well, in any case, I'm glad you're here."

A warm glow spread quietly through Victoria — that feeling of someone wanting her; well, her company at least.

"Me too," Victoria replied, rubbing at her throat, hoping to relieve some of the tension in it that was telling her she should probably leave soon. To get away from the woman who was stirring emotions she had no right to entertain. But she didn't want to. "I'm sorry that I stole your bed."

Clem shrugged, brushing a strand of hair behind her ear. "It's fine. So, what are you up to today?"

Victoria sighed, glancing out the window towards the wharf. "It's supposed to be my day off, but I think I'd better go help Emma."

"Wouldn't she be best helped by hiring a new catering manager?"

Victoria smiled faintly and blew on her coffee. "Emma wants the job. I've given her a two-week trial."

"Oh, really?"

"Yes. Why did you say that?"

"She just seems young."

"She's enthusiastic and passionate about the wharf," Victoria countered firmly.

"Is she qualified?"

"Not really, but then, when have qualifications been essential to someone who is already doing most of the job?"

Clem shrugged. "Fair point. I should get you home then. You can't work like that — not that you don't look totally cute first thing in the morning."

Victoria's cheeks flushed. She tried to hide it by taking

a sip of coffee but failed spectacularly. Clem thought she was cute.

"Are you sure?"

"That you're cute or that I'm giving you a lift?"

Victoria's breath caught at hearing the words again.

Clem gave her a slow, playful smile. "Both, of course. Come on." She moved down the galley, putting things in cupboards and nudging cooling cakes to the back of the worktop. "I could do with topping the batteries up. Florence eats up power."

"I must admit, I have no idea how these things work," Victoria replied, grateful for a change in subject so she could compose herself.

Her eyes caught one of the cakes as she passed, a lemon drizzle with a crisp layer of lemony sugar on top. Her mouth watered.

"Well, running the engine is a bit like running a car: The alternator charges the batteries while the engine's running. I use a lot of appliances, though, so the time Florence spends cruising isn't nearly enough to generate all the power I need in a day. I've got solar panels across the roof, which help top things up, but I still have to plug her into shore power at the house overnight to fully recharge the batteries."

"Sounds like a lot to manage. It must be stressful."

"It is," Clem said, climbing the steps to the stern.

"How do you deal with water?" Victoria asked. She took the last sip of espresso and popped the cup in a bin as she followed behind. It was considerably better than what they served at the wharf.

"I have a five-hundred-litre tank, so it lasts a few days. I fill up from the garden hose, and there are a few filling stations about. But yeah, I'm constantly thinking about it. Even when everything is full, you can't catch a break. I always have to keep an eye on my usage. If Florence was just a home, running out wouldn't be so bad, but with the business, I can't run out of water, gas, or electricity."

"It's not a lifestyle I could manage," Victoria said, feeling overwhelmed just listening to her. "I like my amenities on tap."

Clem sniffed out a laugh. "The problem is I do, too. We definitely take them for granted when we have them." She started the engine and manoeuvred them away from the bank and down the canal. "We have to turn around a little way down here; it's a bit of a nuisance but all par for the course."

Victoria gripped the railing that surrounded the stern to steady herself against the moving boat. "It's fine. I'm in no rush," she reassured her, having no idea what the time was thanks to her dead phone and decision not to wear her watch last night.

"So, when did you decide you weren't so keen on narrowboats?" Clem asked.

"A girls' holiday at uni. I endured it for a week and vowed never again. I was dubious to begin with; they're so small, airless, cramped." She took a breath. "It's the combination of floating on water and it being a bit of a scramble to get out of two fairly small exits."

A boat passed them, sending a slight sway through the deck. "This, too," she said, steadying herself against the stern.

"Couldn't you have left?"

Victoria rolled her eyes and grinned. "No, and I have hormones to thank for that. I endured it because, well, I had a crush on a friend. It stayed one-sided, as it always seemed to back then. Who wanted to be out and proud under Section 28? We hid ourselves. Some of us married the nearest man we found vaguely attractive who didn't look like he'd kill us and hoped for the best. All so we could pretend we were *normal*." She gave a thin smile. "Then you grow up, the world changes, affords you some rights… and you find yourself trapped anyway."

Realising she had perhaps revealed a little too much, Victoria bit her lip.

"You aren't trapped, Victoria."

Victoria squeezed the railing as frustration began to take hold. Had Clem not listened to a word she said? Or simply not understood?

She was about to correct her when Clem added, "Stuck, maybe. Wedged somewhere awkward, where a step the wrong way feels like falling off a cliff edge."

Victoria loosened her grip, the tension easing in her fingers. Clem was trying. She didn't fully grasp what was at stake, but she was at least reaching for it.

"Something like that," she conceded.

"Can I ask… have you ever told anyone about you and Drew? About your situation?" Clem asked gently.

Victoria shook her head. "I've never had anyone to tell."

Clem's eyebrows knitted together. "What about Jasper?"

"I don't want to worry him. Although I'm sure he suspects something is wrong. Especially after spotting Hannah waiting in Drew's car, and the fact that we didn't arrive at the party together."

"Oh. But surely he'd understand?"

"Maybe. But I also employ him. His whole life is in that museum. He knows if we don't make improvements, then we could close, but as for my marriage problems, why drag him into something he can't fix? Especially when I have no intention of losing the wharf."

They fell into silence, both lost in their thoughts, until a boat came towards them in a narrow stretch. Clem expertly navigated past them, offering a wave as they passed.

"You're a natural at this," Victoria commented.

"Yep, it's in my blood," Clem said, staring into the distance. "I've steered bigger boats. My parents' is a wide-beam. That's over twelve feet."

"I must admit, when you mentioned a hotel boat yesterday, it was the first I'd heard of one."

"There are a few about. If you can manoeuvre one that big, you can handle anything," Clem said, her posture sharpening. "Have you ever steered one?"

"No. I managed to avoid it on my week-long trip. Not that I'd remember even if I had. It feels like a lifetime ago."

"Come." Clem stepped back from her spot next to the tiller, one hand still gripping it. "Have a go now."

"Oh, no. I couldn't," Victoria protested, tucking a strand of hair behind her ear, even though she was tempted.

"Come on. For me?" Clem urged.

Victoria felt Clem's hand around her waist, gently drawing her towards her body. It was impossible to refuse Clem when she was this close, and Victoria was enjoying the feeling of her fingers pressing into her too much to resist. She let Clem take control, manoeuvring her beside the tiller and placing her palm on the wooden handle. Clem's warm hand settled over hers, firm and guiding.

Their closeness was making Victoria's chest heavy, and Clem's breath ghosting over her neck only weighed on it further. She knew she should pull away the moment goosebumps prickled across her skin; instead, she leaned in slightly, allowing Clem to take charge.

As they rounded a bend, Clem gripped her hand harder, but as they came onto a straight stretch she removed her hand entirely. Victoria jumped with surprise. Without Clem's touch, everything felt a little less certain. Her pulse quickened, and a tightness squeezed her chest, making it difficult to breathe.

As if reading her concern, Clem placed her hand back over Victoria's. Her body pressing in close again only served to make everything worse.

"You're doing great," she whispered in her ear.

"I think that's enough," Victoria said finally, extracting her hand from under Clem's and stepping away. "I don't want to be responsible for sinking your boat. You might go back to hating me."

"I never hated you, Victoria."

Victoria arched a brow, questioning.

"Not totally, anyway," Clem added.

She huffed a quiet laugh. "Well, I'm sure your parents would have something to say about it."

"Oh, no doubt."

"How do they feel about your recent life changes?"

Clem chuckled. "Don't get me started."

Victoria tilted her head, urging her to continue.

"Well, Mum doesn't stop going on about everything I gave up, but she's coming round — even more now she knows about Florence. I'd kept it as a surprise for her until their recent visit. My dad is fairly nonplussed about it all. He wants me to be happy, though I think deep down he worries."

"I imagine to them money equals security."

"Money isn't everything," Clem countered with a shrug. "I'm a lot happier now, even if I'm more stressed by everything. It's hard to find that happy medium in life."

"Mmm," Victoria mused, wondering if a happy medium was what she had. "As you said last night, you now have the added pressure of not being able to sell Florence."

Clem hummed. "I didn't expect it to be a bed of roses, but early starts, late nights, on my feet all day — it's a bit of a grind. I'm constantly walking into things. Baking in the wharf's kitchen reminded me of what I'm missing: *space*. And I can feel myself getting more frustrated by the lack of it." She sighed. "I'm sure I just need more time to adjust."

"You said yourself that you weren't sure if Florence was the right choice. What if it wasn't?" She pulled her lips to one side. "What do you want out of life, Clem? We talked a lot last night about my pathetic life, but—"

"We barely discussed mine?"

Victoria nodded. "Surely you can't spend the rest of it serving cake and coffee out of a hatch. Not that there's anything wrong with it, but I know you well enough by now to think it's not going to *float your boat* forever."

"Good one," Clem said with a small smile. She paused, thoughtful. "I want to be part of something, but something good. I love drawing people to something… making them happy with cake. Maybe this was a pipe dream, and some things are best left as ideas. Not every dream has to become reality."

"Sometimes we need to change something. If it doesn't work out, change it again. There's no shame in it. If Florence isn't working for you, follow your heart," Victoria said wistfully.

"Like you did here? To the wharf?"

"Yes, exactly," Victoria replied. "It was literally an escape for me. Like you said last night, it was brave. I do see that. I also see that I have people relying on me now for their jobs, and I have to make it work. But I don't regret it for one second."

"Implement some of the things I told you and you'll be fine," Clem said, nudging her arm gently. "If you know your consumer, you've got a good chance of getting it right."

"Well, about that…" Victoria hesitated, turning to face Clem properly. "Your ideas were great — the ones I can remember anyway — but the thing is, I have no idea how to implement them. Would you help me? I could hire you as a marketing consultant or something?"

"Oh." Clem blinked. She fell silent for a moment before replying. "I have my business. I'm not quite ready to throw in the towel."

"You can set your own hours, work around it. I can be as flexible as you need so it doesn't interfere. It might even help see you through the winter. If you hate it or it doesn't work for you, then you've not lost anything." Victoria stopped for a breath, adding more gently, "You were alive when you were talking about all your ideas. I need someone like you. We worked well together for the party, didn't we?"

Clem didn't hesitate. "Yes."

"So?"

"Can I think about it?" Clem asked, scrunching her face.

"Of course. Would you let me show you around the wharf whilst you think? There are parts you've not seen. I assume you haven't been to the museum yet."

"No, funnily enough, I haven't had time."

"Would you come by sometime? Take a look. No pressure," Victoria said, her voice careful, afraid to hope. The last thing she wanted to do was scare Clem off.

"I'd like that. No promises, though."

"Wonderful. I'll ask Jasper to give you a tour."

"Oh." Clem's face fell.

"Then I can show you everything else," Victoria added with a smile.

Clem's expression softened, clearly content with that arrangement.

As they reached the jetty, Clem pulled over and cut the engine. She jumped onto the bank, securing Florence with a rope.

"Thanks for the lift," Victoria said, taking the hand Clem offered as she stepped onto the jetty.

"Anytime."

Victoria couldn't help but grin at what she now thought of as Clem's signature phrase.

"And thanks for everything you did yesterday. I haven't forgotten I owe you dinner."

"Good," Clem said with a playful tone. "That reminds me, I have something for you."

She disappeared inside. A minute later, she reappeared holding a plastic container.

"Here, I baked you a lemon drizzle for your birthday."

Victoria's hand flew to her chest. "Oh, Clem."

The urge to hug her came so fast and so strong that she didn't have time to overthink it. She stepped forward and wrapped her arms around Clem, holding her close for a moment, then another and another. Clem's grip tightened against her own, their rigid bodies softening into each other. Tension Victoria hadn't realised she'd been carrying slipped away in the warmth of the embrace.

Eventually, she pulled back and pressed a soft kiss to Clem's cheek. A flush rose on Clem's face. Either she'd held on too tight, or Clem had enjoyed the embrace as much as she had.

Victoria took the box gently from her, placing her purse on top, and turned towards the gate. As she unlatched it, she swivelled around.

"Thank you."

"You're welcome," Clem replied, climbing back aboard, her broad smile unmissable.

As Victoria made her way up the path, she found her eyes were damp. She wiped them as the low thrum of an engine drifted after her. Florence was sailing away and with her, Clem, leaving a hollow ache inside Victoria. No one had ever baked something for her before. Drew hadn't even given her a birthday present. He probably thought his presence at the party was gift enough.

She forced her mind away from him to somewhere more pleasant... back to that hug. Was it wrong, she wondered, to imagine more? To picture herself in Clem's arms, that warm, tingling rush spread through her chest; the way Clem wrapped around her, made her feel safe and, more than anything, seen?

And what if she let her thoughts drift further? To kissing her. Peeling away her clothes. Touching her bare skin. Would that be cheating? How would it feel to wake up beside her, skin to skin, limbs tangled in quiet contentment? It stirred something deep inside her, something she thought had long since gone quiet. A longing. A desire. But should she even be thinking about Clem like that? Wasn't that wrong?

But why should she hold herself back from something she wanted? Drew hadn't; he did whatever he pleased and more. So why not her?

Because she wasn't him. That was why.

With a resigned sigh, she headed on up the path, leaving the thought — and Florence's fading engine — behind her.

# CHAPTER 17

Clem clutched a weighty box containing a chocolate cake to her chest, trying not to lose her grip on it whilst clutching two heavy bags of delights in her other hand. She should have made two trips to the wharf, as she had on previous mornings, but with only one of her largest cakes ordered today, it hadn't seemed worth it. It was too late now, so she ploughed on across the bridge.

It crossed her mind to pop in on Victoria whilst she was there. Having spent so much time with her over the weekend, Clem felt her absence after a few days apart. Her cheek prickled at the thought of their parting hug and kiss on the jetty.

All the work she'd poured into the party had been worth the effort. So was the last-minute lemon drizzle she'd thrown together while Victoria slept the morning after. It was probably what had earned her that kiss. As much as she enjoyed it, the real reward came earlier that morning with the unexpected news: Victoria wasn't straight. Not that it changed anything. Victoria had made her position painfully clear. She was a married woman and intended to stay that way.

Over the past few days, Clem had found herself overanalysing their conversation that night after the party. She'd started to wonder if she'd pushed too hard, probed too deeply into things she had no right to ask about. It had only served to make herself angry and Victoria upset; forcing the issue helped no one.

It felt too similar to how Victoria's parents had handled things with her, and Clem knew exactly how that had ended. She needed to stop forcing the matter and instead find a way to become what Victoria needed: someone to talk to, someone who would listen, and, most importantly, someone who tried to understand. Victoria's situation was messy — mostly a mess of her own making — but Clem understood it well enough now to try and meet her where she was, as hard as that might be.

"Here, let me help," came Victoria's voice from somewhere ahead.

Clem looked up to see her running from the Jaguar, hair swaying from side to side. Clem sucked in a breath at the sight of her. Just being in this woman's orbit made every cell in her body sing. Victoria scooped the bags from Clem's hand, bringing much relief to her shoulder.

"Thanks," Clem gasped. "Coffee and walnut cake, marble loaf, chocolate brownies, and fruity flapjack are heavier than I thought."

The corners of Victoria's mouth drooped playfully. "No lemon drizzle?"

"Haven't you had enough this week to satisfy you?"

"You know me, I can't get enough of you — I mean, your lemon drizzle — to satisfy me." A sheepish smile crept across her face as she held the wharf's front door wide open. "I've been trying to catch you the last few days, but I always seem to miss you."

"You can text me, Victoria. I'm only over there." Clem nodded in the direction of the canal. "I'd like to see you. I've missed your company," she admitted softly, a statement that broadened Victoria's smile even further as she strode ahead to open the café door.

"Likewise."

"So, what did you want?" Clem asked, desperately curious.

"Oh, just to return your container. I popped it in the kitchen for you."

Clem gave a half smile, secretly having hoped Victoria might have wanted to see her for something more than returning a container.

"There was something else I wanted to see you about," Victoria added, as though she could read Clem's thoughts.

"Oh?" Clem tilted her head, trying not to let her hopes rise too high. She was still waiting on a date for that dinner invitation.

Victoria held open the kitchen door. "I was wondering when you'd pop over for that tour of the wharf."

It wasn't quite what Clem had been hoping for, but it had been on her mind, too. She was curious to see what lay beyond those glass doors and delve into the history of women's undergarments.

"I could come over after I close up. About four-ish?" Clem suggested, setting the cake box down on the kitchen island.

"Perfect. And I really don't mean to pressure you. I want to show you what I've built here — properly, I mean. I know you've seen lots already, well, some of it anyway—"

Clem reached out and lightly touched Victoria's arm to settle her rambling.

"And I'd love to see more," she said, noticing Victoria's cheeks pinking slightly as she removed the cake containers from the bags she was holding. "I'm quite intrigued by an entire museum dedicated to corsetry."

"Jasper has worked wonders with it," Victoria said, handing her the empty container. "Here. The lemon drizzle was predictably perfect. Very thoughtful, too. Thank you."

The sheepish smile was back on Victoria's face, making Clem's heart tug a little.

"You're welcome," she replied softly, remembering again the first time Victoria had thanked her for it. Before she realised what she was doing, her hand had reached up to her cheek — the same cheek Victoria had kissed. She pulled it back quickly, glancing at Victoria to gauge any reaction. Had she noticed? Their eyes met, and Clem felt heat rise to her cheeks.

"I'd best get back to work," Victoria said, her lips curving upwards in a private sort of amusement. "I put out an advert for more catering staff on Monday, and applications have already started coming in."

"That's great. I'll see you later then," Clem said, following her out of the kitchen.

"Looking forward to it," Victoria said, still smiling as she headed off to her office.

Clem stood and watched her as she went. That smile could have meant anything, but it felt like everything. Was she reading too much into it? She stopped her thought in its tracks. It was best not to dream about things that would never happen.

~

Clem arrived a few minutes early for her tour and introduced herself to the woman at the desk.

The receptionist nodded. "I'll let Victoria know you're here."

"Thank you. Do you have a leaflet about the museum?" Clem asked.

"No, sorry, we don't," she replied with an apologetic smile.

How on earth were they promoting themselves to the surrounding area without one?

Moving further into the wharf's reception area, Clem passed a sewing machine on sturdy, cast-iron legs. She'd never noticed it before. Its black enamel still gleamed against the delicate gold trim, and the word SINGER arched proudly across it like a badge of honour. The foot pedal was smooth, no doubt worn out from years of steady use beneath the feet of countless women.

The gift shop offered the usual array of homewares and gardening items. A centre table displayed smaller curiosities. There were corset-shaped cookie cutters, boning-shaped pencils, enamel pins, key rings and postcards bearing slogans like *Tightly Laced* and *My Body, My Rules*. Clem smiled to herself.

Most striking were the bookmarks, fashioned from two pieces of woven fabric and edged with rows of gleaming grommets. Threaded together with fine lacing, they echoed the intricate fastening of a real corset. Another bookmark, made of leather, bore the words *No fashion at the cost of freedom* stamped deep into its surface.

In pride of place amongst the shelves on the far wall were several books bearing Jasper's name. She smiled at one titled *Under Pressure: A Feminist History of Corsetry*. Others — *Unfastened: The Politics of Shaping Women* and *The Queer Understructure* — caught her eye. Beneath them sat sewing guides on how to make your own corset, alongside mugs emblazoned with *Not your waistline, Reclaim the corset,* and *Unlace the patriarchy.* Posters bearing similar slogans adorned the walls. Someone had clearly put a great deal of thought into the merchandise.

She picked up *Under Pressure* and turned it over. Jasper's face stared back at her from a photograph. She'd never known anyone who'd written a book before, let alone an award-winning author, as the cover declared.

A low voice spoke behind her ear. "I thought that one might interest you."

Clem jumped and placed the book back on the shelf. "Victoria. Hi," she said, turning to face her.

"So, what do you think so far?" Victoria asked, looking around the shop.

"It's impressive."

"And all Jasper's work. You wait until you see what he's curated inside the museum. He should be along any minute."

"Victoria," the woman at the desk called out, holding up a phone.

"Please excuse me," Victoria said to Clem.

"Of course." She was about to dive back into the books when another lower voice came from behind her.

"Ready for a whistle-stop tour through the world of corsetry?"

Clem turned to find Jasper smiling at her.

"I'm looking forward to it," she said, smiling back. "Victoria had to take a phone call."

He looked to the reception desk. "Ah."

"I was just admiring your books. Congratulations on being an award-winning author."

Jasper gave a modest flick of his hand.

"Corsetry seems to be your life," she added.

He clasped his hands together, tilted his head, and stared dreamily into the distance. "The first time I laid eyes on one at the Victoria and Albert Museum, at the impressionable age of eight, I became hooked — pardon the pun."

Clem smiled at his exuberance. He was a breath of fresh air in an otherwise stifling world of conformity.

"But I never dreamed where it would lead," he continued. "I thought I would end up as a burlesque dancer, but thankfully, I got my head down at school. I didn't have much choice when the library was the only place for a gay kid to grow up in safety. Fortuitous really, as I don't have the knees for dance."

"Same," Clem said with a grin. "The school library, I mean." Not that she had the knees for dance either.

Jasper smiled. "As for all this, I have her to thank." He nodded towards Victoria, but then his expression soured. "And Drew's investment."

"Urgh," slipped out of Clem's mouth before she could stop it.

Jasper chuckled. "Not a fan either then?"

"Nope."

"Sometimes I wonder if he only backed the project to get her out of London so he could... pursue other interests."

"I think that's exactly what he did," Clem said, lips tightening.

Jasper gave her a curious look, but then his face softened. He seemed comforted by the idea that Victoria was confiding in someone.

"Sorry about that," Victoria said, returning to them. Her gaze swept over Jasper's bright orange waistcoat and tie, her eyes narrowing ever so slightly.

Clem clocked it immediately. Was the colour really that offensive to her?

"Shall we begin?" Jasper asked, grinning as he strode ahead and held the museum door open.

"Why do I get the feeling I'm at an interview for a job I haven't applied for?" Clem whispered to Victoria.

She placed a hand gently on Clem's shoulder. "I said no pressure, and I meant it."

As they entered the museum, a bright, open space welcomed Clem. Light poured in through the large dual-aspect windows. In front of her stretched a long timeline, charting the evolution of the corset from the 1500s to the twenty-first century. Beside it, a silent video played on loop, showing rows of women seated at factory machines, sewing corsets with swift, practised hands.

Jasper led the way as Victoria pressed a hand to Clem's back, urging her to walk in front. All it did was send a shiver up Clem's spine and confuse her legs. She wondered why Victoria had joined them; surely, she knew the museum inside and out? Not that she was complaining. Any extra time with her was a welcome treat.

"The corset is one of the most controversial garments in fashion history," Jasper began, "pulled between power and restraint, elegance and repression, empowerment and victimisation over centuries. A coercive apparatus through which patriarchal society controlled women and exploited their sexuality but also an emblem of beauty, youth, and social status."

He led them through various sections, each themed by historical period. He spoke of the Elizabethans and their stiff stomachers, the Georgians with their panniers and bum rolls, and the Rococo era, when fashion was at its most theatrical, particularly for aristocrats like Marie Antoinette.

Reaching the Victorian section, Jasper continued with his commentary.

"The modern corset, as we know it — a heavily boned, waist-shaping garment — didn't become widespread until the Victorian era," Jasper explained. "It was designed to discipline the unruly female body and reshape it into something more palatable for the male gaze. It wasn't only a reflection of rank, elegance, and chastity; it was a means of control. Women struggled to put them on alone, and it took time, reinforcing dependency and curbing spontaneity. The corset became a metaphor for the broader constraints of womanhood, limiting not only the body but also women's roles, rights, and freedoms."

Clem grimaced at an X-ray showing how tightly laced corsets had compressed the ribs and shifted internal organs. A shiver ran through her.

Jasper leaned in. "Don't worry, tight lacing was only a fad."

He led them on to a display of mannequins modelling corsets beside a full-length mirror. From a table, he picked up a corset.

"Here, Clem, try one on."

She reached out, but Jasper redirected the garment towards Victoria instead. "You'll need help."

Victoria took it, glancing at Clem with eyebrows raised in silent question.

She shrugged and nodded, having always wondered what it felt like to wear one. Turning to the mirror, she raised her arms as Victoria stepped in front of her, reaching around to place the busk over Clem's tightly fitted V-neck T-shirt. Her fingers worked deftly at the front, adjusting the corset around Clem's bust. Starting at the bottom, she fastened each hook in turn, working her way up until her fingers accidentally brushed the curve of Clem's breast.

Clem's breath hitched. Victoria froze, then stepped back. Their eyes met, locking in a moment that felt electric.

"Sorry," Victoria murmured.

"It's fine," Clem mouthed, offering a small, reassuring smile, acutely aware of Jasper's presence nearby.

Clem finished fastening the front, letting her breasts settle prominently atop the corset. Behind her, Victoria was pushing and pulling at the laces, gradually tightening the corset. Clem caught her reflection in the mirror as the corset cinched tighter around her already slender waist. The sensation was strange and unfamiliar. Did it make her feel powerful or confined? She settled on both.

Once Victoria had finished, Clem watched her gaze shift to the mirror. A smile twitched at the corners of Victoria's lips as her eyes narrowed, roving appreciatively over Clem's body. It was enough to send butterflies fluttering in Clem's stomach. It had been a long time since someone had looked at her like that, and she wasn't imagining it — Victoria's eyes were unmistakably all over her.

Jasper coughed, drawing their attention back to him.

"As you can feel, women were severely restricted by a corset," he began as Clem attempted to move about in the garment, "which was fine for those who weren't required to move or breathe much during the day, but for working women, it was a problem. The more physical activity required, the more mobility took priority. Women in rural communities and the very poor would often forego corsets altogether or wear looser bodices or laced stays. Those who did wear corsets were often trying to emulate the elite, creating tension between aspiration and reality."

"I wouldn't want to wear one for more than a few minutes," Clem said, feeling a sudden panic pooling in her chest. With a nod to Victoria, she began untying it.

Her eyes caught something suspended from a steel beam. It was an old-fashioned bicycle.

"What's a bike got to do with corsets?"

"Ah, everything!" Jasper chuckled. "Have you ever heard of the Rational Dress Society?"

Clem shook her head as the pressure released from the corset, bringing much relief to her ribs.

"Founded in 1881 in London, it campaigned for practical, comfortable, and healthy clothing for women. They opposed the restrictive, impractical, and sometimes dangerous fashions of the Victorian era, especially tight-laced corsets, heavy skirts, and high heels. This woman here," Jasper said, nodding at a blown-up sketch of a lady in what looked like a large, puffy skirt with a centre parting, "Lady Florence Harberton, was a vocal advocate for cycling clothing, championing divided skirts and bloomers. It was a sort of 'first wave' of feminism. They even had a manifesto."

Clem smiled, warmed by the stories of women who had pushed back through history. Part of her wished she'd lived then, just to kick up some proper stink.

Jasper pointed to some newspaper clippings displayed in a cabinet. "They were widely mocked in the press. Most people saw them as radicals and eccentrics, but their efforts helped pave the way for the abandonment of corsets after World War I."

"Much to every woman's relief."

Jasper chuckled again. "Don't forget a lot of women went along with them, especially in high society. Some found them supportive, particularly if they were standing for long periods. Others took pride in tight-lacing challenges, seeing a tiny waist as a personal achievement."

Clem's lip curled. "Seriously?"

"One could argue that corsets were empowering. They're no different from heels today. Many women still balance discomfort and damage against fashion and confidence. Remember, fashion opened doors for women back then, so not taking part could marginalise a woman socially."

She hadn't thought of that. There was a lot she hadn't considered about corsets and how deeply they'd woven themselves into society. As they moved on, dummies modelled modern-looking corsets that Clem recognised, though they were more like what you'd find in a lingerie drawer.

"Once a purely functional garment, the corset has become a symbol of eroticism, sexual empowerment, and even an art object, appealing to a wide spectrum of people regardless of age, gender, race, or class. Many modern wearers embrace corsets to reclaim femininity or express autonomy. For some, it's about power; for others, play."

Clem nodded. "I suppose, like anything, it's the reason behind it that matters. If you're doing it for your own enjoyment, by your own choice."

"Precisely."

Having gone full circle around the museum, they arrived back in the entrance, where Clem eyed an old table to one side with small bits of machinery beside an old sewing machine. She hadn't noticed them when she'd entered. A sign above identified them as a hole-punching machine and a bone-cutting machine, then invited visitors to try them out. Beside the machines, small containers held metal eyelets whilst scissors and pieces of fabric lay next to a sewing machine.

"Thank you for a very informative tour," Clem said, turning to Jasper. "It's certainly given me a lot to think about. The corset is no longer a humble item of women's attire to me."

"That's the general idea," he beamed, his body straightening. "I'll leave you two to it — I have another tour starting shortly."

As Victoria led the way back out to the wharf's reception area, Clem wondered if Jasper ever tired of repeating the same information. What she knew of him so far suggested he didn't. He had spoken with passion on their tour, as if it were his first time telling the story.

She and Victoria made their way through a crowd lingering in the reception area and gift shop — no doubt Jasper's waiting tour group — and headed outside. Victoria glanced at her, probably trying to gauge her reaction, whilst Clem's mind buzzed, absorbing everything she'd seen and heard and struggling to process it all.

The museum was a marvel. It wasn't simply about corsets but a broader exploration of women's history and fashion. It was interactive, not too info-heavy, and, above all, fascinating. Clem had assumed it would only captivate those already interested in the subject, but it resonated deeply with her as a woman.

There were, however, a few problems.

"Well?" Victoria asked, clearly impatient to hear Clem's thoughts.

"I loved it, but there's a fundamental lack of information about the female experience within the factory environment. People connect best to human stories; they want to relate to people in the past, to feel what they went through. To try to understand it through someone else's eyes. That's what creates connection." Clem paused, choosing her words carefully. "Jasper focuses a lot on the history, which is great, but this is a corset factory. I'd like to see more about the lives of the women who worked here. How did they feel about their role in that wider, problematic picture of corsets? What were the working conditions like?"

"Why didn't we see that?" Victoria said, shaking her head.

"Sometimes you have to be on the outside looking in to notice these things." Clem tilted her head slightly, hoping Victoria would catch the deeper meaning and apply it closer to home.

Victoria pursed her lips but remained silent.

"It could be as simple as adding some audio clips of factory noises when you enter," Clem suggested. "They would complement the video. I'm guessing it's from the 1920s, so that's why there's no sound."

Victoria nodded, her eyes lighting up. "Yes, and it's actual footage from this factory. I found it in an archive. The tall chap standing with his arms crossed, watching everyone, matches a photograph I have of my three-times-great-grandfather. His brother was an early filmmaker and made a lot of silent films like this."

"Wow," Clem couldn't help enthusing. "What an incredible resource to have! Adding factory sounds would give people a sensory experience, making them feel like they're inside the building in the past. You could even have a woman's voice reading accounts of what it was like working here, even if you need to fictionalise some parts."

Victoria nodded in thought. "When I was doing my initial research, I came across some newspaper articles documenting accidents and events. I'm sure I could come up with something."

"See what Jasper thinks. He's done a great job with it,

but it needs a few tweaks to tie it more closely to the building itself. Where are you in that museum, for example?"

Victoria's eyebrows knitted together. "Me?"

"Yes. This is your ancestry. Your family built this factory from the ground up, yet there's no mention of it anywhere. If you don't want to add something in the museum itself, I noticed a blank patch of wall in the entrance. You could hang a board there, share some information about where the wharf came from and why. Put some photographs on it. Add your family tree. It would make visitors feel like they're supporting something meaningful. Everyone loves a family business story." She took a breath before continuing. "I also have no idea how the factory ended up where it did today. When did it close and why? I get that Jasper has focused the museum on his work, but in doing so, he's forgotten the most important part: the wharf, the history of the building that houses it. It's a museum of corsetry, but why is it here, of all places?"

Victoria nodded again, slowly this time. "Yes. I see what you mean. I gave him free rein with it and rather forgot about myself."

"Sounds like a habit."

The speed with which Victoria's eyes met her own indicated she'd understood Clem's true meaning. Clem held her gaze, raising her eyebrows a little, daring her to challenge the remark. Thankfully, Victoria's face softened.

"When did it close?" Clem asked again.

"In the 1940s. My family sold it in the early thirties when demand dwindled, but it survived until the end of the war because the new owners pivoted into medical garments, surgical supports and that sort of thing. After the war, it fell into decline."

"The world had changed."

Victoria hummed in agreement.

"After that, various people owned it, but ultimately they let it fall into disrepair, standing empty."

"Until you," Clem said softly.

"Yes," Victoria replied with a wistful smile, gazing up at the building.

Clem let out a quiet, peaceful breath as she watched her. The connection Victoria held to the place was clear; it was wonderful to see something in her life bringing her genuine happiness.

"There's no denying you've built something spectacular," Clem said. "Apart from a few minor tweaks, I really believe the wharf could thrive. It's just a matter of drawing more people in. I must admit, I never realised there was so much to corsetry."

"Few do. Which is why the museum is so important — to educate people." Victoria paused for a moment before adding, "You see now how much Jasper holds up his end of the bargain. He's the real asset — the perfect performer — and his knowledge is endless. All the blood, sweat, and the occasional tears in that museum were his. And now it's down to me to make it all work."

"We'll get there; I'm sure of it."

"We?" Victoria arched a brow.

The slip of the tongue made Clem groan internally. She'd allowed herself to get excited, coming up with ideas and ways to implement them, but how would she manage it all with Florence? Otterford Wharf was a good cause, something she'd love to be part of. It wasn't just any museum; it was an important lesson in women's history.

"Let's see, shall we?" Clem said, not wanting to raise Victoria's hopes any further. "And I don't think you give yourself enough credit for your contribution. You got it this far so there could be a museum."

"Mmm," Victoria mused. "Well, you've seen the shop, the café, my office — several times." She flashed Clem a cheeky grin, thinking of their earliest, most fraught interactions. "I'm not sure what else there is to show you."

"What about that?" Clem asked, pointing towards the outbuilding across the courtyard.

"Oh, that. We don't use it."

"Exactly my point."

"We were going to divide it into retail units, but costs overran, and it got cut from the project."

"Is it structurally sound?" Clem asked, her curiosity rising.

"Yes, just not kitted out for retail."

"Is it potential income if you can find someone who doesn't need it to look pretty?"

"Yes," Victoria sighed, "but it still needs a degree of work to make it sanitary. It's clean and dry with good ventilation, but it's not quite ready to move into."

"But with the right tenant who's willing to put in the work in exchange for a couple of months rent free," Clem gently pushed back, "it's a win-win. You wouldn't lose out, and you could gain a potentially long-term tenant. Plus, their investment in your building becomes your benefit."

Victoria's hands fell to her hips as she eyed Clem thoughtfully. "Does your brilliance ever end?"

"I'm sure it must." Clem chuckled. "I might even know someone who would be interested in renting it."

"Seriously?"

Clem nodded. Hadn't Max mentioned he needed space to expand his cider production?

"Want to look inside?" Victoria asked.

"Yes, please," Clem said eagerly, not one to decline poking her head into something interesting.

They crossed the courtyard to the long, stone building with three large, wooden barn-like doors set into the front of it. Victoria unlocked a smaller door to one side, on the end nearest the bridge, and flicked on a light. A beautiful oak-beam ceiling illuminated a red-tiled floor. The space was in better shape than Clem had expected.

Suddenly, Victoria let out a scream. A huge spider scuttled across the floor in front of them. Clem felt strong arms gripping her from behind as Victoria ducked out of sight.

She couldn't help the laugh that escaped her lips. "Wow! I love how you made me your human shield there."

"Sorry," Victoria panted into Clem's right ear.

She did her best not to react to the stimulating sensation of Victoria's closeness, her warm breath on her ear.

Once it was clear the offending spider was gone, Victoria eased off Clem's arms, much to her relief.

"So," Clem said, "you're arachnophobic as well as claustrophobic?"

"No," Victoria replied, shaking her head. "I'm neither. I don't like large spiders or small narrowboats. I only have one fear, and it's neither of those."

Clem smirked, clearly prompting a response.

Victoria rolled her eyes. "Heights, if you must know."

"Ah, a Canary Wharf penthouse must have been fun then," Clem said, pressing her lips together before she could say more.

"Yes, well," Victoria blustered, "you can see why I didn't want to stick around. I prefer my feet to be firmly on the ground."

Before Clem could reply, Victoria shifted the subject back to business. "It's a good size, with electricity and running water." She pointed to a sink in the corner.

"It's a great blank canvas," Clem admitted.

They made their way back outside. Clem looked around as Victoria locked up. The whole atmosphere at the wharf felt welcoming. If you ignored the few staff cars parked in the courtyard and the picnic benches, it was easy to imagine yourself in the past, amid the hubbub of the working factory.

"Well, if that's everything," Clem said, slipping her hands into her pockets.

"Yes. I don't want to keep you," Victoria said, stepping forward and narrowing the space between them. "I can't thank you enough, Clem. You have helped me so much without any reason to."

"I have every reason…" Clem wanted to say she'd do anything for her, but settled for, "To help a friend."

Victoria's hand rested gently on Clem's bicep. "Dinner? Saturday night?"

"Great," Clem replied, her voice a little higher than she intended.

"I'm looking forward to it." Victoria gave a soft squeeze, nearly melting Clem into a puddle before she turned away.

As she watched her go, Clem's hand instinctively went to the place where Victoria had touched her. Afraid she would turn and see her staring, Clem darted to the bridge. She was growing used to Victoria's touches, but each one left her with a simmering frustration. She wanted more than a brush on the arm, a hug, or a kiss on the cheek. She longed to pull Victoria close, hold her tight, and show her everything she was missing out on.

She forced her mind back to the wharf and the endless

stream of ideas swirling in her head. Pulling her phone from her pocket, she furiously tapped them all into a note. The excitement bubbled up inside her as she did. She almost didn't want to return to Florence. She wanted to dive in, work side by side with Victoria, and see her every day.

The woman was to be admired for her achievements. She'd spent her life leaving marks on buildings; all Clem had done was leave her mark on people's waistlines.

# CHAPTER 18

Clem snapped her laptop shut and blew out a frustrated breath. The YouTubers who'd promised to feature Clem's Coffee & Cakes had 'changed artistic direction' and dropped her segment from their video.

She eyed two leftover blueberry muffins and a lone slice of lemon drizzle. She grabbed a muffin and shoved it into her mouth. It was a good job that she'd only baked half her usual batch. What had been forecast as intermittent showers for the last few days had turned into a non-stop downpour. It had eased up today, though not enough for her to risk a full bake.

She placed the remaining muffin and the lemon drizzle slice into a container, then locked up Florence. As she turned, she spied Max closing up shop on his own boat.

"Hey, Max!" she called. "Can I interest you in my last blueberry muffin?"

"Yes, please," he replied, putting a box of vinyl back down and jogging over.

She held the container open for him.

"Oh," Max teased, eyeing the slice of lemon drizzle. "Who might that be for?"

Clem narrowed her eyes at him but otherwise ignored the comment. "I haven't seen you for a few days. Have you been avoiding the bad weather? Or just unable to extract yourself from a certain someone's apartment?"

Max grinned. "Yes, to the weather. I popped around to my parents'. I store my sunshades in their garage over the winter. I figured I'd better grab them, what with all the sunshine we've been having these last weeks. I don't want the vinyl melting. I hit a few record fairs with my dad; he's a bit of a collector, too," he said. "Then he helped me clear out a collection from a music lover's estate — got some great finds."

"Did you shout about your new stock on social media?"

Max rolled his eyes. "No. I will now." He glanced at the dark grey sky. "I shouldn't have bothered opening today, and if you're giving away cake... you probably shouldn't have either."

"I did okay." Clem shrugged. "At least people want hot drinks in this weather."

"Oh! Look what I picked up today." Max grabbed a small, plastic box from his chair and handed it to her.

She opened it to find a stack of loyalty cards and a custom stamp.

Max pressed the stamp onto the back of his hand. "Your idea worked well," he said, showing her a cute record shape in black ink.

"That's great," Clem said, looking at the loyalty cards with ten circles on them and *Buy 10, get £10 off* written across the top.

"So, how was it?" Max asked.

"How was what?"

"Your tour. Jasper said he gave you one."

"It was really interesting, more interesting than I expected. Jasper is great."

"Isn't he just?" Max replied, all dreamy-eyed.

Clem smirked at Max's obvious attraction. "He's so knowledgeable and such a natural tour guide. Everything rolls off his tongue. Did he tell you Victoria offered me a job?"

He took a bite of the blueberry muffin. "He mentioned you were baking for the wharf now."

"Oh yeah, I am, but I didn't mean that. Victoria wants to hire me as a marketing consultant. Only part-time or casual hours — whatever I want."

"No, he didn't mention that. Maybe he doesn't know. Will you take it?" Max turned to her. "Wait. What about Florence?"

"I don't know." Clem shrugged. "I want to take the role. There's something about the wharf; it kind of wraps you in a warm hug."

Her friend laughed. "Are you still talking about the wharf?"

Clem gave his arm a playful punch. "I've got so many ideas to help, and I want to! It's such a worthy cause. It makes sense to get paid for it."

"Then why the hesitation? It sounds like you've made up your mind."

"I have… and I haven't," Clem admitted. "I'm not sure how I'd manage it and Florence."

"Why don't you stop overthinking it and just give it a go?" he suggested. "That's what brought you here in the first place, isn't it? Spontaneity."

Clem bit her lip. It kind of was, but it was more the culmination of years spent feeling stuck. She wasn't exactly unhappy with the way things were working with

Florence. A little unsatisfied and anxious about money, yes. But then there was the prospect of working for Victoria. Would it be difficult, being her employee and having feelings for her? Would she be able to focus? Victoria was very distracting. What if she struggled to keep her mind on the job? What if they disagreed, or worse, gave in to something neither was prepared for? That last thought pulled a smile tugged at her lips. She could dream, couldn't she?

She shook her head, brushing away her unhelpful thoughts. "I'm still thinking about it," she settled on. "That reminds me: Were you serious about needing somewhere to set up your cider empire?"

"Maybe. Why?"

"I might have found the perfect spot. Look." Clem pulled out her phone and swiped to a series of photos.

Max took it from her, zooming in and out. "Gosh, Clem. This is perfect. Where is this place?"

She nodded towards the wharf. "Right on your doorstep."

His eyes widened. "Really?" He passed the phone back, his forehead furrowed. "I'm not exactly in a position to do anything at the moment. Distinct lack of funds, you know."

"Sounds like you need an investor... or an *avid* fan?"

"Jasper? I couldn't. We've only been going out a few days."

"You could draw up a contract to keep that side of things professional. Make him a silent partner." Clem shrugged again. "It's worth speaking to him. Or what about your parents? Could they help get you up and running?"

"Maybe," he mused. "I could sell the boat, but that would mean moving in with them."

Clem couldn't believe she had to walk him through this. "Max," she said slowly, "where have you spent the last few nights?"

His eyes flicked away as he smiled. "Jasper's." He played with his lip. "Can you send those photos to me? It does look perfect. I could sell vinyl from there, too. It looks cool and dry, everything selling from a narrowboat is not."

"And no need for those sunshades! Why don't you stop overthinking it and just give it a go?" Clem suggested, tossing his previous words straight back at him.

"Touché."

"It's not so easy to make potentially life-changing decisions, is it?"

Max rolled his eyes and smiled.

"Well, I'm going to see if anyone around here wants a slice of lemon drizzle." Clem smiled.

"You're desperately trying to get into her good books, aren't you?" Max observed, then slyly added, "Or is it her bed?"

"Still married," Clem called back as she headed off along the tow path to the bridge.

She wound her way through the wharf to Victoria's office, knowing she would be in. Overcast days led Victoria to switch on a light, and it had been on all day. Clem had also happened to spot her at her desk every time she looked out the port side of Florence, which was pretty much every five minutes. What else was there to do on a drizzly day but stare out a window at a beautiful woman who made your insides somersault?

Clem tapped lightly on Victoria's open office door and stuck her head around. "Hello."

Victoria looked up from a pile of papers. "Clem."

The beaming smile on her face suggested she was happy to see her, so Clem stepped inside.

"I have a very lonely slice of lemon drizzle looking for a new owner. I don't suppose—"

Before Clem could finish her sentence, Victoria was on her feet.

"I'll look after it," she said, taking the container and diving straight in.

Clem could barely contain her amusement as she watched Victoria devour the treat in seconds, like a starving dog.

Licking her fingers clean, Victoria passed the container back.

"Hungry, were we?"

"Always hungry for your creations. But yes, salad isn't very satisfying for anything, except the waistline."

"You have a perfect waistline," Clem said before she could stop herself.

Victoria gave a tilt of her head in acknowledgement. "Then thank the salad. It's your fault I have to eat it. I need to counteract all this lemon drizzle with something."

Clem recoiled playfully, clutching a hand to her chest. "My fault?" She poked a finger at Victoria's shoulder. "You could try resisting."

"Seriously? You think resistance is possible? That would require several months in rehab, miles away from you… and your temptations?" Victoria's smile faltered.

"Yeah, sounds a bit extreme if you ask me." Clem winked. "Keep eating the cake and salad; I'm sure it's perfectly balanced."

"I have no plans on stopping. Lemon is a fruit, after all. That's one of my five a day."

"I'm not sure it works like that, but—" Her phone vibrated in her pocket. "Sorry, my phone."

She took it out and saw *Dad* flashing onto the caller ID. "Sorry, I'd better take this."

"No problem," Victoria said, returning to her desk as Clem answered.

"Hi, Dad. Is everything okay?"

The line cut in and out for a moment. She checked her signal; it showed five bars. "Dad?"

"We're at Accid— and Emer— Buckley Hos—. Your mum — X-ray."

A jolt of panic shot through her.

"Dad, is she okay? It's a bad line. What happened?"

Victoria was suddenly at her side. Clem hadn't even noticed her leave her desk again.

"Dad?"

The line went dead.

"Buckley Hospital," Clem muttered, looking at the full signal bars on her phone.

"Who's in the hospital?" Victoria asked.

"My mum, I think." She tried calling her father back, but a series of short, sharp beeps sounded in her ear. "Damn it."

"What do you need, Clem?" Victoria urged.

"A lift to the hospital."

"Okay, let's go." Victoria shut her laptop, grabbed her keys from her desk, her coat from her chair, and was already heading for the door.

"Are you sure? I don't want to put you out. I could get a taxi."

"And wait how long for it?" Victoria muttered as she left the room. "Come on."

Clem nodded to herself, happy to follow. Her brain was racing with thoughts of her mum. Had she had a stroke, or a heart attack? She'd heard the word 'X-ray', so surely that meant she was alive, right? They wouldn't X-ray a dead person. And weren't X-rays mainly for broken bones? More serious things needed MRIs and CT scans. She clung to that thought and that canal-related injuries weren't uncommon.

As she reached the car, Victoria was already holding the door open for her. Clem didn't even remember walking there.

"Get in," Victoria gently urged her, hand on her back.

On autopilot, Clem slid into the passenger seat and clicked her seat belt into place.

"I'm sure she'll be fine, Clem," Victoria said, getting into the driver's seat. Her hand settled briefly on Clem's knee.

Clem took a deep breath. Victoria's reassuring voice and touch brought a flicker of solace. She decided to send a text to her dad. Maybe she could get something — anything — out of him to quell the storm raging in her chest.

As Victoria started the engine, Queen's "Somebody to Love" blared out loudly. She quickly reached for a knob on the RetroSound unit and turned it down. The sudden silence was somehow even louder than the music.

"Hey," Clem protested. "You can't turn Freddie off."

"Sorry. I thought you might want some peace."

"No — a distraction would be great actually."

Victoria turned the music back on, and they made their way down the road, listening to the sounds of Queen. As it was, it couldn't distract her from her looping thoughts. What had happened to her mum? Crushed finger? Broken arm? Something worse? Surely Dad wouldn't call from the A&E for something minor. She tried not to imagine the worst-case scenarios, but they found their way in anyway.

When Victoria finally pulled the car up outside the Accident and Emergency department, Clem was out in a flash. She leaned down through the open window. "Thank you. I really appreciate it."

"Anytime," Victoria replied, with a wink.

Clem dashed through the automatic doors and into the reception area. Glancing back, she noticed Victoria drive away. Spotting the long queue, she approached a passing nurse, giving her mum's full name and asking where she might be. She led her through the waiting room, along a corridor, and into a clinical bay. Clem followed closely behind the nurse as she negotiated uniformed staff rushing among curtained nooks. She discovered her mum sitting a few nooks in, with two fingers bandaged together. Her dad was sitting in an uncomfortable-looking chair to one side of the hospital bed.

"There you are," Clem said, letting out a long, heavy breath. "What happened?"

"It's just a broken finger," her dad called from the other side of the bed.

"*Just!*" her mum protested.

"Oh! Is that all?" Clem said, exhaling with relief.

"What do you mean 'Is that all'?"

"I thought it was serious! That you'd had a heart attack or a stroke or something."

"Well, I wish I had now," she uttered. "At least I might get a bit of sympathy."

"Sorry, Mum." Clem raked a hand through her hair. "I was just really worried, and I couldn't get through to Dad."

"Sorry, love." He sounded sheepish. "The mobile was working fine outside by the ambulance, but I must've lost you when I came in."

"It was *never* working fine. All I heard was Mum was in A&E. At least I caught which one. Why the ambulance?"

"Well, how else would we have gotten to the hospital?" Her mum sniffed.

"They are emergency vehicles, not glorified taxis. How did you even do it?" Clem asked.

"I was cleaning the windows from the towpath. A boat sped past and upset *The Kingfisher*. My hand was leaning on the rub rail."

Clem sucked in a noisy breath through her teeth. She could imagine the rest.

"You didn't need to come." She turned to her husband, exasperated. "I thought you were going to send a text, Tom."

"*I thought* it would be easier to call her. A text message might have worried her."

Clem shook her head at them both.

"How did you get here so quickly?" her dad asked.

"Victoria gave me a lift."

"From next door?" Her mum glared at her. "Friends now, are we?"

"You could say that," Clem said, clenching her jaw to stop herself smiling at the fact.

"I saw those bad reviews."

"You would have seen her reply then, too, Mum," Clem replied, a little too sharply. "It wasn't her — and she wasn't trying to get me moved either."

"What about that mishap that had you both in the canal?"

"A misunderstanding. She's really nice, Mum. I've been helping her out a bit. I'm baking for the wharf, too."

"Is she a lesbian?" her mum whispered, suddenly seeming mindful that they were having this conversation in a semi-public space.

"Seriously?" Clem turned to her dad. "Are you sure she didn't hit her head as well?"

"Not recently." He chuckled.

"Why would you even ask that, Mum?"

"I was only wondering. Are we not allowed to ask that sort of thing anymore?"

"I don't think it's *ever* been appropriate to ask someone that, Mum. It's no one's business," Clem replied, finding the knot that had been forming in her stomach since her dad's call tighten.

Her mum gave a nonchalant shrug.

"Didn't Maud say she had a husband," Clem's dad put in, "though she never saw him around much?"

"Oh, yes, she did."

"She's offered me a job on top of the baking," Clem said, quickly changing the subject.

"Doing what?" her mum demanded.

"Marketing. The wharf needs a little — well, a lot of help to increase footfall, or it might close."

"Oh! Well, it sounds like an exciting opportunity and some guaranteed income, but how would you manage that with your café and baking for the wharf?"

"It's part-time or whatever hours I want, so I can work around it."

Her mum looked ready to respond, but a nurse appeared at the end of the bed.

"You're all good to go, Mrs Wentworth," she said brightly. "The bruising will take a few days to go down. Take some painkillers if you need to, and keep it strapped like this until you see us again. The fracture clinic will send you an appointment for about four weeks from now."

"Great. Come on, Tom," her mum said, pushing herself up with one hand, the other held aloft with a dramatic point. "We're expecting four guests in a couple of hours."

"I hope they enjoy the view out of the clean windows," the nurse called after them with a chuckle.

As they made their way into the waiting area, Clem's heart gave a little leap. Victoria was sat calmly between a single, tired-looking man and a family with rather shouty young children, a magazine perched on her lap. That feeling of joy swiftly twisted into nerves as Clem realised her parents would have to meet her. Properly.

"What's she still doing here?" her mum asked.

"I don't know," Clem said, "but please try to be nice to her. For me." Without waiting for a reply, she strode ahead. "Victoria. Thanks for waiting."

"I wasn't sure if you would need a lift," Victoria said, standing up and putting the magazine on a nearby table.

"Yes, that would be great, thanks," Clem replied with a smile. She hadn't even thought about how she'd get home.

Her parents caught up with them then. Clem took a deep breath.

"Victoria, these are my parents, Tom and Barbara. Mum, Dad, Victoria."

All parties smiled and nodded politely, much to Clem's relief.

"I hope you are okay, Barbara?" Victoria asked.

Clem was surprised to hear a hint of nervousness in her voice.

"I am, thank you," Clem's mum accepted her well wishes. "It's a clean break, so I'm told it should heal quickly."

"Oh. Good," Victoria pronounced.

"I'll go outside and call a taxi," Clem's dad said.

"I could give you a lift," Victoria countered. "Save you the trouble."

"That would be super, thanks," he replied.

~

Five minutes later, the four of them stood in the car park, staring at the Jaguar.

Clem's dad scratched his head. "Erm."

"Yes, sorry. It will be a bit of a squeeze," Victoria admitted sheepishly. Leaning into Clem, she whispered, "How far is it to the marina?"

"About fifteen minutes." Turning to her dad, Clem said, "Dad, you and I can squeeze in the back. You get in behind the passenger seat, and then I'll help Mum in."

"Does this thing even have seat belts?"

"Yes, Mum, of course it does."

"Oh, err, not in the back, it doesn't," Victoria corrected her. "They weren't legally required in cars of this age."

"Well, we're not going far, are we?" Clem said quickly, itching to have her parents as far away from Victoria as possible.

She let the seat fall gently against her dad's knees and pulled the seat forward to give him some room.

"There you go, Mum. Mind your hand."

With everyone squeezed in, they finally set off. Clem wished she'd bundled them into a taxi instead, but as the gentle scent of Victoria's fragrance filled her nose it also soothed the tension inside her.

"I believe I have you to thank for reviving my jumper, Barbara," Victoria said.

"Oh. No need," she replied, ever so politely.

Clem eyed her dad and smirked. He shot a grin her way. It was typical of her mum to be rude behind someone's back and oh so polite to their face.

Much to Clem's relief, the rest of the journey passed in blissful silence aside from her dad giving the odd direction to Victoria. On the way, she checked the weather report to see what she needed to bake for the morning. A large sun greeted her in the app, and she bit back a sigh. The last thing she wanted to do when she returned to Florence was work. Evenings once spent watching TV, bingeing a series, or getting lost in a book felt like a distant memory, sacrificed the moment she started working for herself.

"Here is good," her dad said as they finally pulled into the marina car park.

Victoria got out, allowing Clem to escape and rush around to help her mum out.

"Can you go and get some photographs of what the builders have done this week for me?" her mum asked as Clem helped her out of the awkwardly low car seat.

"Yes. I can go in tomorrow when I—" She stopped herself from saying, *When I go to Victoria's for dinner*, and swiftly corrected to, "When I pass."

Her mum eyed her. The woman could read a book without any words. Clem hugged her, hoping it would serve as a distraction.

"Consider that job," her mum whispered in her ear. "Who knows what it might lead to?"

What did she mean by that? Before she could ask, her dad appeared beside them. Clem passed him her mum's handbag.

"Thank you, Victoria," he said over the car's roof.

"Yes, thank you," her mum added.

Victoria inclined her head. "You're both welcome."

"Let me know how you are tomorrow, Mum," Clem called.

"I will," she called out as they wandered off.

Victoria got back in the car. "Right, let's get you to the wharf."

"Thanks for sticking around and giving us a lift," Clem said, joining her.

"It was no problem. Your mum is…"

"You don't have to finish that sentence," Clem cut in, turning to Victoria.

"Good. I didn't realise until I started that I didn't know how to finish it." She laughed as they drove off.

Clem sniffed lightly. "Mum is Mum. Who knows how she'll cope with a broken finger."

"She'll manage; they both will. They have each other, years of experience, and, from what I've seen of your mum, plenty of determination."

"Yes, she has that in shovelfuls. I'm glad they're giving up, if I'm honest. I do worry about them. They might have experience, but accidents still happen. I know they happen to everybody, and I probably sound ageist, but today was proof that they can happen to them. I'll rest easy when they are safely in the house."

"Where they might leave the gas on because they're so old? Or fall down the stairs? Wouldn't a bungalow be better?"

Clem narrowed her eyes playfully. "I'm sure you know what I meant."

"I do. But you can't wrap your parents in cotton wool any more than they could you when you were growing up."

"Mmm," Clem mused. It didn't stop her worrying.

"More Freddie?" Victoria suggested.

"Yes," Clem replied.

The opening rhythm of "Under Pressure" filled the car — and Clem with a wave of dread. She closed her eyes and leaned back. She wanted to enjoy the music, but concern for her parents and uncertainty about her own future weighed her down. Should she have offered to help them? But how could she? She had her own life to deal with.

A sensation tickling her arm made her open her eyes.

"Clem," Victoria murmured. "We're at the wharf."

"Shit! Did I fall asleep? Sorry." She sat forward and rubbed her eyes.

"There's no need to be sorry. The stress of everything, no doubt, caught up with you."

"I'm certainly feeling it," Clem said, blinking and reaching for the door handle. "Thank you for this afternoon. I don't know what I would have done without you."

"Don't mention it," Victoria replied with a soft smile. "I was happy to be able to help you out for a change. I was beginning to worry this friendship might look one-sided."

"So, you don't just want me for my genius marketing ideas and my lemon drizzle?"

Victoria chose to ignore the comment. "I enjoy helping you."

"Likewise. I'll guess I'll see you for dinner tomorrow night?"

"Yes," Victoria confirmed with a wide smile. "Can't wait."

"Me neither," Clem replied, stepping out of the car feeling momentarily lighter and happier.

But the further she walked from Victoria, the heavier she felt. She'd used the word *friendship*, and as much as Clem treasured it, she wished it were more. Each step across the dusk-lit cobbles towards the canal felt like someone had slipped weights in her shoes.

She was at least relieved that Victoria hadn't raised the subject of the job offer, though she knew there would be no reprieve tomorrow at dinner. Every part of her was itching to get stuck in at the wharf, to implement the changes she'd thought of and watch its fortunes turn around. It was something she was certain she could do; it was who she was, what she excelled at.

Whether she could take that step was another matter. She did miss working regular hours and knowing exactly where she needed to be each day instead of living at the whims of the weather or the passing trade. Not that working for the wharf sounded regular, just whatever she could squeeze between everything she was already doing.

As she reached Florence, her head ached as much as her heart did. A lie down was in order before cruising back to the jetty to start work. She needed to try to reset herself by burying her face in a pillow and blocking out the world for a little bit. It would still be waiting for her, with all its questions and demands, when she awoke.

# CHAPTER 19

*V*ictoria plumped the cushion in her favourite chair for the sixth time, turned the background music off for the third time, and switched a corner lamp back on. She sipped from her glass of Chablis, then refilled it. She couldn't remember the last time she'd felt this nervous — or was it excitement? She struggled to pinpoint the difference. To her, excitement was the anticipation of something positive, and nerves were the anticipation of something negative. But both could have been responsible for her clammy palms, restless limbs, racing heart, and fluttering stomach.

She checked her watch. Her guest was due to arrive in five minutes. She perched on a stool at the kitchen island and forced herself to breathe slowly. It was only dinner. Dinner with Clem, the woman who made her feel things she wasn't supposed to feel.

Why couldn't she keep away from her? She could source cakes elsewhere, find someone else to help the wharf with marketing, and call a taxi when she next wanted a lift. Victoria swallowed hard, trying to suppress the nausea rising in her throat. She didn't want to do any of those things. At least the hospital run had led to making peace with her neighbours. Hopefully they could be cordial from now on.

Clem's words from the tour of the wharf lingered in her head. She'd said Victoria made a habit of forgetting herself. Clem had been referring to the museum, but the way she said it, Victoria knew she was saying something else. And then there was the other thing she'd said: Sometimes you had to be on the outside looking in to see problems. That, too, had a deeper meaning behind it, she was sure. Victoria noticed things, like the slight tilt of Clem's head challenging her to dispute it.

She'd also noticed the way Clem had stroked her cheek that morning when she'd returned her Tupperware, the very cheek Victoria hadn't been able to resist kissing when she'd passed it to her. Had Clem been thinking about it in that moment? If so, did the smile on her face mean she'd liked it? But what could a young, beautiful woman see in someone like her? She had more yesterdays than tomorrows and was desperately trying to cling to the last of her dignity.

A deep sigh escaped her lips. What did it matter anyway? She was still married. Always would be.

The doorbell rang, making Victoria jump and sending her heart racing again.

*Fuck!* Who was she kidding? It mattered a lot. It meant everything.

She opened the door to find Clem holding a bunch of pink roses. Her hand flew to her chest as sudden emotion swelled there, threatening to choke her.

"Wow!" she managed, letting out a breath as she took

them. "It's been a long time since someone brought me flowers. Oh — not that you have, in that way, anyway." Victoria did her best to look less flustered than she felt. "Come on in."

Clem stepped inside, and as Victoria closed the door behind her, she shook her head at herself. What was she thinking? People often gave each other flowers — especially when one of the people was hosting a dinner party. It didn't have to mean anything.

"They can mean whatever you want them to mean," Clem replied softly, eyes locked on her as she turned around.

Okay — maybe it did mean something.

"Thank you." Victoria held the bouquet in front of her face, using it as a shield to hide her moistening eyes. Why on earth was she crying? Okay, she knew why. Clem… had brought *her*… flowers. "Come through," she added, leading the way into the kitchen. "I'll find a vase."

She set the flowers down on the marble worktop and rummaged under the sink, trying to compose herself as she did.

"I'm beginning to think a lemon drizzle might've been easier," Clem remarked, her tone carrying a trace of nervous humour.

"Not at all. I have one somewhere," Victoria called out as she dove into a cupboard under the island. "Ah, here we are." She said, spotting one. "And the flowers are beautiful," she added, setting a crystal vase onto the worktop. As she stood, she took in Clem properly for the first time. Her long, brown hair spilled over her cream, floral dress, and a soft, ever-enticing smile lit up her face. "Just like you," she let slip.

Clem's smile deepened. "Thank you."

*Did I say that out loud?* Victoria scrambled for her brain to deliver something — anything — to move the conversation on.

"Oh, I have something for you, too," she blurted.

She reached for a small, rectangular parcel wrapped in floral paper and pushed it across the worktop to Clem, watching as she peeled it open.

"*Under Pressure: A Feminist History of Corsetry*. Thank you," Clem said, flipping back the book's front cover. "Signed by the author himself, I see."

"Of course," Victoria smirked. "He was very *eager*. Wine?"

"Please," Clem said, not even looking up from where she was perusing the table of contents.

"For dinner, I thought I'd play it safe with a spaghetti carbonara."

"Perfect."

"Did you get everything you needed next door?" Victoria asked, pouring Clem's wine into a glass.

"Next door?"

"For your mum," Victoria clarified, sliding the glass across the worktop to Clem. "The photographs."

"Oh, yes. All sent," Clem confirmed. She placed the book down, picked up the glass, and wandered around the room, taking it in. "Your house is very different to theirs. You wouldn't know they were identical unless you saw the outside. You've opened it up more than Mum and Dad have. Mum didn't want it to be too draughty."

Victoria began arranging the flowers into the vase. "Ah yes, well, I may live to regret it when I'm her age... if I still live here, that is."

Clem flashed her a tight smile; not wanting to linger on the matter, Victoria continued.

"It had lost a lot of its original features by the time we bought it. Rather than install replicas, I decided to embrace more of the building's journey and go for a contemporary interior."

"You've done a great job with it. Original features are lovely, but I know they were giving my parents a headache. I suppose no one knows that better than you, with your career and all."

"Indeed." Victoria grinned. "Why don't you sit yourself over there and have a nose through that book while I make dinner," she suggested, nodding toward her favourite chair overlooking the garden. If Clem watched her cook, she'd probably drop something or cut herself. Her body was barely cooperating now as it was.

"Are you sure I can't help with anything?"

Victoria nodded. "Yes, I'm sure. You go relax."

Resigned, Clem picked up the book and curled into the chair. The soft light from the lamp beside her bathed her in a golden glow. She looked good there. Too good.

"Sorry about the view," she called, trying to sound casual. "The blasted neighbour insists on mooring her ghastly orange boat there. It completely ruins the view of the canal."

"How unreasonable of her," Clem played along. "But you know, narrowboats are part of the canal."

"Oh, I do. Every time one passes my office window, the sound echoes like a foghorn."

"Okay, I'm not biting." Clem laughed, kicking off her shoes and tucking her legs beneath her.

Victoria's breath caught as she watched her. Clem looked so at ease, like she was part of the place rather than a visitor. She opened the book and began flicking through its pages with curiosity. Then she looked over, caught Victoria watching, and smiled. A flutter stirred in

Victoria's chest. She gave a quick smile in return and turned to focus on cooking, heart thudding.

Once the meal was plated, Victoria called Clem over to the dining table. She topped up their wine as Clem took a seat.

"I can't remember the last time I shared dinner with someone," Victoria said, sitting opposite. "You'll have to come again. I always make enough for two."

"I'd like that," Clem said, meeting her eye. "Life can be rather dull alone."

Victoria began digging into the pasta. "And good company is hard to find."

"It is. I often read a book when I eat," Clem added. "Sometimes it's the only chance I can grab fifteen minutes' peace. I'm so tired by the time I get to bed, and then I have to be up early. I'll enjoy reading Jasper's book. Have you read it?"

"No. His books aren't my sort of thing."

"Feminism isn't your thing?" Clem asked, eyebrow arched as she sucked up a strand of spaghetti.

"It's great and everything, and I get behind anyone who is into that sort of thing or musters the energy to be passionate about it, but I don't. I guess I see no hope of ever achieving equality. I prefer fiction — at least that way we can pretend we've achieved it, depending on your genre choice, of course. Some fiction is worryingly becoming reality, increasingly so."

"You don't think an apathetic attitude by too many people might have got us into this mess in the first place?"

"You mean if we all rose up, we could achieve something?"

"If women stopped doing the brunt of the work, or even invoiced for it, the world would be a different place. But we don't," Clem said, getting a little animated with her fork. "We get on with it, all the while enslaving ourselves to our captors."

"Stockholm syndrome," Victoria sniffed with amusement as she wiped her mouth with a napkin.

"Exactly. And each generation of women enables the next set of men when they raise their children. It burdens the women of that next generation because at the end of the day, men have got to want to do something in order to do it. All we ever show them is they don't have to," Clem said with a noisy exhale.

"We only do that because it's easier to do something yourself than watch someone do a half-arsed job — I know that from experience with Drew. And it's not like I'll be raising children. As I've come to terms with not having them, I've realised the simplest contribution I've made to this world is not having contributed to it." Victoria shrugged. "How do you even begin to fix the problem?"

"Women have got to say it has to change, and men have got to agree." Clem pulled a discouraged face. "I can't see that ever happening. The boys of today are the men of tomorrow, but if we raise boys from birth to be dependent on women to meet their emotional and physical needs — and raise girls to believe they need to meet those needs — where does that leave us? It's a vicious circle. I hope things change."

Victoria sighed. "What's the point in being outraged at something if you don't intend to do anything about it? I speak for myself in that."

"And that is why things will never change," Clem replied. "I guess it's easier for you to take that standpoint. You're not burdened by ailing parents, juggling demanding toddlers and hormonal teenagers, or rushing about on school runs, all while trying to hold down a career to feel some sense of self and that you're still

contributing. You just have the wayward husband—"
Clem gave a rueful smile and bit her lip. "Sorry."

Victoria let the comment slide with a casual wave of
her hand as she reached for her own glass.

"Women are so overburdened," Clem continued, "they
don't even have the energy to look after themselves, let
alone rise up and demand better treatment."

Victoria eyed her, appreciating her enthusiasm.

"Sorry. I don't want to come across as a ranting
feminist," she finished, twirling more spaghetti onto her
fork.

Victoria put hers down and reached forward, placing
her hand on Clem's. "It's fine; rant all you want. And for
the record, I don't see it as ranting. You speak with
passion, and I love listening to you."

She loved listening to anyone who spoke with passion
about their interests. It was what she enjoyed most about
spending time with Jasper, hearing his live lectures from
the annals of history. And Drew's shared passion for
bringing new structures to life from the ground up,
transforming forgotten buildings, was what had first
attracted her to him.

"You aren't juggling those things either, so why is it so
important to you?" Victoria asked, noticing that Clem's
cheeks were tinged with pink.

"I'm a woman; it's a woman's issue. You don't have to
be directly affected by relationships with men to be a
feminist, we all live in a patriarchal world. Every woman
thinks in man, but no man thinks in woman. Some may be
able to speak woman, but it doesn't mean they choose to,"
Clem said, glancing down at Victoria's hand. "Why would
they when man is their native language?"

Victoria withdrew her hand, picking up her fork again.
She hadn't even realised she'd placed it there.

"I may not experience the burden in the same way as others, but it doesn't mean I can ignore it," Clem continued, playing with the stem of her wine glass. "I watched female colleagues being treated differently because they had pressures outside of work. I listened to them complaining day in and day out about how much they had to do at home compared to their husbands. If I wasn't a lesbian already, those women would have turned me."

Victoria chuckled.

"We need to fight for equal pleasure as well as equal pay," Clem said, tapping the table with her forefinger. "You know, I was actually overlooked for promotion twice before they finally offered it to me. Both times I was a woman of childbearing age, and both times the job was given to less experienced men who became my managers and expected me to help them. By the time I hit forty, they realised it was unlikely I would be having any kids, and I finally became as worthy as a man for promotion. It helped sway me to walk away from the company when the opportunity came."

"I'm sorry that happened to you," Victoria said, grateful that she hadn't experienced discrimination in her own career.

Clem shrugged. "It's not just me; it's every woman that gets treated like she's a second-class citizen. But we should change the subject, before I get really ranty."

As tempted as she was to hear Clem go into full rant mode, Victoria smiled and did as suggested.

"When did you last have dinner with a woman?" Victoria asked, only to realise it might have sounded like this was a date.

"Oh." Clem hummed. "A long time ago. But... she

wasn't right for me. Sometimes you just know, don't you? What feels right, what doesn't?"

"Mmm," Victoria mused, clearing her plate.

"So I ended it. That was a couple of years ago. It pleased my mum; she never liked her. Said she had sinister eyes."

Victoria laughed and shook her head. "Your mum."

"She was correct, though, about her not being right. Although, I don't know what she had against her eyes. I think parents have a sixth sense about these things." Clem seemed to realise the possible subtext of her words then and blurted, "Oh, sorry. I didn't mean to imply—"

"It's fine," Victoria said, waving her hand. "They do. Whether we wish to see it or not."

Clem flashed a smile and returned to devouring the last of her spaghetti.

"Have you always..." Victoria hesitated, unsure how to phrase her question.

"Been into women?" Clem offered.

Victoria could feel her cheeks colour. "Yes."

"Yeah. Had my first crush around nine. Told my parents when I was about fifteen."

"Were they okay with it?"

"If they had a problem, they never said so," Clem said, placing her cutlery down on her empty plate. "They were more put out by the prospect of no grandchildren. My mum doesn't stop going on about it."

"Tiring, isn't it? A small part of me was almost relieved when we found out Drew was infertile, just to stop the questioning. But then the narrative shifted to me leaving him instead."

"I tried to explain to Mum that lesbians can still have children. She seemed more concerned about me doing it alone. Which I wouldn't."

Victoria chuckled at that. "It makes me laugh, people thinking kids need two parents or that a mum and a dad are like some magic formula. A kind, loving parent or parents are the answer. It doesn't matter what's between their legs if one's beating the kids and the other's neglecting them."

"Too true," Clem agreed.

"So, are kids still on the cards for you?" Victoria asked, genuinely curious.

"I've never made a conscious decision either way. The idea has simply drifted away from me as time has passed. I always thought, well, if it happens, it happens. My mum, on the other hand, would very much like an exact date."

Victoria chuckled. She could quite believe that.

"I'm sure they would make super grandparents. They seem lively enough; they must be fit to do what they do at their age."

"They are. To be honest, at the ripe old age of forty, I wonder if I would have the energy for it."

"Wait until you reach fifty," Victoria smirked. "Then your body turns on you, if it hasn't already."

"What about you? Did you date many women? Before Drew of course," Clem added quietly.

"I dated a few women over the years, but it was never anything serious. Certainly nothing that went beyond the odd kiss. By the time I felt confident enough in myself to even think about telling my parents, I was already working on the house for Drew. Then we started dating, and it didn't make any sense to share. I knew deep down they weren't the kind of people to be overly accepting of it, even if they pretended to be on the surface. They were a little too *conservative*."

Clem screwed up her face.

Victoria shrugged. "Why tell them, only to disappoint them?"

"So they know who you are at your core," Clem said, reaching forward to squeeze Victoria's hand.

It made her whole body fizz. There was only one person in the entire world who knew who she was, and she was sitting opposite her. That felt like enough for the time being.

"I'm not sure they earned that right," Victoria replied softly.

"Wow. Okay." Clem leaned back and took a sip of wine.

Victoria missed the weight and warmth of her hand. "If you don't create a safe environment for your kids to share things, do you have a right to know things?"

"That's a fair point," Clem said, glancing at her watch.

"I hope I'm not keeping you."

"No, you're not," Clem protested with a warm smile. "Sorry, I will have to go soon, though."

"You have to be somewhere? At this hour?" Victoria couldn't help but feel disappointed. She had been looking forward to spending more time with her.

"Yep. I have to bake," Clem groaned. "I can't even enjoy a quiet evening. I've got this customer who'll get annoyed if I don't fulfil her order."

Victoria grinned. "She sounds like a right pain in the arse."

"Oh, she is. She gets very stroppy about signage. You want to watch out for her."

A smirk tugged at the corner of Victoria's mouth. "Sounds like someone who lives by the rulebook."

Clem lifted an eyebrow at her, her face suddenly sullen. "Sometimes a little too closely."

Victoria took a sip of wine and eyed Clem. What did

she mean by that? *Too closely?* Yes, she liked rules; you knew where you stood with them. They made things easier, clearer. Was Clem talking about her marriage?

Victoria stood, deciding to ignore the comment, and began clearing their plates. "Do you always work this late?"

"No, I usually start my last bake about seven. Then I'm up again at six."

"Oh, sorry! I should have thought and had you round earlier."

"It's fine, honestly." Clem shrugged. "It was very nice, whatever the time."

"Can I interest you in dessert before you go? I've got cheesecake — only shop-bought, I'm afraid. I'm not a whizz in the kitchen like you."

"Sounds lovely," Clem enthused. "Yes, I can bake, but that doesn't mean I'm a great chef. That carbonara was delicious, so don't pretend you can't cook."

"I've perfected a few staple recipes over the years."

Victoria plated up the cheesecake and returned to the table. Retaking her seat, she moved the conversation back to where they had left off.

"I much prefer to finish at five and get home to enjoy a glass of wine, especially after working all hours in London. I know there is a lot of work to do at the wharf, but I unapologetically set the pace of my own life now. I've no desire to return to that sort of lifestyle, which is why I cling so tightly to the one I have."

"I can understand that," Clem said, nodding a little awkwardly. She looked like she was about to respond further but thought better of it, slipping a spoonful of cheesecake into her mouth instead.

Victoria wasn't sure if she truly understood or was just being polite. Clem knew where she stood: stuck for now, in a life she didn't wish for but couldn't quite change. Whether her comment was genuine or not, Victoria was grateful she wasn't being dragged through the wringer again, like she had been the night of the party.

"Mmm, that's not bad for shop-bought," Clem said, pointing her spoon at the cheesecake as she swallowed. "I do like the flexibility of my hours, but I miss the regularity of a nine-to-five. To know when your time is your own, you know? When you work for yourself, you end up working all hours and feeling guilty when you're not. You always assume you're not doing enough."

"Until I was full-time here, I was working four days in London, three at the wharf, and working late into the nights. My relaxation time was the couple of hours' drive between."

The memory of that relentless routine, the way she'd used work to numb herself from the mess her personal life had become, made her chest tighten. She'd soon learned that the less time you had for a life, the easier it was to ignore how much of a shit show your own had become.

"That doesn't sound healthy," Clem said. "And not working to someone else's timesheet sounds liberating, but it's not always the answer."

Victoria nodded. "And to reiterate, if you did decide to come and work for me, you really could set your hours. I'm grateful for any time you could give me. No pressure, but... can I ask what your thoughts are?"

Clem took a thoughtful bite of dessert. "I want to take the job. I just... don't think I can."

"What's holding you back? I can sense your excitement about it."

"That I'll love it as much as I think I will," Clem sighed. "Then I'll feel I made a mistake, that I followed a whim with the café and Florence — and that I failed."

"But changing direction isn't failing," Victoria protested. "You could be moving forward to something better."

"You seem to think some changes mean failure when it comes to yourself," Clem observed.

"This is a bit different to a change in a relationship, Clem," Victoria said, putting her fork down, having lost her appetite.

"Is it? Really? Change is change, surely."

"The consequences are different. You'd be closing up a business to work in a sector you're passionate about. That's not the same as me divorcing my husband and risking everything dear to me. If that happens, chances are you wouldn't even have a job at the wharf."

"Then I shouldn't take it. If I did, it would be another reason for you to keep ignoring your domestic situation."

Victoria let out a loud, frustrated huff. "Why is my domestic situation so important to you, Clem?"

Clem didn't hesitate for more than a moment. "You must know why," she whispered. "Every time I look at you, you must see."

Her words sent a pleasant shiver through Victoria's body, but her mind screamed in protest.

"It breaks my heart to see you unhappy," Clem said, reaching for her hand.

"I'm not unhappy," Victoria protested, pulling away before Clem could make contact. It was almost impossible to resist her, which was exactly why she shouldn't encourage her.

"You aren't happy. You can't be. Not about him," Clem said with a disbelieving shake of her head. "You're stuck waiting, hoping for the fairy-tale life you wanted, but it's gone, Victoria. It's already crashed down around you. You're sitting in the ashes, letting them choke you. You're trying to hold together what's already shattered, clutching broken glass that only cuts deeper the longer you cling to it. Like you said yourself, you could be moving forward to something better." She paused and drew a breath. "Sorry, I promised myself I'd try to be neutral, I really did, but it's hard to support someone when you think they're making a mistake."

Victoria took a swig of wine, annoyed that its calming properties weren't kicking in. She could really use them right about now. Everything Clem said was basically true, but it didn't feel great to hear it put so bluntly.

"Well, I'm grateful you tried," she said. "That's more than my parents did."

"Have you ever asked yourself why they kept their distance?"

"I assume they no longer care," Victoria replied with a small shrug.

"Has it ever crossed your mind that they couldn't bear to watch anymore? If all they ever asked was whether you were still with Drew, don't you think that was the thing that mattered most to them?" She leaned in slightly. "I think they were protecting themselves — and trying to protect their relationship with you. What would've happened if they'd stayed? If they kept pushing, kept trying to persuade you to leave him?"

"I would have walked away from them."

"Exactly," Clem exhaled, leaning back. "They didn't want to lose you. And I don't want to lose you either, but I also can't lie to you, so I feel I need to say all this. The people who succeed aren't the ones who never fall. They're the ones who keep getting back up. You *have* to fall to get back up, Victoria. Every step, even the failed ones, still move you forward."

"Says she who is afraid of failure."

Clem rolled her eyes. "You're more powerful than you know. You hold all the power, and yet you won't wield it. You let fear control you. Use it. Take what you want and don't accept no for an answer. There's a reason he hasn't divorced you, and it's not because he cares."

Did Drew not even care about her anymore? Did she care about him? Victoria wasn't sure.

As if sensing her uncertainty, Clem went on. "He showed you how much you mattered when he turned up late to your birthday party — with another woman waiting in the car. He's humiliating you. This isn't an agreement; it's abuse — and you're allowing it. The only person who can stop it is you. If your marriage isn't working for you, then follow your heart. Like you said I should."

She wanted to. God, she wanted to. But it wasn't that simple. Why couldn't Clem see that? She stood, pushed her chair in, and leaned on the back of it.

"I get that you can't bring yourself to hit the button, Victoria, but that doesn't mean it doesn't need hitting. Sometimes we have to rip off the plaster, get it over with. It beats sitting around festering, hoping someone else will so we don't have to feel like we're at fault or a failure. But he won't, and I bet it's because he's more scared than you are. If he was going to divorce you, he would have done it already." Clem got up and walked around the table to join her. "He's not worthy of you."

"I know that," Victoria cried out, pressing her hands against her ribs. Her insides ached with emotion.

"Then why stay?" Clem pleaded.

"Because I'm scared, Clem. Fucking scared. More so than he could ever be."

Clem stepped closer, concern softening her face.

Victoria's breath caught in her throat. "Everything was

fine until you came along," she choked out. "It was working. *My life* was working."

Clem bit her lip. "It wasn't, though, was it?" she murmured.

Victoria shut her eyes. There was a long silence, broken only by the sound of a deep and painful breath. "No."

"He's got you, and he's thrown you away. Discarded you like trash. If you were mine, I'd worship you every damn day. Hell… I will anyway."

The tears came before Victoria could stop them, hot and humiliating.

Clem reached out, gently wiping them from her cheeks, then pulled her into a hug. Victoria let out a long, shuddering breath. God, she needed that — to be held — held by Clem. She wanted to stay in her arms forever.

"I'm sorry," Clem whispered. "This has nothing to do with me. I have no right to demand anything of you."

But she was wrong; so wrong. "No." Victoria pulled back far enough to meet her eyes. "It has *everything* to do with you." Before she could lose her nerve, before doubt or common sense could creep in, she closed the gap between them and kissed her.

Clem responded with unexpected urgency, squeezing her tight, kissing her with a raw, hungry passion that made Victoria's knees tremble. Her soft, wet lips and roaming tongue sent lightning bolts through her, awakening nerve endings Victoria had thought long dead. Never before had she felt so desired by someone.

Hands caressed her, squeezing, kneading, pressing her body so flush against her that she could feel Clem's breasts against her own. The sensation made Victoria dizzy. Or maybe it was Clem's fervent tongue exploring her own, as eager and as desperate. Whatever it was, it was happening, and she didn't want it to stop.

But then a little voice crept into the back of her mind, unwelcome but quiet and insistent. *You shouldn't be doing this.* Regardless of how good it felt or how much she wanted it, she couldn't silence the voice. She was married. She'd given in. She was weak. Nothing but weak. *This isn't you; you have rules.*

She took a step back.

"Are you okay?" Clem asked, eyes full of concern as Victoria stepped away from her.

"I can't believe I did that. I'm no better than him now, am I?" Victoria said, pacing the room.

"What? Hardly! It was only a kiss."

"It wasn't, though, was it?" Victoria said, striking her fist against her heart.

"No," Clem murmured. "But it's not like we've slept together or anything."

Victoria stopped pacing and approached her. "But I *want* to, Clem. That's the point. I want you, and that makes me just like him."

"You are nothing like him," Clem urged, placing her hands gently on Victoria's upper arms.

Victoria brushed her off. "I broke my own rules."

"Rules? For yourself?"

Victoria began pacing again. "Yes. To not be like him. I promised myself I would never break my vow. It didn't matter what he did, that was his choice, but I made a vow, and I was sticking to it."

"But he forfeited his right to that vow," Clem said, trying to follow her. "You made that promise to a different man, someone you thought loved you beyond everything else. He's not that man anymore. He doesn't deserve you or your fidelity."

Victoria turned so fast that Clem had to pull back. "And you do?"

Clem took a moment to reclaim her footing. "That's not the point, Victoria," she murmured softly in response. "I don't want to complicate things."

"It's a bit late for that," Victoria snapped. "It's all you've done since you got here."

"I meant that you need to make decisions for yourself, not because of feelings you might have for me."

*Might have?* Victoria was drowning in them.

"I should go," Clem said. "But before I do, can I ask you something?"

Victoria nodded silently.

"Why did you cry at the flowers?"

Victoria blew out a breath. Trust Clem to notice that. "I like flowers," she demurred.

Clem scoffed.

Victoria took a breath, realising it wasn't going to be enough. "I like being given flowers. I liked it when *you* gave them to me. It means someone cares enough to think of me, to choose something beautiful for me. When someone stops buying you flowers, you notice. You stop feeling cared for. Wanted. That's what they mean to me: that I matter to someone. That I'm not... invisible."

"You matter to *me*," Clem said softly. "I told you before: I see you. *All* of you. You're intelligent, kind, resilient, loyal... and so very bewitching."

Clem leaned toward her unexpectedly. Victoria thought she was going to kiss her again. She tensed, ready to step back, but Clem pressed a gentle kiss on her cheek.

"Thank you for dinner," she murmured.

Victoria had to summon every ounce of strength not to pull her in. Not to feel her warm, eager lips on hers again. Her heart ached for it, urged her forward, but her brain dug in its heels.

Clem walked over to the window, slipping on her

shoes and picking up her book. She paused, looking out over the garden.

"It's such a beautiful view from here," she said quietly. "You've designed something extraordinary. Again. You always seem to curate the most beautiful things. I hope you find it within you to be as brave for yourself as you are for your work. I believe in you; you should, too." Clem turned, her expression pained. "Night, Victoria. I'll see myself out."

Then she was gone.

Victoria ran her tongue over her lips, searching for any lingering trace of Clem, a scent or a taste to connect her back to that kiss. She crossed her arms and grabbed her biceps, holding herself tightly. It had been too long since someone had held her like that, embraced her so fully, like she mattered. No, actually. No one had ever done that.

Now she knew what it felt like to kiss Clem, and she wanted more — so much more. She wanted everything with her, a life she once dreamed of and thought she had. Holding hands on long walks, lazy mornings in bed, sharing meals and discussing the day over a glass of wine. The thought of it all made her insides flutter with excitement.

Then the truth hit her like a slap.

It wasn't possible.

Or was it? Did she want it enough to tear her life apart?

With a sigh, she poured the last of the wine into her glass and slumped into her favourite chair by the window. Clem's scent still clung to the fabric, filling her nose and stirring everything back up again. If she wanted Clem, *really* wanted her, she'd have to risk it all. She'd have to divorce Drew.

Her eyes welled again. She reached for a tissue from the side table, dabbing it against her cheeks. How tragically on-brand it was to be crying into her wine. At least it was something she was well practised at.

Movement caught her eye in the neighbouring garden. Clem was heading down to the jetty, her figure framed against the dying light. Victoria took a large swig of wine, hoping it would douse the feelings inside that were warm, insistent, and terrifying as hell.

lem kicked off her Vans and slumped onto the bed with a guttural huff. Her feet ached almost as much as her heart. It had been almost a week since dinner at Victoria's house and she hadn't seen her since. Unless she counted lunchtime today, when she'd caught a glimpse of her in her office. She was sure Victoria had caught her staring and spun her chair back around before Clem could look away.

They hadn't exactly left things on a bad note — well, unless you called *that* kiss bad, which Clem didn't. Victoria might, but *she* had kissed her. Not that Clem hadn't been dying to do it since the moment Victoria opened the front door that night. She had looked so elegant in a sleeveless, knee-length, black dress that Clem's insides had fluttered.

Victoria's lips against her own had surprised and excited her so much that she kissed her back like it were their last moment on earth. It felt like it lasted forever: wrapped in each other's arms, tongues searching, fingers tingling as they explored. Victoria's guard had slipped just enough to let Clem into a world she kept to herself, and she longed to return to it.

She wasn't even sure if Victoria was ignoring her or if she was the one doing the ignoring. She wanted to give the other woman some space, a few days to process what had happened, and once she had, she hoped Victoria might reach out. But she hadn't. No visit; not even a text. Now she wondered if she should have gone to see her already, but it felt like it had been too long for it not to feel awkward.

At least she knew for certain Victoria had feelings for her, but what was she supposed to do? Step back? Step forward? She didn't want to pressure her. She already felt a twinge of guilt for the harmless flirtations she'd indulged in, knowing full well Victoria wasn't free. But she hadn't forced Victoria to do anything, and it wasn't Clem's fault if Victoria was struggling with feelings she hadn't expected. The way Victoria had hit her chest with her fist and admitted it was more than just a kiss still sent tingles through Clem's body.

She wondered whether the job offer still stood. Had that encounter ruined any chance of friendship, let alone working together beyond her supplying cakes? If so, she regretted it. Not because it wasn't wonderful — it was, possibly the most memorable kiss of her life — but because as much as she longed for her, she wanted Victoria in her life more.

"What do you think I should do, Florence? Any ideas?" She paused as though waiting to hear from the narrowboat. "No? Of course not; you're an inanimate object with no feelings or opinions, and yet here I am shaping my entire life around you."

Then there was the money she'd invested, sinking almost everything she had into her new venture. What was she thinking? Victoria hadn't offered her a full-time job, so Florence and the café weren't going anywhere. Unless she set up a marketing consultancy and touted herself for more work — that was an idea. But she'd still be living and working out of a narrowboat parked at the bottom of her parents' garden. Maybe one day she could move to the marina where Max was.

She groaned and pulled a pillow over her face. There was so much to think about, and her brain was mushy, scrambled by her feelings for Victoria, which prevented any clarity or rational thought.

That night came to mind again. Victoria's house was so warm, cosy, and inviting that she'd felt strangely at home, curled up in that armchair, gazing out over the manicured garden and the canal beyond. If she were lucky, she'd inherit Gram's old house from her parents sometime in the future; not that she wanted to think about that time. She had to think about the now. Right now, she was forty, with little to her name but a narrowboat she couldn't even sell — unless she wanted to crush her mum's spirits.

Clem leaned back against her headboard and sighed. She picked up her notepad and scanned the list of ideas she'd been jotting down for the wharf. She missed marketing — the spark of excitement when a concept landed, the buzz of a strategy falling into place, and the satisfaction of nailing the message. Logging coffees and cake sales on a spreadsheet wasn't quite comparable to measuring the results of a national campaign.

As she turned the page, the stark reality of her schedule confronted her. She'd mapped out every hour of the day, searching for pockets of time. Her mornings began at six, with baking continuing for herself and the wharf until she opened at ten. Then she sold until three, packed down, and returned to the jetty by four, when she would be able to squeeze in a couple of hours' work for Victoria before making dinner at six. Realistically, she'd have to work while eating, which wasn't a problem, but with the next bake needing to finish before bed at ten, she estimated she could give Victoria ten hours a week, if she worked five days.

It would be slow progress at that rate, but progress. Victoria had said she would take whatever Clem could offer — assuming the offer still stood. She wouldn't be petty enough to sideline the wharf's progress simply to avoid her... would she?

Clem knew that once she began working on her ideas for the wharf each day, it would be difficult to stop. She baked automatically, so she didn't need her brain for that. There were also lulls during opening hours and those rainy days giving her quiet spells. Would she start to resent her own business — if she wasn't already? Should she simply move on? There must be other towpaths to trade from. She could forget all about the wharf and Victoria and let her slip back into her perfectly miserable life. That felt like the easy option, to untie the rope and drift away, but it was the last thing she wanted.

She understood Victoria's position, why she had stagnated for years in a marriage like that to keep her world intact. Clem couldn't blame her for patching over the cracks to hold everything together. Still, it didn't stop her hoping Victoria would boot her shitty husband in the balls and tell him to do one. Not because Clem wanted Victoria to take a risk for her, but because she wanted Victoria to take one for herself.

Clem had always thought of herself as decisive. Recent events had shown her that some decisions weren't so easy to make, let alone act on. Once you had, you had to wait for your choice to either implode or work out the way you hoped. When she'd quit her job and bought Florence, it was resentment that had pushed her, years of frustration at work and the lure of finally owning something, even if it was a boat. But the grass wasn't always greener on the other side, and dreams didn't always turn into the reality you imagined. She knew that now.

The small bedroom suddenly felt devoid of air. Casting the notepad aside, Clem got up and opened the bow doors, filling her lungs with cool, fresh air as she stepped out.

She spotted Max passing on the towpath.

"Off to see Jasper?" she teased.

"I'm going to see Victoria, actually," Max replied with a tight grin. "But I might pop in on him."

"What are you seeing her for?" Clem asked, jealousy biting at her as she did.

"I'm going to ask her about that barn. I talked it over with Jasper, and he thinks it's a great idea. So did my parents."

"Tell her I sent you," Clem said, hoping to win herself a few brownie points, "and suggest a couple of months rent-free. I'm sure she'll be open to it."

"Aren't you supposed to be on *their* side?" Max asked with a smirk.

"Currently, I'm on no side," Clem replied with a loud sigh — loud enough, apparently, for Max to climb aboard, concern etched across his face.

"What's up?"

Clem couldn't help it. She launched right in. "I went round for dinner last week... and we kissed."

"Wowsers!" Max staggered back, leaning dramatically against the gunwale. "I did not see that one coming — and certainly not that glum face because of it."

"Mmm." Clem gave a noncommittal hum. "We haven't

spoken since that night. She's clearly avoiding me, so I'm doing what I can to avoid her."

"Well, that always works out well," he teased. "What happened?"

"She's married, remember? I think it hit her hard after we kissed — that she broke a vow, I mean. She said I complicated things."

"Well… haven't you?" Max said gently. "Her marriage might be far from perfect — Jasper filled me in on a few things — but she was probably happily ignoring that until you came along and kissed her."

Clem's jaw loosened. "She kissed me!"

"I bet she couldn't resist you."

Clem sniffed out a laugh, too tired to argue. "She's got these rules she lives by. Rules she sets herself for this sort of open marriage she has."

"Open marriage?" Max questioned. "Jasper thought Drew was having an affair."

Clem shook her head, realising she might have said too much.

"Some people need rules," Max said. "And if that's how she's coped through a shitty marriage, I don't think you can blame her. But hang on — if it's an open marriage, doesn't that mean she could see you?"

"It's a very one-sided open marriage, from what I can gather."

"Oh. Right." He frowned. "She can't love him, surely? He's awful."

Clem shook her head again. "No, love doesn't come into it anymore. But they're financially tied, and Victoria doesn't want to be financially untied."

Max looked up at the wharf. "Oh. Darn."

"Yep."

"I get it. You want her. But if she's not free, you have to

accept it and move on, even if you know she feels the same. Some people's lives are messy. You can't force these things; she has to come to it willingly. All you can do is be a friend, if that's possible. Either that will be enough to entice her away from the dark side, or it won't, but at least you keep her in your life."

"Isn't that worse?" Clem winced. "Being friends when all you want is to be lovers? I *know* she wants me. She even admitted she wanted to sleep with me."

Max tightened his lips and shook his head. "You have to find a way to make friendship enough."

Clem nodded, more in thought than agreement. "You know, she dropped everything last week to take me to the hospital." Noticing his concern, she added quickly, "My mum broke a finger. Victoria hung around at the hospital, then gave us all a lift home. And this was after my parents had been rude to her. My ex wouldn't have even turned the television down so I could take the call."

"Sounds like someone cares about you," Max allowed, "but divorce is a big step. Give her time. I doubt anyone could resist you for too long, especially when the alternative is her creepy husband. He gave me the right ick."

"You and everyone else."

"I'll never understand men like that. All shiny shoes and smiles. Suits filled with muscles, hunting for their next lay so they can feel like the big man. Give me a belly in a flamboyant waistcoat any day."

Clem chuckled.

"What are you going to do about the job offer?"

"I don't even know if it's still on the table," she admitted, "and yet it's all I can think about. I loved history at school and really wanted to do something around it, but I was never very good at it."

"If it was anything like my GCSEs, it was a matter of regurgitating facts."

"Yep. The only knack I have for recalling anything offhand is my recipes."

"Maybe this is life's way of bringing you back to where you wanted to be," Max suggested, "combining your passion for marketing and history in a roundabout way."

Clem chuckled. "A very roundabout way."

"Life takes its time. I've been trading here for a year, almost as long as I've been pining for Jasper. Then you show up, and within a few weeks we're thrown together — all thanks to you."

"I never thought of it like that."

Max gave her a slow grin. "Well, I'd best go see your girl."

"Ha."

"Want me to convey any messages of love?"

Clem was about to kick him in the shin when she paused. "Yes, actually. Tell her I miss her."

Max gave a small shrug; smile gone, his lips were now pressed into a line. "Okay."

She watched as he jumped onto the towpath.

That wasn't adding pressure, was it? A simple statement of fact — she missed her.

Victoria resisted the urge for the hundredth time that day to spin her chair and stare out of the window. The one time she'd done it — without thinking — Clem was at her sink, looking out. Victoria had swiftly swivelled back around. It wasn't like she was avoiding her; she just wasn't making a point of seeing her. Clem hadn't contacted her either, so perhaps she understood Victoria needed some breathing space to think. Now, though, almost a week had passed, and it was beginning to feel like avoidance.

She didn't intend to ignore Clem forever — only long enough to process that kiss and clarify some things with a solicitor, the result of which had done little to ease her concerns. He'd pointed out that the wharf was likely a business asset, not a personal one, and therefore more complicated than transferring the ownership of something like a house.

He had at least reassured her that she was entitled to half of everything. Not that she wanted or needed millions in the bank. She wanted to do an honest day's work in a place she loved and reap whatever rewards there may be. The last thing she wanted was to collapse Drew's empire, lose people their jobs again, or get accused of fleecing him — no matter what she was legally entitled to.

"Knock, knock," Jasper's voice rang out, stirring Victoria from her thoughts.

"Come in," she said, looking up from her laptop.

"Oh, dear. Why the long face?"

"I have to head to London tomorrow for an awards ceremony at The Guildhall," Victoria groaned. "I'm expected to accompany Drew."

"Swanky. Can't he go on his own?"

"No. We keep up appearances for the business, and this is one event where I need to show my face."

"Don't forget to arrive late and then leave halfway through," Jasper said, smirking.

Victoria snorted, grateful for the injection of humour, even if it wasn't funny, more a bleak reminder of what her life had become.

"Not to change the subject, but is Clem taking the job you offered?" he asked.

"I'm not sure." Victoria frowned. "It seems unlikely now."

Jasper took a seat. "Why?"

Victoria clicked the end of her pen in and out, pondering her answer — or whether to give one at all.

"Why?" Jasper asked again, his tone intrigued and insistent.

Victoria dropped her pen onto her desk. "All right?" She blew out a shaky breath and muttered, "We kissed."

"Is there a problem with that?" he asked, eyebrows raised.

"I'm married," she said flatly.

"It doesn't stop Drew."

Victoria narrowing her gaze at Jasper. Exactly how much did he know — or think he knew?

He tetched, then admitted, "I saw him kiss that young woman when he got in his car."

The word *young* made her body twitch. "Why didn't you say?"

He shrugged. "It was your birthday. I didn't want to ruin it completely."

"It wouldn't have been you ruining it," she muttered. "It would have been him, but he'd already done it."

Jasper twisted his lips. "Why have you never spoken to me about it? You didn't need to go through this by yourself. We're a team, on and off the field."

"I was... *am* embarrassed," Victoria admitted quietly.

"Why? His behaviour isn't a reflection of you."

"Isn't it?" She sighed. "I let him do it. I agreed to an open marriage, even if it ripped me apart at the time."

Jasper took a deep breath and perched himself on the corner of her desk. "And why did you agree?"

"I thought if I said it was okay for him to see other

women, it would prevent our marriage and my life from falling apart. I was probably being foolish."

"Wasn't it already broken the moment he asked if you weren't really on board with it?"

She flinched. What had Clem said over dinner about holding on to broken glass and choking on ashes? She did feel choked and lacerated. Victoria nodded, her gaze drifting over her black laptop screen.

Jasper gave her a sympathetic smile. "It doesn't make you foolish. It makes you human. None of this was your fault. You compromised yourself to protect something that should have protected you. Staying isn't failure. Surviving it and walking away… that's strength."

"I can't divorce him," she whispered.

"Why? He doesn't deserve you."

"That's what Clem said."

"And she's right."

"What if he sells the wharf? The house? They're not mine. I'm afraid he might act out of spite," she said, her voice low. "He likes to win, and people can turn nasty during a divorce. They hoard money and use it to hurt each other."

The solicitor had confirmed as much to her and told her she would need to prepare herself if she decided to go down that road.

"Yes, Drew could convert this floor into apartments and sell them off, but he can't take or destroy *us* — what we built. We could move the museum somewhere else. I know this building is your heritage, but it won't be going anywhere. He can't erase your achievement. You saved it, Vic. That won't change. The next chapter might just have to begin somewhere new." He paused, then added more gently, "This is the rest of your life. Don't waste it on him. Don't let stone matter more than living… than loving. This place will stand for centuries because of you. But how long do you have? And how do you want to spend it? Married to that swine or free to do what you want?"

"The museum has always been your domain," Victoria said, "but the building… it's what breathes life into me. It's more than just stone. The wharf gives me everything I need. I always had this connection with architecture. As a kid, I became obsessed with historic buildings, but what we've built together here is something else. It connected me to myself, to my own history, at a time when I felt like I had no future. I've restored so many buildings, brought them back to life, but this one… this one brought *me* back to life when I was at my lowest point."

"And it's time to work on your own restoration now. Rebuild yourself, piece by piece. Start living and not simply surviving," Jasper urged her gently.

"I know it's been over for years," Victoria admitted, "but I found this sort of plateau where things worked — just about — as I rebuilt the wharf and carved out a life away from him. It was working until…"

"Until Clem the Catalyst came crashing in?"

"Mmm. Something like that," Victoria said with a noisy exhale, but she could feel her mouth pulling into a smile.

"It's not our actions we should fear; it's our inactions. They're what keep us trapped. I want you to be happy, Vic, living your best life. If that means divorcing that asshole, do it. Don't worry about me. You think I want all this at your expense? Be happy. See where things with Clem lead."

Victoria raised an eyebrow at him.

"Don't give me that face. Since she moored up, you've looked at nothing else."

"Yes… I have feelings for her," Victoria admitted, knowing those feelings were only getting stronger.

"Feelings?" Jasper prompted.

"Okay," she said on an exhale. "I think I'm falling in love with her."

Jasper threw his hands up in the air. "And finally, she admits it!"

Vic sighed. "I've never met anyone who makes me feel the way she does." Goosebumps rippled over her skin at the thought of Clem. "I love her passion. She's got more substance in her little finger than Drew has in his entire body."

"It's great you feel that way about her. I'm feeling the same way about Max. We should both go for it, and we'll do all we can to keep this place." He gave her a wicked grin and held out his hand for a shake. "So, let's go into battle if we have to, and fight — together."

Victoria was about to accept his cheeky handshake when the phone on her desk rang.

"Hello? Uh-huh. Okay, send him through." She placed the phone back down. "Your young man is here to see me."

"Ah. I believe that will be about our outbuilding."

She lifted an enquiring eyebrow at him. "I assume that has something to do with Clem. She mentioned after her tour that she knew someone who might be interested."

Jasper shook his head admiringly. "She doesn't even work for us, and she's already improving our prospects."

"Mmm," Victoria mumbled. "Oh, that reminds me: She had a couple of ideas for changes in the museum, too. Really good ones."

"Oh, no doubt she has," he said with a wry smile. "I'm always happy to take advice on board. I'll leave you to negotiate." He left the room, only for his head to pop back around the door. "Please think about what I said. And Vic, I'm always here if you want to talk."

Victoria gave him a nod, already tired of talking, tired of going around in circles. What was she even going to negotiate with Max? How much longer would the wharf be within her control to negotiate over? She was feeling increasingly distant from it, like something had shifted inside her. Was it some kind of protection mode coming into play to shield her from the pain of losing it? It was all she'd thought about for the last few weeks. Perhaps the wharf hadn't saved her after all; it had simply become her captor. She wasn't sure anymore.

But she felt the time was coming; she felt compelled to find the strength and confidence to do what she'd avoided for years. Not just because of Clem, with her maddening ability to unpick every thread of restraint, but because it was hanging over her, weighing her down no matter how much she pretended it wasn't. Maybe it was time to leave the strange, suspended state she'd been drifting in since leaving London.

She had left to start over, to dull the pain of a life lost, and to escape the ghosts of hopes and dreams that no longer belonged to her. But even if she'd left, she'd stayed tethered to it all. The wharf had promised her an escape, yes, but it also anchored her — no, shackled her to her old life, a version of herself she didn't feel represented her any longer. A shadow she was too fearful to outrun.

And then Clem had appeared, all intensity and light, stirring something in her she hadn't felt since the day she first roamed the dank, empty floors of the wharf and believed it might be her salvation. Now, she was beginning to see something else. Possibility. Renewed hope, renewed dreams. The freedom to choose; to shape a future with no rules. She needed to accept losing the wharf and the house were real possibilities, but she wouldn't walk away with nothing; that much she knew.

Should she wield the power Clem seemed to think she held? Take what she wanted? If it didn't work out, she could start again. It didn't feel so scary anymore with Jasper's support, and hopefully Clem's. Losing the Primrose Hill house and gaining all that heartbreak had eventually led her to the wharf.

Perhaps the next leap might carry her somewhere even better if she could summon the confidence to take it and the courage to believe. She needed to reclaim her self-respect, set boundaries, and believe she was the main character in her own story. Like Clem had said, the end of something didn't have to mean the end of everything. It could be the start of something new. Maybe that something included Clem, if Victoria hadn't already spoiled her chances.

She might have feelings for Clem, but as Clem suggested, she needed to make decisions for herself. The trouble was it felt impossible to make any decision without considering her. She'd tried to stay away this past week, tried to be sensible, to stay grounded and to think clearly, but her body ached for Clem like a fish ached for water. One taste hadn't been enough. She wanted more.

But did she want it enough to face Drew? To bring her house of cards crashing down? He didn't love her or care for her, and he certainly wasn't driven by duty. All he cared about was money. Maybe Clem was right to question why Drew was 'keeping' her just as much as she was clinging to him.

Was it time to rip off the plaster Clem spoke of, get it over and done with? Face her losses and gains, whatever they might be?

# CHAPTER 21

*V*ictoria closed her eyes, not only to block the view of her husband, but to distract herself from where she was. She always hated using the lift, but climbing the stairs to the penthouse wasn't an option.

"What happened to your old driver?" she asked, eyes still tightly closed.

"He asked for a raise, so I fired him," Drew bragged.

Victoria's eyes shot open in alarm. "He had four kids."

"Five." He grinned smugly as he shoved his hands in his pockets. "His wife had another a few months ago. You'd think he'd have been grateful to have a job instead of trying to extort more money from me. The new driver is single and very grateful for the opportunity."

Victoria sighed inwardly at yet another arsehole move by her husband. She'd watched him all night, puffing out his chest, name-dropping, laughing at his own jokes, clapping people on the back. Clem was right about him; he'd make a great politician. Drew's effortless arrogance was second nature and utterly hollow. What was she even doing there, hanging off his arm like a devoted wife, making him look good? She wanted more than this.

Her mind drifted back to Clem. She was probably asleep by now, curled up in her comfy bed on Florence. The memory of her scent returned, floral and spicy, filling her nose from nowhere. It was so vivid it filled Victoria's mouth with the taste of her, making her chest ache. She pushed it away. It hurt too much to keep recalling that kiss, no matter how fiercely it made her burn.

The lift doors finally slid open, revealing the dimly lit expanse of the penthouse lounge. Floor-to-ceiling windows framed a dark blue sky dotted with city lights that twinkled like distant stars. The view made her knees weaken. She clicked a button on the wall control to close the blinds, then kicked off her heels.

Drew pressed his lips to a gleaming bronze award shaped like interlocking beams, mounted on a slab of polished granite. He placed it reverently on the coffee table, then shrugged off his suit jacket and tossed it onto the sofa. A small table in the corner by the window held a vast array of bottles. She watched as he filled two with whisky. She wasn't sure she needed any more, and he certainly didn't.

"Thanks for coming, Hannah," he said as he picked up the glasses.

Victoria froze. *What the hell!* Okay, he spent more time with her. Was it only natural for him to slip? What was she thinking? She was his wife — his *wife* — not some floozy he'd been screwing for who knows how long. There was her feeling guilty about kissing Clem, and he couldn't even remember her fucking name. She definitely deserved more than this.

He turned, whisky glasses in hand, and caught the look on her face. "Vic, I mean," he corrected. "Fuck! Sorry."

Walking over, he handed her a glass and sank onto the sofa.

"I kissed someone," she blurted out. God, it felt good to say it aloud.

"What?"

His tone sounded more like he wasn't listening than that he cared.

"I kissed someone," she repeated.

"Oh, right," he said slowly. "I kind of assumed you saw other people, too."

"No. I haven't. Until recently, the thought never crossed my mind. I'm not proud of what I did; unlike you, my wedding vows meant something to me. *I* wouldn't bring someone back to our home."

He sighed, as though she were a child failing to grasp a simple concept. "We were heading to Bristol for a meeting, and since we were passing by, it seemed sensible to stay. I didn't think you'd mind since you were at the spa."

"A rule is a rule. No exceptions," Victoria stated, unflinching. "I did mind. I had to wash everything. It made me feel physically sick that she'd been there. You arrived late to my party and left early. We agreed we'd show up for each other when needed — like I have for you tonight — but you couldn't do that. You even had her sat in the car waiting for you."

The look of surprise suggested he thought no one had noticed.

"Yes, Jasper saw you kiss her," Victoria growled. "Others saw you. Do you know how humiliating that was? That was another rule broken — that others don't find out."

"I thought we agreed on seeing other people," he protested. "That was how we wanted things to work."

"We did. But if I hadn't agreed, you would have done it

anyway. So, was it a choice or capitulation? At least by agreeing, I got to set some ground rules, most of which you've broken."

"What are you getting at, Vic?"

At least he finally got her name right.

"I want a divorce," she announced flatly, staring down at him as her heart pounded in her chest.

"That's a bit drastic, don't you think?" He shot up off the sofa, drained his glass, and headed back to the drinks table to refill it.

Her throat tightened at his dismissal. "We don't love each other, and we barely see each other. It's hardly a marriage."

"We can work this out, Vic," he said casually, crossing the room to her side. "We don't need to divorce. Let's start again. Come back to London. We'll sell the wharf and the house."

She knew she didn't want that — there was nothing she wanted less — and she was pretty sure he didn't want that either. There was a rattle in his throat, a slight shake in his hand, and beads of sweat on his skin. Drew wasn't fighting for their marriage; he was afraid of the consequences of it ending. The thought that he was terrified filled her with determination: She was going to get what she wanted.

"Or we could divorce," she said, standing with arms akimbo. "I'll keep the house and the entire wharf — the business and the building — and take nothing else."

He looked up. At first his tired, slightly drunken expression was inscrutable. Was he upset by her lack of emotion? Puzzled? But then relief flooded his face; to Victoria, he looked like a man getting a last-minute reprieve from death row.

"Deal." And then he put his hand out, like he expected her to bloody shake on it.

Victoria's stomach churned. Her blood boiled. How fucking typical of Drew. "This isn't one of your business transactions," she growled. "This is our marriage we're ending — a contract we made to each other."

He sheepishly withdrew his hand as she took a breath.

Clem had been right; Drew was full of fear. Scared she'd take him for half of everything. A small voice wondered if she still should, to punish him, but that wasn't like her. As much as she liked the sudden flicker of power, she didn't want revenge.

"What happened to us? What happened to you?" she said softly.

He shrugged as he collapsed onto the sofa, sloshing whisky over the rim of his glass.

"Knowing I couldn't give you — us — a child, when you so desperately wanted one. It…"

"Changed you? Yes, I noticed."

He glared at her. "Do you know what it felt like? Not being able to have kids?"

"Yes, I do," she snapped. "I knew exactly what it felt like. I was there. It happened to me, too. But that's always been your problem, Drew: You never notice anyone but yourself. It didn't only happen to you. It happened to us. And we went through it alone. I needed support, too, but it was all about you. No one ever asked how I felt. No one saw my pain."

"You should have divorced me when we found out," he replied wearily. "No one would've blamed you. I was always surprised you stuck around. I was grateful you did, though. I couldn't afford to divorce you."

"I loved you," she choked. "What else was I going to do but stay?"

"*Loved*," he sighed. "We did love each other, didn't we? A long time ago."

"In a different life," Victoria mused.

"You might not have walked out, but you did leave," he accused. "Those bloody buildings became your obsession."

"They weren't the reason I left," she replied, eyes fixed on the floor. "And they weren't the reason I didn't come back. There wasn't anything for me to come back to."

He nodded. "I guess our marriage was over a long time before I realised."

That was typical Drew, not noticing the really important things until it was too late. She wondered if that was why he'd never tried to fix their marriage — he was too wrapped up in himself to see there was a problem in the first place. But then again, she'd never spoken up, always convinced it was selfish to let others know she was hurting, too. Maybe they were both to blame. The truth was, she didn't care anymore.

"So, why now?" he asked.

Victoria looked at her feet and sighed. "I'm tired of pretending."

"You said you kissed someone. Is it serious?"

"I don't know," she said honestly, "but I'd like to find out."

She slipped her wedding ring off and placed it gently on the table in front of him.

"Thank you for agreeing," she said gently.

He stared at the ring for a moment, then gave a drunken, dismissive shrug. She hoped he wouldn't change his mind about their agreed terms in the cold light of day.

"The house is my personal asset, so I can transfer that to you," he said. "However, the company owns the freehold over the wharf. I can't hand it over so easily, but

I'm sure I can find a way to make it happen. Keep in mind that you'll be responsible for all the upkeep, including repairs, maintenance, and insurance. I strongly recommend you hire a property management company to handle it all."

Victoria nodded. It was as she suspected — at least in part, realising she would become an unwitting landlord. But at least she would be the owner of the beautiful building that felt like her very heartbeat.

"I could have my team continue what they are doing now," he offered.

"No," she replied quickly, keen to cut all ties with this man. "I'm sure I'll work it out."

He shrugged again and stared into the distance. "Hannah will want us to get married now."

"Oh," Victoria replied, unsure what the right response was. "I hope that works out for you."

"I won't be marrying anyone," he said, taking a long sip from his glass. "I thought you'd take me for everything I had… and I know for certain Hannah would. I won't give her the chance."

Victoria wasn't sure how to feel about it all. A small part of her almost felt sorry for Hannah, but the feeling faded swiftly.

If anything, she felt numb. Beneath that, she felt proud of herself for standing up for what she wanted instead of enduring a life she didn't.

"I'll go to a hotel," she said, placing her untouched glass of whisky on the table.

He spread his arms, dumbfounded. "What's wrong with the spare room?"

"I need some space." It was the truth. She needed to breathe, away from him. She wanted to be alone with her emotions, whatever they might be. She was still numb.

"I'll grab my bag and come back for the rest of my things tomorrow."

He nodded, his face unreadable — sullen or possibly just drunk. Who knew? Who cared?

She walked with purpose to the spare room, where she'd left her overnight bag. When she returned, it was to find him slumped in the corner of the sofa, eyes closed, whisky glass clutched in one hand. Approaching him quietly, she took the glass from his fingers and placed it gently on the table.

Suddenly, his hand shot out and grabbed her leg, making her flinch. He released her quickly, his arm dropping to his side.

"I'm sorry, Vic," he mumbled, eyes half lidded.

"Me too," she replied, though she wasn't sure if she meant it or was saying it to placate him. She paused, then added, "And Drew, I want the wharf. So make it happen. Or I'm coming for everything."

She levelled him with a fierce stare, then walked to the lift, slipping on her shoes, feeling like she was channelling Clem. If he didn't follow through, she was ready to fight.

As the doors closed behind her and the lightness in her body told her she was descending, she laughed. It was an uncontrollable laugh that made tears stream down her face. She was free. Free and finally in control. And for once, the downward journey didn't bother her.

Crossing the large, glass aviary and heading into the revolving door on to the street, the lightness stayed with her. The weight she'd been carrying for years had fallen away. She'd spent so long dreading this moment, only to discover it was over and done with in half an hour. Tiredness mixed with drunkenness likely helped; Drew never had much fight in him when he was like that.

If only she'd trusted herself to advocate for her own

needs sooner or realised that Drew's fear likely ran deeper than hers ever could. She placed no value on his business. It was only money to her; she had no interest in it. To Drew, it was everything, and he didn't want her taking it.

Warm tears began filling her eyes again as the revolving door ejected her into the cool air, but no laughter came with it this time. She felt angry at herself for not asking for a divorce sooner, but fear had gripped her, too, and it was hard to escape when it dressed itself as reason.

Victoria pulled herself upright and wiped the tears away. That was enough. It wasn't worth wasting another ounce of energy on the past. It was time to look forward to the future. A future she hoped would include Clem, who had opened her eyes to new possibilities, encouraged her when she'd been too afraid to move, and tried to support her even when it wasn't easy. Clem challenged her, sowed confidence in her, made her feel desired and deserving of more. She only hoped she was deserving of Clem.

When she woke late the next morning, relief settled over her and wrapped her in a warm hug. Alone in a quiet hotel room, she smiled as the sense of freedom washed over her again. Today was the first day of her next chapter. Still, a thread of sadness lingered for everything that had passed.

She stretched out a slow breakfast in her room, hoping it would give Drew time to get up and leave the penthouse. An hour later, she retraced her steps from the previous night. She punched in her PIN, and the lift took her to the top floor in just enough time for nervousness to settle in and ready her for a confrontation. There was nothing left to discuss, no need to see him again. As far as she was concerned, any further communication could be done via her solicitor.

She let out a breath of relief when she found the penthouse empty. In the bathroom, she gathered the last of her toiletries from the drawers. A few unfamiliar items sat beside them — no doubt Hannah's. Victoria briefly wondered how long Drew and Hannah would last, but the thought passed quickly. It no longer mattered to her.

Five minutes later she was calling the lift, bag in hand containing her toiletries, a few items of clothing, and a pair of shoes. She didn't want anything else; this had never felt like her home. All she wanted was to leave it behind and return to her real home. She welcomed the long drive back to Otterford. It would give her time to think, to picture the life she wanted to build.

# CHAPTER 22

Clem closed her book and dropped it heavily onto the small table in front of her with an equally weighted sigh. She'd read the same paragraph four times, and it was time she gave up. It wasn't Jasper's fault; his book was brilliant. Her mind simply wasn't cooperating after a long day. All she wanted was to enjoy the warm, early evening before the sun set and the chill crept in, driving her back inside.

Tomorrow was a day off. Emma had messaged to say the café was closing for a deep clean and wouldn't need anything. Mondays were quiet anyway, and although no rain was due, and there would be no competition, she knew she needed a break. So, there was no baking tonight, leaving her mind to roam freely. She couldn't settle it. Baking usually soothed the noise, giving her something to create and shape other than her thoughts.

She picked up her wine glass and drained it, hoping it might dull the ache in her chest at Victoria's absence. It didn't. Nor had the glass before. She missed Victoria's steady presence. Not knowing when, or even if, she'd see her again was becoming too much to bear.

She could make her a lemon drizzle. It would give her an excuse to see Victoria, and her brain something to do other than play volley with itself. Clem wanted to push her, to reach out, but she knew she shouldn't. As far as she could tell, Victoria hadn't been home all weekend. Her office light had been off at the wharf, and the house remained dark. Had she gone to London? Was she with him now?

If only she had accepted the job when Victoria offered it, then it would have been impossible to avoid seeing each other. After two weeks of wrestling with the idea, now she'd do anything to snap it up. She wanted to work for her. Around her. She'd find a way; these things couldn't be mapped out on a notepad. Life wasn't so rigid. And if it didn't go as planned, then she would keep changing and adapting until she was happy.

The sound of nearby footsteps startled her out of her chair. She wasn't expecting anyone. But seeing Victoria standing on the jetty, with a cautious smile on her face, caused her breath to catch and then release in a rush of relief.

"Victoria. Hi!" Clem couldn't have packed more excitement into her voice if she'd tried. "How are you?"

Victoria glanced down, then back up. "Can I come aboard?"

"Of course," Clem said, offering her hand out to assist. The dim exterior light wasn't much use beyond casting a glow over the table and the book she'd abandoned on it.

"Have you got any cake going spare? I haven't eaten since breakfast. The traffic back from London was a nightmare. You'd think it would be heavy going the other way, with everyone heading into the city for work tomorrow. There must have been an accident."

So, she had been right: Victoria had gone to London. But why? Clem's impatience got the better of her. She rested a hand on Victoria's arm.

"I'm pleased to see you, but I'm guessing you aren't here to tell me about the traffic. At least, I hope you're not."

"Please fetch me something sugary and" — Victoria picked the bottle of wine up and squinted at it against the light — "a glass for this, please, and I'll tell you."

Clem obliged, returning in record time with a glass and the last slice of chocolate brownie that she'd squirrelled away for herself. She sat watching, leg twitching with nerves, as Victoria devoured it, washing it down with a sip of Chardonnay.

"Thanks, I needed that."

"Why were you in London?" Clem asked, trying to steer the conversation.

Victoria exhaled. "The business was up for an award, which it won. Drew needed a wife on his arm, so I obliged."

Clem tried not to react, but the words punched her in the gut. Of course, she'd gone and played the part. The thought that Victoria might have fulfilled other wifely duties tightened her chest, making her next breaths difficult to take. Victoria wouldn't, would she? Of course not. Clem topped up her own wine glass, only halfway, as much as she desired more.

Victoria turned to face her, declining a top up of her own glass as she did.

"Look," she said softly. "I'm sorry. I shouldn't have kissed you that night. But it helped me understand how you felt. How I felt. It made me feel wanted, desired even.

That I wasn't completely invisible. It helped me see that I wasn't alone."

"You aren't alone anymore."

"I know, but as you pointed out, I was. I have been for a long time. I just couldn't admit it. I felt scared, but you gave me strength. Jasper did, too. He made me see the wharf for what it is — stone. He was right, even if I didn't want to hear it. I think I had to be willing to lose everything before I could finally *hit the button*, as you put it."

Clem shuffled to the edge of her seat, heart hammering in her ears.

"So… you *have* hit the button?" she asked, desperate to understand where things stood. Where she stood.

Victoria nodded. "Yes, I have."

Clem exhaled a deep, shaky breath and slumped back into her chair, relief washing through her. Whatever this meant for them, whatever came next, at least Victoria had made the decision. She had acted.

"And it went okay?"

Victoria nodded.

Clem leaned forward and grabbed Victoria's knee, giving it a firm squeeze. "I'm so proud of you."

"Oh." The word slipped out in a breathless whisper, her brows lifting in surprise. "No one's ever said that to me before."

"Seriously?"

Victoria gave a small, indifferent shrug. "Maybe I never gave anyone a reason to."

Clem squeezed her knee again, gently but deliberately, drawing her gaze. "Other people's emotional voids aren't a reflection of you or your achievements. Have you ever felt proud of yourself?"

Victoria shrugged again.

"Not even for what you just did?"

"Am I proud for ending my marriage?" Victoria questioned firmly.

"No." Clem fell back against her chair, letting go of Victoria's knee. "For setting yourself free."

"I'm pleased I found the strength to do it," Victoria admitted. "That I had to do it at all..." She gave another shrug, turning her head away. "Is that something to be proud of, a failed marriage?"

"Was it your failure?"

"Yes," she said simply. "I should have spoken up. I should have aired my complaints rather than swallowing them down. I had a voice, but I was too scared to use it. Too afraid to say how I was feeling. Instead, I left and hid away here, where life hurt a little less."

"Being afraid to speak isn't failure; it's a trauma response. It's not all on you. If someone has lived in an environment where they don't feel their opinion is of any value, they learn to stay quiet."

Victoria let out a soft sigh.

"Can I ask how Drew took it? And... what about the wharf?"

"He fought it," she said. "Suggested we start again; sell up here and I move back to London."

"What? Why?" Clem asked, her heart lurching. Had she misjudged everything? That made no sense. Unless—

Victoria gave her a knowing look. "You were right. He was terrified I'd take half of everything," she said with a faint smile. "He was more afraid than I was."

"Oh," Clem sighed with greater relief.

"So, he was more than happy to give me the small amount I asked for. Even tried to shake hands on it like it was a business deal."

"Arsehole."

"That he is," Victoria chuckled.

"Will you get to keep the house and the wharf?" Clem asked, needing a bit more clarification.

"Yes. The house, he said, is simpler to transfer, but the wharf is more complicated as technically his business owns it. I told him to make it work, or I'd come for everything he owed me."

Clem gave her an admiring smile. "I knew you could do it."

Victoria raised an eyebrow. "You did?"

"I trusted you'd make the right decision. You're no fool, Victoria. Your passion brought you here, and your determination made the wharf come alive again. You just needed a little push — or maybe a pull — to realise you didn't need Drew and that when you speak up for what you want, you can get it. Fear makes us irrational."

Victoria nodded, gazing out over the water. "It does, and I was full of it. Now I feel like a weight has lifted off me. I feel lighter. Ready to face the future, whatever it might bring. I only hope that it's a little gentler with me."

"Can I…" Clem hesitated, her heart thudding again. She was desperate to know what all this meant — for her, for them — but the fear of the answer caught in her throat. She took a breath, reminding herself of what she'd said to Victoria: to speak up for what you want.

"What?" Victoria asked, her hand now resting gently on Clem's leg, setting her alight. She patted it, urging her on, but it made her lose her words even more.

"I…" she faltered, struggling to articulate everything she wanted to say. "Us," she finally managed. "Might there be an 'us'? We might have only known each other for a few weeks, but it feels like much longer. I really like you, Victoria."

Victoria nodded slowly, giving one last pat to Clem's leg before removing her hand.

"I really like you, too, and I feel the same, but I need a bit of time to be me. Work out who I am. I can't make any promises right now, but I hope you'll stick around whilst I work it all out."

Clem's chest tightened. Was she saying not now? Or not ever?

As though sensing her doubt, Victoria added, "Whatever the future holds, I know I want you to be part of it. A big part. You could even say a main character. But I'm not ready yet. You were right when you said I'm grieving for the relationship I once had. I only ask for a little time to pack it away."

Clem exhaled with relief, a slow smile growing. "I can wait as long as you need. There's no rush. I'll be here." She paused, then added with a grin, "In the meantime, does that job offer still stand?"

"Yes!" Victoria enthused. "And please take it. I'm not sure I can do it without you. We already know we work well together, and it would be lovely to spend more time getting to know you."

"Organising a bit of party food is one thing," Clem said with a raised brow, "but influencing the direction of your business? Would you listen to me? Take my direction? Give me free rein?"

"Of course. I need to make it a success. I own a wharf now, and I've got a house and bills to pay."

"I want to be part of it. I want to help make it successful. Let's get numbers up, and you won't have to worry. And please, no more of this 'I'm not sure I can do it' business. Get to work and show yourself and everyone else you can make this place a success — because I believe in you. And after what you just did, you should believe in yourself, too."

"I think it will take a bit of time to build my confidence up," Victoria demurred.

"Well," — Clem grinned — "I'm always happy to help with that. I'll never get tired of telling you how great you are."

"You've done more than you know. I honestly don't think I'd have made it this far without you. I was… stagnating. But you pulled me out of it. You seem to enjoy pulling me about — like when you dragged me into the canal that day we met."

Clem's grin turned into laughter at the memory.

"You know, I had no idea that canals were so shallow." Victoria chuckled.

"I had to shout at you to stand up, remember?"

"Yes. I was rather flailing around. I seem to do a lot of that."

"You've shown a lot of confidence lately, more than you give yourself credit for. Asking me to work for you, calling out Christine… now that's leadership."

"Ugh, I don't even want to think about her again." Victoria wrinkled her nose. "I'm giving Emma the catering manager role. She's done an amazing job these past two weeks, really stepped up."

"Perfect. She'll need to be ready if we're going to increase numbers."

"How will you manage it with Florence?"

"I think I can give you ten hours a week around her."

"If we boost footfall at the café, can you keep up with cake demand — yours and ours?"

"We'll find out, won't we?" Clem ventured.

"Let's take things slow, see what works, and build from there."

"We can figure it out as we go, together," Clem suggested, wondering if they were still talking about work. "Most importantly, we keep the lines of communication open."

"Agreed. As long as we're both happy and fulfilled in what we're doing, that's what counts."

Clem shot her an affectionate smile. "You've been listening. Good. Now, first off, I want us to have an open day. The Otterford Wharf Heritage Fest. A sort of relaunch. September would give us enough time to get our ducks in a row."

"You've really been thinking this through," Victoria observed.

"To be honest, I've barely thought of anything else the last two weeks — well, except for one other thing I haven't been able to get off my mind."

She glanced at Victoria to gauge her reaction and was relieved to find her smiling. "Did Max speak to you about that outbuilding?"

"He did," Victoria said, taking a sip of wine. "He's a tough negotiator. He insisted on a couple of months' free rent to start with. Funny, though; you'd already suggested that might be a good idea."

Clem smirked and gave a casual shrug, deliberately avoiding Victoria's eye. "Well, you both win, so you're welcome. I need to check with him that he'll be ready to open then. It will be an ideal time for a grand opening. I'm also thinking of asking the landowner to allow some extra trading licences for the day. Bring a few more boats down to the wharf."

"More competition," Victoria said, arching a brow.

"More energy," Clem countered with a grin. "Otterford Wharf is the destination. The traders aren't competitors. Well, maybe one, but she'll be busy that day, so I don't think you'll need to worry. And I'm sure if you ask her very nicely, she'll keep you stocked up with cake."

Victoria laughed as Clem continued.

"You need to see the canal as an asset. It draws people in. I'll speak to the other traders, get them on board. They can help spread the word through their followers."

"I'm sure I've got a lot to learn from you." Victoria beamed. "I'm looking forward to it."

Clem shot her a warm smile. "Me too."

"By the way, Jasper was open to hearing about your suggestions for the museum."

"That's great. And I'm free tomorrow. We could start drawing up a list of what needs doing for the event."

"Nine o'clock?" Victoria said, standing and draining her glass.

Clem nodded, though she was gutted that Victoria was leaving already.

"I can give you a lift, if you like?"

"That would be great." She was reluctant to moor Florence along the towpath when she had no intention of opening. There was passive marketing, and then there was the risk of annoying customers who might wonder if or when she would be open.

"Thanks for the sugar and alcohol hit," Victoria said. "I needed it, but I'm whacked. Thanks for the chat, too."

Clem winked as she stood. "Anytime."

The smile on Victoria's lips faded quickly as she took Clem's hand, giving it a gentle squeeze. "I meant what I said, Clem. Give me time."

To Clem's surprise, Victoria leaned forward and kissed her cheek. She lingered for a second — long enough for Clem to wonder, to hope, that her mouth might drift towards her lips. The soft, hurried sound of Victoria's breathing and the brush of her finger against Clem's hand suggested temptation was teasing at her, too.

Clem eased back. "Night," she said quietly.

Victoria had asked for time, and she'd get it. It was never wise to start something with someone who'd recently come out of a relationship.

"Good night," Victoria replied, her smile seemingly appreciative as she took Clem's hand to steady herself over the gunwale in the dark.

She disappeared into the shadows, leaving Clem suspended between the thrill of possibility and a slow, twisting ache of uncertainty. How long would Victoria need? Would the time ever come when she was truly ready?

All Clem could do now was wait, give her the space she'd asked for, and trust her to come back. Trust in the strength she knew Victoria had and the strength of what was growing between them.

All the same, it was hard not to let doubt creep in and whisper that it could all slip away before it had even begun.

# CHAPTER 23

THREE MONTHS LATER

*C*lem yawned and stretched as she emerged from the wharf into the sunny, late summer morning. Union Jack bunting swayed in the light breeze as people rushed about in the courtyard, unloading items from cars before removing them. Having been baking in the kitchen since six a.m., she was grateful to find the weather mild. It was ideal for the day's event.

She had been burning the candle at both ends for the last few months, and so she was quietly relieved that summer was drawing to a close. Demand for her bakes was only growing, from the wharf and from her own customers, who were making the most of the lingering sunshine before autumn fully settled in. Soon, she could hang up her barista apron for the cold season and focus more on the wharf.

Once today was over, the pressure would ease, though

not for long. The Christmas market needed planning next. That was set to be bigger and better, and there was always more to a Christmas event. A Father Christmas had to be found, a grotto created; a corner of the café might do, and her dad would fit perfectly in the starring role. Clem pushed her ideas to the back of her mind; she needed to focus on getting through today.

Her gaze caught her mum and dad, mid-bicker over the best height to hang a banner that read *Welcome to Otterford Wharf Heritage Fest*. They had been tasked with hanging all the signage, and Clem couldn't help wondering how they would cope now they had nothing to focus on but each other.

Victoria caught her eye and smiled as she directed stallholders to their spots to set up. Hopefully, their tables would manage with the uneven cobbles; that Clem couldn't fix. Nor could she fix her aching heart.

Three months of working closely together, through lunches, dinners, and endless planning meetings, had given her the chance to watch Victoria's confidence grow and bloom. Clem's love for her had only deepened. She was still waiting, hoping that one day soon Victoria might be ready to take their friendship to a new level. She may have agreed to wait as long as she needed, but her feelings for Victoria were threatening to suffocate her. How long did someone need to move on, to heal from their past? There was no answer to that.

Realising Victoria was making her way over, Clem instinctively swept her hair back and tried to stifle the flutter of anticipation in her chest.

"Is your mum still okay to hand out leaflets?" Victoria asked.

Clem greeted her with a smile. "Yes, she's brimming with excitement. She loves this sort of thing."

"Great. Max was hoping your dad would help him in the cider barn since Jasper will be tied up with the museum."

"I'm sure he'll be eager to," Clem said, wondering if her parents would last the day.

Guilt crept in that she'd roped them in at all. With all staffing costs funnelled towards the café for the day, she needed as much free labour as she could get.

"It's going to be tough for them being on their feet all day, though." She sighed with worry.

Victoria quirked a brow. "Aren't they used to that?"

"Yes, but…" Clem twisted her lips.

"They're not children, and they *are* volunteering," Victoria reassured her. "I'm sure if — or when — they've had enough, they'll let us know."

Having her parents around more was going to take some getting used to, but Victoria was right. They were adults and more than capable of looking after themselves, even if her mum hadn't stopped asking for her help with this or that since they moved into the house.

Clem nodded and crossed her arms. Her mind had already jumped to the next task, mentally sorting through everything that she needed to do and in what order.

Victoria rubbed her forearm briefly. "What else is troubling you?" she said gently.

"A few nerves," Clem admitted. "I hope everything comes together and brings the results we need."

This wasn't just the culmination of months of work. It reflected her ability, her performance. It would show Victoria whether she could trust Clem to deliver.

"It will, I'm sure. You've worked so hard. It won't be for nothing."

"I hope you're right," Clem said, letting out a breath. She was nervous, but underlying her performance anxiety, she was mostly excited. "And just think: When today is over, we get to start all over again with Christmas." She chuckled at herself. "If we're making a weekend of it, it's going to be harder work than this. At least Max won't need so much of my time. He's really starting to grasp the whole marketing thing now."

"Good for him." Victoria frowned at her with friendly concern. "Have you thought any more about your schedule? The offer's always open to work full-time or increase your hours. You're more than paying for yourself. You've already made a difference, and today's going to prove that."

Clem sighed. She had thought about it. In fact, it was all she'd been thinking about, sweating through coffee orders and cake slices in the sauna Florence had become during the summer months. She opened her mouth to reply, then shut it again.

"Be honest," Victoria chided. "We agreed on open communication, remember?"

Clem did remember.

"I think… I want to give up the business."

"Oh. Okay." Victoria nodded.

"I'm just…"

"Having a bit of trouble letting go?" Victoria finished for her.

Clem nodded, knowing she would understand.

"The weather is already beginning to change," Victoria observed, glancing up at the sky. "The air's crisper, and the leaves are turning yellow. Transition at your own pace; it doesn't have to happen overnight. Give yourself time to adjust."

Clem nodded again. She knew it made sense. She really did.

"Florence will always be your home, and you'll still be supplying cakes for the café."

That was true, and baking was something she never wanted to give up.

"If I'm not trading, though, I can't moor up in Florence. There's a clause in the agreement."

Victoria shrugged. "Use the kitchen here. Walk to work — or I can give you a lift."

Clem gave her a tentative smile. "That would be great. Thanks."

Having become quite familiar with the wharf's kitchen by now, she found the space really worked for her. It had most things she needed, and the rest she would borrow from Florence. A twinge of betrayal caught her at closing the narrowboat café, but beneath it lay more excitement.

The last three months had been relentless, juggling the two jobs. There was no harm in trialling working full-time for the wharf over the winter, she told herself. She was simply adapting to her environment; that was all. The bonus was that she'd get to spend every day with her favourite person. If it didn't work out, she could go back to her business in the spring.

"We'll make it work," Victoria said, patting Clem's shoulder.

*We.* Clem flashed her a soft smile, but it faltered. When would they be a *we* in every way? Would they ever be?

Her mum and dad joined them, having agreed on the banner height — or, as Clem thought more likely, one of them had given in. Her dad, no doubt.

"It's a great place you have here, Victoria," he said, looking up at the wharf. "I can see why Clem was so keen to work here."

"We were reading the information boards in reception

about your family history," her mum added. "I didn't realise your ancestors built it."

Victoria nodded. "Yes. I consider myself very lucky to have it and to have Clem to help me. She's a real asset."

Clem rolled her eyes playfully at Victoria as her parents beamed with pride.

"The signage is all up," her mum said. "So, what's next?"

Clem was grateful for her parents' enthusiasm — for however long it lasted.

"Dad, you're helping Max in the cider barn today, if that's okay."

Her dad's eyes lit up with delight. "More than okay."

"Mum, I'll take you to meet Max's mum. She's helping you hand out leaflets."

"Thank you both," Victoria said warmly. "I really appreciate you coming to help."

"We wouldn't miss out," her mum said with a smile. "It's all Clem talks about."

A group of people in historic costumes were making their way around from the car park and into the courtyard. Clem nodded in their direction. "I'll leave you to deal with them, Victoria."

"Oh, wonderful, I was beginning to worry they weren't coming." She gave Clem's arm one last pat. "I'll see you later."

"Who are they?" Clem's mum asked as the three of them strode off across the cobbles.

"They're a local theatre company. Victoria invited them to perform some re-enactments of people who worked at the wharf."

Clem recalled how enthusiastic she'd been when Victoria first suggested the idea. The troupe looked impressive all dressed up. She hoped they'd bring an old-world charm to the wharf, telling stories of the lives once lived here. Some were fictionalised, but others Victoria had unearthed from original records held in the town archives.

She led her parents to the barn with its recently installed sign above the doors: *Otterford Cider Barn.*

The large, wooden doors were wide open, revealing a transformed space. Assorted stainless steel equipment and benches filled the floor, along with what looked like a small bottling machine. The air was so rich with the sweet, sharp tang of fermenting fruit that Clem's mouth watered.

"Hey, Clem," Max said from behind a table lined with beautifully presented bottles and filled gift boxes. An older couple stood beside him. "Meet my parents—"

"Graham and Helen Frost," his dad said, stepping forward.

"Nice to meet you both, and these are mine, Tom and Barbara Wentworth."

Everyone exchanged nods and warm smiles.

"Clem has the boat moored next to mine," Max said to his parents.

"The fabulous cake maker!" Helen said. "We've heard plenty about you. I'm hoping to taste one later."

"Well… I can bake a cake or two." Clem laughed, a little heat rising in her cheeks.

"I understand I'm helping you for the day, Max," Clem's dad said, picking up a bottle from the table and casting an eye over it.

Max nodded. "If you don't mind. That would be great, thanks. It's mainly handing out samples with Graham."

"I promise not to drink them all. Although this stuff looks good," he replied, admiring the translucent amber liquid in the clear bottle.

"It is," Graham confirmed.

"That's our strong vintage cider, The Bodice Ripper. And this is our traditional cider, Hard Pressed," Max said, showing him another. "Then we have our medium-sweet, Juicy Squeeze, and our light, refreshing A Little Tart."

Clem picked one up and admired the clear and concise label, noting it was a more reasonable five per cent alcohol now that it was no longer a home-brewed scrumpy. They'd done a fantastic job with the branding, combining clever corset terminology, thanks to Jasper's suggestion.

Right on cue, Jasper waltzed in carrying a large, brown box.

"Don't fear, I'm here," he announced, setting the box down and tearing off the tape.

He patted Graham on the shoulder and kissed Helen on the cheek.

"I was beginning to worry," Max said, looking at his watch.

"These look great," Clem said, pulling a leaflet from the box as it sprang open.

"My love insisted on changing his mind a dozen times before finalising the design, didn't you?" Jasper said, kissing Max on the head as he clocked Clem's parents.

"Oh! Jasper, these are my parents, Tom and Barbara."

He shook their hands. "Congratulations on producing one of the best — if not *the* best — marketing guru in the world. Not to mention baker!"

"Oh, shush, Jasper." Clem smirked. "Shall we get some work done?"

Everyone muttered their agreement.

"Dad, I'll leave you with Max. Helen, do you want to come with me? You are on leaflet duty with Mum."

"Of course. Do you live locally, Barbara?" Helen asked

as they followed Clem out of the barn and across the courtyard.

"Yes, we moved in a few weeks ago. We were having some renovations done, but it's all finished now."

"And are you from around here originally?"

"I grew up here," Clem's mum replied, "but drifted away — as you do."

"Oh, I know. I was the same. Then you eventually drift back. We returned to look after my mum. If you're interested, I've started a women's group. We meet once a week and do something in the local area. It could be something like a nature walk, a litter pick, or even a drawing class. You should join us."

Clem smiled, pleased her mum might have made a new friend.

"I'd like that, thanks," she replied.

"Clem, Max suggested I talk to you about using the café as a meeting place," Helen said.

"Of course. I can reserve some tables for you or cordon off an area if you prefer a bit more privacy. Ask Max for my number and let me know in advance."

Helen beamed. "Thanks."

"Jasper and Max make a cute couple," Clem's mum said to Helen.

"Don't they just?" Helen replied. "We're so pleased he found someone like him."

"It's a shame you can't find love here yourself, Clem," her mum said pointedly.

Clem caught Victoria's eye as they passed by her at the wharf door. Perfect timing, as always, from her mother. She was sure Victoria would have heard.

"You *have* to have one of Jasper's tours, if you haven't already, Barbara," Helen said. "He's such a natural orator, and so knowledgeable about corsets."

"Oh, I will!" she said.

Clem didn't miss the broad smile lighting her mum's face as she took a pile of leaflets from the reception desk. She split them between the two women.

"Ten per cent off at the café on your next visit or twenty per cent off with every guided tour," Helen read from the leaflet. "That's generous."

"We need to drive people in over the next few months," Clem said, "so hand them to anyone who will take one. Take some for your group, too, Helen. I've already distributed a load to the local shops and supermarkets around town."

"Thanks, I'll do that. I saw a video on Facebook about today. It was very well done."

Pleased to hear it after the amount of work the video had taken, Clem thanked her and then checked her watch. It was nearly ten.

"We'll be opening in a minute. If you could each take a gate, and once things quieten down, have a wander around and make sure no one has been missed."

As they stepped into the courtyard, she spotted Jasper heading to the public gate from the car park, ready to open it. Her mum joined him whilst Helen continued with her to the other gate.

Although the empty spot where Florence was usually moored momentarily hit Clem in the chest, the bridge and towpath were teeming with people; Clem had never seen it so busy. Judging by the smile on Victoria's face as she joined them, she hadn't either.

She looped her arm through Victoria's and squeezed it, pulling her closer. "We did it."

"You did it," Victoria replied. "None of this would have happened without you."

"This was a team effort, and you know it," Clem

insisted. "An idea is nothing until it's implemented, and you and I did this together."

Victoria rolled her eyes playfully and gave a conceding shrug.

"Go on then," Clem urged. "Don't keep them waiting."

Victoria stepped forward and opened the gate. Together, they stood back and watched as hordes of people streamed in, Helen handing them leaflets as they passed. Now it was time to hope and pray there'd be no drama or incidents.

By the time lunchtime passed, with a relieving lack of either, Clem found herself back in the kitchen, cooking up another batch of scones and chocolate brownies to the rhythm of an overworked dishwasher. Cakes would take too long to mix, bake, cool, and decorate, so she'd opted for something quick and easy for the event.

"There you are," Victoria said, appearing in the doorway. "I've been looking all over for you."

"I'm just topping up a few things," Clem called over her shoulder. "We were running low. I don't want anyone arriving later to find nothing left."

"You are diligent," Victoria said, casting her eye over the cheese scones cooling on a rack.

Clem beamed at the compliment. "Is everything going okay out there?"

"Yes. I came to give you something," Victoria said, stepping closer and letting the door shut behind her. "I was going to wait until later, but I couldn't wait any longer."

"Okay. What is it?" Clem asked curiously, noticing Victoria had nothing with her.

Victoria moved into Clem's space, making her suck in a breath. She placed her hand gently on the side of Clem's face. "This." Her eyes were intense as she guided Clem's face toward her own, and then she closed the distance until their lips met.

Clem melted into her, unable to do anything but surrender. Her mouth was eager, her tongue even more so, as they kissed deeply.

"Oh, wow," Clem breathed out as Victoria took a breath and dove back in.

Victoria was taking what she wanted — *finally* — and Clem wasn't going to deny this woman anything. The force behind Victoria's kiss reminded Clem of that evening at her house. Clem had matched her energy, kissed her as fiercely as Victoria was kissing her now — almost knocking her backwards.

When they broke apart for air, Clem stepped back toward the island, pulling Victoria with her. She tucked her arms around Victoria's waist, holding her tightly, never wanting to let go again. Their lips locked, making Clem wish the world would disappear right then and leave her with the warmth of Victoria's mouth to enjoy forever.

"Clem!" Her mum's voice called out from across the kitchen. "Oh." She looked them up and down, eyebrows knitted in surprise as they pulled apart. "Aren't you married, Victoria? To a man?"

"Divorced — or at least in the process," Victoria replied matter-of-factly, her cheeks lifting into a smile just long enough to make her point. She turned to Clem, pressed a quick kiss to her lips, and whispered in her ear, "We can resume this later. We have lots to talk about, but now probably isn't the right time. Oh, and I'm not apologising this time."

"Okay," Clem stuttered, still in shock that Victoria had swept in and kissed her, not to mention that her mum was still glaring at them.

Victoria left the kitchen, leaving behind an awkward silence. It didn't last long.

"I thought you said she wasn't a lesbian," her mum said, drumming her fingers on the worktop.

"I didn't say that," Clem said, "and she's not, as far as I am aware."

"How can she not be? Was that little display not evidence enough?"

"Kissing a woman doesn't make someone a lesbian, Mum," Clem said, rolling her eyes.

Her mum shook her head. "I'll never understand the younger generations."

"It has nothing to do with any generation, Mum."

She wanted to point out that just because her mum had never bothered to educate herself on these matters, it didn't mean her ignorance was acceptable. She refrained, tempting as it was.

"Anyway, her sexuality is none of your business."

"It is," her mum countered, "if she's courting my daughter."

"Courting?" Clem chuckled at the use of the antiquated word. "I don't know what we are yet, Mum, but I *do* know she's the best thing that's ever happened to me — as is this place."

Her mum fell silent for a moment before finally saying, "Then I'm happy. Even if she is a little old for you."

Clem swallowed her anger, refusing to rise to her comment. "What did you want, Mum?"

"Helen and I have run out of leaflets."

"There are more in a box behind reception."

Her mum nodded and left the room.

Clem let out a long breath. She wasn't going to let her mum's interruption — or her ignorant comment — get her down. Victoria had kissed her again. *Kissed* her and wanted to talk. It would be a welcome change to speak to Victoria about anything other than signage, marketing copy, stall layouts, or contingency plans. The thought of finally having a conversation about *them* sent a rush of adrenaline through her, which drowned out the flicker of lingering frustration at her mum.

She turned her attention back to filling the trays with rich, chocolatey batter and slid them into the oven. Heading out to a thrumming café, she checked in on Emma at the counter.

"Set a timer for twenty-five minutes on your phone," she instructed.

Emma gave an enthusiastic thumbs-up. She seemed to have everything under control. Packaged sandwiches and rolls had been the right call for fast, efficient service, and the new staff were already easing the pressure.

As Clem headed outside, Max passed her on his way in, a broad smile stretching across his face.

"How's it going?" she asked.

"Great. I have a cider barn, I'm making proper cider, and Jasper's asked me to move in with him."

Clem clasped his shoulder. "That's amazing! Congrats."

"It's all thanks to you."

"Well..." She shrugged one shoulder. "I might have sown a seed or two, but you watered them. What will you do about your boat?"

"I'll transfer the vinyl into the barn in the next few weeks, now that everything's set up in there, then get it sold."

"Wow. Big step."

He nodded.

"I have news, too," she added.

"Tell me?" he said, eyes glinting with interest.

"I'm going to be working here full-time at least through the winter. I can always go back to Florence in the spring, but we'll see. Oh, and… Victoria just kissed me in the kitchen."

He nudged her. "What! Leave that juicy highlight until last, why don't you? I'm so pleased for you. The best things in life are worth waiting for."

"Well, it's early days, and we have a few things to talk about… Also, my mum walked in on us."

Max howled with laughter. "Well, I hope you weren't planning on keeping it a secret?"

"No. I don't think so." Clem chuckled.

"I'm happy for us both," he said, slipping his arm around her shoulder. "To think only a few months ago we were both single boat traders. Now we're both spoken for and living the dream. How far we've come."

"Okay, enough with the sentimental bull crap," she said, shrugging him off with a chuckle.

"Yeah, fair enough. Back to work. I only escaped for coffee. I'm glad Emma's changed it, though my bank account is less than happy. See you later."

He strode off into the café, leaving Clem with a warm glow. She was so happy for Max; he deserved to find love and have his business dreams fulfilled. Having been the one to guide him in promoting his cider, she'd seen firsthand how hard he worked the last few months in preparing the barn, installing the equipment, and somehow producing, bottling, and branding four ciders in time for today's launch.

As for herself, she was ready for a new chapter. There was still so much to do here. Preparations for today's fest had eaten into the few hours she could spare the wharf over the summer months, leaving her barely any time to start on her wider plans for it.

She was eager to start baking in the wharf kitchen, too, though a twinge of guilt lingered over leaving Florence and her business behind. It was the right thing to do, and she wasn't abandoning her completely; Florence was still her home.

Most of all, she was looking forward to working alongside Victoria every day and watching their relationship unfold. Now she needed the day to end so she could be alone with Victoria... and kiss her again.

Victoria had left the kitchen feeling like a naughty schoolgirl caught in the stationery cupboard. It brought amusement to her lips; the thought of the kiss softened it into a satisfied grin. It was something she'd been thinking about doing for days, maybe weeks, if she was honest, but the right moment had never quite presented itself.

Today, with the wharf full of people enjoying the place she'd put so much of herself into, she felt a joy she couldn't hold back. She had to find Clem to show her how she felt.

Before heading back outside, she slipped into the museum and hunted down Jasper. She found him finishing up a chat with a group of women who were promising to book a tour.

"How's it going?" she asked as they dispersed.

"Busy," he said with a tired sigh. "Tours are booked out for the next two months."

"That's great. Our passion project might be flourishing into a fully fledged business."

"Let's hope so," Jasper said, his eyes suddenly narrowing at her. "You've got a bit of brownie—" He reached over and wiped her cheek. "How did that get up there?"

Victoria's face burned as she pulled back and then wiped it herself. Was he teasing, or did she really have chocolate brownie on her face? A small, brown smudge on her finger revealed the truth.

"Oh… well, they're so delicious."

Jasper levelled a look at her, one she knew meant she wasn't getting away with anything.

"Okay, fine. I kissed Clem," Victoria said, throwing her hands in the air.

"Finally! I was wondering when you two were going to get it together."

"There was the small matter of my recent break-up."

"Break-up?" he smirked. "Don't you have to actually be together to break up?"

Victoria narrowed her eyes at him, and he held his hands up in mock surrender.

"We should double-date," he said, still grinning.

"Give us a chance to work things out first," she protested. "I just kissed her! We've still got things to discuss."

"Discuss? Like what, who is having what side of the bed? You love her, and she *indefatigably* loves you. Have you not seen her pining these past months, like a lonesome puppy?"

"Hmm," Victoria replied. "You better go…" She nodded at a group of women all holding his book. "I think your fans want your autograph."

"Will my fame never end?" Jasper said, spinning on one foot and hurrying off to greet them.

Now alone with her thoughts, Jasper's claim rushed back: Did Clem love her?

Victoria had seen the way Clem looked at her when she

thought no one was watching; the look was full of feelings clearly held back. Then there was the careful distance she kept, even as her fingers always seemed to find Victoria's arm or hand under the guise of a casual touch. The way her voice softened when she said her name. Clem had pulled back just enough these past months to give her the time and space she needed, but the warmth and desire in her eyes had always remained.

Had she fallen in love with Clem?

That question had been answering itself for weeks now, in the stir beneath her ribs, in the ache she felt when Clem wasn't nearby. She might have been packing away her past, but her future had been quietly building itself inside her. It was there in the nervous energy she had before they were due to meet, the flutter she tried to suppress when their eyes caught for too long. In the way she took Clem in every time she entered a room. How she inhaled a little more deeply when Clem passed, hoping to catch her scent. How she grabbed Clem's arm or hand at every opportune moment, just to have some physical contact with her.

It didn't feel like falling. It felt like finding something she hadn't realised she was missing. Something that made everything else quieter. Simpler. And still, it overwhelmed her sometimes.

She left the museum and went to her office, in need of five minutes down time away from the bustle of the day. As she was about to close her office door Clem appeared, and that familiar flutter rose in her chest once again.

"Ah, I've been looking for you," Clem said, stepping in "Some people want to speak to you."

"More?" Victoria groaned. "I've already done three press interviews." Her tone softened. "It was a great idea to invite them, though. You really are very clever." She pressed herself closer to Clem and took her hand.

Clem smiled at the compliment, but her voice held a note of caution. "Err… I don't think they're journalists."

An elderly couple appeared in the doorway.

"Oh — Mum. Dad. What are you doing here?"

"They're your parents?" Clem whispered.

"Mmm," Victoria murmured, instinctively stepping away from Clem — only to realise too late she was still holding her hand. She was about to let go when a voice in her head reminded her that she was fifty years old. She didn't need or want their approval. Not anymore.

Her parents' eyes dropped to their clasped hands as they cautiously entered the room. Surprise flickered across their faces, but it quickly faded, almost turning into tentative smiles.

"We thought we should come and see what you've done with the place," her mum said gently.

"Why now?" Victoria asked, not unkindly, but still in a pointed way. She figured she was at least owed that, after many years of silence.

Her mum hesitated. "We missed the grand opening…" She looked down.

Her dad stepped in to take over. "But when we saw this event advertised on Facebook, it felt like the right time to come and see you. We've always kept an eye on things from afar, and we're proud of what you've achieved. Aren't we, love?"

He glanced at Victoria's mum, who nodded.

"We wanted to see you, regardless of…" She looked at Victoria's and Clem's hands again. "It's been too long. All we ever wanted was for you to be happy," she said, her voice almost pleading. "We wanted more for you than you had… with him. A family, for one thing. Not for us, but because we knew how much it meant to you. You were always so adamant that you wanted children. When Drew couldn't give you that, it was an opportunity to leave him."

Victoria sighed. It seemed they were back there again.

"But you were stubborn," her mum said gently, "and we knew we had to let you live your life the way you wanted. So rather than stand by and watch it unfold, we stepped back — to protect all of us."

Victoria's eyebrows rose. They had only ever wanted her to be happy. To them, that happiness hadn't looked like staying with a man like Drew.

"We're sorry if our pushing ever made you dig your heels in further. Or if we made the wrong decision by leaving and not trying to find a better way to support you. You were always so determined to make your own choices." A smile flickered on her mum's lips. "Even when you were little, you wouldn't let anyone choose your clothes. You were so confident."

Victoria remembered. When had that confidence faded? When did she begin to doubt herself so much?

Her mum seemed to read her thoughts. "You changed with him. Always standing behind him, letting him take the spotlight. He drained you. Watching it happen broke our hearts." She paused, then added, "So you see, that's why we had to put some distance between us — to try to preserve the remnants of our relationship with you. We hoped you'd make the right decision eventually. And it looks like you have moved on." She nodded towards Victoria's and Clem's joined hands. "Who's this?"

"Oh, erm—"

"I'm Clem," she said, stepping in smoothly. "I work here, and well…" She lifted their clasped hands slightly. "As you can see, I'm a little more than an employee."

To Victoria's surprise, her mum smiled and glanced at her dad, who smiled back.

"And are you happy, Vic?" he asked.

Considering they hadn't even had a proper conversation about the kiss in the kitchen, she hesitated. Clem gave her hand a small, reassuring squeeze. She looked at her, finding her beaming, not only with pride, but with certainty, like she already knew the answer and was simply waiting for Victoria to say it out loud.

"Yes. Yes, I am," Victoria found herself answering, and she knew that it was the truth.

"Then I'm happy for you," her mum said, looking around her. "Maybe you could show us around the wharf?"

"I'll leave you all to it," Clem said. "Take your time. I can see to everything. It was lovely to meet you…"

"Oh, Mary and Ralph," Victoria's mum said.

They both gave Clem a nod of acknowledgment as she stepped away.

"She seems nice," Victoria's dad said as soon as Clem was out of earshot.

"You don't have a problem with her being a woman?" Victoria asked, carefully watching their faces. She needed to be sure they weren't simply being polite in front of Clem.

"No. Should we?" he said, his tone soft but honest.

Victoria shrugged. "I would hope not. It's early days, but… this is who I am now."

There was a brief pause before her mum asked cautiously, "Can we ask what happened to Drew?"

"I'm divorcing him. I will get the house and the wharf," Victoria informed them, happy in the knowledge it was now all formally agreed between Drew's solicitors and hers.

"Good," her dad said with a relieved smile. "I'm glad you got something out of it."

"Only what I worked for. I didn't want anything else."

They both nodded, their expressions unreadable.

"So, my great-great-grandfather built all this, did he?" her dad asked.

"Yes, let me show you more," she said, leading her parents out of her office. "All the floors above are private apartments now, but we have a museum and café-event space as you no doubt saw. Clem does all the baking for us as well as all the marketing."

Her comment seemed to meet with their approval as she led them into the busy café and through to the museum. To her relief, there was no further mention of Drew, and to her surprise, there was a genuine interest in what she'd built and created in the space. Her parents asked questions, admired details, and listened with the kind of attentiveness she hadn't realised she'd been craving. She felt proud to finally show her parents the culmination of years of hard work.

She'd spent so long believing their absence meant indifference. Now she knew differently, even if Clem had told her as much. They hadn't left because they didn't love her. They'd done it because they did; because it hurt too much to witness her pouring herself into a life that had been draining her.

Now she wished she'd left Drew years ago and saved herself from the slow erosion of who she was. But maybe she hadn't been ready then. Maybe she had needed to walk every painful step of that road to become the woman she was now. Clem's arrival hadn't just offered Victoria another chance at love; she had reminded her of who she was, of her strength and value when she'd forgotten. She wasn't lost in someone else's story anymore. She was finally writing her own.

Her parents' visit was brief; having made a day trip of

it and wishing to return home before dusk. They'd promised to stay in touch and even suggested Victoria visit them in the Lake District to talk some more. She was cautious in her response, saying only that she would think about it. Although the intent behind their absence was finally laid bare, the wound it left wasn't so easily healed. She understood now, but understanding didn't erase the years of distance between them. It would take time to process what had always felt like abandonment.

When she later emerged from the wharf, the energy of the day had dissipated. Stall holders were packing up, and the last of the visitors were leaving the barn with bottle carriers laden with cider. She spotted Clem on one of the picnic benches, taking what looked like a well-earned rest with an almost empty glass of cider.

Sitting beside her, Victoria said, "I hope it works out for Jasper and Max's little cider enterprise."

"Max certainly couldn't have asked for a more enthusiastic investor," Clem replied with a laugh.

Victoria reached out and rested a hand on top of Clem's. "Can I give you a ride home? Specifically, my home. We should talk — and by God, do I need a glass of wine after today."

Clem placed her other hand over Victoria's. "In that case, how can I refuse?"

At that moment, Clem's parents appeared beside them with Helen and Graham, whom Jasper had introduced her to that morning.

"We're all heading to the pub for something to eat if you'd both like to join us?" Clem's mum offered. "Max and Jasper are joining us, too."

Victoria glanced at Clem, hoping she'd decline. She desperately wanted to get her home and kiss her again.

"No, thanks," Clem said. "We're done in. I'll grab a lift back with Victoria; work stuff to discuss, you know."

"We know," Tom said with a cheeky wink.

"I can't thank you all enough for helping out today," Victoria cut in quickly, sparing Clem the need to acknowledge or reply to what her dad had said.

With murmurs of 'you're welcome', the four of them wandered across the courtyard to the bridge.

Victoria nudged her shoulder into Clem's. "See? They survived. And even made new friends, by the looks of it."

"I hope so. I need them kept occupied."

Victoria stood and held her hand out to Clem. "Shall we head back? Emma's locking up the site for me."

Clem took her hand, and Victoria pulled her to her feet.

"I need a shower," Clem said, wafting her T-shirt out from her sticky body.

"Me too. I need to wash the remnants of chocolate brownie off my face."

"Brownie?"

"I think when we kissed, there must have been a transfer," Victoria said, as they walked around to the car park. "Jasper noticed it."

"Oh." Clem smirked. "We haven't been very subtle, have we?"

"No."

"How was your mum about it?"

"She was Mum." Clem shrugged.

"At least that's a known quantity."

Clem nodded. "A very well-known quantity."

Ten minutes later, after discussing the finer points of how the day had gone, they pulled up on Victoria's driveway.

"Why don't you freshen up first and then come over?"

Victoria suggested as they got out of the car. "Spaghetti bolognese suit you?"

"Yes, thanks. I'm starving," Clem replied eagerly, backing away down the drive. "See you soon."

Victoria rushed inside, realising she should have set a time. She had no idea how long she'd have to shower and change, quickly freshen up the house, prep dinner, and pour a glass of wine to help settle her nerves.

# CHAPTER 24

Clem rang the doorbell, her pulse quickening as she eagerly waited. She hoped she'd given Victoria enough time to shower. Impatience had won out, though, and she ultimately couldn't stay away longer than thirty minutes to see her again. A quick glance down at her tight chinos and baggy T-shirt made her wonder if going braless had been wise. Either way, it was too late, and nothing could persuade Clem to put one on right after her shower.

When Victoria opened the door, Clem's gaze dropped instantly to the navy-blue, ribbed vest top, which left no doubt she'd made the same choice. Her nipples strained against the fabric like ripe berries, making Clem's mouth water at the thought of seeing them bare.

"Hellooo." Victoria tilted her head with a knowing smile, pulling Clem's gaze to her eyes.

*Shit.*

"Sorry. You're a little distracting," Clem said, opting for the honest route.

Victoria's low, sultry chuckle made Clem's body tingle and legs weaken. As she stepped inside, Victoria moved to block her path, slipping a hand around Clem's side, fingers grazing the side of her breast.

Clem inhaled a sharp, quiet breath.

"You are a little distracting, too, you know," she murmured, her thumb reaching around and rubbing Clem's erect nipple.

*Oh fuck.* Her head reeled while her body threatened to melt into a puddle.

Victoria's smile softened as she stepped closer. She smelled divine as usual.

Clem tried to inhale her scent, but her breath caught in her throat when Victoria's lips found hers — soft, warm, achingly gentle.

In all the ways Clem had imagined tonight unfolding, having this happen before she'd even stepped fully inside hadn't been one of them. She hadn't dared to dream it. Ending the evening with a single extra kiss would have satisfied her. To have her nipple teased on the doorstep and to be kissed like that, with such hunger and tenderness, made her heart pound hard. It wasn't only desire; it was promise.

Victoria drew back. "Come through to the kitchen," she said casually, as if she hadn't just kissed Clem's face off and robbed her legs of strength. Clem slipped off her shoes, drawing deep breaths as she steadied herself against the wall.

"Is red, okay?" Victoria asked, lifting the lid on a pan of bubbling spaghetti to check it. "I just opened a bottle for the bolognese."

"Yes, thanks," Clem answered as she entered.

Victoria filled a glass with deep, plummy wine and slid it across the worktop to Clem as she settled onto her usual stool. She'd been to Victoria's house often enough over the last few months to feel at home — though tonight, she hoped it would be all personal, no business.

"I think we could call that a successful day," Victoria said, taking a sip of wine.

*Okay, maybe some business, then.*

"Max texted to say he sold out, and I know the café did, too," Clem said, lifting her glass to mirror Victoria's. "Those actors you hired really added to the whole atmosphere. I listened to one telling a group of horrified children about her long working hours and how much pay she got."

"Yes, they were excellent. Oh, that reminds me: The theatre company asked if they could hire the courtyard for some plays next year."

"Seriously? That paid off then! How much do we charge for courtyard rental?"

Victoria's lips pressed together as she gave Clem a blank look. "I'd better work that out. Museum tours are booked solid for the next two months, too."

"Brilliant."

"You are," Victoria said, clinking her glass against Clem's and making her blush. "None of this would have happened without you. We wouldn't have the Otterford Cider Press or cake worth queueing for in the café."

"Emma's been doing a great job," Clem said, ignoring the compliment. "The winter menu she's pulling together looks delicious."

"It is. I'm so glad I took a punt on her and that Christine resigned. I was furious with her at the time for leaving me in the lurch, but I can't imagine how today would've gone with her running the café."

"Just think: If Christine hadn't resigned, you wouldn't have needed me. We might never have spoken again."

Victoria grinned as she stirred a steaming saucepan of

bolognese. "I think our paths would've crossed eventually."

"True. You never could resist my lemon drizzle. You'd have been back, queuing at my hatch."

"Says she who was always gazing out her window in my direction."

"My sink looks straight out onto your office window. I couldn't help it," Clem protested playfully. "And anyway, who could resist staring at a beautiful woman instead of a sink full of dirty mixing bowls?"

"Oh, well, I see. When you put it like that, I suppose *you're welcome*." Victoria winked, then drained the spaghetti. "Let's eat."

"I'm ravenous. It's been a long day," Clem said, taking their glasses over to the table.

"It has, but a genius idea of yours, despite all the work."

Once they'd eaten, they moved to the sitting room, where the large windows welcomed the last of the evening light. Clem sat in what had become her usual spot on the sofa in the spacious room. The teal décor was bold but created a cosy feeling, as did the yellow cushions and throws. A sleek, modern cast-iron stove sat neatly in the brickwork of the original hearth, more for style than for warmth in the summer months. Victoria settled in beside her. This time, thankfully, there was no laptop or spreadsheets to review.

"You didn't say earlier how you felt about your parents showing up like they did," Clem said, taking a sip of wine before placing her glass down on the coffee table.

Victoria shrugged, tucking her legs beneath her. "I suppose I'm glad they came and explained, but it doesn't really heal the wound, does it? Parents should support you. If they couldn't, then I understand why they distanced themselves from me. If they'd carried on as they were, I'd have done the same to them. I think I was beginning to."

"Maybe they sensed you were," Clem offered.

"Perhaps. We'll see how things develop."

Clem smiled softly. "You've got a way with broken things. Giving them a new life."

Victoria arched an eyebrow. "Yes. Buildings."

Clem shrugged and stroked the back of Victoria's hand. "You apply your skills in other areas, too. Take my body, for example; it's very broken after today."

"Then you should rest it," Victoria suggested, with a teasing glint in her eye. "Or… do you need fixing?"

"Well, if you know a way to revive it…"

"I do actually. You're drinking it."

"Hmm," Clem hummed, "it's helped a little."

"In that case, maybe I should try another tactic," Victoria said, shuffling closer and cupping Clem's cheek.

She met Victoria halfway, kissing her first. She would never tire of her lips, the feel of her insistent tongue against hers.

"Does that help?" Victoria asked, pulling back.

"Yes. It's definitely making me feel something," Clem answered, finding the room spinning a little.

"Same," Victoria purred.

Her mouth was suddenly eager again, stoking heat low in Clem's body. Their hands roamed freely as they shed every last inhibition — tugging, pressing, stroking.

Clem sank back into the corner of the sofa, steered there as Victoria straddled her. She was smouldering, alive after what must have been years being dormant. Clem couldn't believe how lucky she was to be the one receiving the affections of this coiled spring as it sprang open.

"I thought we were going to talk," Clem said, suddenly concerned they might have missed a step. Things were heating up a little more than she had expected — not that she was complaining.

Victoria pulled back and looked her in the eye. "Do you prefer to talk?"

Clem pretended to give the question some thought. "Nope."

"Good. My lips… are showing you… everything… I wanted… to say," Victoria muttered between kisses along Clem's neck. "In short, that I want you."

"I want you, too, Vic. You're so beautiful, in every way."

Her words seemed to light a fresh fire under Victoria, who scrabbled under Clem's T-shirt. Clem pulled it over her head, revealing her bare breasts as Victoria mirrored her. They sat for a moment, taking in each other's flesh before Victoria leaned in to stroke and caress breasts. Being eyed so hungrily and touched so lovingly made her body tingle.

"Shall we take this upstairs?" Victoria suggested, her tone tinged with hesitation.

"I thought you'd never ask," Clem replied, hoping to reassure her she wanted this just as much.

Victoria climbed off Clem and took her hand, leading her to the bedroom. She paused as they entered, a flicker of uncertainty crossing her face.

"Are you okay?" Clem asked, stepping closer.

"Yes, erm." Victoria swallowed. "Just a touch nervous."

"I won't tell you not to be, but I will give you every reason not to," Clem said softly, her pounding heart betraying her own nerves. "You're safe. We're safe together."

She stepped closer, gently stroked Victoria's back with her fingers, and kissed her shoulder. The goosebumps rising on Victoria's skin spurred Clem to lightly touch her breast. Victoria's head rolled back in pleasure, nerves seemingly forgotten; Clem grasped it more firmly, teasing her nipple between her thumb and forefinger as she kissed her neck.

Victoria moaned. "Can we lie down?"

"Of course. Whatever you want," Clem replied, stepping back to let Victoria lead.

She walked around to the far side of the bed and switched on a bedside lamp, filling the room with a warm, soft glow. Clem waited for her to settle in before lying down beside her. She admired how Victoria's hair fell around her face, just skimming the top of her breasts. It was noticeably longer than it had been when they first met. Clem brushed it back, letting her fingers trail over her soft, full, perfect breasts.

"You are exquisite, Vic," Clem whispered, her breath catching with emotion.

Victoria's earlier confidence seemed to flare again as she climbed on top, kissing Clem's neck and caressing her breasts. Clem writhed, her lower body trapped between Victoria's thighs. The restraint only heightened her arousal.

"You are exquisite, too," Victoria breathed, her voice low and full of longing.

Clem smiled up at her, hands cupping the breasts she could never get enough of. Victoria arched into her touch with a moan. She pressed Clem's hands firmly against herself, urging her on, guiding the pressure until Clem squeezed harder than she'd dared to do before.

Desperate for release from the fire raging through her, Clem tore one hand free from Victoria's grip and slipped it beneath her trousers, sliding into her soaked underwear.

"Do you need some help?" Victoria murmured, sitting back just enough to start unbuttoning Clem's trousers.

"Yes," Clem gasped, needing all the help Victoria could give her.

She lifted herself as Victoria pulled her trousers down, taking her knickers with them.

Clem kicked them off as Victoria rolled to one side to remove her own. Just one glimpse of Victoria's pale skin made Clem reach for herself again, but before she could, Victoria climbed back on top, pressing warmth and wetness against her and gently taking her hand.

"Don't you be doing my job," she murmured, lifting Clem's moist hand to her lips and sucking her fingers.

Long gone was that nervous, unsure woman of five minutes ago. She had been replaced by a confident enchantress who Clem was sure was going to be her undoing.

"Take me. Please... take anything you want," Clem whispered, her voice trembling.

"Now that's what I call an invitation. But where to start?" Victoria mused, leaning in to kiss her.

Clem pulled her close. The warmth of their breasts crushed together felt like nothing else on earth.

The pulsing between Clem's legs became unbearable. She needed release, and then she needed to build up to this mind-erasing level of tension again. Her hand slid between their bodies, desperate for relief. As if sensing her intent, Victoria grasped it again, and, taking Clem's other hand, she held them above her head.

"Mine," Victoria whispered. Her breath tickled Clem's ear in a most arousing way.

"Fuck!" Clem groaned, feeling like she might implode.

Victoria kissed her way down Clem's neck and chest, where she lingered over a nipple, her tongue teasing out another tortured groan. Clem arched, pressing into the warmth of Victoria's lips as she sucked.

The grip on her hands released as Victoria let go, but Clem left them above her head, on the pillow where they were. She had no issue surrendering herself to this woman; it only heightened her desire — provided she wasn't kept waiting too long. Hope flared as Victoria shuffled back, the warmth of her breasts pressing lightly against Clem's skin as her tongue and fingertips traced a slow path down her stomach.

Clem spread her legs wide, ankles digging into the bed. It wasn't going to take long, but she was determined to savour every second of it. Victoria knelt before her, taking her in with a smile that made Clem feel utterly wanted.

"Please," she begged. As much as she enjoyed Victoria drinking her in, she was well past teetering on the precipice — she was hanging on by a broken fingernail.

Victoria grinned. "If you insist."

She gripped Clem's thighs, her nails digging in just enough to make Clem let out an *ahhh*, somewhere between pleasure and pain.

Clem closed her eyes, feeling Victoria's breath ghost over her skin — a cool wash of air that made her shiver. Then came the heat of her mouth, eager and wet, shooting pleasure straight through her core. Tongue swirling, fingers teasing, Victoria coaxed wave after wave of sensation from her, each one pulling her deeper under. Clem gripped the sheets, pushing herself harder against Victoria's mouth.

Victoria obliged, lapping her rough tongue rhythmically whilst slipping her fingers slowly inside her.

Before Clem knew it, she was trembling, coming hard against Victoria's mouth, pulsing against her fingers as they slowly worked in and out.

"Fuck!" Clem exhaled loudly as her body settled.

Victoria hovered above her, lips moist, a satisfied grin spreading across her lips.

"I love you," Clem said, the words bursting out before she could catch them.

Victoria leaned down and kissed her, her hand stroking Clem's face. "I love you, too. Thank you for waiting for me. For giving me you."

"Anytime." Clem winked. This woman could have her anytime and every time.

She reached up and stroked Victoria's face, running her fingers over the light wrinkles by her eyes. Now it was her turn, but she wouldn't make Victoria wait, not too long anyway. Clem wasn't going to be able to keep herself from devouring the woman.

Victoria collapsed onto the bed beside Clem. She wasn't breathless from exertion — making Clem climax had been no effort — but from the intoxicating intensity of their connection. Clem had given herself to Victoria completely, and any lingering apprehension Victoria had felt melted away with her reassurance. With Clem, she did feel utterly safe.

She curled around her lover, drawing her close as she replayed the moments that had left her in this state. Clem's desperation had been palpable — so much so that she'd tried to ease her own ache. That had stirred something deep in Victoria. She had wanted to be the one to take

Clem there — to coax out every gasp and every shiver; to give her everything she craved.

Clem didn't stay still in her arms for long. Her gaze roamed over Victoria's body, desire flickering in her eyes before her hand followed. Each touch stoked the fire that had kept Victoria quietly simmering.

She could spend a lifetime like this, tangled up with this sexy, naked woman who had appeared from nowhere and almost drowned her in the canal. To hear her say, "I love you," then to say it back and mean it, had made her heart spill over with happiness. She hadn't believed she would ever feel that again in a relationship.

Clem's foot hooked under Victoria's leg, pulling it to the side. With her thighs parted, a rush of cool air swept over the burning skin between them. Fingers trailed slowly down her stomach… too slowly. In that moment, she understood Clem's earlier eagerness and impatience, feeling it, too. She was throbbing for relief. She closed her eyes and surrendered to Clem's teasing fingers, shivering as they slid through her wetness. Every brush of lips along her neck, every gentle nibble of her ear, and the soft whisper of "I love you" sent sparks through her, making her ache for more than just touch.

"Mmm," Victoria moaned back. She writhed at the words. She could feel them burrowing into her core as Clem slipped her fingers inside her — then out again. A whimper of delight escaped her lips, as Clem's rhythmic touch intensified. She was a puppet master, thrusting and rubbing in a way Victoria had never known, bringing her perilously close to the edge. She wasn't ready to fall, not without Clem's mouth on her.

"I need you there," she purred, staring intensely into Clem's eyes as her entire body tingled with anticipation.

"Now who is impatient?" Clem leaned in to kiss her.

Victoria kissed back, then applied a little pressure to Clem's shoulder to encourage her down. Clem's light chuckle tickled her neck as she moved, lips pressing to a breast, then a nipple, tracing down her belly until finally she devoured her completely.

Victoria squirmed with delight, closing her eyes to fend off the dizzying rush that threatened to overtake her. As Clem's tongue teased and coaxed, the ache inside Victoria shifted into a more urgent, all-consuming intensity, one she wanted to savour yet desperately needed released. She grasped Clem's head, not that she needed guiding, but she wanted more connection, to feel her under her fingertips.

With Clem's fingers still dancing inside her and her other hand caressing her skin, she knew she would succumb soon. And she did, moaning, pulsing, and twitching as she tipped over the edge. Her nails gripped Clem's scalp, and she savoured every last shiver as it was drawn from her body.

She felt Clem settling beside her and opened her eyes to take her in.

"You know, you're very much a Victoria sponge. Soft, a little fruity on top..." She looked at her fingers, rubbing them together. "Moist, with a creamy centre." Licking them, she added, "And you taste delicious."

"I'm happy... to hear that... I think," Victoria murmured between panting breaths, heat prickling her skin at what Clem was doing.

Although it was her first time with a woman, the experience had felt entirely natural, better than anything she'd experienced before. It wasn't a performance or a goal to reach on one side, just the slow, deliberate artistry of two women fluent in the language of each other's skin. Clem listened with her hands, read every flicker of breath, every shift in her body. There was no battle for control, no pressure beyond comfort — only an exquisite unfolding. It was softer, gentler, but not lacking in intensity; the fire was there, tempered with care and tenderness, stoked slowly until it consumed her. For the first time in her life, Victoria felt wanted, cherished, and truly seen.

"Where do we go from here?" Clem asked softly, her fingers entwining with Victoria's.

"Shall we take it day by day? See how things develop?"

"I'd say they've developed pretty quickly in the last twelve hours." Clem laughed. "Isn't sleeping with the boss sort of frowned upon?"

"As long as the boss isn't married, what does it matter?"

"Technically, you still are."

"True." It didn't feel like she was.

"Does it bother you?" Clem asked, tone turning serious.

"Not now, no, and we're both adults. If things don't work out, I'd trust we'd still be able to work together."

Clem squeezed her hand. "Let's not focus on things not working out but instead put some effort into ensuring they do."

"I can get behind that," Victoria said, turning to face her. "Will you stay?"

Clem put an arm over her. "Try stopping me, but don't be offended if I leave early. Baking duties await."

Victoria nodded. "He would always leave afterwards and sleep in another room," Victoria said quietly. "And he never was one for cuddling. It made me feel like a… prostitute. If I were one, at least I'd have received payment for my efforts."

Clem brushed a strand of hair behind Victoria's ear.

"I'm sorry," Victoria murmured, looking down, her

eyes inadvertently drawn to Clem's breasts. "I shouldn't be talking about him, especially not now."

"It's okay," Clem said gently. "You can talk to me about anything. We'll always carry our memories with us; they shape us, but we have to ensure they don't control our future."

She hoped the old memories would fade as new hopes and dreams took their place and she rebuilt her life.

"What I mean to say is, well, sex was never like this before," she added wistfully, her hand beginning to stroke Clem's breasts. "I lost interest eventually. It wasn't that I lost interest in sex, only the sex I was going to have with him."

"Ah, yes. The tale of many women, I expect. But he's in your past now. Try to leave him there and focus on the future."

Victoria nodded and leant in for a kiss. With this beautiful woman before her, how could she not focus on what was in front of her? She'd thrown off her shackles, stamped out her fears, and put herself first. She'd reclaimed her life. As Clem once said, *There is nothing that can't be unpicked and something new sewn in its place — stronger.*

She was stronger, and they were stronger for it. A true partnership was about bringing out each other's strengths, not clambering over one another to get ahead or treating the other like dead weight.

With Clem beside her, she felt she could take on the world, but she also knew she could stand on her own now. She didn't need anyone to make her whole; that was something only she could do for herself. If Clem wanted to come along for the ride, she would gladly have her.

# EPILOGUE

## CHRISTMAS DAY

*V*ictoria watched through half-closed, satisfied eyes as Clem's head appeared from under the duvet. A shaft of cold air hit her warm, still quivering body, and the sudden chill rippled across her skin in a shiver. Clem must have noticed, as she pressed her warm body against Victoria's and pulled the duvet tighter around them.

"Would you move in with me?" Victoria asked as soon as Clem had settled in. "You practically live here anyway."

"Move in?" Clem said, pulling back a little to properly face Victoria. "Wow, you're really desperate to get rid of Florence. You know she isn't going anywhere. She's part of the family."

"Ha! Yes, I'm aware she is forever entwined in our lives," Victoria said, lowering her tone to add, "every time I look out the window."

"Hey," Clem retorted, giving Victoria's nipple a tweak.

Victoria shot her a wry smile as a ripple of pleasure shot through her. "I'm quite used to the orange blob at the bottom of my garden by now."

She earned another pleasurable nipple tweak for that, much to her delight.

"Our garden," Clem corrected her.

Victoria's eyebrows knitted together. "Ours?"

"Yes. You just asked me to move in, remember? Or did you forget already?"

"Oh! Very funny," Victoria said, tickling Clem's side and making her squirm. "Does that mean you will?"

"Of course I will," Clem replied, as if it were the silliest question someone had ever asked her.

Victoria was so overcome with happiness that words failed her. Instead, she pulled Clem into her and squeezed tightly, sealing the embrace with a long, lingering kiss.

"You really dislike orange, don't you?" Clem snarked.

"It's not my favourite colour," Victoria replied.

"Did you know my parents named me after her colour?"

Victoria's lips twitched. "I didn't know your name was *Garish*."

Clem narrowed her eyes. "Clementine."

"Ah, right," Victoria said. "I presumed your mum must have been looking at a fruit bowl when she was coming up with names."

Clem let out a low chuckle. "Yeah, I did, too."

"Hmm. Speaking of food, I'm quite hungry. Do you think it would be bad to have Christmas cake for breakfast?"

Victoria couldn't get enough of Clem's homemade one. It was better than any shop-bought one she'd ever had.

Clem pulled her phone from the bedside table. "Breakfast? Brunch, more like. Have you seen the time? If you aren't prepared to eat seconds at Christmas lunch, my mum will take offence, so on your head be it. I think I'd rather tuck into a bit of Victoria sponge again, see how moist it is." She waggled her eyebrows before diving back under the duvet.

Victoria giggled and tried to push Clem's head away as she kissed her stomach. "Come on or we'll be late. I do not want to upset your mum."

"True. We'd never hear the end of it," Clem said as she resurfaced. "I'll fetch us some coffee. Do you want to shower first?"

"Sure."

Ten minutes later, Clem returned with two steaming mugs just as Victoria finished dressing. Victoria sipped from her mug and watched Clem slip out of what was technically Victoria's dressing gown. It looked good on her, but without it, she looked even better. Clem caught her eye and winked as she headed towards the en-suite, sending butterflies tumbling through Victoria's stomach. Temptation gnawed at her to throw Clem on the bed and take her all over again, just as she had done when she'd woken. Fearing a reprimand from Barbara, though, she headed to the kitchen instead.

As she descended the stairs, the gold and silver tinsel wound around the spindles shimmered. She couldn't help but smile, recalling how Clem had spent ages winding it in different ways to perfect the best method. The large Christmas tree in the hallway sustained her smile as she passed it on the way into the kitchen.

She'd never bothered with Christmas decorations before, not to mention a tree. There was no point when it was only her, especially as she always went to London for the festivities. Cooking Christmas lunch for the in-laws had been her job. On Boxing Day, she and Drew would head to the company box at Spurs if there was a match on to wine and dine business contacts. Then they would spend the evenings with the in-laws again, this time at their house in Holland Park.

Today was the first Christmas Day she didn't have to cook, and she couldn't have been happier. It was also her first Christmas in the house — their house, she could think of it as now. She'd loved going out with Clem to pick the tree and decorations, then decorating the house together. It was partly what had spurred her to ask Clem to move in. She missed her when she wasn't there. Clem made the house feel whole — made her feel whole, too.

Opening a kitchen drawer, she took out a large envelope and placed it on the worktop. As she perched on a stool, she sipped her coffee and stared at the official court stamp. She opened it with a deep breath and drew out a single sheet of paper, light as a feather compared to the symbolic weight it carried. It felt like a door closing on another life, one she should have left behind long ago, yet she was grateful for it, too. It had led her here — to another door and to the beautiful woman behind it, the one she'd fallen in love with.

"Don't you have a Christmas jumper?" Clem said, stepping into the kitchen and slipping her mug into the dishwasher.

"No, and I like this one." She fingered the cashmere sweater. "It reminds me of you dragging it out of the canal for me."

"It looked so good on you, draped around your shoulders, all cute and sexy. I had to rescue it." Clem leaned over and kissed Victoria's smiling cheek. "What's that?"

"My divorce papers."

"Oh, when did they come?" Clem asked, taking the stool beside her.

"A couple of days ago. I wanted to leave it for today."

"A Christmas present to yourself?"

"Something like that," Victoria mused.

"'Final Order'," Clem said, reading it. "What does that mean?"

"It's the new term for 'decree absolute'."

"So… that means you're divorced, right?"

"Yep," Victoria exhaled, setting the papers down. "All done and dusted."

"How do you feel?"

"It's time to move on," she said, placing the sheet of paper back in the envelope and tucking it into the drawer. "New year, new start."

"Speaking of which, are you ready to face your parents next week?"

"I'm not really sure," Victoria answered without hesitation, realising she hadn't given the matter much thought. The lead-up to Christmas had been so busy at the wharf that, thankfully, it had kept her from dwelling on it. "Nervous, I suppose. Sometimes I wonder if it's best left alone, but we'll have to see how it goes. There's a lot of work to do."

"On their part?"

"Yes, but probably on both sides." Victoria shrugged. "I'll give them the opportunity to make amends; at least I'll know I've done my part by trying. Then we'll see what happens and how I feel around them. We have to start somewhere, and it will definitely take time."

"I expect it's more than they deserve."

Victoria shrugged again. She'd spent many years trying not to care that her parents had distanced themselves, and she was now quite used to their absence. What outcome she was hoping for, she didn't know, but she was glad she'd booked a hotel nearby and refused their offer of accommodation. That way, they could escape if necessary. It was likely to be a stressful few days, even if everything went smoothly.

"I think I'll need a holiday after seeing them," she opined. "How do you feel about extending our trip? We could stop somewhere for the weekend on the way back, decompress a bit before work starts again. Call it my Christmas treat — and a little thank you for everything you've done for the wharf."

"Do you thank all your employees with cheeky weekends away?"

"Ha. It's not like that," Victoria said, knowing exactly what Clem was implying.

"Oh, it will be. I can promise you that," Clem said, wrapping her arms around Victoria's waist and kissing her neck.

Victoria giggled. "I prefer to see it more as a romantic getaway."

"Okay, it will be that, too. Which reminds me," Clem said, "I have a present for you. Well... I don't have anything to actually give you. Not yet."

Victoria lifted an eyebrow and rose from her stool to put her own mug in the dishwasher. "You have a present, but you don't have one? You tease!"

"Yep," Clem said. Then, unable to hold it in any longer, she blurted, "Every week next year, you'll have flowers delivered."

Victoria gawked. "Flowers for a year?"

"Yes, and you can choose what kind you want each week, too."

"Golly. That's… lovely," Victoria said, feeling her eyes welling up. She wiped them quickly. She felt a little silly in her response, even if it was the most thoughtful present anyone had given her. "I'm not sure what I did to deserve you."

Clem shrugged. "You endured, and then I found you."

"Mmm, you did," Victoria replied, drawing Clem close and kissing her.

Clem's phone vibrated on the worktop. "Ugh, I bet that's Mum wondering where we are." She checked her phone. "Yep."

"Come on then. Best not to keep her waiting," Victoria said, a flicker of unease tightening her voice. "We can share our news."

The rabbit-in-headlights look on Clem's face suggested she was a little concerned.

"If you want to," Victoria revised. "We can wait, if you prefer?"

"No, it's fine. I'm just a bit worried."

Victoria rubbed Clem's arm. "You think she'll fret over Florence?"

"That's exactly what she'll do, but I have a plan I'm mulling over." Clem tapped her head as she stepped from her stool.

"Okay, let's head over then, before your mum marches round."

"Oh, what a thought," Clem groaned. "Can we move?"

"No," Victoria laughed, wrapping her arms around her lover and kissing her, enjoying the warm shiver that washed through her. "But we can tolerate our neighbours together."

"I can live with that."

Clem passed her armful of presents to Victoria and knocked on her parents' front door. Her dad answered almost immediately.

"Ah, there you two are," he said, relief flooding his face as he pulled Clem into a hug and then nodded to Victoria. "Merry Christmas to you both. Your mum was about to send me round to collect you."

"Merry Christmas," she sighed as they stepped into the beautifully refurbished hallway. There were definite drawbacks to living next door to her parents, as she had found out over the last few months. She had to hope her mum was less likely to just pop by once she'd moved in with Victoria. Why did she have to fall for the woman living next door to her parents, of all people?

Her mum appeared, wearing an apron, and wrapped Clem in a hug. "Merry Christmas, you two."

"Merry Christmas, Mum," Clem replied, taking in the festive décor inside.

The last Christmas they had spent in the house hadn't been to celebrate. There had been no decorations then, only the sad task of sorting Gram's belongings. Now, though, everything looked exactly as it had when Gram was alive, as if Christmases past had been frozen in time.

"You kept all the decorations," Clem said softly, her gaze sweeping over the slightly mismatched colours and chaotic mix of treasures Gram had collected over the years. Lanterns Clem had made as a child dangled from the ceiling, and paper chains cut from old scraps of wrapping paper draped across the hall and down the stairs. Every piece held a story, and every piece was in its place.

"Of course I did," her mum said firmly. "She might not be here, but I wanted it to feel like she was with us."

Clem nodded, eyes pricking with tears. "She is with us."

Her mum hummed her agreement and patted Clem's arm. "Go through. Your dad will sort you out with something to drink, won't you, Tom?"

"Yes, dear," he replied dutifully.

"Lunch won't be very long," her mum called out as she trundled back to the kitchen.

Clem dabbed her tears with her sleeve as Victoria slipped an arm around her shoulder.

"What happened to your old car, Victoria?" her dad asked as he led them into the festively decorated sitting room.

"I'm clearing out the last remnants of the past, Tom."

"Good for you. Shame, though — it was a lovely motor. That new one's nice, too. Plenty of space, even room for knees in the back seat." He chuckled.

"Oh, is it a family car?" Clem's mum asked, suddenly appearing in the doorway with a tray of canapés, face alight with anticipation.

"It's just a car, Mum!" Clem tutted. "You know, five seats, goes from A to B. Practical."

Her mum set the tray on the coffee table and headed back to the kitchen, lips pursed.

"Oh, Victoria! While I remember," her dad said, moving closer as she placed presents under the Christmas tree, "I think we should trim the hedge between our driveways."

Clem groaned inwardly. The last thing she wanted was her mum monitoring their comings and goings.

"That's fine," Victoria said. "It could certainly do with tidying up a bit. I don't recall it ever being cut."

"It must be over twelve feet, but don't worry, we won't go too short. I know you'll want your privacy from old

Sticky Beak," Clem's dad said, nodding towards the kitchen.

Clem let out a breath of relief. She could always rely on her dad to circumnavigate her mum and her 'ways'.

As they settled onto the sofa, Clem admired the room. It was such a contrast to how it had felt on previous Christmases. A new cast-iron, traditional fireplace occupied the old hearth, and brand-new furniture filled the space — except for Gram's threadbare old chair. That remained where it had always stood, unchanged, as if time had simply moved around it.

"Do you think you'll need me again next year as Father Christmas?" her dad asked her, pouring champagne into two glasses. "I really enjoyed it."

"I think so, don't you?" Clem said, looking to Victoria for the final response.

"Absolutely. You did a great job."

Her dad beamed and handed them their drinks.

"It was lovely to see all the children's faces, thinking I was the real Father Christmas. Though I'm not sure your mum quite cut it as an elf."

Right on cue, her mum appeared again to top up her own champagne glass. "We were on a tight schedule, Tom!" she scolded. "Left to your timing, that queue of children would still be waiting."

The corners of his mouth drooped, and his eyes rolled. "Yes, dear."

Clem grinned at him.

"Lunch is ready. I think it's best if everyone just helps themselves rather than me dishing it all up," her mum said, heading out of the room.

They all tucked into a delicious lunch beneath the impressive, lantern-style roof in the conservatory extension, and then settled back into the sitting room. As her mum took Gram's chair, stepping fully into her role as the matriarch of the family, Clem decided it was time to share their news.

"I have something to tell you," she began, only to find Victoria's hand in hers, giving a reassuring squeeze. "We have some news."

Clem's mum put her hands to her face, eyebrows arching, full of hope.

"No, Mum! I'm not pregnant. Jeez."

Her mum's expression dropped as quickly as her hands to her lap, much to everyone's amusement.

As the laughter settled, Clem continued. "Victoria has asked me to move in with her."

Her dad shot her a wink. "Congrats, you two. I hope you'll both be very happy together."

"Thanks, Dad."

Her mum frowned. "But what about Florence? You're not going to sell her, are you?"

"Of cour—"

"What about the business?" her mum interrupted. "I thought you'd reopen in the spring."

"There's so much work to do at the wharf, Mum. I need to be there full-time. I enjoyed my time running a business, but it wasn't really for me."

Clem looked to Victoria, realising she should have probably run the idea past her first, but she had only just decided. "If that's okay with you, I mean."

"Of course it is." Victoria smiled. "More than okay."

"Is this her doing?" her mum said, nodding at Victoria.

Clem grimaced, wishing her mum wasn't quite so blunt.

"This has nothing to do with Vic, Mum, and everything to do with what I want. I've been at the wharf full-time leading up to Christmas, and I don't want to go back to serving coffee and cake out of a hatch. I love working at the wharf, and I love working with Vic." She gave Victoria's hand a squeeze and received one in return. "I'm sure I'm going to love living with her, too."

"Well, as long as you're happy, that's all we care about. Isn't it, Barbara?" her dad affirmed.

"Oh yes," her mum muttered. "Haven't I been telling you all along you needed a steady job in marketing?"

Clem rolled her eyes. It was typical of her mum to now make it sound like it had all been her idea and she'd just been waiting for Clem to catch up.

"You'll keep Florence, won't you?"

"If you'd let me finish what I was trying to say," Clem said through a gritted smile, "you would have heard that I'm giving her back to you."

Her mum blinked. "To me? Really?"

"Yes. I have no use for her now, and I can't think of anyone else who would look after her as well as I do. Although… maybe if I can persuade this old landlubber to an occasional boat trip" — she nudged Victoria — "we might borrow her occasionally."

Her mum began to flap her hands, but her dad was already there with the tissues. Clem rarely saw her mum cry; the only times had been when she was moved by Florence. It was nice to see that, buried beneath her fussiness, there was a heart after all.

"I'll look after her," her mum said, sniffling into a tissue. "I've missed having a boat these past months. We can take her out, Tom, cruise around like we used to."

"I thought you could open her as a B&B or hire her out," Clem gently suggested. "It would give you something to do, Mum."

"What a good idea. It would supplement our pensions

nicely, wouldn't it, dear?" Clem's dad said, winking at his daughter.

Clem smirked back at him and mouthed, "Merry Christmas."

Her mum blew her nose and took a breath.

"I lost my home of twenty years, and now I'm living back in my old one while another bobs about at the end of the garden," she said, a note of melancholy in her voice. "But... without Gram..." She sighed deeply, unable to go on.

"Mum," Clem said, sharing a wary glance with her dad and Victoria, "how much have you had to drink?"

"Not enough, but, yes, that's enough sentimental stuff." She shook her head briskly, then slapped her knees. "We were thinking of holding a New Year's Eve party, weren't we, Tom?"

"Yes, dear, you were," he drawled.

She knocked him with the back of her hand. "Helen and Graham said they'd come, and Jasper and Max." She looked at her watch. "In fact, they should be joining us shortly for a few drinks."

"Oh, sorry, Barbara," Victoria said tentatively. "We won't be here for the new year. My parents have invited us to the Lake District for a few days."

"Oh, right. Well, not to worry. I'm sure we'll survive without you both," Clem's mum replied, her smile a little too tight to be convincing as the doorbell rang out. "Oh, speak of the devils!" She leapt from the chair and staggered to the front door, her brief disappointment at her daughter's absence for New Year's Eve vanished.

Jasper and Max filed into the sitting room a few minutes later, weighed down by bags full of chinking bottles. Helen and Graham followed, each carrying a couple of bottles of wine.

"Does anyone want a Juicy Squeeze?" Jasper shouted over the hubbub, holding up a bottle of cider.

"Not so soon after lunch," Clem's dad called back, "but maybe you could give me one later."

Everyone laughed as they found seats, and Clem's mum fussed around with handing out glasses.

"You all missed Clem's news," she said once everyone had settled. "She's moving in with Victoria."

Words of congratulations filled the room.

"And I've got Florence back," she added.

"What?" Jasper and Max exclaimed in unison, looking between Clem and Victoria for clarification.

"Yes," Clem confirmed. "I'm going to be working full-time at the wharf now, so Florence is going to be looked after by Mum."

"That's great news," Jasper said jubilantly. "We're more than happy to have you. You're still baking, aren't you?" he added, concern lacing his tone.

"Of course," Clem replied. "I wouldn't leave you without your coffee and walnut now, would I?"

"I'm glad you finally made a decision," Max said with a wink.

"Does anyone want anything to eat?" Clem's mum offered. "We've got loads left over from our Christmas lunch."

A resounding no came as everyone patted their stomachs and shook their heads.

She opened a sideboard and extracted multiple boxes and tubs of chocolates. "Well, I'll just leave these on the table in case anyone wants one."

Within seconds, everyone was diving forward, grappling for the treats.

They settled into an afternoon of charades, board games, and laughter in front of a roaring fire. As the evening crept in, and feeling full of finger food, Clem felt Victoria's hand pressing against her leg.

"Shall we head off soon?" Victoria whispered. "That Victoria sponge you left in the oven is going to be over-baked soon, and I know how you like it moist in the centre."

Clem shot her a wide-eyed, very interested look. "Okay, let's go," she said, standing up quickly. "We're going to head off."

Tired groans of protest echoed around the room.

After they'd all said goodbye, Clem's mum and dad walked them to the door.

"We'll give you some money for Florence," her dad said, giving her a hug. "It's only fair we buy her from you."

"If you're sure," she said. "I could certainly use the cash."

"We're sure," he replied firmly.

"Maybe you could use it at a sperm bank," her mum slurred in a tipsy whisper.

Clem spat out a laugh. "Mum! You did not just say that."

Her mum giggled guiltily, but soon they were all laughing. Clem reached out her hand for Victoria and was given a steadying squeeze.

"Come on, Vic," she said as she tried to regain her breath. "We should leave before she tries to lend us her turkey baster."

Having said their goodbyes, they walked across the drive hand in hand, swaying a little as they walked.

"That went better than I expected. It was lovely to see everyone," Clem said, feeling content with the world and the life-changing decisions she'd made in the last twelve hours.

"It was," Victoria agreed. "I really enjoyed it... bar a few of your mum's comments."

"Yeah, sorry about that," Clem said with a sheepish smile.

"It was still far better than previous Christmases, that's for sure," Victoria said, her tone thoughtful as she gazed up at the dark sky. "I'm not sure where I'd be now if you hadn't *barged* into my life the way you did."

"Oh, we're doing canal puns, are we? Anyway, you were the one doing the *barging*. You came for my sign, remember?"

"Only because you *barged* into my territory. There I was, happily minding my own business, when Storm Clem whipped along the canal, stopping right outside my window."

"Like I said to you then, no one was forcing you to look," Clem teased.

"Oh, but you were, and I couldn't keep my eyes off you," Victoria said, kissing the back of Clem's hand as they reached their front doorstep. "Just like you couldn't keep yours off my nipples after Max fished me out of the canal."

Clem laughed. "I remember. And you don't have to keep your gaze off me, anymore, you can *lock* eyes with me every morning,"

"And I couldn't be happier," Victoria said, kissing Clem under the mistletoe hanging from the porch. She pulled back suddenly. "Hey, was that another canal pun?"

"Might have been." Clem smiled as she stole another kiss. "And now you see you were wrong. Love isn't overrated — or for the young. It finds you when you least expect it. And sometimes, it's the best thing you could ever hope for."

Victoria's lips curved into a soft smile as she unlocked

the front door and pulled Clem inside. "I'd say you're that best thing," she whispered.

"I think you already did, multiple times," Clem teased.

The scent of home enveloped her, as Victoria closed the door behind them.

359

THE END
Keep turning for a free book!

# REVIEWS

If you enjoyed this book, please consider leaving me a review on Amazon, BookBub or Goodreads. Just a rating or a line is fine. Reviews are life-blood to authors, boosting visibility and connecting new readers with our books.

AMAZON REVIEW LINK

# JOIN MY READERS CLUB

If you'd like to hear about my new releases, sign up to my newsletter and receive a FREE sapphic romance, *The Third Act*. Download here…

*At the suggestion of her daughter, Amy, widowed Fiona attends an art course at the local college where she meets the confident, inspirational teacher, Raye.*

*Raye awakens feelings long suppressed, but as Fiona rediscovers her sexuality, fear grows over how Amy will react.*

*Can Fiona find the courage to follow her heart, or will she be destined to spend her third act alone?*

## REVIEWS

*5* Absolutely loved this book! Great story line, well developed characters and beautifully crafted. It is really refreshing to see the older lesbian represented for a change!*

*5* A beautiful story of love knowing no age.*

*5* A very well written, heartwarming novella that challenges the absurd belief that people over a certain age are "too old" to crave intimacy, to start fresh and fall in love. I thoroughly enjoyed this story and I wish it was longer.*

# ALSO BY

## THE SOUTH DOWNS ROMANCE SERIES

### BOOK ONE: Broken Beyond Repair

GOLDIE WINNER 2024: AUDIOBOOK NARRATOR (ANGELA DAWE)

GOLDIE WINNER 2023: THE ANN BANNON POPULAR CHOICE BRONZE AWARD

GOLDIE FINALIST 2023: CONTEMPORARY ROMANCE LONG NOVEL

WINNER OF THE LESFIC BARD AWARD 2022: ROMANCE

WINNER OF THE LESFIC BARD AWARD 2022: COVER DESIGN

WINNER OF THE QUEER INDIE AWARDS 2022: CONTEMPORARY ROMANCE

*Sydney MacKenzie, personal assistant to the rich and famous, is looking forward to a well-earned break to go travelling in her beloved VW camper van, Gertie — that is, until Gertie cries off sick. When her boss calls in a favour, one that will pay Sydney handsomely and put Gertie back on the road, she can't refuse.*

*Internationally renowned actress Beatrice Russell — adored by her fans and despised by those that know her — is splashed across the tabloids, all thanks to her broken leg. She limps back to her palatial English country estate to convalesce for the summer, where she finds herself in need of yet another new assistant.*

*Enter Sydney, who doesn't take kindly to the star's demands, attitude, or clicking fingers — much less her body's own attraction to the gorgeous diva. If not for that, and Gertie's worn-out engine, she would leave tomorrow. Or so she tells herself.*

*As the summer heats up, the ice queen begins to thaw, and Sydney glimpses the tormented woman beneath the celebrity bravado, drawing her ever closer to the enigmatic actress — sometimes too close.*

*Can Sydney reach the real Beatrice and help heal her wounds before the summer ends and she returns to filming in the States, or is the celebrity broken beyond repair?*

**BOOK TWO: Reality In Check**

GOLDIE FINALIST 2024: CONTEMPORARY ROMANCE LONG NOVEL

*Sculptor Arte Tremaine is thrown into the hospitality industry when her beloved late grandmother bequeaths her and her sister a charming yet rundown country hotel with zero guests. Arte is determined to make a success of the business, despite her sister snapping at her heels to sell it and painful memories confronting her inside.*

*Charlotte Beaufort, heiress to a hotel empire, television celebrity, and self-confessed city woman, hits the countryside to film an episode of her reality television show, Hotel SOS, where she immediately clashes with the overwhelmed Arte and her inquisitive Labrador, Rodin.*

*Arte doesn't take kindly to Charlotte's attitude and frank opinions about her hotel, but when they are thrown together, she begins to realise not everything is as it seems with her attractive nemesis. As Arte begins to chip away at Charlotte's icy exterior, both women begin to realise dreams and reality rarely entwine and that, sometimes, our dreams are not even our own.*

*Can the artsy dreamer and ambitious heiress face the reality of their* situations and discover their true paths? And if so, can those paths lead them toward true love?

**BOOK THREE: Beyond Her Manner**

*Gillian Carmichael is grieving, not for the loss of her husband, but for what his death has cost her — Kingsford Manor, her beloved home. To make matters worse, she can observe the new 'Lady of the Manor' from her small abode in Kingsford Lodge, and observe her, she does.*

*Viola Berkley, an internationally renowned classical singer, retreats to the quiet of the countryside after her mother's sudden death, seeking peace and anonymity. What she finds is an unwelcome adversary in her outspoken neighbour Gillian Carmichael, who is quick to critique Viola's suitability for her new role and her lack of village sensibilities.*

*As their worlds collide, both women realise they have more in common than divides them, and the line between animosity and attraction begins to blur. With Gillian shackled to her past, unable to let go of the life she lost, and Viola carrying the weight of her grief, can the pair find a path forward, or will the shadows of the past keep them apart?*

*and move forward? Will a curtain-twitching busy body curtail any blossoming attraction before it even has a chance to bloom?*

**Spend Christmas in Nunswick with TRUST IN TRUTH, the enthralling follow-up to LOST IN LOVE.**

*After the events of the summer, Katherine and Anna are looking forward to spending a quiet, cosy Christmas together before hosting a New Year's Eve party at Nunswick Abbey.*

*When a romantic weekend away for Anna's birthday doesn't go to plan, it proves to be the beginning of their Christmas woes, and as workplace pleasantries grow too friendly, a cloud of jealousy and suspicion forms.*

*As Anna plans the most important party of her career, can she convince Katherine their co-worker has more than pub lunches on the brain? Can Katherine keep her composure as the tension rises at Abbey House?*

*As they count down to the New Year, will Anna and Katherine's relationship survive the calamitous Christmas season?*

**Join Anna and Katherine as Nunswick Abbey opens for the spring amidst building work, archaeological excavations, and vandalism.**

*When an old school friend returns to the village with her family, Anna begins to question her long held vision of her future.*

*Old wounds are reopened for Katherine when she's presented with an opportunity. Can Anna convince her to take it and finally confront her past head on?*

*With Anna dreaming of the future and Katherine consumed by the past, can they get on the same page and decide what life they want to build together?*

### PRAISE FOR THE SERIES

*This is one of the best books I've read in a very long time. I laughed out loud, cried, and even became indignant at one point. I love a good age-gap slow burn and this checked all the boxes!! Well done!!*

*A splendid read. It had the perfect amount of laughs, tears, and feels! Can't wait to read the others in the series*

*LOVED this quintessential English romance novel!! Beautifully written, the plot is tight and the main characters - and those around them - precisely drawn. It gripped me from the very first page and I finished it less than 24 hours!*

*I do not think there is a heart string left that this author didn't strum. I am a mess of happy and sad and just all out of sorts hahaha. Superb writing. Everything the characters feel, you are going to feel so maybe a few tissues, a pint of ice cream and a hug from a friend should be added to your list of things you'll need after enjoying this book.*

*I rated this book 5 stars because it's absolutely breathtaking, the atmosphere of the quaint little village with the ruins of an abbey is such a beautiful picture and reminds me of a town near to where I grew up. It's so hard to find sapphic books in general and it's even harder to find one as good as this! I'm in love with Katherine and Anna's relationship and I'm so excited to continue the series. Also this was such a fun book to read that I read it in 1 day and I'm usually a slow reader.*